D0777154

ANGELS

AT THE

GATE

T.K. THORNE

CAPPUCCINO BOOKS

Maps, List of Characters, Author's Notes, and Bibliography
may be found at the back of this book.

ISBN 978-3-906196-02-2

Published by Cappuccino Books
Cappuccino Books, Alter Postplatz 2, CH 6370 Stans, Switzerland
www.cappuccinobooks.com

Interior book design by Neuwirth & Associates, Inc.
Cover design by Laura Katz Parenteau
Maps by Patricia Martin

Printed in the United States

10 9 8 7 6 5 4 3 2 1

For my sister, the wind beneath my wings.
And my father, who taught me to ask questions.

ACKNOWLEDGMENTS

A HEARTFELT THANK-YOU to all who helped me in this endeavor: Margaret and Giora Duvdevani for their warm hospitality in Israel; Ronin and Asa-el Helman for sharing their wisdom and love of the Negev desert, and for helping me find the right spots; Avishay Levy for his energy and enthusiasm; and Dr. Sandy Ebersole, James Lowry, Dr. Norman Rose, and Jessica Papin for their professional advice and expertise.

To editor, Catherine Hamrick, of the keen eye; proof editor, Paula Marshall, who took on the daunting task of making everything consistent; and Patricia Martin for the perfect maps.

My thanks to my publisher, Adriano Viganò, for his openness to "a good story," and to Marisa Lankester for her warm welcome as a new friend and fellow author at Cappuccino Books.

I owe the moon to my sister, Laura Parenteau, for the beautiful cover and constant underpinning, encouragement, and editing skills. Her partnership is a gift I can never repay.

To my "first-reader" friends, for their support and editorial input— Jimsey Bailey, Clarence Blair, Fran, Lee, and Scott Godchaux, Debra Goldstein, Warren and Sarah Katz, Dottie King, Judi Miller, Dianne Mooney, Joyce Norman, Jessica Papin, Laura Parenteau, Harriet Schaeffer, Dale Carroll Short, Roger Thorne, Sue Brannon Walker, and Alice Hart Wertheim. If I have left anyone out, I beg his/her forgiveness.

To my husband, Roger Thorne, who supports me in so many ways— from his editorial help and patience with my need for solitude to work, to picking up a camera and accompanying me to Israel, where he endured treks through museums, the desert, and the perils of the West Bank to snap pictures of rocks, cliffs, trees, artifacts, and anything else he thought I might need.

I am also grateful to all the readers of this book, for entrusting me to take you on this journey.

But Lot's wife looked back as she was following behind him, and she turned into a pillar of salt.

—Book of Genesis 19:26

PART

I

CANAAN, 1748 BCE

CHAPTER

1

In those days, and for some time after, giant Nephilites lived on the earth, for whenever the sons of God had intercourse with women, they gave birth to children who became the heroes and famous warriors of ancient times.

—Book of Genesis 6:4

I F THE PATH OF OBEDIENCE is the path of wisdom, it is one not well worn by my feet. I am Adira, daughter of the caravan, daughter of the wind, and daughter of the famed merchant, Zakiti. That I am his daughter, not his son, is a secret between my father and myself. This is a fine arrangement, as I prefer the freedoms of being a boy.

At the head of our caravan, my father and I walk together beside our pack donkeys, the late day sun casting stubby shadows before us. Our sandaled feet raise a cloud of dust along the dry path that winds through Canaan's white-and-taupe hills, studded with shrubs and spring flowers. We are taking a gift of sheep to our tribe's elder, along with a portion of our recent purchase of olive oil and wine. I am less than enthusiastic. Father sees this in my face. He reads me well—often, too well.

"You are not happy to see Abram and Sarai?" he says, giving my donkey a pat. "Why not, Adir?" He always uses the masculine form of my name, even when we are alone. He is afraid if he does not, he will forget one day when he is angry or tired.

I shrug. "I am happy to visit with my cousin, Ishmael, but Abram is old and likes to talk."

"He is a wise and learned man," my father says, resting a hand on my shoulder. "You should listen to him."

I should do many things I do not. But a visit to old Abram is not without benefits. His wife, Sarai, produces very fine weavings; one of bright russet covers my head. Also, and more importantly, his second wife, Hagar, makes excellent honey cakes.

I glance at the three strangers, the northmen who joined our caravan less than a moon ago when we traveled through the north hills of Canaan. They, too, are on their way to see Abram, whose herds graze in the valley of Hebron. These northmen tower over everyone. The oldest man is very thin and wears an odd, peaked hat. The two younger men do not wear hats. One, who walks with a tall staff, has hair and a full beard of a bright copper and eyes as green as the fronds of a date palm, and the other, the more handsome, is golden-haired and clean-shaven with eyes the blue of the Galilee deep. At their appearance, rumors darted like hungry fish through the caravan: They are giants; they are Egyptians; they are El's angels. Their donkeys carry an object covered in thick black fur among their possessions. I am curious to speak with them, whoever they are, as I have a skill with languages and a yearning to learn about other peoples, especially mysterious ones, but they have kept to themselves.

The sun knifes through my fine headdress. Inside my robe, the pup wriggles, adjusting his position before settling back for a nap. I stole him from the litter, afraid he would not survive Chiram's pot, having overheard our cook complain about wasting food on the pups when they are weaned. I take a peek when Father is not looking, amused at his tiny gold-brown paws and black nose nestled against my chest. His little eyes have not opened, and he smells of milk. It is fortunate for me my breasts have only begun to swell, though I am fifteen summers. Otherwise, there would be no room for pups or baby geese or any of the creatures I hide there.

Father has told me often enough not to carry animals in my robes. I think he is trying to ease me into the idea that I am no longer a child but, as I have mentioned, I do not excel at obedience. Fortunately, the heat of my body has lulled the pup to sleep. My job with the caravan is to help manage the animals, and I am good at it because I pay attention, a skill

I learned at my father's side in negotiations. Father says understanding comes when the right question has been asked.

"What is the right question?" he asked me the first time I went with him to a trade.

I said what came to my mind, certain I was correct. "How much will they pay?"

"No."

The next time I gave greater attention to the process, trying to discover the right question. This time, when he asked me, I said, "The right question is this: What is the price that makes both buyer and seller happy?"

"No. Pay closer attention."

"I did!" I protested.

Father stroked his beard, considering me. "So what did the man from Harran wish to purchase?"

"Salt," I said at once.

"Any salt?"

"No, only the finest. He was very adamant."

"Why?"

I had no answer.

"Find the answer to this question, and you will know the answer to my question."

It took two summers of studying. My father would question what I saw at each trade, what I heard or smelled or felt, and then he would return to the subject of the man from Harran, the man who wanted the finest salt. For two summers, I thought about this man before I went to sleep each night. I went over everything I could remember from the encounter, time after time. Though I would tire of worrying over the problem and try to forget it, the puzzle always returned to plague me.

Finally, I woke abruptly in the middle of the night and knew the answer. That day I studied the negotiations with different eyes, and when my father made me recite all I had observed, he asked, as he always did, "And what is the right question?"

Excited, and fearful I was wrong, I said, "The man from Harran said he wanted the finest salt, but that was not what he truly wanted."

I had trapped my father's attention. "And that was?"

My heart drummed. "What he truly wanted was to be seen as a man who knew more than others and who watched out for the interests of his people."

The slightest of nods. "He wished to be seen as a leader. And how did you decide this?"

"When he spoke, he angled his body to be sure his words carried to the crowd around him. He studied and tasted the salt with large movements, so they could see."

Now my father gave me the rarest of gifts, a smile of approval. "And so, in negotiations, what is the right question?"

"Not how much we will give or they will pay," I said carefully, "but what they want."

"Yes," my father said.

I felt as if I had climbed the highest mountain in the world and brought my father the prize he desired most. "And you, Father, gave him that by praising his eye for salt in a loud voice!" I laughed. "And he announced he would buy all the salt we had."

Now I understood why my father made me attend to every nuance. People speak in many ways other than with their words—the catch of emotion in their voice, a twitch of cheek, or a brush of hand across the mouth, even the way they position their bodies. Animals also "speak" in these ways if you watch and listen and have a good nose. I will say that for my knotted beak—it can smell.

One of our goats is about to birth her kid, and Father decides to stop for the day. When dusk falls and everyone is busy making camp, I sneak my pup back into the litter to let him suckle. Chiram has already chosen the evening's fare and has no need to cook puppies tonight. His burly son, Danel, is helping him, so I am relieved of that duty for now.

Nami eyes me reproachfully, knowing one of her pups has been missing. She is new to the caravan and new to motherhood, but I am not sorry I took him. There is no way to be certain when Chiram will decide to be rid of the litter. They crawl blindly over one another to get to her teats. I wish I could save them all, but I am not even sure how I will save the one. Chiram knows every handful of grain, every pomegranate in his stores, and I am sure if he considers these fat pups as a future meal, he knows how many there are.

When my borrowed pup wriggles himself between his siblings, I stroke Nami's head and tell her what an excellent mother she is. She thumps her plumed tail and licks my hand. She is indeed a beautiful creature, a black hunting dog, prized by the desert people. Standing, she comes to my thigh. Just looking at her is a pleasure—the graceful curve of her, like a cresting wave from her slender hips to her deep chest. My first glimpse of her standing on a hill took my breath. Wind caught the long, silky flow of her ears and the white feathering on the back of her forelegs. She stood like a carving, like a dog of the Egyptian kings, barely deigning to notice the world.

Because of her size, some of the caravan boys feared her when Chiram first brought her into the camp, but I saw a sense of humor in the expressive golden-brown tufts over her eyes and the smiling line to her mouth. We became friends at once, and she followed me around the camp until she had her pups. Then she spent her time as we traveled anxiously pacing beside the donkey that bore them, lifting her slender nose every few moments to check the sack where Chiram had stuffed them.

Chiram ignores her. She belongs to him, but she does not seem to know it. Only two of the many animals of the caravan are truly mine—my aging donkey, Philot, and a brown horse with black legs. We purchased the horse in a small city north of Harran. Father did so for a trade, but I begged to keep him. He relented, though Chiram grumbled greatly about how useless it was and how it ate food meant for the goats or donkeys. I am not supposed to run the horse, but I love the feel of the wind in my face and the slide of powerful muscles beneath me.

My tasks are easier without worrying about the pup squirming under my robe or crying out in hunger. I see to the goat, but she is not ready after all, and her kid will come another day or most likely in the middle of a night. Once the animals are settled, I turn the spit for the roasting meat, changing positions to avoid the shifting smoke. The moon is a pale shadow in the darkening sky. I unwind my headscarf and pull it around my shoulders.

My father emerges from the tents to put a hand on my shoulder. From the firmness of his grip, I know I am in trouble. "Our tent after the meal."

I nod. "Yes, Father." I can tell by his parting squeeze my attempt at respectful acquiescence has not relieved him of whatever parental burden he carries. I *am* in trouble.

This is not a new condition.

"Adir, you are burning the meat!" Chiram's shout from where he stands outside his tent snatches my attention back to what I am doing—or supposed to be doing. I turn the spit, then my mind wanders again, this time to the puzzle of the tall strangers. Who are they? Where are their lands?

As if I have conjured him, a cloud of smoke parts, revealing the clean-shaven stranger, the one with the gold hair, now more bronze in the fire-light. The smoke fills my nostrils. I cough but do not speak, remembering the rumor that El has sent the tall men. What does a god's messenger want with me?

"You are Adir, Zakiti's son?" he asks.

It was the first time he had ventured from the company of the other two. I nod, unable to pull my gaze from the broad forehead and jaw and the hair that gleams in the firelight. How does he know my name? Then I realize he has just heard Chiram shout it, and relief floods me. It is not necessarily a good thing to come to a god's attention. I think of Abram, praying day and night and making sacrifices on his high place. Not a very interesting life, in my opinion.

My glance drifts to the skein of fire. I want to have an interesting life—to see the world and its mysteries, to relish its surprises.

Boldly, I look back up at the northman, all the way up. "What are you called?"

A smile makes his face radiant, and a pulse throbs in my throat.

"I am Raph."

"Raph," I repeat to make sure I have the accent right. "And your companion?"

"Mika."

"Where are your lands?" I ask.

His smile turns wistful. "A simple question, but easy answer no." It is clear his mother tongue is not our language.

He gestures toward the fire, a graceful movement that makes me aware of my awkwardness, despite my father's assurances it is only a matter of my age and height. "Should you . . . circle?" he asks.

Grateful for the warning, I twist the pole that impales the carcass, just in time to save the skin from blackening and avoid another curse from Chiram. Raph moves to the opposite side of the fire to assist. With both of us on either end, the pole turns easily.

"Thank you."

"Nothing to speak." He changes from kneeling to a more comfortable squat. The smoke starts to follow him but switches directions abruptly. I keep my eye on it, watching to see if it provides evidence of El's favor on this man, or if he gets smoke in his face like any other.

"Where are your people from?" I ask.

"Ah, this wiser question, Adir," he says, and I am reminded of the lesson of the salt negotiation and my father's teaching: Understanding comes when the right question has been asked.

Struggling for the words, Raph says, "Now live they many places, but most in north mountains."

His phrasing stirs my curiosity. "You imply they come from elsewhere?"

Again, his smile stirs more than my curiosity, and I wonder at my body's acute reaction on so little information.

"Yes," he says. "They do."

At that moment, Chiram strides over to check the meat, and at his aggressive approach, Raph rises in one swift move to his feet. *Warrior*, I realize. That grace belongs to men whose muscles are tuned to obey in the most efficient manner, like the gallop of a horse or the quick turn of a herding dog. I still see no sign of weapons, but I have no doubt he could use them.

Chiram is a large man; a layer of fat covers his muscles, but I have seen him lift with ease a downed ibex onto his shoulders. Still, even the meaty cook comes only to Raph's chest. Chiram's hand tightens on the knife he holds. What has riled him? Raph moves only slightly, but his body now edges to Chiram's. Whether Chiram notices this, I cannot tell, but he seems to lose a bit of his bluster and turns to carve off a slice of meat. "Ready," he proclaims, and my mouth immediately begins to salivate. I am hungry. I am always hungry.

Raph takes his share and a portion I assume is for his companions, and disappears into the night. I eat slowly, not relishing my father's summons.

2

Then the men [angels] got up from their meal and looked out toward Sodom.

—Book of Genesis 18:10-16

WHEN I CAN AVOID IT no longer, I go to our tent, a knot in my chest. My father will be right to punish me, as I have disobeyed him, but more than his punishment, I dread facing his disappointment.

I pull aside the hanging and duck through the opening. Our tent is not lavish, but it is home. My section is small, only my blankets and bag of clothing, everything always rolled and ready to pack in the morning. We rarely stay in a camp more than a night.

My father waits beside the small fire that warms the interior, the remains of his own meal beside him in a clay bowl. Trying not to be awkward, I kneel before him on the hard ground, my bottom resting on my heels. I wish to be still, but my fingers, which have their own will, twist the braid of the rug. It is finely made with reds and blues in patterns my trader's eye identifies as a piece from the east Father has acquired.

"Adira," he says, and I catch my breath. My true name! This is indeed serious.

"Father, I am sorry," I whisper.

He frowns. "For what?"

Confused, I meet his eyes and then look away. Why does he make me say it? Is he angry at something else I have done? My mind races through the past few days, and I can bring nothing else to mind, at least nothing he could possibly know of. He can't know about the aloe juice I added to Chiram's wine. Chiram thinks I do not listen when he talks about his herbs, but I do. I bite my lip to keep from grinning at the thought of him, straining to keep his thick bowed legs together, running at regular intervals to the camp's edge for two days. It served him well for speaking of cooking puppies. I decide I will start confession at the lesser infraction. "I am sorry for my disobedience in taking the pup."

"Ah yes, that," Father says, as though distracted from another chain of thought. "You must return the dog to Chiram."

"But Father," I say, though I do not still have the pup in my possession, "he is going to *cook* him!"

He snorts. "Adir, the bitch is his and thus her litter is his. To steal from another in the caravan is a stoning offense."

"But—"

His right hand slices the air, which means he will hear no more on the matter. No amount of begging on my part will change his mind once he has made that gesture. I have seen him use it many times in negotiations when he has made his last offer.

"We are a tribe of laws," he says, oblivious to the terrible cramping of my chest.

I stare into the fire and try not to see those tiny, warm balls of fur nuzzling into their mother's belly.

"There is else I wish to speak of," he says.

"What?" I ask, trying to dam the tears that have welled in my eyes.

He shifts and holds his closed fist toward me, palm up. Despite myself, I am curious. "What is it?"

He opens his fingers. On his palm lies a small cylinder seal made of a black silvery gemstone. I pluck it from his hand, admiring the small carving of a woman in long, tiered robes.

"Lama," he says. "A goddess of protection and intercession. I gave it to your mother long ago in Ur. Now it is yours, your personal seal."

A slender piece of rawhide threads through the hollow center. I hold it in my hand for a moment, trying to feel some connection to my mother, and then tie it around my neck.

"When your mother died, I did not want to give you up. You were my only connection to her. But you have not stayed a child, and I fear I have kept you for myself too long."

"What are you saying?"

"I am saying it is time you claimed your birthright as a woman."

"But you always said you did not want the caravan to know I was a girl. I have never told anyone. Why would they suspect now?"

He gives me a sharp glance. "They will suspect soon. How are you to hide your woman's bleeding?"

I flinch. I have tried to keep that from him, apparently without success. "It only just began last moon."

He sighs. "I should have left you with Sarai long ago. She asked for you, but I could not bear to give you up. Each time I thought, one more journey, so I can become used to the idea."

Give me to Sarai? "Why can I not stay with the caravan? There are women here."

"There is not a man here worthy of you, and you need a chance to have your own family."

I rise to my feet, breathing hard, betrayed. We travel to Abram and Sarai so he can dispose of me. "I have a family. You are my family. The caravan is my family!"

Once again, the hand slices the air, but I am not silent, not obedient. "No, I will not go. No matter where you send me, I will not stay. I will follow you."

He does not answer. I expect his rage, but the look on his face is not anger, only a great sadness, and that fills me with more despair than I can hold.

I turn and flee into the night, grateful for the bite of cold air. The need to run, to feel the wind's push on my face, pulses through my flesh. Since I was young, I have been drawn to rocky inclines and hills. No feeling can match standing in a high place and receiving the wind's embrace. My father truly named me daughter of the wind.

Oblivious to stones and without my guidance, my feet take me across the camp. No one pays attention or tries to stop me. Boys often run about, dodging fires and chasing each other. I chase no one, but my future pursues me.

When I approach the herds, I slow to a walk. To run here would start a stampede, and that is not my purpose. Only now do I even know my purpose. I have fled without thought, but now I take a camel-hair bridle from the cart and slip through the donkeys, moving slowly out of habit, though the ache to run still pounds in me.

Above, clouds veil the half moon, but I know each creature by the shape and the lighter markings that distinguish them. A soft neigh ahead changes my course, and my hands find the familiar silky skin of the gelding I have named Dune. His breath is sweet on my face, and he lowers his head for the bridle. He is not young, but he still loves to run.

Glad for my height, I swing onto his back and guide him away from the herd. The desire for speed is still strong, but I am no fool to run a horse in rocky terrain at night. A fall and a broken leg would mean Dune in Chiram's pot. Instead, I drop the reins and lay my head on his mane, wrapping my arms around his neck and letting him take me up and down the hills where he will.

Before my tears finish soaking his mane, Dune snorts, lifts his head, and halts. Sitting upright, I search for campfires, but none are in sight. I check the sky, knowing I headed west originally, but clouds now blanket the stars, and I have no idea how much of the night has passed while I wrapped myself in misery.

A shadow moves in a nearby clump of brush, and Dune's muscles tense beneath me. Before I can react, he rears and jumps sideways. I am slipping off. I make a desperate grab for mane, but most of my weight is off to his side. With a frightened snort, Dune leaps again, and I hit the ground.

I cannot draw breath or move for long moments. Dune is not in my line of vision, but I imagine by the sound of pounding hooves, he has fled back to the caravan. He is gone, and I am alone. There is not enough light to follow his tracks. If I stumble around in the dark, I risk becoming more lost. It is best to wait here until morning breaks and Zakiti realizes what has happened and comes for me.

It is the best plan I can think of . . . until I hear something move in the brush and catch the faint, greenish gleam of watching eyes.

3

At that time a severe famine struck the land of Canaan, forcing Abram to go down to Egypt, where he lived as a foreigner. As he was approaching the border of Egypt, Abram said to his wife, Sarai, "Look, you are a very beautiful woman. When the Egyptians see you, they will say, 'This is his wife. Let's kill him; then we can have her!' So please tell them you are my sister. Then they will spare my life and treat me well because of their interest in you."

—Book of Genesis 12:10-13

I WIPE THE DIRT FROM MY mouth, my gaze locked on the last place I saw the gleam of the wolf's eyes. Every breath jabs sharply into my side. I have fled from a future I do not want and found a present with fangs.

What a fool I am.

With one hand pressed tightly to my side, I roll to my knees and try to stand. Pain stabs me so fiercely, my vision blurs and nausea churns my belly. I let out a cry. Perhaps it will frighten the wolves, or perhaps someone is coming to look for me and will hear.

But that is not possible. Dune has not had time to return to the camp. What are the chances someone will notice he is bridled? That I have disappeared? I should have ridden Philot. My faithful donkey would not have left me. I should have paid attention to where I was going. I should have—

A cloud moves from the moon's face and I see my death less than a stone's throw away. I scrabble about with my hand looking for a stick, a stone, anything for a weapon. Even uninjured, I could not outrun a wolf.

There is nothing within my reach.

Warily, the wolf approaches. It is lean and muscular, with short fur a mottled gray. The copper undertones are barely visible in the moonlight. I put a hand on the cool, smooth surface of the seal that hangs around my neck, hoping Lama will protect me, or at least intercede with El on my behalf. But one does well not to rely completely on the gods, as I have heard Chiram say, and I yell at the advancing wolf, the loudest shriek I can manage, which sends another bolt of pain into my side.

He hesitates, head cocked sideways in a canine question. The wolf appears to be a lone male. A human is not his normal prey, but a wounded human is another matter. He is thin without the advantage of hunting with a pack, and hungry. In the cock of his head, I read he is weighing the risk of waiting until I weaken further against the possibility of another predator finding me and robbing him of his meal. Competitors abound in these hills—lions, leopards, a pack of wolves.

I am indeed a fool. My father is better rid of me.

The wolf lifts his head, sniffing, and then moves forward, his lips pulled back, exposing sharp teeth. His instincts are wolf, not hyena. He will make his own kill.

My breaths are ragged from fear and shallow to keep the pain from stabbing my chest. He hears that and probably my galloping heart. I try to slow my breathing, hoping to appear less vulnerable.

He circles.

On my hands and knees, I scramble to remain facing him, knowing his preferred attack is from the rear, onto the back of my neck to break my spine between his powerful jaws. To keep from crying out in pain, I bite my tongue—and realize another mistake with the coppery taste in my mouth.

Now, the smell of blood stains the air.

Without taking his cool eyes from his prey, the wolf sniffs again and growls, a low, rumbling sound that freezes my heart.

I scrape my fingers against the hard ground, gathering dirt to throw in his eyes, a meager defense.

Moonlight gleams off his teeth. They transfix me. So white, so pure.

As he charges forward, I throw my pitiful handful of dirt and raise my hands to shield my face. So quick is his spring, he appears only a blur of motion. But as fast as he is, a slender black shape meets his leap like a thrown lance.

Ferocious snarls, flashes of teeth—

They fight over me, until both abruptly stop, regarding each other with lips peeled back and low, ominous growls. I peer closely at the intruding wolf. Nami! My throat clamps with gratitude and with fear for her.

Locked in a standoff, both canines vie for dominance with their posture. Nami's swollen tits hang low. She has left her pups to follow me. I do the only thing I can to help her. Grimacing, I growl low in my throat. *We are pack*, my bared teeth warn. *I may be wounded, but we are pack.*

The wolf's eyes flick to me and then back to Nami, who stands tall because of her long, slender legs.

Perhaps it is the threat of both of us, or perhaps he defers to Nami as a female he does not wish to fight. I do not know, but slowly he turns his head aside. Nami holds her position, not yielding, the short fur on her shoulders stiff with warning.

With a slow, deliberate movement, so as not to provoke her, the wolf turns his back and stalks away.

Nami waits until she is certain he is gone and then limps to my side, licking my face and taking my chin delicately in her mouth for a moment, something I have seen her do with her pups. She has turned in an instant from fierce predator to adoring dog. I hold onto her and for the second time that night, I cry into an animal's side.

"Nami, thank you."

She gives me another worried lick.

"I promise I will save your puppies. All of them, I swear on El, my god."

Unimpressed with my oath, Nami stretches beside me and tends to her bloody paw.

Exhausted, I ease down and rest my head on my arm, draping the other on her back. She lies by my side, but when she finishes cleaning her wound, she keeps her head raised, alert for the wolf's return or any other danger that might appear.

We are pack.

CHAPTER

4

And . . . when Abram arrived in Egypt, everyone noticed Sarai's beauty. When the palace officials saw her, they sang her praises to Pharaoh, their king, and Sarai was taken into his palace.

—Book of Genesis 12:14-15

M Y FATHER AND CHIRAM FIND me just after the sun rises above the hills to copper the sky. I am most grateful to Lama and El for letting me see it. My father kneels beside me. "Are you hurt?"

"A little." I put my hand to my side.

With care, he gathers me into his arms to hold, enveloping me in the familiar, salty smell of safety.

From over his shoulder Chiram growls, "Idiot boy!"

Father's grip on me tightens, and I catch my breath with the pain, but bury my head against him and say only, "I am sorry, Father."

He sighs.

I have said those words often. I always mean them, but somehow, despite my best intentions, I find them on my tongue with greater frequency than any other child I know. And I am soon to be beyond childhood. That thought is a reminder of what drove me from our tent the previous night. I do not want to be a woman and leave my father and the caravan. The way he holds me tells me he feels the same.

"One more trip," he whispers in my ear.

I clasp onto that promise. *One more. I will not be abandoned!*

When my father releases me and tries to help me up, I cannot stop the cry that wrenches from my lips.

He again kneels beside me. "What happened?"

"Dune scented a wolf and threw me," I admit. "My chest hurts. Did he return to the camp?"

He shakes his head and my heart sinks. This can only mean my horse fell to predators or perhaps, I comfort myself, he wandered to another camp.

Though I am fifteen summers, my father scoops me into his arms and carries me, a watchful Nami at our heels. The sharp stabs in my side are preferable to Chiram's grumbles. "The sheep dropped her kid while you were off wandering around."

"Enough, Chiram," my father finally says. "Adir is punished enough. Let it lie."

With a last grunt, Chiram acquiesces.

AT THE CAMP, father lays me gently on his own pallet and gives me water. My mouth is parched and cracking. Chiram is wrong; I am beyond idiot. I did not even take water with me. I am no longer in the desperate grip of the despair that drove me out of our tent only last night. The moonlit gleam of a wolf's teeth has altered my view of things. I still do not want change, but I have another, more pressing, desire.

"Chiram will tend you," Father says.

I groan. "No, please. I will be fine." I do not want Chiram's greasy hands on me.

"He has the most knowledge of medicines."

"Only because he butchers animals," I retort. "Please, not Chiram."

At that moment a shadow appears at the tent entrance. "May we enter?"

I recognize the accent, but not the voice.

My father pulls aside the hanging to reveal Raph and Mika, two of the messengers of El. "Be welcome in my tent," Father says, stepping aside and gesturing for them to enter. They have to bend to avoid brushing their heads against the tent opening.

Raph glances at me and then addresses my father. "We heard your son was injured."

I close my eyes, unwilling to face the humiliation of hearing my father tell what I had done.

"He fell from the horse," he says simply, and my heart swells anew with love for him.

Raph gestures to Mika, who is even taller. If Mika had worn the peaked hat the third giant wore, he would not be able to stand upright inside the tent. "Mika is learned in medicine and healing. He is willing to examine Adir with your permission."

Mika glances at me as if I am a sheep or goat. I imagine Raph has talked him into coming.

Father looks relieved and then concerned. I know what he is thinking. He does not want to give permission for a man to touch me. I certainly do not want to be touched, especially by this cryptic stranger who may be our god's messenger and looks at me with such cold assessment that I want to stomp his foot.

But the alternative is Chiram.

"It is all right, Father." I lift my outer robe, revealing only my ribs, which already have begun to turn a pale blue.

Mika takes only one step to reach my side. He kneels without the warrior grace I observed in Raph. Despite his cold manner, Mika's hands are gentle, though it takes my breath when he prods.

"A rib—" he searches for a word and confers with Raph in a tongue I have never heard.

"Bruise," Raph offers.

Mika nods. "Bruise. Perhaps hair-crack, but no broken." He hands my father a small package wrapped in cloth. "Boil this and give to him." He pauses and confers with Raph, now in the language of the northlands, which I understand. "How do you say twice daily for the next hand of days?"

Raph shrugs.

Mika turns back to us, holding up his forefinger. "Morning." Another finger joins the first. "Night." Then he splays all of his fingers. "Days. Understand?"

Father nods, but my eyes narrow at this brusque order given without the least pretense of politeness. Perhaps a god's messenger does not need to be polite, but I do not like this man.

He has me sit upright and wraps a wide strip of cloth tightly around my lower ribs. He does it expertly enough, and the pain eases.

Mika rises. "Check in morning." I am not certain if he means we are to check it or he will.

"Thank you," Father says. "May I pay for your—?"

Mika's back stiffens. "No." He turns and strides from the tent.

Raph smiles and holds both his palms up in a gesture that apologizes for his companion. "Mika not mean rude. Just . . . way."

"He can be any way he pleases," Father says. "I am grateful for his aid."

CHAPTER

5

Then Pharaoh gave Abram many gifts because of her [Sarai]—sheep, goats, cattle, male and female donkeys, male and female servants, and camels. But the lord sent terrible plagues upon Pharaoh and his household because of Sarai, Abram's wife. So Pharaoh summoned Abram and accused him sharply. "What have you done to me?" he demanded. "Why didn't you tell me she was your wife? Why did you say, 'She is my sister,' and allow me to take her as my wife? Now then, here is your wife. Take her and . . . [go]!"

—Book of Genesis 12: 16-19

INDEED, THE NEXT MORNING Mika returns to check my bandage. Raph also, and I wonder why, since he is hardly needed. Father has gone to attend to caravan business, so I am alone in our tent.

Mika scowls at me, as though irritated I am taking his precious time, and I scowl back at him.

Raph grins. "Adir is not impressed with your displeasure, brother," he says in the north language.

Mika does not acknowledge his comment.

So they are brothers. This is something I did not know, and the plan I birthed last night requires I know all I can about them.

Mika inspects the bandage, sliding his fingers beneath it to check for tightness and then pressing a hand against my flesh below it. I flinch at his touch.

He looks at me for the first time. His eyes are green. Father says mine are grey-green, flecked with tawny bits, but his are just green.

"I check skin heat."

I nod. A bandage wrapped too tightly means the blood is not flowing well and must be adjusted. I have wrapped enough donkey legs to know this.

Mika stands. From my perspective sitting on my pallet, he seems more like a tree straightening in the wind. "You live."

The words are edged with sarcasm, as my wound is not major. I start to retort he should not bother with me anymore, and then I remember I need his assistance and hold my tongue.

Raph rests a friendly hand on my shoulder. "You dash soon about."

He is much the handsomer of the two. They are both exotic, but when Raph gets close, I can feel the pulse in my neck throb. I have never had romantic notions toward any boy, but this man with his sun-gold hair and blue eyes is different. I wonder what it would be like if he leaned down and brushed my lips with his—a custom of the Egyptians, the people of the Black Land—a custom I thought disgusting until this very moment.

Startled, I realize they are unaware of my dreaming and are almost out the tent. "Wait," I say, too loudly.

Both turn.

"I have a proposition."

Mika lifts an eyebrow. Raph gives me a kind smile that makes my heart leap.

"Proposition?" he asks, and by the way he says the word—as if it is a strange fruit in his mouth—I know he does not know what it means.

"A barter," I say.

"You have nothing to want," Mika snaps and starts to turn.

"I do."

He hesitates. "What?" His hand has already brushed aside the entrance hanging, and a gust of wind sweeps into the tent, carrying the smells of the caravan—the sweet musk of donkeys, the pungent aroma of goats, and the dizzying allure of simmering soup. My stomach whines.

"I do not know your business," I say, which I do not, other than some mission of El's, or perhaps they are finished with that and now pursue their own goals. "But whatever it is, you would do far better speaking Akkadian."

Mika stiffens. "We Akkadian speak."

I shake my head, "I have sat at more negotiations with my father than I can number, and I have seen this happen. Men perceive you as vulnerable if you do not speak the language with skill."

Raph nods and says in the northern tongue, "Adir has a sharp meaning there, brother. One's language carries more than words. You have often said this to me."

Now I spread before them the most persuasive element of my argument. "Besides, your Akkadian words are those of the northern dialect. Where we go, you will need the southern dialect."

Raph and I both look to Mika, who stands very still. Finally, to me he says, "And want you?"

Well, there is hope for him as a bargainer. "I want a young goat."

With a wave of his hand, Mika says, "No goat we."

"You have things of value," I counter. "Buy one of our goats."

Mika presses his lips together and points a finger into Raph's chest. "You." Then he strides out of the tent.

Raph returns and squats near me. His eyes sparkle with amusement. "You understand northern tongue, yes?"

"I understand it," I say, taking care with my accent.

"You know others?"

I beam. "Many." It is not a boast. Since I was three summers and my mother died, I have traveled with my father, who took advantage of my young mind and had me learn from various peoples, many of whom traveled with us for a time. It is dangerous to travel alone. Bandits and thieves prey upon travelers, and kings sometimes decide to make war on their fellow cities. That happened summers ago, and Abram's nephew Lot was taken prisoner. Abram had to rescue him. After that, Lot decided every word of Abram's came straight from El, and he became a most devoted and ardent follower of the god of Abram.

"When you teach?" Raph asks.

I have already thought of this. My tasks are mostly finished by dusk when the animals are settled. "In the evenings after the night meal," I say. "I can come to your tent."

Raph considers. "And when your goat?"

This is the tricky part. I do not want to wait long. "In three days," I say in his language to further impress my skills. "I will teach you for three days, and then you will say if my lessons are worthy. If not, you owe me nothing, but if you wish to continue, you must purchase my goat."

With thumb and forefinger Raph rubs his clean-shaven chin. "This fair."

"A pact then," I say, holding out my palm.

He nods and presses his palm into mine. "A pact."

CHAPTER

6

Abram was very rich in livestock, silver, and gold.
—Book of Genesis 13:2

As SOON AS RAPH LEAVES, I roll onto my hands and knees and carefully rise, taking shallow breaths to avoid the pain. To my relief, Mika's bandage helps. I will not run and jump for a while, but this is manageable. I eat the breakfast of flatbread, dried dates, and goat's milk my father has left, clean my face with a damp cloth, and go to find Chiram.

Chiram has already begun to pack, which means bread, dried meat, and dates for the mid-meal. He sends Danel to find something. As he passes by, Danel shakes his head. "Stupid boy."

Chiram kneels before the bronze pot that is his pride and looks up at me from beneath the black forest of his brows. "So, you live."

I look down at the grass and shift a stone with my foot.

"Idiot," Chiram grumbles. His voice is gravel. "You cost me." He places a long wooden stirrer into the pot for traveling, protecting it with leather packets of spices and dried food. Between them, he lays a couple of knives. Chiram is most fond of his knives—he always tucks at least two into his sash. His favorites are two matching daggers with ibex-horn hilts. When he is not busy with matters of the pot, he sharpens or practices throwing them. He is quite skillful.

My foot rolls the stone back over. "Cost you? How?"

"Lost the pups to hyenas while that bitch was out chasing you." His brows slide together, forming a single dark ridge over his eyes. "You owe me."

His words seem to float somewhere above my head, refusing to sink into my head. *Lost the pups?*

My chest hurts with a different kind of pain than the fall from Dune imparted, my mind filling with images of each pup—the perpetually sleepy one with a white splash on his throat; the female who was a reflection of her mother, black face with golden brown on her brows and under her muzzle; the playful silver-gray one with black splotches; and the sweet one with a golden nose I had taken with me yesterday.

The pain in my chest twists up into my throat, and I have to wait long moments before speaking. Finally, I say, "I am sorry."

I am sorrier to Nami than to Chiram, who intended to cook them all. "I will pay for all of the pups in three days with a young goat."

"A goat?" Chiram looks up.

I quickly add. "And for Nami."

Chiram considers. "That's a costly dog."

I stare at him. "Why did you buy her? Surely, you did not purchase such a dog to eat her pups. Better a goat that will give milk every day. A goat is a very good bargain for a dog." He has no use for a dog anyway.

He shrugs. "Won it. Let some desert rat stake it in a game."

Chiram does not think much of the desert nomads. My people are wanderers too, but our customs are different, and we do not traverse the deep desert, but stay in the hills and grasslands with our flocks.

"Meant to put it back in," Chiram grumbles, "but the former owner passed out." He runs the knife expertly along the sharpening stone. "So I was stuck with the scrounger."

Scroungers. That is how people in the city look at dogs. Herders and farmers, and, of course, the desert people see dogs through better eyes. I do too, but Chiram is originally from the city and thinks them dirty beasts of little use, other than as delicacies for the pot.

"Where are you getting a goat?" Chiram asks, his wide forehead bunched in suspicion. "Your father has no need for a dog to feed."

I pull myself straighter and do not mention I have been feeding Nami in any case. She can hardly live on the tiny amount Chiram gives her, even though her breed subsists on less food and water than others. They are desert creatures, like the camel. "I am working for the goat. I will bring it to you in three days."

Chiram rubs the fold of skin at his neck and then pulls on his dark, coarse beard and looks down at me. "Three days, then."

DESPITE THE STONE in my chest, I hurry to a hollow in a hillside where Nami had settled with her pups when we first arrived. She is curled up in the place where their scent lingers. I remember how she paced beside the donkey that carried them, checking every few moments to make sure she could still smell her pups. She did not leave them, even for water. But the past night she spent with me, and hyenas had killed them all. My shoulders sag with the burden of that as I kneel beside her. Her teats are tight and swollen.

"Oh, Nami, I am so sorry." I offer the back of my hand, half hoping she will bite it, as I deserve. Instead, she sniffs my hand and then solemnly licks it, which makes me cry. And that makes my chest hurt anew.

"Adir, what are you doing?"

I look up at my father, unaware until that moment of his presence. "How do we deserve them?" I ask.

"What? Why are you out here and not in the tent resting?"

I hiccup.

"Come," he says more softly. "Back to the tent. I have told Chiram to unpack. We are staying a few days."

I let him lead me, casting a glance over my shoulder. Nami is nosing the place where her pups had lain, searching for them, feeding her longing with their scent. My heart is breaking for her.

THE NEXT MORNING I go about my chores, despite my father's protests. "They are just bruises," I tell him. "I am fine." But the only thing that convinces him is, "A *boy* would not lie around because of a few bruises. Do you want to ignite suspicion?"

My father told the caravan he wanted the animals to graze another day or two before we left. I suspect he wanted me to rest, but the caravan master's decision is not questioned.

I hate staying in the tent. I love the early morning when mists rise in the hills, kissing the grass with dew. A magical stillness wraps the world before the heat descends.

Philot always greets me with a bray. My donkey nuzzles my hand before scooping up the date treat with his big lips, nodding his head as he eats, as if he has never tasted such an odd thing before, though I bring him one every morning.

"You have another day or two to eat and doze," I tell him. "No packs or traveling, a gift from my stupidity. But," I add, "that part you do not have to share with anyone."

Philot sniffs my hand to make sure he has not missed a date.

Nami had accompanied me when I checked the animals, but now she will not leave the place she last saw her pups. After the animals are accounted for, I go to her. She lies on her side as if her pups will appear at any moment, eager for her swollen teats. Her tail thumps once at my approach, but she does not move. I kneel to stroke her head. How does a dog express grief? I let my tears fall for us both.

THAT NIGHT, WHEN Raph indicates I may enter their tent, I am surprised at my reluctance to do so. It is as if I feel the future splitting here—a stream encountering a stone that forces it to a different course. But I enter. I have made an oath.

Their tent is simply furnished. I expected something more lavish for El's messengers, but only a rug, bedding pallets, a bronze bowl, and two plain cups furnish the interior. At the far side is the object covered by a black fur they have carried with them. Whatever lies beneath appears to be about as long as my arm. If I had a fur that thick, I would have it on my pallet for the cold nights. Perhaps it had been, but now it covers something—something they do not wish me to see and gossip about?

Curiosity is another of my faults. It has gotten me in difficulties as much as my lack of obedience. The older man, the one who wears the pointed hat, sits beside the object. He has removed his hat; his hair is sparse and gray, his beard as long as his hair.

"This is Anan," Raph says, indicating the old man. "He not speak Akkadian and not receive the lessons. He soon returns north."

I bow my head to acknowledge him. He does not return the gesture.

Raph waves a hand to a spot on a rug. "Be seated." I sit on the rug, disappointed it is of ordinary weave. These exotic travelers should have more interesting possessions, so by this I know they are not traders.

Mika lowers a cup at his lips and scowls, obviously disapproving of me or of the plan to instruct them. One of the rumors that swirl about them is they are very learned men. It would be insulting to allow a caravan boy to teach them. I must tread carefully. If Mika throws me out, Nami will stay Chiram's dog, and any future pups will die in the pot, if she does not end up there herself.

This is a serious concern. I am not good at treading carefully.

"Tea?" Raph offers a cup.

"Thank you." It is rude not to accept.

"So," Raph pours a brown liquid from the bowl into his own cup and hands it to me. "How begin?"

"Perhaps," I say, "if I know your purpose, we can start with the words you will most need."

"Not concern you," Mika says.

I bite my lower lip and bow my head. "No offense or intrusion is intended. I only wish to be useful." *And earn my goat.*

"A good plan," Raph says. His grasp of our language is more sophisticated than Mika's. Perhaps Mika considers himself too holy to bother with a language not his own.

Raph rubs his chin. "Begin with only words."

So I translate their words into my tongue. It is an odd list, including "star, white, daughter, stone, morning, storm, dream," and several more, but Raph will not proceed until he and Mika can say each with the correct accent. I explain that pronouncing a word differently can change its meaning, and so it is important to get it right.

Despite his surly attitude, Mika is quicker than Raph and remembers everything almost the first time he hears it. This annoys me, but it gives me an excuse to look at Raph more.

He is very pleasant to look at.

7

He took his wife, Sarai, his nephew Lot, and all his wealth—his livestock and all the people he had taken into his household at Haran—and headed for the land of Canaan.

—Book of Genesis 12:5

AFTER TWO DAYS OF REST, we resume our journey. Nami trots alongside the donkey that had carried her pups and sniffs the empty bag. Heartbroken, she whine-sings her anxiety and returns to my side. We travel quickly all the morning, and approach the oak trees and the tents of Abram while the sun is still high. The rich scent of roasting lamb fills the air, along with the high-pitched laughter of children, and I identify Ishmael's voice. My cousin is twelve summers, and a head shorter. I spot him among one of several sheep herds that belong to Abram and his family. Ishmael waves, but he is busy with the sheep and does not run out to meet us.

Convinced at last that her pups are not with the donkeys, Nami follows me like a shadow inside the largest tent, and I follow Father, already almost his height. Sarai knows I am a girl, but she keeps our secret out of respect for my father's judgment. Though considered an elder, Father defers to Abram. They grew up together in the city of Ur. I have been to Ur, Babylon, and Egypt. I have traveled the world, at least the most important parts of it.

I sit at the back of the tent on one of the sheepskins spread throughout, scrunching my nose at the smell of men's bodies in a cramped space. I would rather be outside with Ishmael. Instead, I play the part of Zakiti's only son. Nami drops beside me, resting her head on her paws. My fingers work on the mats under her ears.

Father looks back over his shoulder and shakes his head at me. I regretfully decline the offering of fermented camel's milk, but grab a handful of dates from the copper tray a slave offers.

Ishmael wriggles in beside me. "Nice dog," he says, eyeing Nami appreciatively, and then tilts his head at Mika, Raph, and Anan, who have settled along the tent's edge. "Who are they?"

"Giants," I mumble ominously.

I see Ishmael eyeing their broad foreheads and shoulders and skin reddened from the sun. "Do they carry weapons?" he asks.

"Many." I watch in amusement as his eyes widen.

My cousin, Lot, who is almost my father's age and nephew to Abram, takes his place beside my father. "Zakiti, how is the life of a rich merchant?" he bellows.

My father grunts. "Rich? Have you ever seen my gold-trimmed robes, Lot? Abram is the one with wealth." He nods at the finely worked hangings along the tent walls, "I have not the stomach to acquire it as he did."

He speaks of Abram's journey into Egypt in the days of famine before I was born. The king gave Abram sheep, oxen, donkeys, camels, and servants in exchange for Sarai, whom he took into his harem, thinking she was Abram's sister.

The story is that El struck the king and his household with illness whenever he tried to touch Sarai, until he begged her to explain what was happening. She told him she was Abram's wife, and her husband was beloved by El. Then the king let Abram go, laden with riches. If I were the king of Egypt, Abram's trick would have angered me. But I suspect Sarai talked him into releasing them with their possessions. She is as smart as she is beautiful. She runs the household and all the business of the flocks—even Abram's steward answers to her—while Abram goes off to his high place to talk with El.

With another hearty laugh, Lot slaps my father's back. "You should come to the Vale and give up all this traveling back and forth across deserts and mountains. The grass is plentiful and yields rich crops of barley.

The sheep graze and fatten. A much more peaceful life than dodging bandits and herding donkeys."

"Ah yes," Father says with a twist of irony in his voice. "I hear you are fond of the peace of your lands."

"Such a tongue you have, Zakiti! All right, you have caught me. It is no secret I prefer the city walls. It is peaceful out in the fields, true, but sometimes a man needs more than peace to keep life spiced."

Before my father can respond, sudden quiet descends. All heads turn toward the draping cloth parted by two young boys as Abram steps through, flanked on his right by his first wife, Sarai. Abram's head is gray, but his back is straight. He is tall, though not as tall as the northmen, and other than the color of his eyes, his features are like mine, perhaps my legacy from the blood of his line. Except, of course, his nose has no knot. When I was five, I broke mine in a fall from a rocky incline my father forbade me to climb. My fingers stroke the bridge of my nose, finding the familiar coin-sized place where it knitted together without grace.

As Abram comes closer and takes a seat on a wooden bench, my regretful thoughts about my nose fade, captured by the burning intensity in his eyes. They are the color of a deep pool reflecting a night sky, and I find I cannot look away from them. Why do I not remember this? Our previous visit was three summers ago, when I was twelve. I only remember playing with Ishmael, studying with Sarai, and sitting in agitation as the men talked on and on . . . and, of course, Hagar's honey cakes.

Abram spreads his hands, palms out, over the crowd. "My friends, my tribe, I thank you for gathering in my humble tent. You are a special people under the eye of El, your god."

"Tell us the story!" one man shouts from a corner.

"Yes," Lot adds roughly. "The story; let us hear it again."

I know he will tell of how a storm and shifting of the earth broke all his father's idols except one, the statue of El, and how El spoke to him and said, "*I am your god, Abram. From your loins will come my tribe, and I will be their god.*" And then El told Abram to break the remaining idol because he was not to be contained or managed by human hands. El said, "*I am without boundaries, beyond the limitations of clay or stone.*"

To follow a god that refuses to inhabit a statue or belong to one place is an idea even some of Abram's tribe still struggle to hold. Abram has embraced it, and he offers it to us at every gathering. Many have accepted, including Mamre the Amorite, who lives on this land, and his brothers and families who had ridden in battle with Abram. This was my teaching since I was young, so I too worship El-without-a-form, though he has never spoken to me.

Ishmael's elbow finds my ribs. His eyes glaze over with boredom. We do not need to speak. The attention of everyone is fastened on Abram. Being the youngest allowed in the tent, we sit in the very back. Ishmael carefully works the edge of the woven camel-hair fabric just enough for us to crawl under it. Nami belly-crawls after us.

Outside, the sun bears down on us, but we don't care. "You have grown a foot length, cousin!" I say, as soon as we have run beyond hearing range.

Ishmael beams. "Mother says I eat enough honey cakes to grow tall as a mountain." He shakes his head. "But I will never grow as tall as those giants." His eyes shine with admiration. "What do they eat?"

I grin. "If I told you they eat grass, would you go join the sheep and graze?"

"Yes!"

I follow Ishmael to a hillside overlooking the sheep and donkeys.

"I remember the last time you came," Ishmael says, his dark eyes gleaming. "My father told the same stories, and I was so bored. Then, when everyone was hushed and intent on his words, you suddenly squealed, and a gosling poked its head out of your robe." He sighs. "It was wonderful!"

Ishmael was the only one who thought it "wonderful." I believe this is a story he will repeat as many times as Abram tells his. "How could I forget?" I say with a wry grin. "The little beast woke up and bit my nipple!"

We both laugh. I definitely had been in trouble that day. My father forbade me to ride Dune for a moon-cycle as punishment. My cousin continues to laugh, holding his side, and I realize how much I miss him. Seeing him often would be the only good thing about staying here with Sarai. I wonder, however, what Ishmael's reaction would be if he discovered I was not the boy he thought, but a girl. Having no siblings, he looks up to me as an older brother. The other boys in the tribe shun him because his mother is an Egyptian.

As if he heard my thought, a heavyset boy appears over the ridge. He is about my age, but much larger. "So," he taunts, his hands on his hips, "why aren't you in the tent with the other high-ranking men, *special boy*?"

Ishmael stiffens. "What I do is no concern of yours, Talmet. Go away."

"Perhaps I should tell Eliezer that you are shirking your duties."

I feel Ishmael twitch at that name. Eliezer is Abram's steward and not a man to be displeased. "Leave him be," I say, as another boy, a head taller than Talmet, appears.

"Oh, it is the *Egyptian* boy," the newcomer says with a sneer at Ishmael.

I feel my cheeks flush with anger. "He is not Egyptian. He is Abram's son!"

"His mother is an Egyptian concubine. How many men did she know before she lay with Abram?"

Ishmael throws himself at the taller boy, catching him by the knees and toppling him. Talmet jumps on Ishmael and begins to pummel him. Nami whines. I snatch up a rock and strike Talmet's shoulder. Nami dances around us, whine-singing her anxiety. I don't see Talmet's back-swing, which catches me in the mouth and knocks me onto my bottom. I taste blood, and a sharp pain lances through my still-bruised ribs. In a flash, Nami is between me and Talmet, all the hair on her back stiffened. At that moment, I would have been happy to see her tear into Talmet, as she had the wolf. But I grab her, afraid that her teeth might slash Ishmael in the tangle of bodies. "No, Nami!"

At that moment, Danel appears. I am happy to see someone from the caravan, even though he does not care for me as much as I do not care for his father. He is the cook's son, and all we have in common is the loss of our mothers at a young age. He is two years older and a size that will soon match his father's. I can tell by the danger in his eyes that he saw Talmet strike me, and he grabs Talmet by the throat, throwing him aside. The other boys leave Ishmael and attack Danel. My hands are full with Nami.

"What is this?" The sharp bark of Abram's steward halts the fighting as though a bolt of El's lightning stabbed the ground before us.

The boys separate. Eliezer's glare travels the group and stops on Danel. "Who are you?"

Danel straightens his shoulders. "I am Danel, son of Chiram."

"Why are you fighting?"

Danel glances at me. "To defend the caravan's honor."

I sigh. Now I owe him.

And Father will not be happy.

CHAPTER

8

Terah took his son Abram, his daughter-in-law Sarai (his son Abram's wife), and his grandson Lot (his son Haran's child) and moved away from Ur of the Chaldeans. He was headed for the land of Canaan, but they stopped at Haran and settled there.

—Book of Genesis 11:31

TO MY RELIEF, ELIEZER DOES not relate the incident to my father. I suppose a little fight among children is not worthy of bothering him or Abram and, in fact, Eliezer lectured the boys about the duties of hospitality. "These are our *guests*," he said to Talmut and the others. "If you were older, your punishment would be severe."

I asked, as a guest, that the episode be forgotten. Of course, I must explain my swollen lip and the red splotch on my face from Talmet's hand. Fortunately, my shrug and mumble about being clumsy come at a moment when Lot appears, insisting that we travel with him to Sodom and stay at his home. I do not care for that stinking city, but I am grateful for the distraction.

That night Abram has two lambs butchered, and we feast on the tender meat, along with plenty of milk, cheese curds, and dates. Ishmael and I try to see who can eat the most. I win. Father often laughs at my ability to eat and not put on fat, but my belly hurts most of the night.

In the morning, when I make my sleepy way to the cooking area, I can see that Ishmael's mother has been awake a long time. Hagar eyes my robe, as if wondering what creature might be hidden there. At my outburst on our previous visit, I was banished to the women's tent. When the gosling again stuck his tiny head out from my robe, Hagar only laughed and helped feed and water. She does not disappoint me this morning. Honey cakes appear for breakfast! I forget my recent vow to stop eating.

As I stuff yet another in my mouth, Nami watches attentively, but does not beg for scraps.

Hagar throws her long dark braid over her shoulder and frowns at me. "Adir, how did your lip get bloodied?"

"I . . . fell and hit a rock."

She skeptically tilts her head. "Well, it has not affected your appetite. You shouldn't eat so many cakes; you'll be sick."

I answer her in the language of her homeland, where some say she was a slave and some say a princess. "I will stop eating your honey cakes when you prepare them right. But for now—you must keep trying." I sigh in mock dissatisfaction.

An old joke between us. She laughs and waves me out. "Go find Ishmael!"

I go, but not before grabbing the last flat cake for later and leaving a small bundle. It is a colorful scarf from the Black Land to cover her head. Father allowed me to trade in the market there, and I did well, so he gave me leave to purchase it. I have a fine eye for cloth.

Outside, dawn paints the sky, not in the bold colors of sunset but with pale rose. Only the moon and the morning star are still visible. Abram's tent sits on the highest edge of the hills above the valley where his flocks graze. The sides are rolled open on the east and west to catch the sunrise and allow a breeze in the heat of the afternoon. Ishmael sits with his father. Spread before us are spectacular views—to the south across a wilderness of cinnamon-brown boulders and to the east, down into the great rift in the earth that cradles the Dead Sea. I lift my face to the morning sun and the wind's caress.

Nami and I sit with them until Sarai calls us to lessons. Women are the keepers of history, but all children must learn it. This is what makes us a tribe, tracing our lineages and our past back to First Man and First Woman. As cousin to Abram, I am descendant of Noah and Na'amah through their first son, Shem.

"Begin with Enoch," Sarai says, pointing at me.

I take a breath and recite the first part of the Telling of Enoch.

Ishmael scowls when I finish. "How do you remember it all? You have no mother to prod you."

"No mother," I say, "but a father who thinks he should be a mother."

Taking that as a complaint, Ishmael is somewhat mollified, until Sarai points at him. "Now, you—the lineage from First Man."

I notice she never calls Ishmael by name, but always "you" or "that boy." Father says her heart is broken because she has been barren. Her duty to the tribe is to produce heirs, and so she gave her handmaiden, Hagar, to lie with Abram, as is the custom in Babylonia. As soon as Ishmael was born, that elevated Hagar to the position of second wife. I do not understand why that infuriated Sarai since it was her idea in the first place.

Ishmael stumbles.

"Start again," Sarai snaps.

I am almost guilty that I learn with ease. Perhaps it is a result of all the languages I have learned. Like a bladder bag, my mind has expanded. Now, it is not much trouble to put more in there.

Ishmael focuses his gaze on the weaving behind Sarai, so her stern glare does not undo him and, on this attempt, he correctly names the entire list. Through Abram, he also descends from Noah's son, Shem. I wonder if Hagar makes him recite the Egyptian side of his lineage.

And so the entire morning passes.

SEVERAL DAYS LATER, when we leave the tents of Abram, only Raph and Mika join us. Anan, who is the oldest of the three tall men, travels north with a small group of herders. Without being obvious, I watch Raph and Mika working their packs onto two donkeys, balancing the object wrapped in black fur on the largest. I have never seen a live bear. Such fur is rare. They could get a good trade for it.

I pat my bags, pleased they bulge with honey cakes. Hagar made extra for me.

Lot travels with us to Sodom. He brings six sheep to add to his own herd and a string of young black donkeys from Harran that we will sell for Abram. The finest donkeys are bred in Harran, and they will bring enough to make his journey worthwhile.

Almost fifteen summers older than I, Lot is coarsely bearded, with skin
the color of a walnut and large thumbs. Every time I see him, I must fight
to keep from staring at his thumbs. They seem too large for his hands,
and I cannot help but wonder if the giggling tales of young girls as to the
significance of a man's thumb size bear any truth.

I have seen plenty of male organs. The boys of the caravan consider me
one of them, and they don't hesitate to fountain their water in front of
me. That I manage to avoid suspicion is due to my reputation as a strange
boy who keeps to himself.

Eliezer counts the donkeys, and has Lot press his seal into a clay tablet
to account for them. This is also a practice taken from Babylonia. In Canaan, only the wealthy carry personal seals. I touch the form of my seal,
hidden under my clothing. It makes my mother real, if only for a moment. She too would have worn it next to her heart.

"A safe journey to us, Zakiti!" Lot bellows to my father, though he is
not a donkey's length from us. "I will hold you to your promise to sleep
beneath my roof when we arrive in Sodom."

Philot, my donkey, flicks his long ears in agitation at Lot's strident
voice, but he is a sturdy, dependable animal and does not move while Father checks the straps of my packing. I scratch his forehead, and he closes
his eyes in pleasure.

"Thank you, cousin," Father says. "We would be foolish not to accept.
Your graciousness to guests is famous."

A smile craters Lot's cheeks, deepening the scarred pits that make a
rough landscape of his face. A man's honor is judged by his hospitality to
guests. That is a law of the desert, and my people abide by it as strongly
as any nomad tribe.

Father smiles and gives Philot a pat, satisfied with my efforts. I sigh
in exasperation that he still checks behind me, as if I were a child who
would leave a strap loose.

Lot moves closer, his voice lowering. He runs a thick thumb along the
coarse hair of his chin and gives a furtive nod toward the tall strangers.
"Watch your words around those two." Lot's words are for my father's ear,
but I have sharp hearing. "Abram says El sent them."

"Yes, so the rumors have been and so Abram told me, as well."

Disappointment floods Lot's features. Clearly, he had wished to bear
such interesting news. He tries again. "The third man—the one who

returned to their lands in the north—is a priest, a shaman, maybe even a king."

I smell an embellishment.

Father waits.

Lot chuckles. "Word among the tents is Abram asked them to make Sarai's womb fertile."

Both my father's brows rise at this. "Sarai is still a beautiful woman, but is she not past the age of bearing children?"

Satisfied his gossip had induced a reaction, Lot chuckles and spreads his thick hands. "Not for me to say. If they are truly El's men, what is not possible?"

At that moment, Lot spies Abram emerging from his tent and hurries to his uncle's side. Abram has come to escort Raph, Mika, and Anan as far as the last oak tree, showing them honor. I consider the men who walk beside my tribe's patriarch. They have not confirmed they are messengers of El, at least not to me, but I may not be of sufficient importance to confide such a thing. I think through the strange list of words they wish to know in the southern dialect of Akkadian, but I am unable to parse a meaning from them. If they are angels, they keep their mission to themselves.

The call to move out distracts me from such questions. My job is to guide the newly acquired donkeys, which are not inclined to leave. I cannot blame them. My life, since I was three summers, has consisted of moving from place to place, but these young animals have never left their mothers' sides.

At the braying of one of the donkeys, my mind returns to my task, and I circle around to stand between the new ones we are taking and the lure of the familiar, positioning myself at the herd's back flank to discourage them from making a quick reversal around me. Animals attend primarily to body movements. I raise my staff. "Hiya!"

They move off, ears flicking in consternation, but following the donkeys that Chiram's son leads. I will stay in this position between them and their home until we are well out of sight of Abram's tents. I must stay alert and anticipate the first testing move from one of the donkeys. They do not have the strong herd instinct of sheep, being more independent. But if one gets away with turning, another will do the same, even if they do not go the same way, and chaos will erupt. The staff extends my range a bit, and if I keep my mind from wandering, I can manage. Philot does not need me to lead him, so accustomed is he to our traveling.

Nami is no help. She only looks at me when I signal her to move the donkeys. I wish our old herd dog had not died. He was a wonder, and I still look for him whenever we break camp or need to move the herds. From habit, I also look for Dune, but he is gone, a victim to my foolishness. At the cost of my horse and my ribs, I have bought another summer with my father and the caravan. Then Father will surely insist I stay with Sarai . . . but I cannot worry about that. Who knows what will happen in such a space of time?

9

This was the same place where Abram had built the altar, and there
he worshiped the Lord again.

—Book of Genesis 13:4

THAT NIGHT WHEN I AM with my students, my father sweeps into
the tent without requesting entry. I have a cup of tea to my mouth
and choke on the strong liquid.

Mika, who is the one I would expect to react to this rudeness, looks
up calmly.

It is Raph who jumps to his feet, his hand flying to his left hip,
the movement of a swordsman, but he carries no weapon. He has also
stepped protectively in front of me, which I notice, even though I am
coughing.

"Why is my da—" My father catches himself, and his cheek spasms
with the effort of control. "Why is my son in your tent?"

Raph quickly drops his hand and takes a breath before answering. "He
teach words, so we speak more skill. Is this a difficult?"

"Difficulty," I correct.

Raph amends, "A difficulty?"

I admire how he smoothly slips from battle-ready to negotiator, though
he remains in front of me.

Father's mouth opens and then closes. "Yes, it is. He is too young, too—"

He struggles to give a coherent reason. "We leave tomorrow. He must rest." With a glare at me, he says, "Adir, go to our tent."

"But father, I—"

His hand slashes the air in the gesture that cuts further discussion.

"It is late," Raph says to me. "You filled my head to sloshing."

I cannot help a smile at his analogy, though my stomach is starting to clinch with the expectation of my father's anger and an end to my plans.

IN OUR TENT, my father turns his fury on me. "What are you doing?" he hisses to keep from shouting.

"What Raph said I was doing, teaching them our language. Why are you so angry, Father?"

His fists knuckle in frustration. "Why?" He turns and paces into the depth of our tent where my pallet lies in the shadows. Whirling back, he approaches me, keeping his voice under control with an effort. "That is exactly the problem. You have no conception of danger!"

Danger? I am lost to his meaning. "I thought they were El's messengers and friends of Abram. Why would they mean me harm?"

My father blinks. "They are men, Adira. *Men.*"

Finally, I understand. This is related to my father's worry about raising a daughter alone. If my mother had lived, he would probably not be so anxious about the subject. I suddenly wonder why he never married again. Most men would have. Why have I never questioned this before?

"Why didn't you marry another woman, Father?"

My father appears to swallow the barrage of words he is about to spew, though his mouth remains open. "What?"

Feeling bolder, now we have left the tents of Abram behind, I say, "All this deception about my gender would have been unnecessary had you married and let me grow up as other girls."

His face slackens, all the anger drained away. "Have you been unhappy? I thought you wished to be with me, or was it more you did not wish to stay with Sarai?"

I want to laugh, but I see the pain in him and do not. "I have been most happy, Father. I would not trade my life for any other."

He brightens, until I add, "I just do not want to be a woman."

"That is not a choice you have."

This time I stop the fear that uncoils like a serpent in my belly, remembering the last time I thought to run from my fate. A wolf almost ate me, and Nami lost her pups.

Eventually, I must deal with the fact I am a woman, but it is not important at this moment. "Neither of the strangers knows I am a girl," I say quietly in the most reasonable voice I can muster. "I am just a boy to them."

Father sighs. "Perhaps, but I forbid you to go alone into their tent. One day you will want a husband, and your reputation will matter. I want no one spreading falsities about you."

I grind my teeth. This is exactly why I do not want to be a woman, at least not one of our tribe. Men never worry about such things. They do exactly as they please, but let a woman step her toe beyond the boundary men mark, and she is ruined, not worthy of being a wife. Concubine, perhaps. For a moment, I consider that possibility. Is it any better a choice than being a wife? Or perhaps one of the priestesses in the five cities of the Vale or Babylonia? The followers of the goddess in the cities are free to lie with any man, and it is a holy act. The priestesses hold property and make important contributions and decisions. No king would quickly act against their advice. Nomad and city dweller alike respect the power of the goddess. Her figurine has a special place in every woman's tent. Even Sarai asks for the goddess's blessing on her empty womb. El may not dwell in any form, but the goddess likes her slender carvings, her trees, and her high places.

I sigh. Father would not approve of my being a priestess; besides, I wish to remain with the caravan.

"Adira," my father's voice, still low, so we will not be heard beyond the tent walls, calls me back from my mind's wanderings.

"Yes, Father," I say, trying to sound obedient and calm him.

"I forbid you to go alone into the tent of the strangers."

I can only stare at him.

"Into any man's tent," he adds, his dark eyes boring into mine with all the force of his authority as my father.

"But this is important," I say. "You do not understand."

"Nothing is as important as your honor." He grasps me by the shoulders.

"This is for your own happiness. It may not seem like it now, but I do this for your happiness."

I realize it will change nothing to explain about Nami. It will seem a minor issue next to my honor and future happiness.

I do the only thing I can—bow my head in acquiescence.

10

The Lord said to Abram, "Look as far as you can see in every direction—north and south, east and west. I am giving all this land, as far as you can see, to you and your descendants as a permanent possession. And I will give you so many descendants that, like the dust of the earth, they cannot be counted! Go and walk through the land in every direction, for I am giving it to you."

So Abram moved his camp to Hebron and settled near the oak grove belonging to Mamre. There he built another altar to the lord.

—Book of Genesis 13:14-18

But the land could not support both Abram and Lot with all their flocks and herds living so close together. So disputes broke out between the herdsmen of Abram and Lot. . . Finally Abram said to Lot, "Let's not allow this conflict to come between us or our herdsmen. After all, we are [brethren]!

—Book of Genesis 13:6-8

W E TRAVEL SOUTHEAST FROM ABRAM'S tents through the hills. Lot rides beside my father, talking most of the way. He is a great talker, mostly a great complainer. I stay as far from them as I can. I wish I could simply travel with Raph and Mika and instruct them as we go. In that way, I could fulfill my bargain and obey my father, but that would mean failing my duties. We are short two men, so I must stay with the animals.

At least I have Nami's presence again, although she periodically runs to the donkey that carried her pups to sniff in worry and hope. I distract her by trying to teach her to keep the stubborn donkeys in a pack. My hand signals confuse her. I am certain she has been trained as a hunter, but I do not know what signals she understands. She knows I want something, but is not particularly interested in herding donkeys. I think she would, however, be happy to chase them, as she is off after any sight of a rustle in a clump of grass.

Danel comes to walk beside me. For the first time, I wonder how he sees me—as the favorite of my father, the caravan master, while he is merely the son of the cook? I cannot help being that, but perhaps it is a source of discontent for him. I have never tried to be nice, as I despise his father, Chiram . . . but Danel did fight for me, earning a few bruises too.

"Thank you for coming to my aid," I say stiffly.

"I didn't ask for your thanks."

"No," I reply. "But I give it."

He grunts, sounding exactly like his father.

"Why did you come to walk with me, then?" I demand.

He shrugs. "I don't know." He looks at the sky and the hills. "Well . . . I came to thank you for asking Eliezer not to report our fighting."

I laugh. "That was more for me than you."

He grins, and I am surprised at the happiness that gives me. I do not have friends among the boys of the caravan, perhaps because I need to keep my distance to protect my gender or perhaps because they all resent me as Zakiti's son, much as the boys of Abram's camp resent Ishmael.

"I have a grandmother in Sodom," Danel says.

"Is she nice?"

"She is tiny and frail, but full of spirit."

I envy the love in his voice.

Danel helps with the donkeys until Chiram calls him away on some errand.

Despite the distraction of Danel's presence, my belly has stayed in a tight coil at my predicament over Nami. I should obey my father, but he has also taught me to honor my oaths, and I have made one to Nami. She followed me, sacrificing her own pups, and she saved my life. I do not know what to do. I cannot let her future pups be destined for Chiram's pot.

That night after the evening meal, I claim weariness and pain in my ribs. Neither is a lie. I crawl into my pallet and wait. Father is late coming to the tent and I chafe, but keep my back to the fire. When he calls my name softly, I do not answer.

I wait until his breathing steadies, and then I ease from my bedding, leaving the large lump of stone around which I had curled my body. Satisfied it will be taken for my form in the shadows, I slip out of the tent.

I love the morning, but I also love the night—the stars caught in the gauzy veil spun across the ebon sky.

A hyena coughs and is answered by the stuttering bleat of a doe goat. Not far away, a campfire burns, silhouetting the shape of men that stand between it and me. The wind shifts, and I smell something familiar and not pleasant.

Lot.

"Adir," he bellows, and I move quickly away from our tent, lest he wake my father. "Where are you off to, boy?"

I shrug.

He squints at me. "Not going to ride out into the night again, I hope?"

"No."

"El does not tolerate such foolishness. He demands obedience to him through a child's obedience to his father. Obedience is honor."

These words feel like an arrow through my throat. Does he know I am disobeying my father as I stand here before him? Does El speak through him? I am not certain whether El is angry, but Abram says he is a jealous god, and I do not wish his anger with me to fall on my father's back.

"I hear you, Lot, my cousin," I mumble, looking humbly at the ground.

Chiram approaches. He gives barely a glance, acknowledging my existence without commenting on my worth or lack thereof, and puts a hand on Lot's shoulder. "You said to call you when we were ready."

I smell fermented camel's milk on Chiram's breath and know he has not waited for Lot.

When their attention is off me, I slip into the shadows and make my way to Raph and Mika's tent. A stab of pain stops me at the opening, and I press my hand against the bandage. They have lowered their tent sides, though it is a hot night.

"It is Adir," I say when the pain has subsided. "May I enter?"

"Wait," I hear, then some shuffling noises. When they bid me to enter, I do not look directly at the bear fur covering the object, but I notice it is not in the same position as the previous nights.

"Adir," Raph says, "it is late. We thought you not appearing." He is on his feet, but Mika remains seated, a distant look on his face.

"My apologies for the time," I say. "My duties kept me. I hope it is not too late for you?"

"Late," Mika says.

My heart freezes.

Raph rolls his eyes. "No, it not too late. We need words. Come, sit, Adir. I think today I need know many. I told all to my grumpy brother; he remembers better. Truth, Mika?"

Mika scowls at him, which makes Raph grin. "So settled. Sit, Adir."

And so far into the night, we talk and practice. I stay intent and focused despite the weariness tugging at my bones and the pain in my chest. Finally, Mika holds up a hand. "You are pale."

I take a careful breath. "I am fine." *I want my goat.*

Mika rises and steps before me.

"No," I say, suddenly panicked. "I am fine. I need only to rest."

But he ignores my words and kneels beside me. "Lift robe."

My heart pounds. If my father wakes and finds a stone in my place and me here and Mika's hands on me—I cannot even complete the thought. Yet Mika is not to be dissuaded. I know this somehow. Unless I jump up and run, which I do not think I can even do, I am trapped.

Reluctantly, I lift my robe the minimum amount, glad I still wear a young boy's pants beneath it and thus can expose only the bandage. In a move camouflaged to look as if I am merely keeping my free arm out of the way, I press my little breasts flatter than the narrow band I tie around my chest. Surely, they are too small for him to notice, but I want to cover the band as well. Mika's fingers press against the flesh below it.

I think my heart will burst through the cloth. Dispassionately, he checks the other side. "Too cold," he snaps and stretches his open palm toward Raph.

With no further instruction, Raph hands him a worn leather bag. From it, Mika selects a slender knife, which he applies to the bandage. There is instant relief when he removes the pressure. Quickly, I lower my tunic. "The bandage felt much better at first." My voice makes it a question.

"Sometimes swelling," Mika replies. "Should checked."

I am not certain if he is blaming me or himself for this.

THE FOLLOWING MORNING I bring my goat to Chiram. His thick brows lift in surprise, and he examines it suspiciously. I am not worried. I picked her out myself, and she is perfect. I step between him and the goat. "For Nami."

A frown arcs his mouth. He has thick lips like Lot, mostly covered by the black hairs beneath his nose. "She is worth silver, that dog." With the nail of his last finger, he picks something from between his yellow-stained front teeth. "I won her in a game of senet."

"You told me that before, but we have a bargain." I cut the air with the blade of my hand in my father's gesture.

With a snort that passes for a laugh, Chiram concedes. "All right, the bitch is yours then. Good riddance, I say. She has not brought any silver to me. Just another mouth to feed."

The thought of touching Chiram makes my skin twitchy, but I press my palm into his to seal our trade.

My heart is lighter than it has been for days when I go to tell Nami. She is less dejected, picking up my mood, though her almond eyes are still sad. If I had my own tent, I could bring her inside. This is the first time it occurs to me to wonder what I will tell my father.

CHAPTER

11

Lot took a long look at the fertile plains of the Jordan Valley in the direction of Zoar. The whole area was well watered everywhere, like the garden of the Lord or the beautiful land of Egypt. (This was before the Lord destroyed Sodom and Gomorrah.) Lot chose for himself the whole Jordan Valley to the east of them. He went there with his flocks and servants and parted company with his uncle Abram. So Abram settled in the land of Canaan, and Lot moved his tents to a place near Sodom and settled among the cities of the plain.

—Book of Genesis 13:10-12

As it happened, the valley of the Dead Sea was filled with tar pits. And as the army of the kings of Sodom and Gomorrah fled, some fell into the tar pits, while the rest escaped into the mountains.

—Book of Genesis 14:10

AT LENGTH, WE REACH THE cliff's edge bordering the great rift. In the fog-shrouded distance, facing us, stands a sister cliff. The two mountain ridges run straight as lances, north and south. Between them, far below us, lies the Dead Sea, sparkling like lapis lazuli in the sun. We will descend here, but first we stop at the temple to pay our respect to the gods and toll to the priests, so we may enter the oasis of En Gedi.

Afterward, we make our way carefully down the steep slope, our presence scattering a family of ibex. One male stops to regard us, the scraggly beard under his chin quivering as he continues to chew.

Danel loosens a quickly strung arrow that ensures dinner and the prize of the horns.

A small settlement exists at the cliff's foot to support and protect the priests. The men here make a balsam from the resin of a thorny plant that grows at the cliff's base. Its making is a highly-guarded secret men have died to protect, and the scent is meant only for use in the temple, but an exception is made for one trusted trader—my father. We stop long enough to share a meal and procure a tiny bronze vial of it.

We leave the oasis too soon for me and head south, following the line of cliffs, banded in colors of spice, that rise to our right. On our left, the Dead Sea gleams in the harsh sunlight, its depths ending abruptly in green shallows as clear as dragonfly wings. We camp in caves set into the cliff walls. Father knows the ones that hoard fresh water in their hidden recesses.

In the days that follow, we cross the broad, flat valley that wraps the southern end of the Dead Sea. The cliffs we leave behind are now hazed, and the eastern bluffs rise before us. Beyond their heights, toward the rising sun, stretches a desert and beyond it, the great cities of Babylon and Ur. Of course, no one is foolish enough to travel straight across the desert. The caravan route to Babylon and Ur lies along the Kings' Road, following the great, verdant arch that begins in Egypt and ends in Babylonia. But this day, we go to Sodom for a load of pitch and salt to carry to Egypt.

We come at last to Lot's southern pastures. Fed by fresh waters from the east, this land is said to be as lush as the region tipping Egypt's great river. As an experienced traveler, I say this is not so. Still, it is rich grazing and dotted with yellow, white, and red flowers eager to take advantage of spring rains.

We set up tents for our return. The caravan will stay here. We take only what we need for the short journey to Sodom. As much as I want Nami with me, I decide to leave her at the tents, because I do not know how welcome she will be at Lot's house. Besides, wild dogs—eaters of rats and garbage—roam city streets, and I do not want her mixing with them or getting into fights with a pack.

Danel agrees to make certain Nami has food and water and a chance to relieve herself. I do not like trusting him, but we have talked more on the journey from Abram's tents than we have my entire life, and he is my best choice.

"I will return, Nami," I tell her, but I have to tie her, as much as it pains me. She strains against the camel-hair rope as we leave. It is the first time she has not been at my side since her pups died, even when she belonged to Chiram. So far, I have not mentioned her change in status to my father, and I do not think Chiram has thought to, either. Why stir trouble into a pot already salted?

We travel along the southern shore of the Dead Sea. When Sodom looms before us, I can also see Gomorrah in the distance. Lot has a house inside the city gates of Sodom. He insists that we be his guests. As we approach the main gate, we are careful to stay on the path. To our right are the charnel houses and shaft tombs of the dead. To the left, between us and the sea, pools of bitumen dot the rocky landscape. The stones glare white in the sunlight, a stark contrast to the black pitch they cup. Some call this the land of Mot, the underworld god.

"Here is where King Bera fell, in the wars before your birth," Lot instructs, as though I am a child bereft of any learning.

I wrinkle my nose. I hope Bera died of a sword and did not drown in the slimy pits. It seems an unworthy death for a king trying to defend his people.

We enter through the main gate. Two towers built on stone and wood foundations flank the gate and loom above us. The area just inside spreads out around a central well into a large open square, known as the Gate. All along the city's wall, merchants sell wares, livestock, and food. Men and women crowd the area, as eager for the exchange of gossip as for the purchase and sale of goods.

Roads radiate from the Gate, like spokes of a wheel, where the sellers of finer goods have more permanent structures or even houses for their merchandise. People, mostly of Canaan, fill the streets. I note some wearing the garb of Hittites and a couple of Hurrians, men of the Horse Tribes. Not long ago, Egyptians ruled here, but I see no sign of them now. My father says they are busy with their own problems, but that does not mean they will not turn their attention again to Canaan.

Sodom prepares for the Spring Rites. Gold and red flowers adorn the women's hair, and red ribbons gaily decorate slender asherah poles honoring the goddess.

Many eyes turn to Mika and Raph, who are noticeable even in this crowd. I am busy watching the women who are busy watching Raph.

Mika seems lost in his own thoughts. Raph bends to pluck a handful of dates from a basket set between the owner's brown legs. The man looks up to protest, but as his gaze continues up, he seems to think better of it and waves his hand, as if it were his idea to offer dates to Raph, and in fact, Raph should help himself to more.

Raph tosses him a small nugget of copper, more than fair compensation for a handful of dates, and turns to Lot. "Abram claims Asherah is El's consort, but these people speak of a Baal?"

I had not thought him interested in talk around us. From this, I tuck away the knowledge that he hears, even when he appears not to be listening.

"Asherah *is* El's wife," Lot says, "but these people wrongly believe that she is Baal's wife."

I am happy not to have to understand the intricate politics and pairings of the gods. Gods do what they wish. Should a son take his mother as wife in our human world, it would be considered an abomination. Sister and brother, of course, are another matter and almost common among royalty. Sarai and Abram are half-siblings. Still, the ways of Sodom are not the ways of my tribe.

As if in agreement, a small brown dog, stinking of offal, barks at us from an alley. Aside from Lot, we are all strangers here.

MY COUSIN'S HOME in the city is opulent, with several rooms. He is a wealthy, influential man, thanks in large part to Abram's generosity. Of course, Sodom is not Ur or Babylon, and it has not mastered the art of plumbing. The smells offend my nose, though I must endure them without the agonized facial expressions of my youth. Otherwise I risk my father's pinch and a lecture. The hot wind shifts, making me thankful for the loose outer robe that offers protection from the burning sun.

Mika and Raph must duck their heads to enter Lot's house. "The area just inside the doorway is called the little gate," I say, wishing to impress them with my knowledge. Perhaps they will realize I can be of more help than just as an interpreter, and they will decide to stay with us. At least, that is the dream in my head.

Lot's wife, Hurriya, waddles to the front room to meet us, her arms spread as wide as her hips. "Be welcome!" She is light-skinned and plump, her face rosy with sweat.

Behind her are two women bearing bowls of water. They are introduced to Mika and Raph as daughters of Lot and Hurriya. I met them on a previous visit, but they paid little attention to me, and I had no particular interest in them. Lot has another daughter who lives elsewhere in the city with her own family.

"Not yet married," Hurriya says pointedly of her daughters, as she pours water from a pitcher into a bowl, making certain Raph and Mika hear. We sit on benches made of the same white limestone as the walls, and the daughters wash Mika and Raph's feet, as is the custom for honored travelers and guests. I am last, as the youngest, and have to wash my own feet. Also, I get the dirty water.

Hurriya, however, comes to me. "Be welcome to our house, son of Zakiti," she says. She reaches down, taking my chin and cheek in one big hand and tilts my head. "Hmm," she mutters, "a good thing such a flaw resides on a boy's face and not a girl's. A nose like that would take a flock of goats to buy a husband!"

She laughs. Lot and his daughters smile. My father does not, nor do the honored guests. Raph looks confused, and I have never seen Mika smile at anything. I am surprised at the sting of her words. Father has told me the knot on the bridge of my nose is barely noticeable and that I will be a beautiful woman. Does Hurriya suspect something and wish to put her own daughters in a better light?

Hurriya directs us to the interior courtyard where we sit on fine rugs. The floor in the other parts of the area—the domain of the chickens that wander freely about—is covered with fresh reeds. Hurriya leaves the door open to encourage a breeze, and my gaze finds a window at the far end of the room through which I can see the salt formations at the water's edge and, beyond them, the sparkling surface of the sea itself. I remember my father's warning when I was old enough to want to wade into it.

"Don't taste it," he said.

Of course, I immediately did. It burned my mouth, and though I tried to hide my tears, my father laughed, knowing exactly what I would do. Then he pointed to one of the small, irregular white spires along the shore and quoted. *"All her tears came to naught, leaving only a pillar of salt."* It was a saying I had heard all my life, but I was amazed to see the pillars of salt. What giant lady had wept so many tears to leave the dazzling white crystallized lumps, encrusted stones and salt towers, some

as large as I? The wonder of it dried my own tears from the bitter bite
of the water.

"Did she cry into the water and make it so bitter?" I had asked.

"My apologies," Hurriya says, pouring hot tea from a copper vessel and
pulling my attention back into the present. "There is no use in polishing
copper when the sea belches pitch."

"What mean you?" Mika asks.

"The Dead Sea releases . . . pungent odors."

"Mot's farts," Lot says.

I laugh, but Hurriya looks annoyed.

"A story told of pitch from sea?" Mika, normally quiet, has expressed
curiosity about everything since entering Sodom. Instead of answering,
Hurriya looks to her husband to explain, while she putters about seeing
to our meal and comfort, assisted by a small young woman with skin the
color of cinnamon. A slave brand marks her upper arm. She is not named
and does not speak.

"A true story you were told," Lot says. "Pitch from the pits is used for
mortar and waterproofing and such, but the sea produces a finer quality
and more of it. The people of Egypt use it in the preparation of the dead."

Mika raises an eyebrow. "How so?"

"I don't know all the details. They wrap the bodies in linen. A secret
mixture containing pitch preserves the cloth and what lies within it. Of
course, only the wealthy can afford such an elaborate procedure. Abram
says it is better to return to the dust from which we were made."

"How do harvest it from sea?" Mika asks.

"It rises to the surface and floats, then the boatmen gather it. We often
have unwelcome warning of this event through our noses." He scrunches
his face.

I am still pondering why anyone lives here. Men will put up with anything for wealth, I decide. Not all the pitch in the world could replace a
clean wind on my face.

"And the copper—" Hurriya reminds him.

"Ah yes." Lot shrugs. "Everything tarnishes. No point in cleaning it—
the green always returns. We normally stay away during this time, but I
wanted to show you my home."

More, *show off* his home.

We settle on the rugs, my mind as much taken with the quality of their weave as the heady smells of roasting lamb, heavily spiced with turmeric and cumin. The aroma intoxicates. Chiram is much stingier with his seasonings, as they are imported and costly.

The younger daughter, who is several years older than I, presents the first platter, just as a dark shape bounds through the open doorway. Hurriya cries out in fright. The chickens squawk and flap, and Raph leaps to his feet, drawing a knife hidden in his robe. I had thought him unarmed, because most men wear their knives proudly displayed in their front sash.

Waving her tail in tired pleasure, Nami trots to my side and collapses, panting. She knows she belongs to me, or I to her, and she was apparently not to be left behind, as evidenced by the piece of chewed strap dangling from her neck.

Everyone has frozen, except Mika, who chooses a date that interests him and lifts it to his mouth. Hurriya sputters, unable to form words for her thoughts. Her daughters cling to each other, as if Nami might decide they looked tastier than the dates. She is a large dog.

My father's brows rise, and he looks at me.

Raph's shoulders settle, and he slides the knife back into its hiding place with a laugh. "I thinking wolf found us!"

My father leans toward me. "What is this about, Adir? Why is Chiram's dog here?"

My first thought is to ask him why he is asking *me* why Chiram's dog is here, but I swallow and decide truth is better served than a clever retort.

"She is my dog, Father," I say as humbly as I can, casting my gaze at his feet.

A stolen glance reveals he is not impressed with my humility. "Your dog?"

I nod, my fingers playing with the edge of my robe. Nami's timing could not have been worse. As if she feels my attention on her, she lifts her head briefly and looks up at me, still panting, her mouth gaped in a pleased-at-myself smile, and I wonder at my initial assessment of her sense of humor. Does she know she is getting me into trouble?

"Yes, Father. My dog."

"How could that be?" he demands.

"I . . . bought her."

He scowls. The others sit in silence, unwilling to intervene. "With what?"

"A goat." I hate that my voice is small, but I also hate displeasing my father. I want him to be proud of me, but I seem to always be mangling that possibility.

He sits back and takes a swallow of his tea. I glance again at his face, and hope sparks. Is the corner of his lip twitching?

"And how did you obtain a goat, Adir?" he says without looking at me.

My gaze flicks to Raph, who makes no attempt to hide his amusement. Mika chews the date thoughtfully, his face, as usual, unreadable.

"I earned it, sir, instructing the messengers of El how to speak the southern dialect of Akkadian."

"This is true," Raph offers. "He did earn the goat."

Father considers him and seems about to say something before changing his mind. I remember how furious he was to find me in their tent. Perhaps we will not have to enumerate how many visits I made, and he will assume the time he found me was the last.

"It would please us if you let the creature stay," Mika says, stunning me.

Hurriya sputters again. "In my house? A dog—?"

But Lot holds a flat hand in her direction, cutting off her protests as quickly as Father's slicing gesture halts further discussion of an issue with me. "If it pleases El's messenger, it pleases me—" He glares at his wife before adding, "—and those of my house."

She stiffens, but makes no further objection. The household is under the wife's dominion, but a matter of guests takes precedence.

With a dip of his head, Father acknowledges Lot's graciousness. "My apologies for the disruption caused by my son."

Lot beams, looking to Mika for his approval, but the northman, in his usual manner, retreats to his inner self. He has no allegiance to social niceties.

12

Sodom's sins were pride, gluttony, and laziness, while the poor and needy suffered outside her door.

—Ezekiel 16:49

WE SPEND THE NIGHT WITH Lot's household. The following day, Chiram comes into the city and speaks with my father, who calls me to him. "Adir, the caravan requires my presence. I will return there with Chiram and will arrange for the pitch in exchange for our wine and oil as I leave, but scout the market here to see if there is anything else worth taking with us. I will send for you soon." He gives me two small bags. One, I know has only a small finger ring or two of silver for my belt. The other has more, and I hide it in a fold of my robe.

Proud to be entrusted to the task, I nod. "I will, Father."

He puts a hand on my shoulder. "I will tell Danel that *your* dog is with you."

"Thank you, Father."

That afternoon I take Nami with me to scout the goods for sale along the gravel-and-sand streets of Sodom. Perhaps it is the flowers in the women's hair or the ribbons, but soon I become inured to the city stench.

Although I have worked with Nami to teach her the rudiments of herding, I wish to learn how to communicate better with her. There is no question in my mind she has received some training. Desert tribes raise such dogs with great care as companions and hunters. I just do not know her signals or the words she knows. I was delighted to find slapping my thigh brings her to my side . . . most of the time. She is alert to everything, but stays beside me if I signal her thus, unless a creature needing chasing dashes by. Then she has as much trouble with obedience as I. But, otherwise, if I stand still, she stands beside me, and if I walk or even run, she matches my pace with delight. The faster we go, the happier she is.

I suppose we make a sight together, the lanky boy and attached desert dog. Several of the street vendors nod and wave at us, in a good mood because of the flux of people—and thus business—arriving for the Spring Rites. One even slips me a treat, a meat stick, which I share with Nami. With great care, she takes the offered morsels from my sticky fingers.

Then I begin my duty to find bargains for trade. The cloth vendors are my favorite stops. Although I do not have skill with weaving, I know a fine work from a sloppy one and can tell where almost any cloth originates from the texture, dyes, and knotting.

I eye the ruins of several buildings that have partially collapsed and wonder what caused such, and why they are not repaired. Sodom is not a sophisticated city, not like Ur or Babylon or the Egyptian port cities where rare items are to be found—ingots of gold, tin, or even cobalt blue glass, tortoiseshell jewelry, and elephant or hippopotamus ivory. I love the port cities—the smell of the sea and exotic spices. Here in Sodom, the displays are mostly locally grown food, weapons and pottery, although there is one vendor who has a few pieces of nice ebony from Egypt. Since we are headed there, I am not tempted. The main source of wealth for Sodom is the pitch which we are prepared to transport. Pitch, as Lot explained to Mika and Raph, is harvested from the sea where the water cools it into a gooey mass, but it also oozes up through the ground. The primary hazard of night travel from the city is not predators, but the likelihood of stumbling into a pit of pitch or one of the old grave-shafts, if you do not stay to the paths.

I stop to watch a potter folding the edges of what is to be a small oil pot, admiring his skill. I do not have such a skill, though I have a good eye for what is well made, be it pottery, metal, or weavings.

At the far end of the main street, near the city wall, I skirt a row of large jars of pitch and stop at a cloth merchant's shop. It appears to be a house as well as a shop. I give only a cursory glance to the pieces stacked outside. The least-worthy items are usually displayed there to minimize any loss by a snatching thief.

I signal for Nami to stay outside and wait for me. She appears willing to do so, at least as long as I don't tie her and leave her for long. Inside, I let my fingers choose what to study. They stop on a fine piece and only then do I look at it. It is a small rug in deep reds and blues. I pull it from its heap of fellows and take it out to the daylight with another mediocre piece to study. The owner steps out with me. A shaft of light angling over the stone wall reflects off a tiny silver ring that curves through his left nostril.

"You have an eye, boy," he says, cocking his head at me.

Once my gaze rests on him, it is captured by the strange travel of his left hand across his body. His fingers draw up his chest, through his oily beard and along the side of his face to touch the top of his balding head before starting the cycle again. He seems unaware of the ceaseless tide of his hand, but it is distracting. "You know your weave," he says. "Finest pieces I have."

Of course he would have said that about anything a customer chose, but I have no doubt for the one piece, he is correct. The double knot weave and pattern identify it as originating from the north, where young girls weave their family pattern into dowry rugs. The dyes are rich and pleasing. As we are bound for Egypt, this would be a worthy item to obtain.

I shrug, beginning the ever-fascinating game of negotiation. "It may be, but I have not the funds to buy a fine piece. Perhaps you have others more in my range. It is a gift for my mother."

"Perhaps it is not as expensive as you think," he says. "And a gift for your mother should be as fine an item as you can manage. How much do you have?"

Only an amateur trader or a herder or farm boy would fall for that, but I put my hand to my pouch as though to pull out my coins to count and then stop, letting my head fall, as if shamed I am not learned enough to tell how much I have and do not want to embarrass myself.

Again I shrug. "Not much, but what is the price for this small rug?"

Thwarted, the merchant names a price, less I am certain, than he would have ordinarily begun with, but something above the range of this ignorant boy who cannot even count his coins.

"I do not know," I stumble.

"Perhaps you should consider this piece," he advises, indicating the other cloth. Its price is not worth mentioning—a pile of salt."

Salt is highly prized in the desert and mountains far from the sea, but here it is as common as dust. His hand continues in its absorbing path of stomach-beard-cheek-head, as though too unhappy to rest anywhere.

"Perhaps I should look at something entirely different," I say, half turning back into the store and then pausing to look at the piece in my right hand. "But my mother would like these colors."

"They are very fine," he agreed. "If I knew how much you had to spend I could advise you better."

At that moment, I notice through the opening of the house that Nami has her jaws almost level with a large chuck of raw pig meat at an adjoining stall, and I slap my thigh loudly. She turns her head and hesitates before trotting to my side, her flowing ears flat in shame I have caught her in a transgression or thinking of one.

The merchant's hand pauses in its journey, caught in an invisible web at his chest. "This is your dog?" There is a note of disbelief in his voice.

"Yes," I say, suddenly alarmed, although I cannot name a reason.

"A saluki," he says, as if to himself. "So the rumors are true."

My free hand drops to stroke Nami's head. "What rumors?"

Abruptly, the merchant's hand resumes its nervous path and he ignores my question. "I might know of a man who would be interested in such a dog. Perhaps we can come to an agreement about the rug."

Curious now, I ignore the scent of danger. "Who would be interested? She is terrible at herding donkeys."

He flinches. "Herding donkeys?"

For the first time, I pay closer attention to his features. He could be of a desert tribe. Some gave up the nomad life for a place in the cities, although their people disdain them.

I run my fingers through the long, silky hair of Nami's ears. "Yes, I am training her."

He straightens. "This dog was not bred for herding." An angry tone has crept into his voice. I find this interesting, as professional traders do not allow anger to show in the midst of a negotiation. We are into personal territory here, and I should move us back to a discussion of the rug or leave.

Perversely, I instead sink us deeper into the trench that has opened before us. "Oh," I say, all innocence. "Tell me what you know of such dogs."

He scowls, and the hand moves faster in its predetermined path. I should leave, but I want the rug and I have a wedge now. Besides, I would like to know more about Nami or at least her breed. The desert nomads prize their dogs, but they do not share information about their training. My hope is this man, perhaps ostracized by his tribe, might do so.

"You should not have this dog."

"But she is a good dog. Why not?"

"If you will not sell her, then you had better leave."

There is no mistaking the danger that weighs in the air like the pressure of a storm. His hand stops again and slips to one of the two daggers prominent in his sash.

"Leave my premises," he says.

I take a deep breath. "I have decided I do want the small rug."

"Go."

"My mother will like the colors."

"Go now." Menace rumbles in his voice.

"I think since I have seen it, I will be happy with no other piece," I say, as if unaware of his anger. I want this rug to show my father I can be trusted to find and negotiate fine goods.

My hand still rests on Nami's head, and I feel, rather than hear, her warning rumble. The man's hand has tightened on one of the hilts. He freezes at her growl.

I name my price for the rug in my hand, a fair one, holding out the copper rings to him.

His face suffused with rage, he snatches them with his free hand.

I take two steps away, still facing him, not wanting a knife in my back. Nami, to my amazement, also backs, keeping a watchful eye on the merchant.

Slowly, his gaze locked on her, he releases his grip on his knife, perhaps finding his temper or perhaps not wishing Nami to attack him if I am harmed.

Only then do I turn, but not without a backward glance over my shoulder, and I realize my fingers, which clench the small rug, are drained of blood.

CHAPTER

13

Everything is in flames—the sky with lightning—the water with luminous particles and even the very masts are pointed with a blue flame.
—Charles Darwin (aboard the *Beagle*)

THAT NIGHT, THE SCENT OF rain rides in with the wind that now blows from the west. It is greatly welcome. Lot, being a wealthy man, has his house in the eastern quarter of the city, right on the sea's edge and within sight of the cliffs. The window is an unusual feature, but it helps draw cooler air into the house and up the roof over the courtyard, which is shaded with fronds laid over thin logs, but not so tightly as to block the flow of air or smoke from the cook fire. Our house sits on a rise, and I can see the shimmering of the Dead Sea.

At the evening meal, I feel Hurriya's sharp eyes on me, and I make sure to keep my gestures bold. It is easy to spot a girl who merely dresses in boy's clothing. A girl's movements should be graceful and her glance, shy. I have studied this for many summers. If I miss a detail in telling Father what I observed during his negotiations, he snorts and tells me I have much to learn. As a child, this motivated me as no beating or harsh words would. I want above all to please him, to have him proud of me . . . and to stay with him. Always, the fear of being sent away looms over me.

It is rare I miss anything, and it has become a game between us. Afterward, in the privacy of our tent, we query each other. In the past few summers, I have sometimes caught what he has missed and make a point to snort, which makes him laugh.

I slip a piece of meat from my bowl and hide it in my robe. Nami's head remains on my foot, but her dark eyes follow the move.

"What your father keeps?" Raph asks around a mouthful of flatbread.

"What keeps my father?" I correct him and shake my head. "I do not know. He said he would return in a few days, if he can."

Lot frowns. "Perhaps there is a sickness among the animals."

I wipe grease from my mouth with the back of my hand, a gesture no properly raised woman would do, and Hurriya's tight sniff rewards me. She is watching me as closely as I watch others.

"I do not think so," I say, without interrupting my chewing, "or he would have taken me with him."

"Well, he hardly had a chance to taste our hospitality!" Lot booms, and I flinch before I can stop myself. Does he think we all have bee's wax filling our ears? He slaps a hand on his thigh. "I am known for treating my guests well, am I not, wife?"

"Well known," Hurriya admits, glancing at the large portions of food set before Raph and Mika. She does not seem impressed to host El's messengers. They do eat a lot. I wipe the last bit of grease up with my bread. By the width of Hurriya's hips, she might give them an honest competition. I, myself, am no idler in the task of eating, but no matter what I eat, it does nothing to alter my shape.

Leaning forward, Lot addresses his guests. "We are most honored to have you in our home."

Raph wipes his fingers on a moist cloth. "Thank your welcome."

Lot scratches at his chin, his fingers brushing his bottom lip, a gesture that often means a man wants to speak but is unsure of the reception of his question. "Meaning no disrespect, but I wonder at your origins."

Mika stiffens so slightly I am sure no one else notices.

"Despite my manner," Lot continues, "I am an educated man, born and raised in Ur, though not the scholar my uncle, Abram, is. So I must wonder if you could be descendants from the giants of old who escaped the great flood with our ancestor, Noah."

To my surprise, Mika answers. "Yes."

Lot takes a deep breath. "Then our peoples are connected."

"Connected," Mika echoes. He seems to consider the word and looks at me. I repeat it in his language, and he nods. "Yes, peoples connected."

"I understand now," Lot says, "why El chose you as his messengers." He leans back and slaps his thighs again, this time with both palms. Then he gestures to his oldest daughter. "Pheiné, play for us!"

With one hand, Pheiné sweeps her thick auburn hair over her shoulder and smiles boldly at Raph. "Will you be participating in the Spring Rites tonight?"

My cheeks and throat burn with a hot flame, and my hand goes on its own accord to my short curls and then to brush the knot of bone on my nose. I suppress the urge to throw a lamb bone at her. With great difficulty, I keep my attention on my food, but I watch every nuance of her manner from the corner of my eye.

Raph occupies the other side of my gaze. He smiles back at her. "We are strangers in your city."

This is not a satisfactory answer to my mind.

Mika frowns, and Lot says at once, "Play for us, Pheiné."

Pheiné raises an eyebrow, but lowers her head in obedience. "As you wish, Father." She places a lyre in her lap. It is a beautiful nine-stringed instrument of Egyptian ebony. Fortunately, her voice is ordinary, and Raph seems only politely interested.

I love music, though I cannot play. Father feared to let me sing, lest it reveal my gender. This never stopped me from singing to myself or to Philot or the goats.

When darkness claims the land, I lie on my pallet, listening to the city. Nights in the hills are full of sound—wind whispers in the grass or the scrub trees, night birds call, and wolves howl. Last night I fell asleep in Lot's house to the slosh of sea against the shore and the rustle of a city curling into slumber—muted voices calling, doors shutting, a dog's bark. But tonight is different. Tonight, the city is alive with sharp sounds and smells. Feasting and drinking will go on into the morning for days leading up to the rites. It is interesting to imagine coupling everywhere and anywhere in celebration of life, people echoing the wanton burst of blooms that entices bees, the abandon of grass seeds offering themselves to the wind, and the coming together of Baal and the goddess, Asherah.

Muffled voices in the far room catch my attention. At first, I think it must be Lot and his wife practicing the rites, but then I realize the sound comes from Pheiné and Thamma's room. An image of naked Pheiné entwined with Raph incites my heart to a swift gallop. My first impulse is to jump up and confront them.

Confront them with what? What claim do I have on Raph? He does not know what I have just decided—I love him; I want to be near him forever. He does not even know I am a woman.

Sensing my distress, Nami, curled beside me, licks my hand. Then two figures pass me in the darkness, and I realize the story in my head is only a story I have imagined, because there is no mistaking those tall shapes. Where are they going?

A stupid question. They are going to join the revelry. But I think again. Raph, perhaps, but Mika's disapproval of the Spring Rites has been obvious, so much so that Lot has declared he and Hurriya will not participate in them. Questions continue to pour into my mind. Where are El's messengers going? Are they on El's business? It is too much to endure, and I climb to my feet and slip on my outer robe. Nami's feathered tail whips my leg; she is eager for an adventure. I signal her for quiet with a claw gesture, a sign I taught her, though she rarely barks.

The slave girl, whose name I have learned is Lila, lies by the fire. She appears to sleep soundly. I strain to see in the room lit only by the moonlight seeping from the open window and through the small gaps in the fronds over the courtyard. The oil braziers no longer burn. When Mika and Raph settled on their pallets earlier in the night, they set between them the fur-covered object they have carried throughout the journey. A pull stronger than a current draws me toward the spot. If necessary, I can move very quietly, a skill I learned in order to slip out of the tent without arousing my father. I squat next to the object, my fingers exploring its dark shape.

I wish the light were better. The fur covering is gone, and I can only see it is a chest. My fingers slide across fine wood polished with oil. I fumble with it, my heart thudding, and open the lid. Only then does it occur to me what lies inside might be cursed . . . or alive, and I rock back on my heels.

Nothing jumps out at me. My skin does not melt with El's fire. The faint scent of cedar touches my nostrils. Tentatively, I reach inside. The interior is lined with thick sheepskin, but nothing is there. Disappointed, I close the lid. They must have taken it with them.

Sleep is far from my reach. I move to the door. Fortunately, Lot's door, well greased with fat, opens soundlessly. Nami trots out beside me. It is night, but it is not dark. Torches burn everywhere, making me blink stupidly for a few moments in the unexpected brightness.

People have spilled into the street as if it is midday market, but they are dressed in their finest clothes. Women wear Egyptian kohl around their eyes and have twisted their hair into oiled braids. It is a chaos in which I cannot find pattern, and there is no sign of Raph or Mika, though by all rights, their heads and shoulders should have been visible above the crowd.

Frustrated, I decide not to wade into such confusion to look for them, but to seek a higher point where I can perhaps spot them. Not far to the east, the land rises sharply. I start that way, Nami at my side, her head high, nose to the wind, eyes bright. It lifts my heart to see her out of her brood for her pups.

The northeastern gate is normally closed by dark, but tonight the gates are thrown open, as though inviting the world to partake in the celebrations. This gate is smaller and less elaborate than the south gate where we entered the city. No one stops me or questions me as I pass through.

Beyond the bright areole of torchlight, I pause to let my vision adjust to the darkness. There is a well-worn path to the right, but from the other direction, a flash of light on an outcropping arouses my curiosity. As though she knows my desire, Nami leads. We are not the first to come this way. It is clearly a path, though not as wide as the first one. I am thankful for the white markings on Nami's legs, because otherwise, she is a brush stroke of darkness in the night.

We wind our way up the steep trail until it splits, the main trail continuing up, and a less traveled path heading toward where I saw the flash of light. That is the way Nami chooses. As a sight hunter, Nami's sense of smell is perhaps not as keen as other breeds, but it is still far superior to mine. I follow until we gain an outcropping, a flat expanse that looks out over the city and the Dead Sea. Light from multiple torches halos the sky above the city walls below and blocks the stars from view. The moon is a bright egg, but its edges are ragged with dark clouds.

I settle on the edge while Nami explores the dark recesses of a cave behind us.

To my surprise, I hear a soft laugh and a gentle, "Your nose cold, Nami." I turn swiftly to see a tall shadow unfolding from the even darker shadows.

"Do not start, Adir. It is only me, Raph."

My heart starts a patter. Raph? Did destiny guide my steps, or perhaps El? Then I catch sight of the polished silver disc hanging from his neck and realize the flash of light I had seen from below must have been a reflection of moonlight from his pendant. I manage to croak, "Are we alone?"

Raph drops to sit beside me. "For short time. Mika relieves himself."

This means I have only moments to win his love forever. I, an inexperienced girl he thinks a boy, a daunting task I have no idea how to begin.

He puts a friendly hand on my back, and my heart catches.

"What brings you here? Curious of the rites?"

Trying to remember how to breathe, I am far too distracted to answer. The spot on my back where his hand rests burns, as though with fire.

Is it a holy fire?

And, just as important, does it linger longer than a friendly man-to-man touch?

And yet again, that would be a matter to be judged in light of one's customs, and how would I know the customs of his people? All these thoughts race through my mind until I remember he has asked me a question.

"What?" I say stupidly.

Nami, who sits at my left side, gives a quiet whine, her attention on the trail.

A portion of the light from the city is blackened by the column that is Mika. He stops, seeing me. "What are you here?" Disapproval stains his voice.

I ignore him because I am busy being furious with myself. I have Raph alone and do I reveal my soul, my longing? Do I uncover my true self so he can see past this disguise of my boyish dress?

No, I sit in silence, unable to answer even the simplest question. The lost opportunity carves an ache in my belly.

Mika remains standing, but Raph and I sit at the outcrop's edge while the moon rises, silvering the sea's dark waters. Raph waves a hand toward the salt formations at the water's edge. "Like snowdrifts."

As traveled as I am, I have heard stories of snow, but never seen it. My mouth is dry, but I clear my throat, taking advantage of an opportunity to engage Raph in conversation, even if it is about the weather. "I have never seen snow. Is it like white sand?"

Raph smiles. "More fragile, but hold in your hand."

I frown. "It is frozen water, is it not? Ice?"

"Yes, it a form of water is. If apply heat, it melts to water, but snow is lighter, like—?" He looks to Mika, who stands on Raph's other side, holding his staff, a long rod that is taller than his head.

Mika shrugs. "Clouds?"

I am intrigued by the concept of holding clouds in my hand, but the wind shifts, bringing the scent of coming rain and roiling dark clouds to obscure the moon's sliver. Before the night is over, I fully expect to be soaked by a downpour, but I am not willing to leave Raph's side. We are close enough that he has actually brushed my arm twice.

While we watch, a line of firebrands forms in the streets below. From our vantage, it appears a blazing snake, weaving a path through the town toward the temple. The sound of drums slides under my skin, pounding my blood to match its rhythm. If it were not for my desire to stay with Raph, I might have heeded the pull to join them.

Over Raph's shoulder, I hear Mika's voice. "This is not The Way."

Lightning flashes across the sky, and for a moment, night is day.

"They are not our people, brother," Raph says. "You cannot expect them to honor our truths. They have their own."

I like that.

Another burst of light in the sky.

"Truth is truth," Mika says stubbornly.

Below, I see someone exit Lot's house and recognize the almost square shape of Lot. Is he sneaking off to the rites or looking for his missing guests and kin?

Nami whines and presses against me. I stroke her and find she is trembling. "What frightens you, Nami?" I whisper.

At that moment, the air sharpens, lifting every hair on my arms and the back of my neck, as though the sky has drawn a breath. From the corner of my eye, I catch a flash and look up at Mika who stands beside us, looking down at the city. His staff is alive with a corona of light. I have never seen anything like it. Countless tiny particles of blue light dance at the tip, down the shaft, and over his hand and arm.

I grab Raph, digging my fingers into the muscles of his upper arm. He glances at me in puzzlement, then follows my gaze up to Mika, and I hear the suck of his breath. We are silent, all of us, frozen at the wonder and beauty of the softly sizzling light.

Twice more lightning stabs white fingers into the dark sea below us. Thunderous blasts follow, but we cannot take our gaze from the cobalt fire that engulfs Mika's staff and hand.

When the corona fades away, a third bolt crackles into the sea, accompanied by a loud clap of thunder. Lightning ignites a patch of floating pitch the size of Lot's roof, which floats slowly toward Sodom. Wind spreads the fire's oily black breath over the walls and into the city like an augury, where it entwines with the torch smoke of the marchers winding their way toward their destination—the temple where Baal waits for the appointed day to join with his Asherah and arouse the earth.

14

The Lord appeared again to Abraham near the oak grove belonging to Mamre. One day Abraham was sitting at the entrance to his tent during the hottest part of the day. He looked up and noticed three men standing nearby. When he saw them, he ran to meet them and welcomed them, bowing low to the ground.

—Book of Genesis 18:1,2

WHEN WE RETURN TO THE house, Lot is waiting and falls on his face before Mika. When Lot turned and looked up into the cliffs, he must have seen the holy fire on Mika's arm and staff.

"I and my family are yours to command, angel of the most-high god," he says, lifting his face from the dust, but keeping his gaze averted.

"Angel" in the old stories can carry a connotation beyond a god's messenger, acknowledging a people a step closer to the gods than we, and it is clear Lot is using the word with this meaning.

Mika puts out his hand, "Rise up, Lot."

"I cannot, lord," Lot insists, trembling. "Is El angry at the rites of Sodom? My family will not partake of them. I will speak against them!"

I, too, am shaken by what I have seen.

"I am not your lord or your god," Mika insists.

"You are the mouth through which El speaks. I saw you hold holy fire. I saw it!"

Mika starts to speak again, but then stops and shakes his head. There is nothing he can say. I saw the fire too. Even Raph seems affected, his reddish complexion almost pallid.

If Mika is really Mika-el, an angel of my god, does that mean his brother Raph is also an angel? I do not know how to digest this. Am I in love with an angel? In the stories Sarai had us memorize, such did not turn out well.

Only Nami appears unaffected by the presence of holiness. She strides into Lot's house with regal poise, as if it is now part of her territory.

Finally, Lot composes himself enough to stand, and I slip off to my pallet, though I am unable to sleep. I keep seeing Mika's staff and arm engulfed by cold fire and the black smoke from the burning pitch spreading across the city. What does it all mean?

THOUGH I SLEEP fitfully, the city's dawn catches me dozing. Nami's cold nose on my neck rouses me from the warmth of my pallet. I throw on my garments. Everyone appears to sleep deeply. Raph has his arm thrown over his cheek. Mika's back is to me. I am certain whatever they carried to the overlook is back inside the box that lies between them. Perhaps they meant to hide it in the cave, but my presence changed their plan. When we came down from the cliff, Raph carried it wrapped in the bearskin that now again covers the chest. I would love to slide that skin aside and open the box, but I do not dare. Raph is a warrior and probably sleeps as shallowly as a wolf. I have not decided what Mika is. But whatever is underneath the fur, it is something they wish to keep secret.

Alone, Nami and I slip onto the street that runs the length of the city from the northeastern gate to the southern gate and out to the massive burial grounds. The road is stark, deserted by all but an occasional reveler staggering back to his house. Even the dogs are still asleep, and we are not challenged. The east tower gates remain open, and just outside them, we turn this time to the right, walking beside the eastern wall to the river that runs down from the cliffs. It turns with the slope of the land and feeds the fields below. If the Vale relied on water from the Dead Sea, it would be a desert. Most wadis are dry gulches or riverbeds that only fill when the spring or winter rains come, but a few, like this one, are fed from sweet water whose source is underground.

Sodom's idea of plumbing is the privacy behind one's house. I prefer a place between boulders. Nami is not so particular. The fresh waters of the wadi run nearby, and we both are happy to drink from it. I take the opportunity to wash.

It is still early, and on our return, I climb the cliff where the blue fire struck Mika. Below, a thick mist covers the calm silk of the Dead Sea. Like the city, she gives no indication of the violent storm that plowed her surface last night. Nor is there sign of what burned, although not far out from shore, I can see men in small boats hauling in the pitch that floats like black flatbread on the surface.

The wind shifts, and the stink of rotting eggs rides with it. The Dead Sea's nature is complex. It is beautiful, yet poisonous. No life can survive in it. From its depths comes the black pitch and noxious gases, yet the pitch has made many men wealthy, including my father, despite his protestations to Lot. The run to Egypt is a long, hot journey but one with great rewards. With such a dowry, even the problem of my slightly flawed nose can be overcome.

I slap my leg and Nami bounds to my side. My heart is light. Somewhere in the turmoil of the night, I have decided to shed my persona as a boy and marry Raph, although I will not do so until I can speak with my father. He will be pleased and know what to do. No one is his equal at negotiations. I will talk Raph into joining us. Mika can come too, if Raph wishes and if his angel's mission allows it. And then I will not have to leave Father or my beloved caravan. How can my father not approve? Though Raph is not of our tribe, his people and ours are connected, as Lot said, and he is an angel's brother. That has to be something of account.

THE FOLLOWING DAY, Chiram's son, Danel, arrives with instructions from my father. With the money earned from the black donkeys, we are to buy five camels for the desert journey to Egypt and return with them and with the pitch pots he has purchased to Lot's tents.

Lot advises us on the location of the best pitch, and we purchase the camels outside the city gates where traders come with livestock to sell or trade. Other merchants who cannot pay the tax required for a place inside the Gate are here as well. Young slave boys run about bare-chested, identifying customers for their masters and hawking the extraordinary quality of their particular animals or merchandise.

We hire help to pack the camels with the pitch and our water, which are the heaviest items. The rest goes on our donkeys. Danel brought Philot and two other donkeys with him. Though Mika and Raph left most of their possessions at the tents on Lot's land, they brought one donkey between them to carry their belongings and the box of mystery. Raph has retrieved that beast from the stable and piled the fur-covered chest and their pallets atop her. Between the donkeys and the camels we have purchased, we do not have much we have to carry ourselves, a luxury.

We are careful to stay on the road after we leave the city. The stone surrounding the Dead Sea is easily tunneled, and people have brought their dead here since ancient times. Before the more modern mud-brick charnel houses were built, families brought their dead to the shaft-graves that still pocket the land.

Once we have reached Lot's tents on the plain and rejoined my father and the caravan, we will carry the pitch to Egypt. It is no small task to journey to the Black Land, and it is not one I look forward to. But since it appears Raph and Mika will travel with us, this trip will be different. My confidence in my father's negotiations skills is high. Zakiti is not a poor man. He will be happy I have a solution to the problem of my being a woman.

BY MIDDAY, WE are well past the burial grounds and into the lush plain. It is constant work to keep the camels from grazing. I prod their legs with my stick to encourage them forward. Raph matches pace with me. As always, his presence makes my breath short.

"Adir, you miracle are with animals."

I smile, pleased. "But I know little of weapons, as you do."

The look he gives me is one of surprise. "How know you?"

At that moment, the lead camel angles her head toward a succulent patch of grass, and I raise my rod, stepping to her flank. She mouths, as if chewing, a sign of submission, and turns back to the path. I shrug. "It is obvious."

"How?" he asks.

"In the way you move."

He arches an eyebrow. "I see. And Mika? What your wise eyes do see in him?"

I consider his question. "Mika moves more like a prince or king, as if everything he does is special, only he does not realize it."

"He not king is."

"'King' is not the right word," I admit, "but I do not know what the right word is."

"You asked him?"

It was my turn to be surprised. "No." My gaze finds the back of Mika's broad shoulders. "Would he tell me?"

A fond, amused smile flickers across Raph's face. "Not hopeful. He shares little."

I look up at Raph, following the square lines of his jaw, covered in copper beard. He is so beautiful. Will he mind having a wife who is not?

My gaze returns to Mika. "You saw the same thing I did . . . on the cliff?"

He hesitates. "Yes, I saw."

I wait, sensing his discomfort.

"I not know," Raph's gaze also wanders to Mika's back. "I think he not knows, but I heard tale of such once."

"Of someone holding blue fire?"

"No, but herder told of storm where blue lightning danced on his horns."

I frown. " . . . danced on his horns?"

Raph shakes his head in frustration. "The horns of his rams."

I consider this. I don't know what the blue fire was, but I don't know what lightning is either or how a flower blooms. That is the gods' business. And priests' business to determine what such things mean or if they mean anything at all. Lot, however, has decided it meant Mika was El's angel, but if blue fire has played on rams' horns—I will wait and decide my own mind.

IT IS DUSK when Nami alerts us to trouble. We left the city later than planned, and our pace has not been swift, so Danel has decided we will camp for the night and reach Lot's tents in the cool of morning. I lie my pallet against the back of one of the kneeling camels. Through the night, her body will give off the heat she has soaked up during the day. Because there is plenty of dried food for a meal, we make a fire only for warmth. When fresh, pellets of camel dung make an excellent fuel, as their bodies suck all the moisture out before making the deposit. When we travel through the desert, I will collect it with the other boys . . . or perhaps not, if I announce myself as a woman. Collecting camel dung is not my favorite task. This is a compensation, I suddenly realize, for giving up my boyish disguise.

Nami, who had curled beside me, is suddenly on her feet, a low growl in her throat. Raph and Mika have noticed and come to stand on either side of her, staring into the darkening landscape. I am not concerned. Raiders do not come into the Vale. It is when we brave the desert, their land, that we must have guards and wrap ourselves in wariness.

With that thought comes the rumble of hooves out of the gloaming, and my heart rises to my throat. I am wrong. There is just enough time for me to grab Nami when a raiding party of armed men erupt from the dark beyond our fire and surround us. Small horses with arched necks and wide, flaring nostrils pull four chariots.

I am stunned to see such here. A horse this far south is rare and a chariot rarer still. All are dressed for war, three men to each chariot. The drivers keep their attention on the horses, but the black eyes of the bowmen and shield bearers glare from beneath their pointed helms. Drawn arrows menace our hearts. I have examined such bows in Egypt and Mira. Made of horn, wood, and sinew, they have extraordinary power. At this range, one might pierce me completely. I gape at the arrows' bronze tips. These are not the people of the desert with whom we normally trade. They are warriors and somewhat familiar, yet I cannot place them. What are they doing here? And, more importantly, what do they want?

Raph slowly releases the hilt of his dagger. Resistance in the face of such numbers would be a foolish gesture . . . and certain death. When the chariots halt, Raph steps forward.

Two men ride their horses, one a gray mare and the other a black mare. These men do not carry bows because they cannot easily shoot arrows from horseback. From their dress and the easy skill with which they guide their horses, I know them to be Hurrians, horsemen of the north. When I was eight summers, my father engaged a Hurrian to teach me to ride.

I begged him for a horse of my own, and he purchased Dune, despite Chiram's complaint that the horse was clumsy compared to the donkeys and ate too much.

Casually, the man riding the black swings a leg over and jumps down. Unlike the charioteers who are clad in a heavy linen shirt sewn with metal disks, he wears the lighter robes of a desert nomad. A curved sword and axe hang at his belt, but he touches neither weapon, well aware of the arrows ready to spring should we pose a threat.

"What you do want?" Raph asks. He seems calm. I fear for him and admire him for posing as our leader and putting himself at risk for us.

The man looks Raph over with a steady eye. "What do you have?"

Danel steps forward then and shrugs. "Only what you see, a few camels, a few worthless items, but know they belong to Zakiti, son of Yakud, a friend to the desert people."

"I do not know this man or care whom he calls friend." The warrior turns his attention back to Raph, but the sweep of his gaze includes Mika, who has stepped forward to stand with his brother. "Who are these?" he asks Danel.

"They are holy men," I say quickly.

The man's gaze flicks over me, as though I am an annoyance unworthy of his attention, but he signals his men, and several leap from the chariots to pilfer through our belongings. One discovers the fur-wrapped box from Raph's donkey. He pauses to finger the thick bearskin, itself worth several donkeys and maybe a goat too, and then unwraps it, revealing the box of polished wood. Though my fingers have run across the smooth surface in the dark and known it to be skillfully made, this is the first sight of it. The wood is a fine cedar with a carving of a crescent moon positioned like a smile, cupping a five-pointed star.

"Take box only." Raph says, "A worthless thing inside."

"It is yours, eh?" The head raider signals, and the box, unopened, joins the pile of goods stripped from Philot and the other donkeys. I am not surprised when they take the camels, but horror stabs my heart when the head raider strides to me with a rope and loops it around Nami.

I start forward as he drags her away, but Danel's strong arms grab me and hold me back. "He will kill you, Adir," he whispers harshly in my ear. "Do not be an idiot."

Nami turns her head toward me with a whimper but, half-strangled, she cannot fight the man.

As if my misery is not complete, Raph, too, is taken, stripped of his hidden knives, his hands bound behind him, and forced to mount one of the camels, who protests loudly at having to kneel and then rise with his weight added to her burdens.

Mika steps forward in protest, "He my brother. Take me where you take him."

The raider eyes him. "I do not wish for another mouth to feed. Or should I kill you?" he asks with no change in his voice, as though asking if the day will be hot.

"No!" Raph shouts from the camel. "He lies. He my servant."

The raider shrugs and turns his back on Mika. In two steps, he is beside his stallion and mounts with a graceful leap. With ululations of triumph, the raiders turn their chariots, leading our camels and goods, and disappear into evening gloom.

We are left with the donkeys and our clothes, and I am left with a desert in my heart.

15

She sobs through the night; tears stream down her cheeks. Among all her lovers, there is no one left to comfort her. All her friends have betrayed her and become her enemies. Judah has been led away into captivity, oppressed with cruel slavery. She lives among foreign nations and has no place of rest. Her enemies have chased her down, and she has nowhere to turn.

—Lamentations 1:2,3

I BURY MY FINGERS INTO PHILOT'S coarse, upright mane to still their trembling. Raph is gone. I am a woman who has opened her arms in anticipation of embracing her lover, only to discover he has dissipated into smoke. Not that I have ever had a lover and, at this moment, it seems doubtful I ever will. My heart is torn between losses—Nami and Raph.

But a glance at Mika's stony face reminds me I am not alone in my abandonment, though for long moments, not a muscle on his face or lanky frame moves.

Danel is the first to speak. "We have our skin intact, and the donkeys. It could be worse."

Only then does Mika turn and, for a moment, I wonder if he will pull a dagger and slay Danel right in front of us, but he only says through tight lips. "Who were they?"

Danel frowns. "Horse people. Hurrians and foreigners."

"Where have they taken my brother? And why?"

His question goes unanswered. I, too, do not understand why the Horse People are raiding this far south and who the charioteers with them were, but a sudden realization shakes me from my shock. "They came from the direction of Lot's tents!"

Danel exchanges a glance with me, and I know he understands my agreement that things could indeed be worse. My trembling has spread to my legs.

"I will take a donkey and ride ahead," Danel says.

My need for action courses through me like a flash flood through a wadi. I wish for Dune's swift legs. "I will ride with you."

"No," Danel shakes his head with the same finality of Father's hand slicing the air. Then his face eases a bit. "I need you to manage the rest."

I start to insist, but he says, "Adir, my father is also at the camp. I will ride quickly, I promise."

I swallow and nod.

From the corner of my eye, I see Mika striding toward his donkey. "I am going after my brother," he says, taking up its halter rope.

"Do not be a fool!" Danel calls. "They have taken all our water. You will not last a day where they go without water. You can resupply at Lot's tents. It is not far."

Mika hesitates and then, seeming to understand he cannot help his brother if he is dead, nods.

I pick up my camel stick and wave it at the donkeys. "Hiya! Hiya!"

Mika goes ahead. His long strides would have soon taken him beyond our sight, but it is clear from his frequent stops where he squats and examines the ground, he is not merely leading us to Lot's encampment, but making certain we follow the trail the raiders left. This only confirms my fears. I push the donkeys, my heart squeezed between concern for Raph and for my father. Nami is a prized animal. They will not hurt her, but I miss her already.

WHEN WE NEAR Lot's encampment, I race ahead. The raiders have been here. Goods are scattered; goats and people mill in confusion. I run to father's tent, my legs clumsy with dread. Danel meets me before I can enter, grasping my shoulders.

"Is he all right?" I demand, panting.

For a moment, his eyes cannot meet mine. "Chiram fought them," he says. "My father was wounded too."

Wounded too. The words are unreal. Blood drains from my head, leaving it as light as air, and my knees wobble.

"Zakiti is . . . bad, Adir," Danel warns.

I start to tear from his grip to enter the tent, but he holds me. "He is not here."

"Where?"

"In the tent of the strangers."

How I get there fuzzes in my mind. Only when I duck into the shadows of the tent, do the sharp edges of reality re-form. A woman I do not know kneels beside my father. When she looks up, her eyes are thick with sympathy.

I drop to my knees at his other side.

Slowly, he opens his eyes, though neither of us has spoken of my presence. "Adir?" His hand lifts, seeking, and I grasp it with both of mine.

Amazed that even now, he protects me with my boy-name, I manage, "I am here, Father."

His eyes are curtained with film. I hold his hand tightly, keeping him here with the strength of my grip.

He tries to speak, but coughs; a spittle of blood edges his lips.

"Do not speak," I beg.

For a moment, his eyes grow fierce again. "I will," he rasps. "And you will listen."

His features blur. "I am listening, Father."

"Take my knife."

"No."

The woman pulls the dagger from his belt, holding it with both palms cupping the blade, presenting it to me as Zakiti's first-born son. It has a silver-worked hilt and bronze blade, curved at its tip. All my life it has been in my father's sash.

I take it, but it is not real. None of this can be real.

"Go to Abram," Father says. "Obey Sarai."

I nod.

"Swear to me."

I swallow. "I swear to you."

"Swear by our god."

"I swear to you before our god."

"Name him." He insists.

My father asks me to do this on his dying breath. I cannot refuse him. "I give my oath by the name of El-Elyon."

"Remember that your name means "strength.""

His eyes close then and warmth fades from the rough hand enfolded in mine.

IT SEEMS A long time later Mika enters.

The woman has gone. I sit alone with my father, still holding his dagger. "Adir?"

The voice seems to come from afar, some distant place I used to know. "Adir."

I blink at him, and my mind belatedly puts a name to the sunburned face. Mika. El's man. The angel who held blue fire in his hand. His face, which has never showed emotion of any kind, softens, and there is aching in his beryl eyes. "Your father fought in tent ours."

My father fought the raiders because Mika and Raph were guests, charged to his care by Abram, but not only guests—sacred visitors. Holy men. Messengers of our god.

Anger churns in me.

"My father is dead because our god chose to *honor* us with you!"

He bends his head. "I sorrow."

"I do not want your sorrow. I want my father!"

"I know."

"How do you know? How could you know?"

He looks to the tent's far wall. "My brother," he says, reminding me of his own loss.

"It is not the same. He is alive." I cannot see for the fury that rises in me like a sandstorm. "My father is dead."

Without another word, Mika backs out of the tent.

I LIE, SLEEPLESS, on my pallet, seeing only my father's face before me, even when I close my eyes—especially when I close my eyes. Once, my hand even lifts of its own accord to touch it, that beloved face with its sun-creviced lines and gray-flecked beard, with its stern eyes that melted when he thought I did not see them on me.

Vaguely, I remember the woman coming in to check on me, but she only runs the back of her hand softly across my cheek and does not disturb me.

Finally, I rise, gathering my belongings and find Philot. His cool nose and soft muzzle graze my face. His breath is a familiar comfort. I load him quietly, taking all the water and food he can carry.

I have given an oath to my father, but there are things I must do first. I must find my husband-to-be, my dog . . . and my father's murderer.

16

For his friend, Enkidu, Gilgamesh
Did bitterly weep as he wandered the wild.
I shall die, and shall I not then be as Enkidu?
Sorrow has entered my heart!

—Epic of Gilgamesh

WHEN I RETURN TO THE place where the raiders found us, the moonlight is bright enough that I can follow the tracks. They first go west and then south. Philot and I follow, moving quickly in the night's cool and on through the morning, resting only when the sun is high.

The following evening, we approach the place where the dry wadi from the Zin Valley spills into the Vale. Turfs of grass cluster in the folds cut into the hills by spring and winter floods. This is the only way through the mountains to the west. Once across the mountains, they could go straight to the sea or perhaps they would turn north to the King's Road or south. I find traces of a camp and the droppings of the horses and camels that lead along it. To get through the steep cliffs, we must travel in the middle of the wadi, through the growth of blue-silver and dull green plants waiting for the gush of water that will descend upon them. It is still spring; there is a possibility of rain. If it does rain, water will sweep down from the higher ground, often with no warning. The chance of this is higher in the winter, but as soon as we are able to travel beside the wadi instead of in it, I do so.

Of course, without the fresh water near Sodom and floods in winter and spring, the land below the Dead Sea would be barren. It is, I suppose, the gods' way to grant boon with a price. But Lot is fortunate to have rich lands to graze his herds. Before my birth, Abram let Lot choose where to take his flocks after their men came to blows over a grazing dispute.

Grazing is no minor matter in the desert. Many battles have been fought over who has the right to graze land or drink from wells. This I learned early at my father's side. We have traveled often with nomad guides, and I learned desert ways from them. Father said I swallow knowledge like a thirsty camel. A thirsty camel can drink a well dry, so I know many things.

Unfortunately, there are also many things I do not know, and I miss my father more than my tongue could ever explain. I am adrift in a wasteland far drier than the one of hard brown dirt and stone my feet tread.

At night, I lie on my back without making a fire. The cold is a welcome pain, and I want to see the stars. It is said when tears dry, only salt remains. I have wept enough to salt the sky. My dried tears stare down, glimmering in the endless dark of the night.

Around me, the desert awakes—the soft call of a distant owl, a scuttle of rodent through the stunted, twisted shrubs, the beat of my own heart. I am surrounded with life, yet so alone.

In one sense, Abram, Sarai, Hagar, Ishmael, Lot, and his family are all my family, but in another, deeper sense, my father was my only family. Even when I disappeared for a time from his presence, I was back soon at his side; he was always the center of my dance. I cannot believe he is gone. My mind knew he would not always be with me, but not my heart, not any part of me that lived day to day. In the same way, I know I will die someday, but my body does not truly believe it. I stare up into the stars, and the same thought circles—*I will never see him again.* Never hear his voice chiding me for some disobedience, some recklessness. Never feel his strong arms around me.

I remember when he lifted me into them after my fall from Dune, and how he carried me next to his chest, as if he would tuck me there against the world, against anything that might try to harm me. I thought I was dry of them, but tears run down my temples, into my hair and then onto the ground that drinks them greedily. Water is not a thing to be wasted in the desert.

...

IN THE FOLLOWING days, the trail grows more difficult to follow, as shifting winds gnaw at the soil or the riders pass over the hardpan, leaving only droppings or some sign of a camp. I use the skills I learned in negotiations to observe every detail of the land. The land speaks if you listen, but always I hear my father's voice in my mind asking—*What is the right question?*

The right question is not, where is the path they took? Nor even, where are they going? The right question is, "Why?" Why did those warriors come to Lot's tents? And why Hurrians? They took little from the tents. What were they looking for? Was it the chest Mika and Raph carried? Why take Raph too? My questions spawn too many other questions, and the ache and numbness of my loss keep any answers from my grasp.

I want to stop and rest, but it is better to move steadily because of the flies, although at midday I must seek shelter from the battering heat for me and Philot, and I try to sleep in the shadow of a shrub.

The Hattians of the north believe the sun is a goddess, but Egypt's Ra is male. Whether god or goddess, the sun shows no mercy here.

Mercy.

Do any of the gods care about such things, or only that their contracts and agreements are fulfilled? I saw the gods of Ur once on their stage in the Great Temple. I could not tell anything about what the stone images thought or were doing, though it was explained they were going about their daily lives, waited on by servants who seemed to know when they wanted to eat or love or sleep. I wondered how the priests could tell such things.

Our tribe's god does not wish to be confined to a stone image. So I wonder, what does he look like? What if he speaks to me through Raph? Will I have to fall down at the feet of my husband?

A little bubble of laughter rises from the pit in my chest. "Philot," I say aloud, and my little donkey turns his head at the sound of my voice. "Do you hear the concerns I have? My love is so only in my mind. He does not even know he has my heart, and may not wish to. And worse, he is taken from me to unknown places by unknown people, and yet here I lie worrying what to do if El speaks through him."

Philot chews on a turf of grass, as if considering my comment.

I trust my safety to Philot's long ears and keen nose, and I close my eyes, but it is a long, long time before my mind slips from the grip of grieving and allows sleep to quiet it.

A WET SENSATION in my left ear awakens me. For a moment, I see only a vast, blue dome and think my grief has pulled my spirit from my body and cast it into the sky. The wetness in my ear moves to paint a stripe along my cheek. Against that endless blue background, a nose appears, a black, moist nose followed by teeth that gently grasp my chin and release it. *Nami!*

I sit up and hug her neck, feel the beat of her pulse, the silk of her coat beneath my fingers, and somehow her presence, the life within her, stirs the deadness from my heart. She is alive and so, I am alive.

As when she found me in Lot's house, a strand of leather dangles from her raw neck. She looks very pleased with herself. Despite her obvious hunger, she takes the piece of salted meat I pull from my pack with great gentleness.

I can think a bit better now, and I consider returning to Lot's tents and letting Chiram take me to Abram and Sarai, so Nami will be safe. But images of my father dying and Raph taken prisoner are burned into my mind, and I go on. I am not being disobedient to my father and my oath, just postponing when I will honor it.

The land climbs steeply upward. We come upon a settlement where Egyptians mined copper. The mine is abandoned now, but a few families have stayed. I stop at the cistern, and a woman hauling water tells me she heard mounted men pass the night before. Nami and I follow the direction she indicates.

The wind and hard dry ground have stolen most of the raider's trail, and so we move very slowly, searching for any sign of an encampment or tracks of camels or horses. When the camel prints were fresher, I studied them. A desert man can tell much from a spoor—the age of the animal, the weight of the load it carries, and, of course, whether it is of his own herd. He can tell from its droppings and the smell of its urine when it last drank water and what it has fed upon. I do not have such skill, but one of the camels has an in-turned stride, and I am certain we are following the same beasts we bought outside of Sodom.

The land is brown as long-buried bones, dusty, full of hills, valleys, and stone. Nami, not impressed by my pace, runs ahead, sometimes disappearing from my sight. The second day after her return, she gallops back to me from her scouting, her entire body speaking excitement.

Wondering what she has found, I leave Philot and follow after her. At the wadi's edge, she stops and looks back to see if I see what she does. It is almost midday, and dark clouds are forming far ahead of us. A dust demon whirls by, and I move quickly from its path. Ill fortune to see one, much less be touched by it. A storm is coming or perhaps even now dropping its burden of rain, and that is no time to be near a wadi. Still, Nami is practically dancing in place, and I follow her down into the dry gulch.

With care, I make my way around the stones and rough ground. There is more growth here, as plants cluster where there is water . . . or hope of water. A misstep could mean a broken leg, and in this land, that means death. There are a thousand ways to die in the desert.

Perhaps I am here because I want to find one. Do I know the true reasons for any of my choices? Father often told me I asked more questions than there were answers. Perhaps that is why he guided me to ask the right ones.

I see now what so excites Nami, and my heart flutters. A man's legs protrude from behind a boulder. Without a sound, I draw my father's knife. Distant thunder rumbles, chasing a cold line down my spine. I know better than to be in a dry gulch. Spring rains can come suddenly, and the weather is always unpredictable, other than being hot. But Nami will not budge until I see what she has found.

My knife held before me, I step around the boulder far enough away from the body to avoid a surprise lunge. When I have a fuller view of it, I lower the blade. There is no mistaking that long figure or the red hair. Mika's face is raw from the sun, his lips crusted. I drop to my knees beside him and press a hand on his forehead. It burns with more heat than the sun's kiss.

A distant boom of thunder at my back. An ominous rumbling. Nami whines.

"Mika," I call to him. "Can you wake?"

Nothing.

I shake him. "Wake, Mika. We must get out of the wadi!"

A quiet moan. His eyelids flutter. I am not sure he sees me. I slide my knife back into my sash and give him water from my skin, only a small amount, not wishing him to choke. There are no supplies around him, only his medicine bag attached to his belt. I search him for injuries and find matted blood on his head and a swollen area on his ankle that might be a scorpion sting. My heart stutters.

El's angel is dying. Why has our god abandoned him? Has he been disobedient? Is that why Raph was taken? Father is right. I ask too many questions. This is not a time for questions. I must get Mika out of the sun. What the gods do is their business.

But Nami whines-sings her anxiety again, and the rumbling becomes a growing roar. I look over my shoulder. Bearing upon us is the reason one does not go into a dry wadi during the spring rains.

CHAPTER

17

I have placed my rainbow in the clouds. It is the sign of my covenant
with you and with all the earth.

—Book of Genesis 9:13

I HAVE ONLY ENOUGH TIME TO grab Mika under his arms and shout,
"Run, Nami!" before the churning wall of water is upon us. With all
my strength, I hug Mika's upper body to my chest and snatch a breath
as the wave hits. It lifts us, tumbling our bodies as though we are bits of
scrap cloth. I clutch Mika to me.

Underwater, something crashes into my thigh, sending a jolt of pain all
the way up my chest. Mika's long legs catch, dragging us deeper. I twist
and kick. Another sweep of water does the rest, wrenching us free and up
into the air. I gasp for breath. The leading edge of the wash is past now,
and I roll onto my back and kick hard for the wadi's edge. The current is
far too strong to go a direct path, but I angle toward the shore. A flash of
black races alongside us. I hope it is Nami, but I cannot spare my balance
or attention to look.

Thank El, Mika is still and does not fight me. With each breath, our
heads go under, and I kick and fight back to the surface and another incre-
ment toward the bank. Exhaustion wraps me.

"Let me go," Mika moans in my ear.

Every part of me calls out to obey him. He is right. He is dying. Without him as a burden, I can reach the edge . . . and I might live.

We go under again and for a sweet moment, I stop struggling and just let the water carry us.

No!

The voice is my father's, so loud and clear in my head, I do not doubt his presence. For once, I obey without question. A jolt of strength surges through me, the last I have. I fight for the surface and reach for a stone outcropping, but a surge of water pushes us past it—*I am sorry, father. . . .*

Then, to my surprise, the water spits us up onto a patch of ground.

For long moments, I cannot move. Mika and I lie on our sides, my face buried in the wet hair at the back of his head, my arms locked around his chest. The rhythmic expansions of his chest confirm he still clings to life. My own ragged breaths finally slow to match his.

A soaked Nami stretches out beside us. My heart lifts to see her ribs also rise and fall. The rain has reached us. It patters us with drops that pool and run down into the raging current. I turn my head to the churning water where El has stitched a rainbow into the foam.

I AWAKE COMPLETELY dry in the hot afternoon sun. Mika is still in my arms. I extract myself with difficulty and stand to see if I can determine where we are. Though the sun is almost overhead, I know we are now on the far side of the wadi, which has slowed to a sullen stream, innocent of the terror it wielded only a few hours past, but it could easily flood again without warning. I cannot risk crossing it again, especially with Mika.

Above us, canyon walls the color of wool gleam with moisture. Already the desert has responded to the rain. The usually dull scrub and brown clumps of grass and brush are vibrant, and flowers have opened again, greedily suckling every bit of moisture. They spend the wealth given to them in the moment, though tomorrow all will parch again.

Kneeling beside the stream, I refill my water skin and Mika's. I still have my father's knife and my belt bag. My next priority is to get him out of the sun. I bathe his face, trying to wake him. He is far too heavy for me to carry, and Philot, with all my supplies, is lost.

"Mika," I say, leaning closely. "Can you hear me? Can you wake up and walk? It is not far."

He stirs only a bit. We are surrounded by steep walls. I must move us to higher ground. We cannot climb the steep cliff but, a stone's throw toward the bluff, there is a flat rise and a lone acacia tree. It is tiny compared to the oaks of Mamre; I could not stand beneath its branches, but it offers a little shelter from the sun. Mika is very heavy. I work him into a sitting position and once again wrap my arms under his, my chest to his back, locking my fingers and pulling him along. Nami circles around us, clearly wanting to help.

When I stand, I almost tip over from his weight, but somehow manage by stages to drag him the length of his body. That is all I can do without resting.

After a moment, I grasp him again in the same manner and pull. Then rest. There are rocks in the path I must move if I can, or go around. Then pull and rest. He has lost his headdress, so I cut a section from his robe and wet it, wring it over his mouth and then tie it loosely over his face and head.

Pull.

Water.

Rest.

Move stones.

Pull.

Finally, we are at least far enough to be safe from another flood, although the presence of the tree just beyond us means sometimes water reaches this level. I collapse beside him, trusting Nami to warn me if danger comes. I am too exhausted to think about fire or food or even water.

THE HEAT OF midmorning wakes me. Mika is not responsive, though his eyes move behind their lids. He seems worse. His pulse is racing, his muscles twitching. I find dried blood matting his hair. He must have fallen and struck his head. Perhaps that is why he doesn't waken, but I am certain the greater danger is from the scorpion. Whether he lives or dies is dependent on what kind stung him . . . and the will of the gods, most particularly El's.

Nami pants, and I share water equally with her and Mika before rising on wobbly legs to assess our location. Not far away in the harsh landscape is the lone acacia tree, its branches shaped like an inverted bowl. I sigh, but there is no other choice than to haul him again. Mika cannot survive in the sun. He is still unconscious.

When we finally reach the scant shade of the acacia tree, I drip more water into Mika's mouth, rest, and then gather fallen branches from the tree to start a fire. At least I can clean his wounds.

When my arms are full of sticks, I return to Mika and fall to my knees beside him, realizing I have no bowl. How can I heat water?

Disgusted at myself, I sit and brood. Then my eye catches sight of Mika's medicine bag. The knots are tight from their soaking, but I work them free with my teeth. Inside are several tiny but very sharp knives rolled in thick leather, packets of herbs, kept dry by the oiled camel hide, a small bowl made of an unfamiliar hardwood, and a stone mortar, as well as flint and a striking stone. I have one in my bag too, and a little food, but not much. Most of my supplies were on Philot who, at best, headed back to Lot's tents. I hope he does not fall to Dune's fate, and makes it to our people before a predator finds him.

Every child knows how to light and tend a fire with a flint stone, but my hands shake, and it takes me several tries before my little pile of tinder ignites. When the fire is stable, I look for the right size stones. Nami puts her nose on every one, trying to figure out why I am interested in them. Finally, in exasperation, I wave her away. "Go hunt something!" I shout.

To my surprise, her mouth gapes in a dog-grin, and she is off into the wadi, now mostly dry. Other than our little acacia tree, the ground here and the cliffs behind us are dry and barren. The danger of another flood has not passed, but we have no choice. Only in the wadi does anything grow.

My heart sinks watching her. Surely, she will come back. She has always returned, even when taken against her will. Of course, she will come back. What is wrong with me? I walked out into the desert alone, but now I am afraid of being alone.

I glance at Mika. He is still unconscious, but restless, his limbs jerking periodically, and he has soiled himself. Not good. I put aside my fears and concentrate on what little I know to do. The stones go into the fire. While they are heating, I cut strips from my robe and clean Mika's wounds. He does not seem aware of what I am doing, and that is probably good. Though I thought he was unconscious when we were in the water, he spoke to me. Perhaps the poison has frozen his limbs. I have heard of such.

When the stones are hot, I pick them up with a forked branch and drop them one by one into the small bowl of water until it steams. I lay out all Mika's herbs. "Which ones?" I ask him, on the chance he might hear, but he does not answer. I choose the pouch that smells like onions. Onions are good for snakebite. That is something I learned once in Egypt, but I do not know if it will help a scorpion sting. Chiram came as close to a medicine man as our caravan had. I was interested in his herb lore, but I usually kept my distance from him. Why my father trusted him, I will never understand. Anyone can look at him and tell there is something mean in those small eyes enfolded in skin. He is always in a bad temper. When I was small, he frightened me.

I soak the onions in the boiling water and let it cool just enough not to burn skin or tongue, and then use a strip of cloth from my own robe to soak in the tincture and wrap Mika's wound. With a smaller piece, I drip the broth into his mouth. He swallows reflexively when it hits his tongue. Has he slipped away because of the sting or the injury to his head or a combination? I wish now I had asked to learn about healing, even from Chiram. Mika is dying. It does not take much skill to see this. Perhaps he will be gone by the morning. I will wake up, and his face will be set in stony stillness like my father's . . . and I will be alone.

"Do not die," I whisper, leaning close to his ear. "Fight, Mika. *Fight*. Your brother needs you."

Surely, he had been searching for Raph, desperate to find him before the spring winds and floods obliterated the tracks. Why else would he have come this way alone? I came alone because I knew Chiram would insist I go to Abram and Sarai immediately, and I could not.

Mika does not move, and I do not know if he heard me. It is for priests to petition the gods, not youths like me. Abram has the ear of El, but Abram is far away. I have no lamb to sacrifice, no animal except Nami. If El himself demanded it, I would not harm Nami.

But what if she does not return?

What if the moon falls down? That was my father's question when I voiced some worry that had no solution.

"Father," I would whine, "What if a wolf kills my goat-kid?" or some other such concern.

"What if the moon falls down?" he would reply, and I would always smile at this absurdity.

But now, it does not make me smile, only ache.

. . .

NAMI RETURNS BEFORE sunset with nothing to show for her adventure. Either she caught something and ate it herself, or she didn't catch anything. Or perhaps I just imagined she responded to my command. Still, we have leaped from a bed of snakes into a nest of scorpions. We may not drown, but we will starve if we do not find food.

I do not give Nami any of the last bits of salted meat in my bag. I have now only one dried date left. She sits before me, her bright eyes following my every move. Always, I have shared with her, and it is difficult to withhold the food, even though what I have put in my belly does not begin to ease its gnawing. When it is obvious there is nothing for her, she gives a soft whine and approaches to lick my fingers.

At my insistence, Nami lies close to Mika, on the side away from our small fire, I curl on his other side, pressing my body along his, hoping we can keep him warm. Mika trembles and moans. I hold him tight when his body jerks. Only twice do I doze, with the same dream of the Dead Sea belching pitch that ignites into blue fire.

The following morning, when dawn paints the sky pale orange, I reach with trepidation for Mika's face, fearing what I will find. But his breath moistens my fingers.

He has lived through another night.

AGAIN, I FEED nothing to Nami and send her out at dusk, the best time to hunt, when creatures stir from sleep or come out to feed in the evening cool. My day is spent dripping broth into Mika's mouth, cleaning him, and changing his poultice, much as the day before, except there is no more dried wood on the ground, and not another tree in sight.

After filling our water bags, I venture across the wadi to the far side to search for what I need. I have no choice. Most of the morning is gone before I find what I seek—droppings from ibex and wild camels. Camel dung burns very slowly and repels flies. I gather all I can, including camel thorn to start the fire, using my robe as a basket.

Other than that foray, I leave Mika's side only briefly to get water where it has pooled in the wadi's deepest spots or to hunt on my own, returning with my robe full of little snails that cling to some of the low brush and the little fishes that emerge from the sand when there is water. I thought I spotted a bush farther away that might have lentils. I throw the snails into the wooden pot with more dried onions.

Nami returns panting, but with nothing. She watches me crack and eat the snails, though it hurts me to disappoint her. She is barely more than a pup herself. I am certain the litter she lost was her first. Her training to hunt would have begun by putting her in the company of other seasoned dogs. She may never have made a kill on her own. But it is clear she recognized the words, "Go hunt!" and possibly the gesture with it.

I take her long, elegant head between my hands and look directly at her. She is still for this, listening, her bright eyes fixed on mine.

"I need you Nami. You are a desert dog, bred to hunt. Find something or we will die here together, the three of us."

Her dark eyes are intent, as if she is trying to read my soul. I have no problem reading hers. She wants to understand, to please me. My belly moans loudly. The snails were not enough. My head feels like a cloud, and I release Nami and lie down beside Mika.

He is hot again.

I try to think. I must do something. I could return to Lot's tents, bring back help, but I am days away. Mika would be dead before I returned. "But," I murmur, "we will all be dead if I do not."

A strangling sound comes from Mika's throat. Has he heard me?

Nami licks his outstretched hand, either in sympathy or for the salt.

THE ONE THING we have is water, but less and less of it every day. There may be more flooding, or no more rain until winter. The heat has descended. Everything goes still at midday, and I drag Mika around to keep him in the scant shade of the tree. The flies are a bother when we move out of the smoke from the burning dung or the handfuls of weed. Both stink, but I am used to the smell.

WE HAVE DEPLETED the dried onions, and I fear to eat the other herbs, as I do not know their use. Mika's leg is still swollen and red. He sweats constantly, and tears leak from his eyes. He needs more water than I can spare.

· · ·

I AM WEAK from hunger. In the evening, I hunt into the now-dry wadi as far away as I dare, keeping Mika within sight in case a predator comes. Once, I was most fortunate, stumbling upon a porcupine that was agitating a horned viper into attacking it. The snake struck over and over at the raised quills until, exhausted and wounded, it lay inert. I snatched it up, though the porcupine escaped, but now—a feast! Nami whines when I give her nothing. I can see each one of her ribs. "Go hunt," I snarl.

I AM SO tired. I just want to lie beside Mika and drift away, but he moans, his muscles seizing up in a cramp, and I drip water into his mouth . . . the last of it.

Then I do lie down. I should go and try to find more water while it is cooler, but I am so tired. My bones ache. Is this how it feels to slowly starve? Oddly, I do not feel panic at the thought. It is almost as if I am watching myself from somewhere outside my body. A fleeting shadow pulls my gaze upward to the unmistakable wingspread of a vulture.

Mika stirs. His lips are cracked and raw, as is the skin of his face and hands. His people were not meant to live in the desert. Where then? Where did this chosen one of my god come from? And where is Raph, my beloved?

My beloved. The words now seem strange, as though their power has lifted like steam into the sun's heart. Even the loss of my father has buried itself beneath my attention. I have not thought of love the past days, only how to survive and how to keep Mika alive. I consider the long length of man beside me.

His god has abandoned him, but I have not.

CHAPTER

18

Who is like you among the gods, O Lord [Yahweh]—?"

——Book of Exodus 15:11

The average layman, whether Jew or Gentile, still believes that the official Hebrew religion was a strict monotheism beginning with God's revelation of Himself to Abraham. Scholars date the origin of Hebrew monotheism a few centuries later, during the days of the great prophets.

——Raphael Patai, *The Hebrew Goddess*

NAMI'S DEEP BARK WAKES ME instantly. She does not bark except to alert. My hand grips the knife that sleeps in my grasp, and I am on my feet before I even remember where I am.

Moonlight, so clear it casts shadows, illuminates the world in grays and blacks. I see no danger, only Nami sitting close by, her gaze intent on me, her ears pricked toward me.

"What?" I ask her.

Only then do I see the bloody heap before her. It is the length of my forearm and dead. That is all I know at first. That is all I need to know.

"Oh, good girl, Nami," I breathe. *"Good girl!"*

This acknowledgment is what she has waited for and she jumps up, forgetting her dignity, to wash my face with her joy at pleasing me.

"Great hunter," I say, stroking her and praising her over and over. She has a wound on her leg, but seems to have licked it clean, and I leave it alone.

"Let us see what has given you such a fight," I say, and turn to the hunter's prize. Nami accompanies me to inspect it, her nose close. I push her back, full of love for her. She could have eaten it herself. She was even hungrier than I, but other than battle bites, she has not touched it. My eyes fill with tears. I have starved her, but she has shared her prize—all of it.

Are we worthy of such companions?

The animal has a dark underbelly and a back of silver-white fur. Wicked teeth. "Nami, you could have chosen a less ferocious prey for your first kill! This is a honey badger. No wonder you are wounded." I stroke her again to make sure she knows how proud I am.

Nami sits nearby, watching my preparations avidly. I make her wait for the meat to cook, grilling it over the fire, but at a slant, so the juice drips into my bowl. It does not seem wise to give her the message it is fine to eat the meat raw. I want her to bring the spoils of her hunt to me. It might not matter, but our lives balance on this, and I will not chance a mistake.

The smell of the meat makes me dizzy. Nami's eyes water from the smoke because she will not move from its path. I hope that is not a bad omen.

After we have feasted on the cooked badger, I drip the meat's juice into Mika's mouth. My strength returns. Nami curls at my side for a well-deserved sleep. Dawn is not far away, and I wait for it, watching with reverence, keenly aware of the closeness at which death hovers over every moment. I feel privileged to be alive, to see the morning star pierce the dark blue-black of the sky.

Mika's groan startles me from my trance. This time his eyes open. At first they do not see me, but dart around as if he is a trapped animal. Then they fix on the morning star shining in her glory, and he calms at once.

"Mika?" I am at his side with a damp cloth and run it over his face, clearing the night's crust from his eyes and mouth. Slowly, his gaze pulls from the star to me. I answer the unspoken questions in them. "You fell, and a scorpion stung you. You have been unconscious for days." Still he stares, and I shake my head. "I do not know where Raph is. We have lost his trail."

Then his eyes close, and he drifts away. I feel for a pulse at his neck. It is stronger. This is not the last moment of strength before death, as I feared. He is only asleep. My heart hammers with elation. *He will live.*

I watch over both of them—Mika and Nami—until the sun, rising behind the acacia tree, tips its low branches with light. Then Mika wakes again, and Nami ambles to him to lick the salt from his face. It is a morning ritual. A smile cracks the dried skin around his swollen mouth. He lifts a hand to Nami's coat for a moment and then lets it fall, his expression stricken with the realization of the extent of his weakness.

With some trepidation, I move to his side. "Do you need to make water?"

He swallows and nods. I help him roll to his side. Long ago, I stripped him of his clothing, just letting him lie naked beneath his robe to ease my job of keeping him clean. The ground slants here, so his urine pools away from him. Usually I drag him to another spot afterward, but this time, I just cover it with dirt. It is only a tiny amount and enough indignity that I must do this.

There is still a little badger broth. I throw the head and skin to Nami to gnaw and take the bowl to Mika, setting it aside to help him sit, but soon realize I cannot keep him upright. It requires sitting behind him, and it is too awkward. "No!" I say when he reaches for the bowl with a trembling hand. He will spill it before it ever reaches his mouth. "I have an idea."

Gently, I lower him back down and move the precious liquid to safety. Then I grasp his upper body to my chest in a well-practiced movement and drag him closer to the tree. After some maneuvering, he can sit, supported by the trunk. Despite his burned skin, he pales and faints.

I push his head down between his legs so the blood can return to his brain, and I wipe his face and the back of his neck. After a moment, he groans, and I help him back to a sitting position.

Fearing he will spill the broth, I say, "Just sit for a moment and let your body get used to the position."

Again, he nods and leans back against the tree.

When finally I hold the wooden bowl to his mouth, keeping my own grip on it, he can drink only a portion of its contents. We do not speak, but his eyes track my every move like a nursing infant. I am his connection to life.

Twice more he awakens, and we repeat this. He *is* an infant. I must continue to do everything for him.

He does not know I am a woman, so it is perhaps less humiliating for him. But now I find myself blushing, even though I have handled and wiped clean his manhood without thinking much of it for days. Now it is different. I feel the burn on my cheeks and wonder if he notices. He says nothing. It is as if he has forgotten how to speak. A new fear worms into my chest. What if the poison has attacked his mind and he cannot speak? What if he never recovers and I must care for him forever?

What if the moon falls from the sky?

Yes, Father. I hear you. For the first time, the thought of him makes me smile instead of weep.

19

I have blessed you by Yahweh of Samaria and his Asherah.
>—Hebrew inscription on storage jar
in northeastern Sinai, 700–900 BCE

To Yhwh and his Asherah
>—Tomb inscription in Judea, 700–800 BCE

MIKA DOES NOT SPEAK FOR a long time. I remind myself he spoke little before the scorpion stung him, but still I am relieved when he does, even though he makes little sense.

"Must find it," he mutters, thrashing his arm to the side.

"What?" I ask.

"Must dream . . . Raph."

These utterances do not connect. I touch his forehead to see if fever has replaced the chill of his limbs, but it is only warm from the desert heat.

At last, he sleeps.

WHEN HE OPENS his eyes, he sees me. I know because he calls my name, "Adir."

I tell him again what happened. "Yes," he says. "I remember told me."

"I think you will live." El had favored him, my father would say, but I would not call allowing a scorpion to bite me a great favor.

"I will live," Mika whispers through cracked lips, "because you." His eyes are upon me in a strange way. It is said saving a person's life binds you to him. I am not certain I want to have such a connection to this man. Suddenly his presence is akin to standing close to a windstorm that blows you where it will.

I shrug.

At that moment, Nami arrives with her prize, a fat mouse, which she drops before me. Mika's brows arch in surprise. I praise Nami as if she has delivered an ibex, skinned and ready to cook. Her plume tail switches in pleasure, and she lies before me, paws crossed, focused on her mouse—plainly inviting me to do my part.

But before I can begin to skin it, I catch a movement at my vision's edge. "Be still," I tell Mika. He follows my gaze and stiffens.

A brown, many-legged creature, larger than my fist, climbs over the bandages of his wound. With a quick flip of my hand, I swat it off, and Nami jumps to investigate. "No, Nami!" Despite my warning, she pokes her nose at the creature.

Mika looks pale.

"Just a camel spider," I assure him.

With a sharp yelp, Nami trots to my side and sits, pressing against me for comfort. A tiny bit of blood wells on her sensitive nose, and she licks it off.

"It bites, but it is not poisonous." I do not laugh at Nami; she is quite pitiful. I understand the pull of curiosity over obedience.

"In my homeland," Mika says, "spiders decency to be small."

At once, I ask the question politeness has kept from my tongue, "Where is your land?"

Mika reaches out and strokes Nami's chest. "Born in mountains north, but ancestry—land of my people, homeland, is far across sea."

"Tell me of it."

But he falls back, his face pale from the small effort of stroking Nami.

"Later," I say. "Rest now."

His eyes are already closed.

WHEN MIKA WAKES again, I smile encouragingly, but a new worry presses my mind. Not really new. It has been there from the beginning; I just have not had time for it.

I have made a broth from the mouse, the last of our water, and a handful of lentils I picked from another scraggly bush, sharing with Mika and Nami. I know what I must do, but it is too hot, so that task must wait.

Draining the cup, Mika puts it aside and insists I remove the bandage so he can look at his leg. I do so, careful not to let it touch the ground. We have no water to clean it, and the wadi is dry.

His mouth grim, Mika examines the leg as if it belongs to another. Finally, he grunts and leans back against the tree. "You good job, Adir. I see was infected. What use?"

"Onions. At least I think that's what they were. From your bag."

"Good choice. Now, try else."

My head drops. "We do not have the water." I do not want to look at him, afraid he will read in my eyes what this means. His recovery is still fragile. He has not shared much about himself, but a man who will leave an encampment alone in the middle of the night to find his brother and perhaps revenge his host—is a man who will not lie on his back and die slowly.

"We must travel," he says. "When cooler."

I swallow. "You cannot travel."

Mika starts to speak and then turns a critical healer's eyes on his leg. "No," he says so quietly I almost do not hear. "Not on leg." He eyes the tree branches overhead. "Perhaps a stick to hold weight."

I bite my lower lip. He has been unaware of his state, unconscious for most of the time we have been here. Even with a crutch, my guess is he could hobble only to the edge of the wadi, at most, without collapsing.

In the end, he does just that. It takes that to prove to him the impossibility of travel.

"You alone go," he says slowly after he has rested for a while. "Do know way to Lot's tents?"

"I know the way."

"Then must go . . . tonight."

He is right. A person could live without water maybe three days if travel is limited to night's cool. It is unlikely, but possible I could make it to Lot's tents. I am not certain how far the river swept us in that direction. But I would never return in time to bring help to Mika.

"I am not leaving you," I say, stroking Nami's head, which rests on my thigh.

"You must." Mika's gaze on me is intent, as if by the power of it, he can force me to his will. I suspect, by the easy assumption in his voice, he is a man accustomed to commanding others. Is that, I wonder, because he is El's messenger or because of his position in his own land? I know little of this man—or his brother who holds my heart.

I feel a wistful smile curve my mouth. "I am not good at obedience, but even if I were, I could not go."

His glare shifts into puzzlement.

With a sigh, I look up through the branches of the tree that have shattered the sun's dazzle into daggers of light. "Perhaps your ways are not ours. Perhaps you do not understand." I look again at him. "My father gave his life for honor."

Mika's head shakes. "Raiders slew him."

"They did. But he died in your tent."

Perfectly still now, his eyes fixed on me, Mika waits for my words. When they do not come, he asks softly. "Why, Adir?"

Long moments pass before I can continue, before the terrible clench in my throat releases enough for air or words to pass. Nami's gaze lifts to my face, though she keeps her head on my thigh. There are idiots who say a dog does not understand. Nami's understanding is silent, but deep.

At last, I can speak, though my voice emerges as a hoarse whisper. "My father went to your tent to defend your belongings, because you were his guest. That is our way."

Silence hovers between us while Mika considers this, and then I say, "You are still our guest, wounded and in need of aid. I will not leave you."

20

We find our Spirit in the wisdom spoken in the wind.
—a Pablo elder

WHEN THE SCORCHING HEAT SUBSIDES, but good light remains, Nami and I set off down the wadi, looking for pockets of shadow in the rocks where water might have pooled. My eye scans the stones and pebbled ground for areas thick with vegetation, particularly cane grass that might signal the presence of sweet water. I avoid the scrubby pines, because they can live in areas where the water dries faster and leave more salt.

My lips are already cracked and the back of my throat is parched. I used the last of the water to cook the mouse. There was really no choice in the matter. We had to eat, and Mika could not have handled raw meat. Mika drank his portion before I told him our situation, or else he might have protested. He may not know the ways of our people, but he is not a selfish man. In that, El chose well.

I am glad, because guest or no, I would not wish to die for a selfish man.

At my side, Nami pants. I watch her because animals often can smell water where it appears there is none. Her nose disturbs a hare, which bursts from beneath a shrub. Nami gives chase. She matches the quick changes of directions with an agility her lanky, puppyish play has never revealed. This is not play; this is life or death. The days of no food have awakened this focus in her muscles and sinews. Her need drives her to anticipate the hare's movement, and instinct guides the decisive snap of her jaws that breaks its neck.

But it is her love for me that keeps her from devouring the meal, the warm flesh and scent of blood so tantalizing in her mouth—love that makes her turn and bring her prey to set at my feet.

And it is thirst that drives me to cut into it and drink the blood. It will not long satisfy my body's need for water, but the hot liquid wets my throat. I share it with Nami, then bind the hare's hind legs and attach it to my belt, and we continue the search.

The sun has almost touched the earth's lip when I find a place beneath an overhang of rock that shelters a tiny pool of water, not much more than Mika's bowl will hold. Nami noses among some bushes, no doubt hoping to find another hare. I fall to my knees and with hands that tremble in relief, lay my water skin down in it.

When my skin is half full, only a small puddle remains. Even my eyes are dry and gritty, and I long to splash my face, but instead, I call Nami over and let her drink what remains. It is not much, and I know she wants more. I take one long swallow from the skin and tie the cords of the bag. It is dusk and will be dark by the time I return to our tree.

THE FOLLOWING MORNING I find the pile of stones I left to mark the tiny pool. It is dry, but my hope is that water has soaked into the ground. Sometimes there is a rock shelf beneath that pools or channels water. Nami remembers she drank here yesterday and begins to dig, spraying me with grit. I smile and let her. When she tires, I do the same, using my dagger and a stone. This dulls the edges of my weapon, but it cannot be helped.

Throughout the morning, Nami and I take turns digging. Up to my elbow, the ground is dry, but after that, I am encouraged by a hint of moisture. Now the sun is half the distance to center sky and sucks the sweat off any bit of exposed skin. My robe and head wrap cover most of my body except for my eyes. I absorb a minimum of the sun or wind's hot breath, but I can feel my thirst as an ache throughout my body, viciously focused in my throat. The skin on the back of my hands is ridged with veins, like an old woman's.

Nami has given up on this game and lies in the deeper shadow of the overhang, her forepaws crossed, tongue lolling, watching me. I want to tell her to close her mouth, that she is losing moisture, but I know she cannot sweat, and this is how she cools herself. She would die quickly if she could not release her body's heat.

We will all die if I do not find water.

This knowledge drives me, even through the swelter of the overhead sun. Over and over, I place the end of the dagger into the dirt and drive it down with a stone against the hilt, praying to El the bronze blade does not break, praying water is there. I shake my head to dislodge the flies that crawl into the corners of my eyes, seeking moisture.

The blade does not break, but there is no water.

I stop when the dirt in my hole turns dry again. Then I know it is useless to dig deeper. My fingers drop the knife and stone. There is a buzzing sound in the distance and a queer feeling in my belly. I do not have the strength to shake my head, and the flies cluster. Vaguely, I face the thought that I cannot return to Mika. I am sinking somewhere, somewhere deep and cool. I want to be cool. Perhaps there is water in the depths of this dark well.

My last thought is the realization my face has fallen into the hole I dug.

CHAPTER

21

Now Sarai, Abram's wife, had not been able to bear children for him. But she had an Egyptian servant named Hagar. So Sarai said to Abram, "The Lord has prevented me from having children. Go and sleep with my servant. Perhaps I can have children through her." And Abram agreed with Sarai's proposal. So Sarai, Abram's wife, took Hagar the Egyptian servant and gave her to Abram as a wife. (This happened ten years after Abram had settled in the land of Canaan.) So Abram had sexual relations with Hagar, and she became pregnant. But when Hagar knew she was pregnant, she began to treat her mistress, Sarai, with contempt.

—Book of Genesis 16:1-4

A DOG BARKS IN THE DISTANCE. This is annoying, and I ignore it. Then there are more sounds—voices—and strong hands lift me. My eyes blink to a flash of men in dark, flowing robes, the underbelly of a camel, and a long, braided tassel that swings beneath it. The smell of blood. A wet tongue on my face and in my ear. *Wet*. That captures my attention. I force my eyes open to see Nami standing over me and, beyond her, desert men clustered around me.

"Look," one says, "the boy is awake."

"Water?" I croak, and a skin is placed in my hands. The warm liquid is the sweetest I have ever tasted. They let me lie still while life returns to my body, awakening like the desert opening to rain.

"Many thanks," I gasp. "I ask your hospitality and help for myself and my friend."

The young man nearest me frowns. "Your friend?"

I point. "Under the acacia tree that grows close to the wadi's edge."

"I know the place," the man says, nodding.

WHEN I NEXT awake, my memory is like a stream that runs beneath rocks, appearing for a ways and then disappearing underground. A fragment of riding on a camel, someone's arms around me to keep me from falling. Mika under the tree. More riding. Snatches of words floating around me. A tent. A woman kneeling next to me. Mika's weak voice.

I wake to a familiar view—wisps of coarse goat hairs protruding from the weave of a tent roof. Black goat-hair walls surround me on two sides. Down the middle of the tent, dividing the space in two, is the long woven wall that separates the men's area from the women's. I know my secret is still mine because I am privy to the beautiful finished patterns. The back of the weaving always faces the women's partition. Strangely, this does not relieve me. I am unsettled, but I cannot name my feelings.

The deep, throaty bellow of a camel and the smell of cooking goat stir me, and I roll onto my knees. Only then do I notice Mika, asleep on another of several palm-braided mats. I smell him too . . . and myself. With great relief I see a large bowl and clean clothing set out for us.

I see no one nearby, so I quickly wash my body and the binding I keep around my breasts and put on the clothes without an attempt to dry myself. The desert air will do that soon enough. What a joy to be clean!

I stand, my ears buzz, and I must catch myself on a tent pole, but after a moment, my head clears, and I walk out. The area near the tent is empty, though I can see women inside other tents. A small boy, perhaps six summers of age, catches sight of me and approaches.

"Greetings," he says with a lopsided smile, in the language of the south desert. "I am Shem. I offer you the hospitality of my tribe."

"I am most grateful," I reply. And I am, but a fear gnaws my belly with the pangs of hunger. "Do you know what happened to my dog? She is black with gold brows—"

"Yes-yes," he says quickly. "She is well. My father took her hunting. He has a fine falcon. You will see."

I smile, relief pouring through me.

"Do you want milk?" Shem asks.

"That sounds very good."

"Our camels give beautiful milk, and they are the most beautiful camels in all the world. You will see." A gap-toothed smile flashes across his face.

I laugh, charmed by his enthusiasm and loyalty toward his family's camels. It is, I realize, the first time I have laughed since the day the raiders came. I also realize it has been days since I thought of Raph, and guilt plucks at me. What has happened to him? Is he even alive?

Following Shem around the scattered array of tents, I see he has not spoken in bravado. The white camel is not particularly happy at the process of being milked or at being separated from the herd, which is not in sight. Shem rests a large bowl on one raised knee and uses both hands to milk, hopping on one leg without spilling a drop when she moves. A small replica of the mother camel hugs her opposite side, all wobbly legs.

When he finishes, Shem approaches with the bowl. "This milk will give you and your companion health," he pronounces with surety.

"I have seen many camels," I say, taking the clay bowl with both hands, but this one is the most beautiful I have ever seen."

Shem beams, bouncing from foot to foot on thin legs. "Yes-yes. Her name is Niha. I can recite her lineage for generations. Now drink!"

I do, gulping down the sweet, sharp liquid, still warm from the camel's body. I am grateful for every drop. There is more there than my belly can handle, and with care, I carry the remainder back to Mika.

I find him awake and sitting up. He looks terrible, and I wonder if I am as burned and swollen as he. I glance down to inspect my hands, which appear normal. Perhaps the deeper color of my skin protects me. I have seen people in Egypt whose skin is as dark as kohl. They readily endure the sun and heat, walking about in midday when everyone else retreats to whatever shade they can find. Even Shem wears kohl about his eyes to guard against the harsh glare of sun. I pity Mika for his light skin that even his wiry red beard cannot protect. He does not belong in this Land of the Sun. Not for the first time, I wonder why El brought him here.

Mika has recovered enough to hold the bowl and drink without assistance.

Shem squats beside us, eyes bright. "You will be well now."

Wiping the back of his hand across his milk-stained lips, Mika turns to Shem and then to me to interpret. When I do, he smiles and nods, returning the bowl to the boy with a look of thanks that needs no translation from me.

Shem takes it in his earth-brown hands and leaps to his feet. "I go now to return Niha to the herd."

In a moment, he is gone, and Mika and I are alone in the tent. Though I have tended him as a mother to an infant for many days, I do not know what to say. Finally, into the awkward silence, he speaks. "Adir, my life I owe you."

I lift my hand in a gesture of dismissal, but he shakes his head. "No, more is here than my life. You have right this to understand."

"What is your meaning?" I ask, confused.

He does not reply at once. After a moment, he says. "I owe you answers, but I still not speak well this language. Perhaps easier if you ask."

I could remind him that I speak his language fairly well, but I consider his offer. There are many questions frothing in my mind. What is the right question? What do I want to know most?

With a deep breath, I say, "What did the raiders seek and why did they take Raph captive?"

Mika considers me. "You go swiftly to heart, Adir."

I wait for his answer.

When it comes, it is not what I expected, although I cannot say what I expected. "In my land, I am—" Mika stops and begins again. "Raiders wanted what inside the box we carried. It great value to my people, yet no value without understanding how to use."

"And Raph understands how to use this thing of great value?"

"No, he not. But raiders think so." Mika's swollen hands knot. "They should taken me. I am eldest. They should taken me!"

The agony creasing his face stirs my own guilt. I feel the same about not being at my father's side when he was threatened. He died defending our family's honor. He would have said nothing was more important, but I would rather have him alive than hold an empty cup of honor.

"You tried," I say, remembering how Mika had stepped forward when Raph was taken and cried, "Take me with him!"

Why didn't they take Mika with Raph? Apparently, the raiders thought they had the right person. "So Raph cannot use this thing of value and . . . power—" I pause to see if he will object to my use of the word. He does not, and I continue, "If you had gone with the raiders, they would have been able to use this object?"

Again, he stares at me. Then, as if his internal anguish was a fire that has burnt low, he says in a voice so quiet, I am not certain I hear it, "I do not know."

This is not helpful, and I am still full of questions. "Who are you, Mika?"

The intensity of his expression melts into a wry smile. "Again question straight as spear." His eyes lift to mine—such a sharp green in daylight; they are darker in the shadows of the tent.

"I from the north mountains, but my people from very far land, land with mist and rain, hills like green carpets, not gray-green of this land, but green, like—" He struggles to find an adequate word.

"Like your eyes?" I ask.

He smiles. "So I told. Hills that roll like waves into distance and forests thick."

I close my eyes, trying to imagine such a place.

"My people very ancient, Adir."

I keep my eyelids shut, floating into this land of green and mists.

"Our oldest name is 'Watchers.' We watch sky from beginning of time. My ancestors built temples of stone that"—he searches for a word—"measured heavens and brought goddess into them."

"Stones that brought the goddess into them?" I do not understand what he means, but in my mind's eye, I see a structure of stone, vague, but massive, surrounded by an aura of mystery as thick as the fog that obscures it.

My eyes open and, for a moment, I am startled to be here. "You are weary," I say, noting the dark craters around his eyes. "Lie down again and sleep. You can tell me more later."

He does not lie down, but leans against the pole and closes his eyes. I watch him for a long time, wondering about his people and the land I glimpsed in my mind's imaginings. Do any of those stone temples still exist? Are they like those in Ur and Babylon or different? I feel a pull, a longing to see them, to see the land of emerald and mist.

22

Then Sarai said to Abram, "This is all your fault! I put my servant into your arms, but now that she's pregnant she treats me with contempt. The Lord will show who's wrong—you or me!" Abram replied, "Look, she is your servant, so deal with her as you see fit." Then Sarai treated Hagar so harshly that she finally ran away.

—Book of Genesis 16:5-6

B Y DUSK, THE CAMP REPOPULATES with the camels returning from grazing and men from their hunt. Nami runs happy circles about me. I kneel to embrace her, and she promptly begins washing the ear closest to her mouth. "Nami, it is clean!" I protest. "Cleaner than in many days."

At the sound of a gruff snort, I look up at the man standing before me. I did not hear his approach. He wears the loose black trousers, robe, and headdress of the desert people. A leather sash studded with silver holds several knives, both straight and curved. His bearing marks him as the head of a family or possibly a clan.

"So," he says, "you are recovered."

"Yes, sir."

He nods at Nami. "Your dog is a good hunter. Did you train her?"

"She trained herself," I say and then amend. "Someone began her training before she became mine."

His piercing eyes narrow. They are a light, almost translucent brown. "And how did she become yours?"

My breath catches. The carpet merchant in Sodom had been insulted I owned such an animal as Nami, who clearly was a desert-bred dog. Possible explanations fly through my mind as the man waits, but I decide upon truth. "My father's caravan assistant won her in a gamble, and I bought her from him."

The thick brows above his falcon eyes rise. "You bought her?"

I feel my mouth slide into a stubborn line. "With a she-goat."

He rubs a hand over his own mouth. "I see." He considers Nami, who now licks my other ear. "Well she is a fine dog, and there is no doubt she thinks you belong to her."

My mouth relaxes into a smile.

"That is the important thing," he says. "But I have been rude. You and your tall companion are my guests. You must come to my tent and eat with my family. The dogs have brought down a gazelle. We will feast."

Pride swells my heart that Nami has done well, and my mouth waters at the thought of the gazelle. It seems a long time since Shem and the camel milk.

The man dips his head. "I am Yassib, the grandfather of this family." A woman steps to his side. She is also clothed in black and wears a headband with bits of gold nuggets dangling from it. Gold and silver bracelets begin at her wrists and extend up both her arms. She wears more wealth than do many kings, I would wager. I have no doubt Yassib is a clan chief, perhaps even a tribal one. His arm extends to her. "This is my wife, Mana, who has born me many sons."

The woman smiles down at me. "Be welcome in our tents—?" Her voice trails, and I realize they do not know our names.

"I am Adir, son of Zakiti," I say out of habit, but in that moment I realize when I awoke in the tent of Yassib, it was as Adira, daughter of Zakiti. The time in the desert, grieving for my lost father and lost life, has changed everything. Like the butterfly, I am ready to shed my cocoon, but I do not know how to take back the words, to transform who I am in these people's eyes. I know their ways are strict in regard to men and women, and I have slept alone with Mika and possibly with others on the men's side of the tent. The desert people cherish their women, but kill them if their honor is questioned.

Better now to keep my secret.

When he leads us back, I learn I have indeed slept in Yassib's tent. The other woven mats belong to him, another son, and his grandson, Shem. I speak with the men and drink tea while the women roast the gazelle, trying not to show what torture the wafting smells evoke in my belly. One good thing about staying a boy—I can eat as much as I wish without criticism.

As Mana and her daughters serve us, I am thankful not to have been a girl raised in a desert tribe. Never do they meet my gaze, their heads downcast, although the youngest steals a frank stare when she thinks no one is looking. A girl child is almost an embarrassment, and some are even put to death as a burden on the family if times grow hard. Until a woman gives birth to a son, she is not truly recognized as a wife, although she has the power to divorce a man by simply turning the entrance of her tent. Yassib introduced Mana as the mother of his sons. The two daughters before me do not even exist in his eyes, or so their customs say. I wonder if he might truly love them, but by custom cannot acknowledge them.

It is not so in my tribe or in the cities. Sarai manages the household, and Abram listens to her counsel. My father never would have withheld his love or approval from me because I was a girl, though he chose to hide my gender to keep me safe and at his side. In the cities where the goddess is worshiped, in Egypt, and in the northern lands of the Hatti, women own land and businesses, and their wealth is passed to their children. Why do the ways of people differ so much?

For so long, I have not thought much about such things, but now anger rises in me. Why should a girl child be so unwelcome? Life in the desert is difficult, but without women, men would not be able to hunt. Women birth and care for children, prepare the food, and make the garments, the tents, the saddles, and the bags necessary for such a harsh life. Why are their contributions less worthy?

A cold worm of unease works its way into my chest to nestle with the anger. What will happen if my guise is uncovered among these people?

Finally, we feast on the gazelle cooked with dates soaked in camel's milk. I think I can eat forever, but my belly is not used to so much food, and it rounds in protest. Mika is not much better, but I watch every bite that goes into his mouth until finally he turns to me in humorous protest.

"Adir, you not mother!"

I start at his words, and then my cheeks flush.

Yassib gives me a questioning look, and I translate. Everyone laughs. They think I am embarrassed because I am a young boy being called a woman and a mother. I relax and laugh with them.

"The desert," Yassib says, tearing meat from a leg bone with his teeth, "is a cruel mother."

It is a well-known saying, and the truth of it is now in my bones.

AS THE DAYS pass, Mika gains strength and begins to walk in the evening when it is cooler. At first, he can accomplish merely the distance from one tent to the other, but gradually his strength returns, though he still favors his leg. I always walk with him, worried about his being alone, stumbling onto another scorpion or a snake or pushing himself too hard and growing faint. Also, he needs me to translate for him.

"Why not they speak Akkadian?" he asked on one of our first walks beyond the tents, clearly annoyed after all his studying, he cannot speak to Yassib's people or understand their words. "Is not that language of trade?"

"For many, yes, but Yassib's people do not bother with the cities. They trade with other desert tribes for food the camels and goats cannot provide."

"And how other tribes have those things?"

I smiled a bit at his ignorance of desert ways. "Not all of the tribes are nomads. Some choose to settle near low fields where rain water pools."

"They grow here crops?" he sweeps his arm across the landscape, his brow raised in disbelief.

"Yes."

"What?"

"Lentils, wheat, barley, even dates. Yassib's people must wander to secure grazing for their animals, but they find plenty of trade for what they make from camel hair and leather."

"Well, not be here long enough for learn another language."

I know he wants to pursue Raph's trail. But he is still very weak, and where would we go?

As he grows stronger, we have made it a habit to walk every evening after the meal to a rock-strewn dune and sit to let him rest before walking back. From here, we have a good view of the ragged, wild landscape, buff-colored hills, and valleys stretching as far as one can see.

Shem came with us the first few times, but quickly grew bored with our talk and found other things to amuse him. But Nami always accompanies us, and I am glad for her nose and sharp hearing, as many creatures come out to hunt in the evening cool.

Mika has insisted we continue working on his Akkadian, and he has become much more proficient. Only rarely do I have to correct him. He is not a man of many words in any language, but I hold him to his promise of answering my questions. I have asked him about his childhood and about Raph and told him of mine, except the part about my gender. I fear he might not understand that these people—who have saved our lives and treated us with such hospitality—might kill me for being a woman or for lying to them.

"Do not sit there," I say, guiding him away from a cluster of saltbushes.

He looks around for signs of scorpions or snakes, a good habit he has acquired.

"That is a salt bush," I say in explanation.

He pinches off the rounded leaf and puts it to his tongue. "So it is salty, why should I not sit near it?"

"If the sand flies bite you, it will leave an ugly round sore."

"I have seen you sit near such bushes."

I smile. "And I could show you the sore on my buttocks from it."

He lifts an eyebrow, but moves to a flat stone a distance away.

"As can every member of this tribe," I add.

"All on the buttocks?" he asks.

I can tell his healer curiosity is aroused. "Yes."

"Sand flies only bite there?" The brow is arched higher in disbelief.

"They bite whatever they can reach, but a few days after its birth, every desert baby is wrapped with only its buttocks exposed and laid in the dust beneath a salt bush."

"So the flies only bite the exposed flesh!"

"Yes. Otherwise, you might bear a scar on your face or other places more . . . sensitive."

"I see, and once bitten, you do not get rashes anywhere again?"

I nod.

He rubs his chin through his thick red beard. "There are certain illnesses that once they strike a person, never repeat themselves."

To change the subject to one more interesting to me, I settle beside him with Nami between us and ask to hear more about the connection between our tribes.

Mika lies on his back and cushions his head with an arm, his eyes full of the haze of bright stars that needle the fabric of sky. He takes a deep breath and expels it as a teller would before beginning a story. "Long ago, when the Watchers saw a star approached the world, they remembered."

He pauses, and I think this a strange way to begin a story. "Remembered what?" I ask.

"Ancient time when star falling brought ruin to earth—great fires and floods. My people lived on island, and all knowledge almost destroyed. They worried of it happening again, and so seeded their knowing throughout world."

Mika rolls over onto one elbow and plucks a small stone, tossing it at one of the rock-paved trenches that collects water from the hillside when it rains and deposits it onto the fields where the tribes graze their animals. The thrown pebble strikes the rocks with a sharp ping and tumbles down the shallow, dry channel.

"How?" I ask, experience having taught me Mika needed prodding. "How did they seed their knowledge?"

"They sought wise men to give it." He looks up again at the stars. "Enoch was such a man."

"Enoch? The ancestor of Abram and my people?"

"The same. The father's father of Noah."

As usual in conversations with Mika, my question has led to an answer that grows more questions. I do not know which to pursue. Finally, I ask, "What do you mean, 'They saw a star approaching the world?' "

His forehead wrinkles. "Do you remember I told you of the stone temples built my people by?"

"Stone temples my people built," I correct. "Yes, I remember."

"These revealed time with— " he scowls, searching for the word he needs. "Openings framed with stone."

"Portals?" I suggest.

"Yes. The stars rose through portals, and my people tracked them."

I do not need Watchers and portals to tell me that the stars wheel across the sky in predictable patterns and that the location of star clusters in the bowl of night indicates the seasons. "Why do you need a temple when you can just look up in the sky?"

He smiles. "Seasons revealed by eye, but with time-keeper temples, Watchers saw future . . . predict seasons to the day and tell people when to plant and when to harvest. My homeland was rich with much rain, but winters harsh and long. If plant sprouted too soon, frost killed it. Such knowing meant life for them."

Mika looks up again to the night sky. "Every star has its path."

This is something my father also said when I whined I did not want to be a girl or ever leave him.

He points toward the north sky. "Look there!"

I follow his finger to catch a streak of light across the firmament. In a moment, it is gone. "Is that what the Watchers saw?"

"Yes, but saw it every night grow closer before it burned day sky." He points to the spot where the light had disappeared. "That time only a moment. A star fell, but yet"—he waved his arm from horizon to horizon—"all still in place, no star fallen." The awe of this mystery edged his voice.

"So what did we just see?"

"My people think a flaming rock, eaten by own fire. The sky has wept many flaming stones, and sometimes leaves black, pitted rocks, holy stones, on ground."

"I have never seen such a stone," I say, and then amend, "or if I have, I did not know it came from the sky."

"They fall without warning, but twice in my people's time, stars come in line with us. First time, Watchers tracked seven growing, night by night, until struck."

Growing night by night. I say the words over to myself, trying to imagine it and what it could mean. I can feel my brows knit together. "A distant object grows larger as it approaches."

He reaches out his free hand and taps my head with a knuckle. "Adir, you have makings of Watcher."

My thoughts are afire. "And black rocks would not be visible in the night sky. They must have been burning."

"Yes, they burned. Grew large as sun."

I inhale sharply. "Did the seven strike the world?" A phrase from Enoch's Telling rose in my mind though I did not say it aloud: *"I saw there seven stars like great burning mountains. I saw many stars descend and cast themselves down from heaven."*

"Oh yes," Mika says quietly. "So long ago, only memory now in the stories, but terrible memory. Water rose from deep; sea swallowed land and all on it."

My hand seeks the warmth of Nami's coat for comfort. "Like the great flood in Noah's time?"

"Legend-memory in every tribe my people has met."

Beneath my hand, the hairs of Nami's back bristle, and a low growl issues from her throat. Mika and I glance at each other, and then we are both on our feet. Mika's knife has found its way into his hand. Nami starts toward a large rock, but I lean down and grab her around the neck.

A trail of cloud veils the half moon. Wind nudges the cloud aside, and moonlight pricks white teeth from the dark. The shadows behind them resolve into a pointed muzzle, a round head with pointed ears and a bristling mane. The creature steps stiff-legged from shelter of boulders, revealing black stripes along its downward sloping torso.

Hyena.

"Stay, Nami," I caution, my hand in her ruff. I do not want her to tangle with the carrion eater.

Mika's hand tightens on his knife.

"It will not attack unless something is wrong with it," I say quietly. "They are lone hunters and eat the kill of other animals."

"In north, hunt in packs," Mika says, keeping his knife at ready.

Though she is compliant to my restraint, Nami's growl deepens into an unmistakable warning.

With a show of teeth, the hyena backs away into the gloom, eaten by the night.

Wisely, Mika moves so our backs are touching to prevent the hyena from slinking around behind us, but after a while, the ruff of Nami's fur flattens, and I release her. "Do not speak of this," I advise.

Mika slips his dagger back into the sash at his belt. "Why?"

"A bad sign to the desert people. A demon."

"You believe so?" Mika asks.

"I do not know," I say, but I cannot deny the cold that has speared my spine.

23

And the angel also said [to Hagar],"You are now pregnant and will give birth to a son. You are to name him Ishmael (which means 'God hears'), for the Lord has heard your cry of distress.

—Book of Genesis 16:11

THAT NIGHT, THE MEANING OF the hyena's presence becomes clear.

As we finish our evening meal of flatbread, red lentil soup, and the staple of every meal—milk-butter served in wooden bowls—Yassib wipes his mouth and announces, "We will move tomorrow. The camels have grazed enough here. We will start the summer-trail."

Jerah, one of Yassib's sons, looks up. "But the hunting is still good here."

"We release the birds tonight," Yassib says.

There is some grumbling at that. Unaffected by it, Yassib picks up his bowl and drains it. "Summer's fire is almost upon us. The birds suffer. Would you have them die in the heat?

A younger man, Kerit, nods in agreement and then turns to Jerah. "Remember brother, it was the dogs who found the gazelle."

"That is true," Jerah agrees, reluctantly. "The dogs can still hunt, but my bird is the best I have ever had."

"Next spring, can I catch a bird?" Shem asks. "I am almost old enough."

Yassib plucks a dried fig from a dish. "Next spring is next spring."

When we finish the meal, all of the men and boys of the clan gather on the highest point near the encampment—the hill where Mika and I trek every night. Kerit allows Shem to wear the thick leather bindings on his hand and arm and carry his falcon. Shem radiates pride at being given this task. Jerah bears his own bird, as does Yassib. All three falcons are hooded.

I walk beside Shem, admiring the glossy feathers. Shem's chest expands. "My grandfather's bird is the best hunter."

"I have never seen a capture," I say. "How is it done?"

"With a net. My mother and sister wove it. You tie the bait to a stake and wait. When a falcon strikes, you wrap it in the net. You must be careful not to harm the bird because it is frightened and fights."

"I would be too," I say.

He nods. "Yes-yes. It takes much skill and patience to train a falcon. My grandfather is the best. He is known throughout the land. I would be good because I am very good with the camels."

Yassib laughs and puts a hand on Shem's shoulder. "Enough, Shem. Too much chatter."

When we reach the hill's summit, the men make a circle. Kerit takes the bird from Shem, and he and Jerah stand in the center with Yassib, who raises a hand to the sky. "We thank the sky gods for the loan of their winged hunters, and we now return their gift." He pulls the hood from the regal bird and holds him aloft. "Go now to your summer place, to the cool of the hills, to the high places."

Jerah and Kerit repeat the words.

A sudden wind brushes my face, lifting my headdress. I turn into it without taking my gaze from the falcons, which watch with haughty eyes and shift restlessly on their handlers' arms. Kerit's bird lifts his wings and then settles them—a signal he is ready to fly, or that he does not wish to leave his master?

My question is answered as Yassib, Jerah, and Kerit lift their arms in assist. Wings snap the air, and Yassib's bird gives a piercing shriek, a wild cry that declares it has never really been tamed. I hold my breath, feeling for a moment as if it is I who flies into the wind.

We watch them until they are lost in the sky.

LATER THAT NIGHT, we sit around the fire outside Yassib's tent. Even though his tent is the largest, it is too small for all to gather there.

It is also cooler outside in the breeze. The women serve us fermented camel's milk, something for which I am acquiring a taste. The night is peaceful, and I have forgotten the hyena until Yassib's youngest daughter, who is four summers of age, waddles to where I sit next to Mika and points at me, announcing, "He is a girl. I saw him squatting to make water."

My heart stops.

Everyone looks at me.

"She is a child," Mana says quickly. "She is confused."

Yassib silences her with a gesture, his gaze fixed on me, studying my features with the intensity of a leopard measuring its prey. Slowly, his face infuses with blood.

Mana grabs the girl into her arms and backs away. The others watch intently, but do not speak or move. My heart is racing. I sit very still.

In a smooth movement that belies his summers, Yassib stands and draws his dagger, the curved one, its golden bronze blade catching the firelight. It will fit nicely around the arc of my neck.

Mika, whose attention had been on his drink, hastily rises and steps forward at an angle to Yassib. "What is happening?" he says, facing Yassib, but wisely not drawing his own weapon. Instead, his hands are spread before him, palms open, signaling a desire for peace.

"Talk," I say in Mika's native tongue.

"What do I say?"

"Anything, just talk quickly in your own language."

"I do not know what is happening," Mika says. "Please explain to me why you have drawn a knife and are staring at Adir with such anger? Has he displeased you?"

I translate: "Most excellent host, why are you angry? How have we displeased you?"

Yassib shifts his gaze from my face to Mika's. "I opened my tent to you, yet you have deceived me. The boy is a girl, a woman." The last word is almost spit, as if it is a bitter taste in his mouth.

"Talk more," I say to Mika, again in his own language. "Say anything; just speak in the northern tongue. Do not try Akkadian. This is delicate."

Mika widens the space between his hands in a gesture of confusion. "I wish I could understand you, but I do not know your language. I am most grateful to you, but I will not allow you to harm Adir."

Despite my fear, my heart warms at Mika's brave words. He towers over Yassib, but he still favors his leg, while the desert man is no doubt swift and his blade at hand. I glance about the fire at the young men watching the drama. All are armed, most with more than one weapon. These are men hardened by a harsh land. They seem confident in Yassib, but should Mika harm their grandfather and leader, I have no doubt there would be many knives and swords at his throat in an instant. Everything depends on what words I put in Mika's mouth.

"My customs," I say, "are not as yours, yet I ask you to stay your hand and let me answer you." Despite the recent tang of fermented milk, my throat is dry as dirt. When did the girl see me relieving myself? Why have I not prepared for this moment and thought of some explanation?

"Answer then," Yassib says, and I hear nothing but death in his voice.

Mika needs no further prompting from me. "I come from distant land. . . . "

I do not pay attention to his words, only to the cadence. When he stops, Yassib flicks his eyes toward me, indicating I have permission to translate. I have ceased to exist to him as a human being. I am only a woman, a woman who has deceived him and violated his customs.

"Men seek our lives," I say with sudden inspiration. "Powerful men. They have stolen my brother and now they pursue me and my wife."

Yassib's knife lowers slightly. "Your wife?"

I look to Mika, and he babbles on about rivers and green hills on an island across the sea.

"Yes. These men look for me and my wife. That is why you found us alone in the wasteland with no provisions. We had to flee. I instructed her to wear a man's clothing to confuse them when they ask if we have been seen. She is obedient to my wishes."

For a long moment, Yassib stands where he is, breathing slowly, as if to regain control of himself. Finally, he slips the dagger back into its elaborately decorated sheath. "Why did you not tell me this?"

Mika's posture relaxes slightly, but he keeps his position. "By goddess, I wish I knew what is happening, but I suppose my part is just keep talking. You seem to be handling it, Adir."

I clear my parched throat and speak formally to remind Yassib of his obligations. "Excellent host who has granted us the hospitality of his tent and his protection, I did not wish to bring danger to you and your family and so I kept this from you. I ask your forgiveness and that you allow us to continue to deceive our enemies."

Yassib takes a deep breath and extends his arms. "You are my guests. Forgive me for my anger. Your enemies are my enemies."

Mika allows himself to be embraced and does fairly well at keeping the bewilderment from his expression.

24

Uriel, the holy angel who was with me, who is their guide, showed me, and he showed me all their laws exactly as they are.

—Book of Enoch

PERHAPS IN PENANCE FOR DRAWING a knife on his guest, Yassib allows me to continue to wear a boy's clothing and sleep on the men's side, but my mat is moved between Mika and the divider weaving. At the first opportunity, Mika asks me, "What happened in the tent? I only understood a few words."

I open my mouth to tell him, but what emerges surprises me. "I made an error and insulted Yassib."

"How?"

"It was a language issue. Not intended." Where did I learn to lie so glibly? Perhaps when my father first caught me sneaking out of the tent to ride Dune?

"Is this why you moved sleeping position?"

"Well, I did not do that. I think Yassib had Mana do it. I gather he wants me further away from him. He has not completely forgiven me."

"I notice he avoids you now."

I nod.

"This is not good. Adir, you must be careful."

Oh, how many times had my father said those words? "Yes, I promise. I will."

Why do I not tell him the truth?

I am not certain of the answer. I desire to shed the persona of a boy, but now I am trapped. I cannot dress as a woman because of the story I gave Yassib that dangerous men pursue us. So now I am pariah—both the men and the women avoid me as if I am diseased. Everyone but Shem.

"Are you really a girl?" he asks me, peering at my chest to see if there are breasts hidden behind the folds of cloth.

"Yes-yes," I say, and he smiles, recognizing his own favorite phrase coming back to him.

The smile at once transforms into a frown as another thought occurs to him. "Then I am not supposed to talk to you."

I frown too. "I think you have another year or two before that is a problem."

He looks affronted and then relieved. "Good, because I like you."

"I like you too, Shem."

WE BEGIN THE trek northward for the summer. We camp only long enough to graze and rest the herds. The sheep and goats and people need the rest more than the camels. A camel is at home in the desert, storing food in its hump and able to go for days without water.

Gradually, my status has changed to one of tentative acceptance. Everyone seems to find comfort in forgetting I am there, or I am a woman, or alternately, a boy, depending on where I am and who I am with. I live as both boy and girl with the tribe of Yassib. As Adir, I help watch the camels, sitting with Shem and the other boys, listening to their tales of heroes and how they will grow up richer and more powerful than any before them.

Shem has his own small bow and practices daily. Yassib has told him he must bring down game before he can fly a hunting bird. He teaches me the hunting signals for Nami, for which I am very grateful, and she is excited that I am now "saying" things she can understand. Shem tries to teach me to use the bow, but I am clumsy with weapons. Perhaps I should have hidden my distaste for Chiram and let him teach me about knives.

As Adira, I sit with Mana and the other women, and they show me how to weave on the flat looms that sit just above the ground. I have always had an eye for texture and pattern, but never imagined I would have the patience to work the threads. At first, I chafe at it, but I am determined, and when my fingers finally learn their task well enough, I find it soothing.

Rarely do the women work in silence. Their talk is a constant flow, though I am not included. How can I be? I do not know the dilemma of what to do with a childless bride, whose daughter needs to be wed, or the finer details of how personalities tangle a disagreement.

On a day I feel I have finally mastered the weaving knot and can keep up with at least the slowest, when Mana's oldest daughter, Petra, looks my way with a cock of her head. "And how did you marry, Adir? Were you both bride and groom?"

My fingers freeze over the loom. The other women fall silent. I snatch a breath. This is the first overture . . . or insult. For the most part, the woman have ignored me. I look directly at Petra. "Indeed, I gave myself a bride price."

There is a shared pause, and then the tent rocks with laughter. The sound washes warmth over me. I am a part of something I have never experienced before—the bonding of women. Women, I have learned, speak of their lives, sharing details and feelings that men do not. And now, I am one of them, despite my clothing and the fact I sleep on the man's side of the tent.

The women are the physical manifestation of the nomad tribes' honor. They bear this burden with easy acceptance. For a girl to violate tribal custom, even if forced upon her, would bring dishonor on the clan and tribe, and that would be intolerable.

At first I believed all the power rested in the hands of the men, but listening carefully, I begin to recognize that many opinions or decisions I hear as Adir in the company of the men originate around the looms and cook fires. The elder women hold the future of the tribe in their hands, for they are the ones who discuss and determine who should marry whom.

I tell Mika I sit with the women to learn more about the art of weaving to increase my knowledge of cloth and my acumen as a merchant. He shrugs and says I do not have to answer to him as to what interests me. In turn, he spends much of his free time with the shaman who knows a little trade Akkadian, filling in with gestures when the shaman's knowledge of the language fails him.

Sometimes I interpret. The shaman never inquires as to our status or mentions the fact I am a woman. And Mika never belittles the shaman's beliefs or ways, seeking instead the common threads in their practice of medicine and religion. Through our conversations, I have concluded it was not the beliefs of Sodom that bothered Mika, but the fact that the populace emulated the holy rites, and he suspected the intention of all was not to engage in a holy act, but to take advantage of the custom. Or perhaps his time in the desert has altered him and caused him to judge less harshly.

Here, with the shaman, he finds a culture that, similar to his, looks to the stars for guidance, and the morning star is a goddess to both peoples.

This seems right to me. El is the god of my people and the creator of all, the highest god, yet every people my father and I encountered have their own gods and spirits. Who am I to say they do not exist, merely because they are not mine?

DURING THE MATING season of the camels, I am especially glad to have the reprieve of weaving. I am used to the stench of goats at such times, but that fades in comparison to male camels in rut. Mika is particularly offended, having little experience with camels. "What is that terrible smell?" he asks, holding the edge of his headdress over his nose.

I point to the bulbous, swelling neck glands on the bulls' necks. "What is wrong?" I tease. "The female camels, the cows, find it irresistible."

He scowls at me.

Another source of the stench comes from the bulls beating their manhoods with their tails and then flicking the scent onto their backs. When they do this, they become aggressive, attacking other bulls for supremacy. Shem and I have to pull Mika back the first time he sees them wrestling, each wrapping his long neck around another's until one is forced to the ground. It is an amazing sight, and I understand Mika not thinking about the danger. In this, he reminds me of myself, but at least I know better than to approach wrestling bulls!

• • •

WE ARE SOON to reach the refuge of the cooler highlands where we will spend the remainder of the summer. I busy myself on the morning of one of our last traveling days, helping to take down the tents, a woman's job. Mana appears apprehensive about something. Finally, I ask Shem what he thinks is wrong with his grandmother.

"She is good with the weather. Perhaps a storm comes."

I look up into the turquoise pan of sky. Not even a wisp of cloud is visible.

He shrugs.

On travel days, meals are quick affairs of flatbread and the milk-butter curd. By late morning, everything is ready to load onto the camels and to begin the trek to the next waterhole. The beasts are milling just outside the camp, and I go to watch them, Nami at my side. Shem trails a measured distance behind me, so it looks as if he just happens to be going in the same direction as I, and not actually following a girl.

I sit on a stone a little distance from the herd and watch them, a breeze wafting their scent to me. Nami does not sit, a trait I have observed in the tribe's salukis. She plops on the ground, her head on her paws. The camels move with graceful deliberation, lifting their noble heads on occasion to check for predators. There are none that would attack a healthy camel, though a lynx or lion might stalk a calf.

As they mill about, my mind wanders.

Mika is doing well now. He has healed. I am no longer bound to stay with him or to stay here where, despite my progress with the women, I am more tolerated by the men than wanted, and I do not know where to search for Raph. It is time to honor my pledge to my father and return to Sarai. She will find a place for me among her household. I can learn to be a woman. Perhaps another will take Raph's place in my affections. I am young yet. I will wed and bear children. I glance over at Shem who sits several feet away, busy not looking at me.

Children.

I have never thought about having children of my own. It is a concept full of mystery. How can men think women weak when they have within them the power to create life?

I consider what I have learned of the desert people, even in this short time. I wonder if their way of ignoring a girl until she marries and bears children is a way to pressure her into such a fate. Perhaps the customs that seem to estrange women are born of a secret acknowledgement of their power and necessity.

I cradle my belly with my hand. A baby could grow there. A baby with potential to be . . . anything. When I die, I will have left the world something precious that will live on, perhaps bearing his or her own child, and they the same, far into the misty future. That seems a gift worthy of giving and would honor my father.

It is settled then; I will return to Mamre. Now, the only question that remains is how? I must have supplies. I eye the camels. I have the means to buy a camel, no doubt, from what my father has left me, but no access to it. Would Yassib take my word in lieu of payment for a camel, food, and water? And what about protection from raiders? How am I to manage that?

This is a prudent thought, but one which apparently fled my mind when I left the tents of Lot. I was crazed with despair at my father's death and the loss of Raph and Nami. I drop a hand to Nami's silky head. She looks up at me, her tongue lolling from the side of her mouth. "Faithful Nami," I say softly. "You will not abandon me, will you?"

She runs her tongue around and lets it fall out the other side of her mouth, panting in the heat. Her tail thumps at my voice, but something catches her interest in the distance. I follow her gaze but see nothing. The camels become agitated. The dominant bull makes his way to stand between the females and whatever attracted Nami's attention, alerting me that perhaps a predator lurks in the dusk.

"Something has disturbed the herd," I say to Shem who is drawing in the dirt with a stick.

He does not bother to look up. "Yes-yes. Probably they know we are going to move out. They always know."

But Nami is on her feet now. The wind is at our back, but she is a sight hunter, so she may see something or hear it. I rise to look where she does. At first, nothing, and then a stir of dust. More camels coming in? I do a quick count of the herd. No, they are all here.

I watch a moment until I am sure, then I shout. "Riders!"

The two young boys watching the herd look at me and turn to peer in the direction I point. But the horsemen are on us so quickly the boys' own calls of alerts are lost in the cries of the raiders. Within moments, they have surrounded half of the camels.

Nami presses against my side, not certain what to do. I order her back and quickly look for Shem. He is not running back to the settlement as I hoped, but toward the *raiders*, yelling furiously. I cannot say I have blame for him. Those camels are the difference between life and death to the clan, and Shem's beloved white camel Niha is among those being stolen.

I run after him. "Shem!"

He pays no attention to me, and I see Nami has not either. I am not the only one who lacks the virtue of obedience.

My longer legs close the distance to Shem, who has somehow managed to grab the leg of a raider. His head is no higher than the man's foot.

The black horse spins as the raider lifts his curved sword to strike Shem, and I am suddenly on the opposite side. I do the only thing I can—grabbing the man's other leg. For a moment, it is a tug between me and Shem. Confused, the horse lowers his head and kicks out with his back legs.

Nami leaps forward, slashing the animal's sensitive nose, and it rears, hooves pawing the air, neighing in panic. Shem is knocked aside, and I realize I have won the tug, as the man, unbalanced by the horse's kick and rear and my weight, totters and falls over on me. I twist as we fall, trying to be free of him, but we hit the ground, locked.

I struggle wildly, sure a blade of some kind will find my flesh, but Yassib is suddenly there, rolling the raider's body from me. Blood is everywhere. Is it mine? I stand on shaky legs, staring stupidly until I notice the wound, blood on the raider's temple, and on a sharp rock nearby.

Yassib seizes Shem and pushes him into his mother's arms. Confusion reigns as angry men and boys run toward us with weapons drawn, shouting their anger. A few arrows fly after the raiders, but fall short. The clan has no horses, only the camels, and no way to chase the raiders and reclaim their property.

Behind me, the horse snorts and I turn, surprised it is still there. The black horse stands on spread legs. Blood flows from his nostrils where Nami's teeth sank into them. His eyes are wide, ringed with white. For a moment I cannot understand why he has not fled, until I realize his reins are caught beneath the man.

That is when I see the strip of carpet the raider used as a pad. It lies on the ground between the raider and the frightened animal.

At that moment, I lose all sense.

25

The orbit of Venus [the Morning Star] is such that it produces a very strange but interesting effect when viewed from Earth against the backdrop of fixed stars that we know as the Zodiac. The planet appears to move in the form of a five-pointed star with the sun at its centre, taking a 40-year cycle to repeat the process . . . the five-pointed star was the ancient Egyptian hieroglyph for "knowledge."
—Christopher Knight and Robert Lomas, *Uriel's Machine*

W ITHOUT COHERENT THOUGHT, I SNATCH the horse's reins and yank them loose from the beneath the rider. Already terrified, the horse backs, throwing his head up, and rears again. As his front hooves touch the ground, I vault onto his back and dig my heels into his sides.

If I had not grasped his mane with both hands, I would have tumbled off with his explosive response. Within a breath, I am flying after the raiders, the magnificent beast beneath me leveling into a hard gallop as though a demon chases him. I do not even care if that is so; the fire in my belly that drove me to this horse's back keeps my attention ahead, where a cloud of brown dust marks the raiders' path. I guide us in that direction, but Wind—as I have silently named him—needs no encouragement to join his fellows. Their speed is hampered by the gait of the camels, which as individuals can travel quickly, but are less inclined to speed in one direction as a herd. The bulls are sluggish, and the females are not happy leaving their calves behind. Also, the raiders' herding efforts have disrupted their normal, single-file mode of travel.

I am soon alongside them. At first, I am not noticed. The dust is heavy from their passage, and I am dressed in a similar manner to the raider I downed. The others assume I am he. I make my way to the front camel, Shem's prize white camel, Niha. Pressure on the reins and a shifting of my weight slows Wind to match her pace. The bulls protect their family, but it is a female who leads. The others will follow her and will not go faster than she, and she will not go faster than her calf.

I apply a steady pressure to Wind's right flank with my leg. He balks, snorting. Horses do not care for the scent of camels, but I am insistent, with little nudges of my heel, and he finally obeys, moving away from the pressure and into Niha's side.

"Hiya! Hiya!" I cry, waving my hand in her face, since I do not have a stick. She turns away and I stay at her side. All the riding skill I have is called upon to turn Niha, but she finally acquiesces. Shouts rise up from the other raiders who still think I am one of them and are calling to me, asking me what I am doing.

Now Niha is moving in a wide arc, the other camels, stringing out behind her, following.

"Hiya! Hiya!"

She acquiesces, trotting with long languid strides in a direction at a sharp angle to her previous course. Now, the other raiders, realizing the deception, are racing toward me, swords drawn. I glance over my shoulder to check their progress. Close. Too close. I am still caught in the sweep of emotions that hurtled me onto this wild course. I will not give up my position.

"Hiya!" I wave my hand into Niha's face, threatening her eyes. She jerks her head away, toward the encampment and finally completely turns that way. Some of the raiders are trying to circle the remainder of the herd back, but Niha has decided she has had enough of all this and wants to go home, and that is where she is going. And the other camels are ignoring the shouts and following her.

I turn too, just as the unmistakable whoosh of a sword blade slices the air, close enough to shave the fine hairs from my ear. Had I not turned at that instant—

There is no time to dwell on this. Wielding a sword from horseback is almost as difficult as trying to shoot an arrow from there, but I do not wish to put that to the test. I have only my skill at riding and my lighter weight to keep me alive. My heels drum Wind's side. He tosses his head, flinging a string of bloody mucus from his torn nostril into my face. But he responds to my need, bursting through the ragged line of loping camels. I lean low on his outstretched neck, half closing my eyes against the sting of his mane, squeezing speed from him with the muscles of my calves. I am counting on the raiders' anger to compel them to follow me.

But if they catch me, I am dead . . . or worse.

It is a race. A glance behind me—too close of a race. My pursuers' mounts had only to match the slower pace of the camels and are better rested than Wind. The swaths of the raiders' headdresses cover their mouths, but their dark eyes brim with rage. Fisted hands brandish raised swords that gleam in the sun's ruthless glare.

I focus between my horse's ears, straining to see our goal, but the wind has added to the stirred dust of our passage, blowing in a sudden burst that blurs the figures running toward us. Perhaps the windstorm that concerned Mana has arrived. My hands grip the strands of Wind's mane. I have no whip, but I free one hand to rest on the side of his foam-streaked neck and lean further forward in a plea for more.

From somewhere, he finds more to give. His stride lengthens, lowering us closer to the ground. The pounding of Wind's hooves are my blood's beat, the rushing earth a dry flood, flashing the colors of brush and stone and loess. For a moment, I lose fear and even the wild thing that drove me to jump on his back. For a moment, I am only horse, running.

I am daughter of the wind.

Then a stumble pitches me forward, catapulting me up in an arc . . . and then down. The earth that rushed past me a moment ago now rushes toward me. I tuck my arm and head, as the Hurrian horse trainer taught me, to let the blow strike the back of my shoulder, something I had no time to do when I fell from Dune's back so long ago—how could it have been so long ago and yet not long ago at all?

There is that thought and air and then . . . impact.

Walls of pain pin me from every direction. I cannot move, cannot breathe. If a sword descends to slice my head from my neck, I can do nothing to stop it. I cannot even turn my head to see it. I can only wait for the pain to stop, for my breath to return, or for this brown dusk to turn to a forever night.

Finally, I can suck a breath into my lungs.

A second one.

Through the pain, I hear the sound of hooves. I am not certain what direction I face. Where is the enemy? I am at his mercy, but there was no mercy in those black eyes. Does he know I killed his kinsman? I want to roll over and face him. I want to meet those eyes and tell him what I did. Tell him it was for my father. I want to see my death come, not lie trussed like a lamb for slaughter, my face in the dirt.

And then I will go meet my father. I feel his presence near. His hand on my shoulder. Through a blur, I see his face, and now I am glad to see it, rather than my slaughterer. *Wait for me, Father.*

My ear is pressed against the ground. The sound of feet, many feet. The clang of blades meeting. Curses. A dog's low growl. Now, all around me, the sounds of battle. My mind struggles with this, as if it cannot comprehend anything different than what it has imagined will be.

I blink, and through the thick dust I see a thin stick planted beside my head—two sticks. They resolve into slender black legs, feathered behind with white, and I realize Nami stands over me. The blanket of dust that covers us is a gift of the wind. While I cannot see my enemy, they cannot see me either. The pain eases enough for me to gather my knees and attempt to stand, but hands grasp me and haul me upright.

26

There were the giants famous from the beginning that were of so great stature, and so expert in war. . . .

—The Book of Baruch

THE WORLD SPINS, AND I am only semi-aware of walking, supported on either side by men whose headdresses protect all but their eyes from the swirling dust. Bodies lie strewn across the ground, and we must navigate around them. Nami presses against my calf, and that alone would have sent me sprawling to kiss the ground if hands were not holding me upright. I try to think through the haze in my mind. Are these raiders or Yassib's men?

The wind is strong. My headdress is gone, and bits of grit sting my face, making me wish for the camel's extra milky lid and long lashes. I blink. Through the dust, figures approach and I recognize the shape of a very tall man among them.

Yassib's clan has become a camp again, though only a few tents are back up. We are not moving out today.

Mana and one of her older daughters rush out to relieve me from the men's arms. Yassib's tent is one of those reassembled, and I stumble between the women to my mat, which has been laid out for me. Then I am down. My eyes close, but I drift in and out of sleep.

When they open again, I see Nami curled with her head across my foot. Alert to my movement, she pricks her ears, thumping her tail twice on the hard ground to tell me she is happy I am back.

"How you feel, Adir?" The voice is Mika's. He sits cross-legged just out of my line of vision, and I have to twist my head to see him.

"Thirsty."

He moves closer and helps me sit up to drink. I take the bowl of water from him, grateful that my hands are steady. The tent flap is rolled up, which means the dust storm has passed.

He has me move arms and legs and starts to feel my ribs, but I push his hands away. "I am fine."

He does not insist. "Does it hurt to breathe?"

"No." I take another long swallow. "What has happened?"

"Good question. I heard shouts and noise, but saw men rushing after cloud of dust. I followed, but most of battle finished and camels returned to camp. Then you brought in, and I waiting for you to waken."

I tell him about Shem, my wild ride, and the fall.

His face pales. "Why you do such a foolish thing, Adir?"

His question hangs in the air. I take another swallow of water and try to explain. "The weaving that ignorant raider used as a pad. It slipped off when he did."

"You risked life for of a piece of cloth?"

I took a breath. "It was the cloth I bought in Sodom."

His eyes widen as the meaning of that settles in his mind. "It was among goods stolen by those who took Raph?"

I nod.

He is perfectly still, except for the pulse that quickens in his neck.

"Yes," I say, my voice hard as stone. "The raiders who took Raph and killed my father."

Before another word is spoken between us, Mana appears at the tent's entrance. "A traveler has come, asking for you by name and description. He seeks a tall fire-haired man and a boy. He has touched our tent pole and asked for hospitality, but Yassib has suspicions he might be one of the men who mean ill toward you." She looks me full in the eyes. "You saved my grandson and our herd. We will not allow harm to fall upon you."

My thoughts are racing. No one is chasing us; that was just the story I told to keep Yassib from cutting my throat in outrage at my trickery. It

was a made-up tale, but—I glance at Mika—could there be some truth to
it? What do I truly know about the business of Mika and Raph?

"Someone has come looking for me or us," I say, translating. "Could it
be someone wishing you harm?"

He is thoughtful. "If they have learned Raph was not useful, they
might come for me."

I turn back to Mana, "Thank you for your warning. Can you describe
the man?"

"He is thick-bodied, with black hair and a full beard. A lot of hair and
thick brows, also black. A gravelly voice."

"Chiram!" I stagger to my feet, and Mika moves quickly beside me, a
hand under my arm, in case I am dizzy.

"Chiram?" he says, confused.

"The cook from my caravan."

"Do you trust this man?" Mana asks.

I hesitate. Since I was a child, I have found Chiram distasteful. He
was with the caravan before my birth and has never said a kind word to
me. Yet, my father often trusted the caravan to him, and he had been
wounded fighting the raiders. I bite my lower lip, and my mind spins,
still not recovered fully from my fall. Chiram's wound was not a serious
one. How hard had he fought to protect my father? Was the raid of Lot's
tent a random happening or had they come looking for El's messengers
and perhaps the mysterious box they carried? How had they known Mika
and Raph traveled with us? It suddenly seems odd Chiram had gone off to
gamble with desert men after the two strangers joined us on our journey
to the tents of Abram.

Troubled, I say, "I am not certain if we can trust this man. Please ask
Yassib not to kill him, but not to grant him hospitality either, until we
can learn if he is with the men who wish us harm."

If Yassib gave Chiram hospitality, he would be obliged to protect him,
although Yassib had almost violated that most sacred code and killed me.
Perhaps, if the moment had been allowed to play out without my inven-
tiveness, he would have stayed his knife, bound by desert code, but I am
glad not to have relied on it.

Mana nods and disappears in a whirl of black dress.

Mika, seeing I am steady, drops his hand from my arm. "What she
say?"

I tell him.

He rubs his chin. "It seems you making habit, Adir."

"What habit?"

"Of saving lives. Now Shem and I both owe ours."

I do not want his life. I want my father back. I want—my thoughts stop on their way to proclaiming my love for Raph. Do I truly love him? Now, after so much has happened, I am not certain. I am not even certain what love is. It is not a necessary ingredient for marriage, though desert tribes are famous for their poems of love for women . . . and camels.

I can imagine Shem telling a love poem about his white camel. Mika cocks his head at me when I break into a laugh. "I confuse words?" he asks.

As out of place as my laughter is, it is difficult to stop. I wipe a tear from my eye. "No, you spoke well. Let us go see Chiram."

CHAPTER

27

Keep your friends close and your enemies closer.
—Sun Tzu

OUTSIDE THE TENTS, THE MEN of Yassib's clan sit in a circle around the communal fire, though it was extinguished for our move and is only ashes now. The sun has started its descent, extending shadows toward the eastern hills. A few paces away, the man I pulled from the black horse kneels, his hands tied behind him to a stake driven in the ground. I thought I had killed him, but apparently the blow to the head was not fatal. His dark eyes track us as we enter the circle.

Though I am a woman, Yassib beckons me forward to sit beside him. It is a place of honor. It has not been long ago that his knife thirsted for my blood. *So does the world turn head-below-feet.*

Upon seeing me, Chiram climbs to his feet. "Adir! You are here!"

He starts toward me but, to my surprise, Kerit, Yassib's son, leaps to stand between us. Chiram stops, his thick brows knotting. He glares at Kerit and then me. "Adir," he demands, "tell him who I am."

Who *are* you? I want to shout. Did you truly fight to defend my father or did you lead those raiders to his tent? I see the healing wound that runs from his check to his neck—a slash from battle or a carefully opened line made to look so?

Instead of shouting at him, I respond calmly in the tongue of Yassib's tribe, "Why are you here?"

His mouth twists as he realizes events are not proceeding as he imagined they would. "I have been searching for you since you disappeared."

"Why?"

The men sit silently watching.

"Speak in the language of the desert men," I say. Chiram knows it as well as I. How else would he have gambled for Nami . . . *or arranged for a raid on Lot's tents?*

Realizing he is being judged, Chiram turns both palms out in the sign for peace. "I looked for you because that was what your father would have wanted me to do. He made me swear I would watch over you and see you to Abram and Sarai."

I have only recently decided that is where I was going. Now, because it comes from Chiram's mouth, I balk. "I will decide where I am going and when. I am a wo—" I halt the word before it escapes. "I am of age to do so."

With the back of his hand, Chiram wipes his mouth. It is a rough hand with splintered nails, fingers stained from the grease of a thousand cook fires and calloused from wielding his beloved knives. "Danel and I set out for you as soon as we realized you were gone. We tracked you until I lost the trail."

"Where?" I am curious.

"At the edge of a wadi. We feared you had drowned, and we returned to Lot's tents."

I close my eyes. Help had been so close.

"Then how did you find me?" I ask.

"Word came to the city through a traveler that an unusually tall man with hair the color of the setting sun and a young boy were guests of this tribe. I came in the hopes it was you."

He looks around at the solemn, hard faces. "It seems, for a youth, you are highly thought of here. Are you planning to stay with these people?"

Yassib twists a short camel stick in his hands. "Adir may stay with us as long as he wishes."

I am stunned. Such an option has not occurred to me. Yassib and this tribe know I am a woman. This fact, which had been such an offense to them, is now accepted. In gratitude for saving the clan's camels, he offers the protection of his people for as long as I wish. I have a place, a home should I wish it so. Like my beloved caravan, this home is not bound to one location, but moves with the wind.

Chiram presses his fat lips together. "You will not honor your father's wishes?"

I ignore him and turn to Yassib. "You honor me with a generous gift that is more than I deserve."

He gives me a curt nod. Not a word has been spoken of the camels or my actions, but enough has been said. He waves at Chiram to return to his seat. "You may stay here three days." This is the mandatory hospitality requirement period of desert code.

Chiram glares at me, but keeps his anger to himself. He is familiar with this culture, and I am sure he is waiting to confront me later.

"We have a clan matter to determine," Yassib announces to all, extending his arm to the bound man outside the circle. Two men cut him free from the pole and bring him to stand in the center of the circle where they bind his wrists behind him and then move to rejoin the circle of seated men, leaving him standing, alone.

Yassib's eyes are hard. The prisoner's are equally so. Whatever either feels is hidden beneath that harshness demanded by this land.

"You have sought to take our camels," Yassib says. "Is there reason to ransom you?"

He straightens. "I have value."

It is the beginning of a possibly long negotiation for this man's life. Yassib would seek recompense for the lives that have been lost. But first, his gaze travels over the faces of the men around us. He does not consider the women who have lost sons and husbands. His question is for the men only, though perhaps in the privacy of their tents they have heard their wives' tears.

"Do any claim blood price?" Yassib calls out formally.

It is the right of those who have lost value to claim the man's death. In doing so, they would gain personal vengeance, but in giving up that right, they allow the tribe to recoup some value by ransom. The addition of even a single camel can mean much if the balance of people to resources is at stake or a water hole has dried or a trade soured. The clan respects the right of a man to extract the death of an enemy, but there is a cost to the clan to do so.

No one speaks.

Then, into the silence, I speak.

By the granting of the right of status, I am part of this tribe. As a woman not married to a clansman, I could not claim this, but by some strange twisting, I have been accepted as a man, an honored man, no less. It is as if by ignoring my gender, the dilemma is put aside. This is a puzzle to ponder later.

I stand. "This raider stole my goods and camels and my . . . friend's brother." I indicate Mika who sits in the second row of men, loathe to call him my "husband" and break my fragile acceptance as a man of status or betray my story that we are hiding our "true" relationship. "The same men raided the tents of my cousin"—I take a breath—"and killed my father."

Yassib considers. The stealing of the camels and the death of his clansmen occurred before his own eyes. But I was claiming some past injury of which he has no knowledge. "How do you know the truth of this?"

"This man," I say pointing at the raider, "whom I pulled from his horse, sat upon a piece of cloth I purchased in the city of Sodom, a cloth that was taken from me on the road to the tents of Lot by the same raiders who killed my father."

There are murmurs among the men of the circle, and several discussions break out. Yassib is the head of this clan and tribe, but he is not a king or ruler. His wisdom is sought, but every man has the right to his opinion and to voice it. My welcome into the tribe, likewise, would not have been Yassib's decision alone.

One man's voice rises above the talk. "You have proof this man stole the cloth and your camels and took a man for ransom. That gives you the right to recompense, but why do you speak for this man Lot? Were you there when his goods were taken and your father slain?"

The others quiet for my answer.

I understand the reasonableness of his question. I have a right to a portion of a ransom to help buy back Raph, but blood right—the life of this man—is only reasonable if he were linked to my father's death, and I have no proof of that.

A familiar, gravelly voice speaks from the opposite side of the circle, and I realize Chiram is on his feet. Despite his bulk, I did not notice the movement, with the bound raider standing between us. "I have such proof."

All gazes turn to Chiram. He points at the man's back. "I fought with this man in the tents of Lot." Chiram lifts his hand to the red welt tracing a line down his cheek and neck. "This man slew Zakiti, Adir's father."

Blood gallops through my veins, blurring my vision. Images of my father play before me. *Lost. Lost to me forever.* That which was most precious in my life, stolen by this man. And worse, he took from my father that which was most precious to him. Zakiti would never feel the thrill of a new land opening before us, the satisfaction of a hard-won bargain, the wind upon his face . . . or his daughter's kiss.

My hand moves of its own accord to the hilt of my knife, my father's knife. My gaze locks on the prisoner's, as if some invisible force draws us together. Still, I wait for the clan's judgment. I have no right to avenge my father's death without that. No right in their eyes . . . but in the darkness of night I can claim my right.

Yassib calls for silence. "We have Adir's evidence this man rode with raiders who stole camels and goods, and Adir's opinion that one of them killed his father." He pointed at Chiram. "We have a guest's word that this is the man who did that deed." He turned to the prisoner. "What is your name?

"Sidilk of the Hurrians."

"What do you say, Sidilk of the Hurrians?"

Though bound, he shoves out his chin. "I slew your clansmen in battle, but we had no intent of it. We would have taken only four camels and turned the rest back. Because of this boy—you lost men."

Only a twitch of cheek beneath Yassib's left eye gives notice of any reaction. "And this boy's father?"

A shrug. "He fought over a few items. He was not desert people."

A flush crawls through my body. There is more talk around me, but I hear nothing. It is as the buzz of distant bees. My eyes lock on the raider's, and his cannot escape mine. He knows I am his death, here before this council or in the arms of night, should they leave him tied or should he sleep. If they give him his life and ask for his honor in exchange for being untied, he will search me out in my sleep . . . if he is wise.

Yassib's raised hand tells me they are finished with the discussion. "Because Adir is of this tribe, so is his family. It is not a matter of a tribesman killing a city dweller, but a family matter." He points at me. "Blood right is yours."

The world hazes at the edges, and I realize I am on my feet, my knife in my hand. Nothing exists except the bond between me and the man who stole my father from me. Without direction, my feet move me toward him until I stand close enough to share his breath. His beard is black and closely cropped; a small oval mark stains the skin below his left eye. He has not moved, but a pulse beats in his throat. His chin is the height of my nose, so I look up and he down, but we are together, alone. His life is mine.

As though from a long distance, I hear, "Adir!" and realize Mika has been shouting my name over and over. Slowly, I turn my head, to find him held between Kerit and another man. I feel myself take a breath and wonder vaguely if it is the first one I have drawn since Yassib granted me blood right.

When he realizes I see him, Mika shouts, "Adir, this man knows Raph's fate."

I stare at him.

"Raph's life inside your hands," he says, his mouth shaping each word precisely.

My eyes fall to my hand where I hold my father's knife. A shaft of sunlight flares off the bronze blade; a kindred spirit, it blazes with the same fire that burns inside me.

Inside my head the meaningless words spin: *Life. Raph. Raph's life.*

I raise my blade to the raider's neck where the blood pulses beneath the sun-browned skin, stilling my hand's tremble against that throb. My gaze lifts to his, and I pull words heavy as boulders from a deep crevasse. "Ransom then," I say. "But for knowledge."

The briefest of nods from him.

"Where is the man you took when you stole the cedar box wrapped in black hide?"

Considering me, Sildik's tongue edges his mouth.

"Where is he?" I press the blade against his neck. Skin dimples with the pressure.

A word emerges from his lips, but no more follow, as though the rest are wedged in his throat.

Disoriented, I watch his knees slowly buckle and a tiny crimson pearl well from his left nostril. Only when he pitches forward do I understand. Protruding from his back, like trees planted in his flesh, are two ibex-antler hilts.

Chiram's thick arms are still thrust before him in the follow-through to the throw. He drops them to his sides, his mouth grim. "Zakiti's slayer does not get to choose life."

I turn back to the man at my feet.

Somehow Mika is at my side. "Did he speak?"

I am empty, dry as a wadi in summer's heart.

"Adir, for the sake of my brother!"

"A word." My voice cracks. "Only one."

"What word, Adir?"

"Babylon."

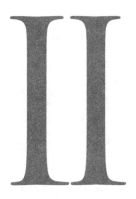

BABYLONIA, 1748 BCE

CHAPTER

28

Marduk [god of Babylon] considered and began to speak to the gods assembled in his presence. This is what he said. "In the former time you inhabited the void above, the abyss, but I have made Earth as the mirror of Heaven, I have consolidated the soil for the foundations, and there I will build my city, my beloved home. . . . It shall be BABYLON.

—Babylonian hymn

YASSIB WARNED THAT TO CROSS the desert to Babylon in summer would be death, but the journey would be much swifter in winter than following the King's Road and safer from those who might hurt us. We heard rumors of men in chariots along the King's Road, searching for a tall man with flame hair, so we stayed with Yassib's tribe in the highland valleys until the weather turned. In gratitude for his hospitality, I gave him the black stallion as a gift. The horse has a great heart, and Yassib and his clan will treasure him.

I left them with a mixture of regret and relief. Although I was treated with esteem and acceptance, fear of making a misstep was a constant companion. It tore my heart, however, to leave Shem, who forgot he was supposed to ignore me and embraced me as a sister. He came with Yassib to the edge of their territory to pass us into the hands of another tribe.

Our caravan would never have attempted to cross the eastern desert, but Yassib assured us it was possible with the right guides. Our course was not straight, as we traveled from watering hole to watering hole, places we would never have found on our own. Thus, we made our way across the desert—a long journey of dirt, sand, heat, and thirst, but much shorter than the normal caravan route that would have taken us north and then curved in a frown's arc to the east.

Chiram gave up trying to get me back to Abram and Sarai, but insisted on traveling with us. His presence was good for one reason: He had brought my little donkey, Philot. I was happy to know Philot had found his way back to Lot's tents when I lost him at the wadi. He is ever patient, and when there was not enough grass for him in the deep desert, he drank camel's milk for sustenance. Still, he is very thin when we reach the mud huts and irrigated fields that surround Babylon. Aside from Chiram, who seems amazingly unaffected, we all are.

NEVER HAVE I been so glad to see a sight as I am the walls of Babylon. The glazed slab-brick gates were not here when I visited as a child and are only partially completed, but it is clear they will be a wonder. Across the rich shades of blue, golden bulls, dragons, and lions march. When we pass, I cannot resist putting out my hand to touch the glazed surface and marvel at the craftsmanship that has managed to raise the images, as if catching them just emerging from the smooth brick to claim their birthright as the gods and goddesses of Babylon.

The gates of the city are open the morning we finally arrive. We do not enter as beggars. Yassib gave us gifts of value, beautiful weavings that would bring good prices here, and Chiram brought a veritable treasure of silver with him, my inheritance from my father, although he insists on "holding" most of it for me. Metals of any kind are greatly valued here, as they must be imported.

It is an odd feeling to walk a city again, particularly this one. The streets run true as spears, crossed at regular intervals by equally straight ones. To our left, the River Euphrates flanks the road, its shore lined with date palms that grow with their feet in the water. To our right, tall, windowless walls of baked brown brick rise far above even Mika's head. The towering ziggurat and temple cast deep, welcome shadows along the streets.

People of all ranks—landowners, merchants, commoners, and slaves—fight for rights of way. Enticing rows of goods fill blankets laid next to the walls—great baskets heaped with grains or fish; dyed cloth and rugs; items of bronze, silver, even gold; bags of salt; hanging meat; pottery and jewelry. The fragrance of fresh and dried herbs, cooking meats, and spices mingle in the air, thankfully masking the underlying smells that belong to all cities. Every block contains altars and shrines to the gods—which one is for which god would require a lifetime of study.

Sounds jumble into a cacophony of voices; lyres and cymbals of street musicians; the bleating of sheep, bray of donkeys and squeal of pigs—all punctuated by the cries of vendors. There is little room on the narrow dirt streets off the main way. Men with carts pulled by small donkeys or large dogs shout at blockages ahead, but must wait with the rest of us to push through. Nami presses against my leg. Philot's long ears flip back and forth.

I understand. I have become accustomed to the silences of the desert, breached by the lone screech of a hawk or morning hoot of an owl, or by the soft spit of sand sent by the wind to brush against a tent. After the generous expanse of open sky and land, this cluster of sensations is smothering. Even Mika, who rarely shows emotion, seems unsettled. People are no different from animals in most ways. A swish of a donkey's tail can be meant to chase a fly, or it can be a warning, depending on the context. So the brush of a hand to the nose or the pulling of a beard or shifting of weight can be for a man. My father taught me that these things speak truer of a man's mind than his tongue.

Mika, though he has tried to disguise himself with a hooded robe and walks bent over a staff like an old man, carries tension in his shoulders, and his gaze scans the path before us. Some of the men in the great city are almost as tall—men with bold noses who wear pointed or carefully curled beards. And then there are smaller black-haired people—Sumerians, my father called them.

Among the diversity of peoples, Hurrian and Hittite merchants pass, rousing no rancor, despite tensions between them in the lands to the west. Desert nomads also stride unchallenged—warriors who prey on farmers outside the city, but here exchange their goods for items brought from the ends of the earth. *Trade is the great peacemaker*—more of my father's words proven before my eyes.

Most of the traders who come to Babylon camp outside her gates, but we are wealthy, at least for the moment, and Mika insists we purchase the use of rooms in a modest house. While we crossed the desert, he perfected his skill with the language and speaks now as well as I. Still, by unspoken agreement, I negotiated for the house. The less he is noticed, the better. With a generous offer of silver, its owners are more than pleased to go live with cousins and promise to have their slaves bring us water, a daily breakfast, and an evening meal. Stone is not easily found here. Like the houses of Sodom, these dwellings are made of bricks and sealed with pitch. In this land, the tarry substance oozes up through the ground in pools and is said to be of a finer quality than that found in the Dead Sea. Like that of every other house, our doorframe is painted a fiery red to ward off demons.

At my insistence, we bring Philot inside. I do not trust leaving him tethered at our door. People of the city are ruled by law, not tribal honor, which means their integrity is based on the odds of being caught.

Inside the small central courtyard, we shed our burdens. The flat roof, buttressed by cedar and packed mud, is loosely covered with palm fronds, creating shade and a relief from the heat. Nami, who has learned to take rest where she can, sinks to the floor at my feet, her tongue panting in an effort to cool herself. I follow her, weariness a weight in my bones that belies the hollowness of my belly. Like the animals of the desert, I have learned to survive on small amounts of food.

Without a word exchanged, we extinguish the clay lamps that have filled the house with the scent of sesame oil, lay out our pallets, and sleep through the night.

Sometime before dawn, Nami alerts me with a low growl. Visible in the soft moonlight that filters through the overhead palms, a man enters, carrying a large clay jar. He freezes as Nami rises to her feet, and I place a hand on her to let her know I see him. The man is slender and wears simple, rough clothing. His step is soft. Neither Mika nor Chiram has wakened.

Slowly, he raises the jar. This gesture is for me, to show his purpose, though his gaze is fixed on Nami. I nod, noting the slash of a brand on his upper arm that marks him a slave. He lowers his burden just inside the courtyard where we sleep and leaves as silently as he entered. Nami's attention stays on the door and after a short time, the man returns with a tray of food, which he leaves by the door, backing out to keep Nami in his sight.

After a moment, Nami lies down again at my side. Any of the dogs on the street would have gone to gobble the food, but Nami has more manners than most people I have encountered. I drift back to sleep, knowing she will keep watch for us, and that breakfast will be where it was left come the morning.

DISORIENTED, I WAKE to small patterns of sunlight through the courtyard roof. Beside me, Nami does not move her head, which still rests on her forepaws, but her eyes follow me. I put my hand between her shoulders, stirring a layer of dust.

"We need a bath, Nami."

She gives my nose a solemn lick.

I snort. "That's a start, at least."

First, however, I share with her a portion of the flatbread, cheese, and dates the slave has left for us. I throw the pits and Philot's dung out onto the alley street. The dogs will graze on edible waste, and slaves are already working to cover the rest with a layer of clay and straw. This explains why the street level is above the entrance to the house. Eventually, they will have to add more steps inside to climb to the level of the street.

Mika stirs, but then settles back into sleep, and I risk the luxury of the bathing room where the slave left fresh water. The floor and lower parts of the wall are baked brick covered with a finely ground stone mixed with pitch. All is angled to slope to the center of the room, where the water can drain off in small runnels of glazed tiles.

I strip and dip water from a small bowl to pour over myself, using a scraper to slough away dead skin, and then rinse again. It feels wonderful. Then I confront the problem of my clothes. Preferring to be clean over being dry, I wash the undergarments and put them back on wet. They will dry soon enough in the heat. I will buy another outer robe so I can clean this one.

Mika is waiting with impatience when I emerge, and tends at once to his own ablutions. I am surprised he did not join me in the bath, but perhaps his customs are different. It is a good thing, as my secret would not have remained so. Chiram shows no interest in cleanliness. I imagine he has emptied his water against a wall outside. Having already breakfasted, I take Nami for a walk.

It is just before dawn, and a light mist gliding in from the river hazes the city, which lies silent as a hunting leopard. Few people are out. It is too early for the children to be at the tablet houses studying with scribes. A few merchants are setting up their goods. Dogs scavenge through garbage, giving Nami quick assessing looks and then ignoring her when they determine she is not competition. The quiet is welcome.

I learn quickly to seek the inner walkways, the nicest being alongside the Euphrates River, which cuts through the city. The streets that run along the outer wall are choked with the stench of those who have used them as Chiram did, and other unpleasant smells that the dogs apparently perceive as delightful perfume.

Since we are out, I decide to refresh my memory of the city's layout. It has been many summers since I was here. Abram often told us the story of his father's disillusionment with Babylon, how King Hammurabi stole a millennium of knowledge and culture from Abram's home city of Ur. But I have always been intrigued with the laws of Babylon's previous king. I remember my father taking me to see the great black stone edifice that stood near the Temple of Marduk, the chief god of Babylon.

I let memory guide my feet in that direction, toward the city's heart. Nami, more relaxed and herself in the early morning quiet, briefly investigates a small pile of refuse and then trots back to my side. I love the airy grace of her gait. She moves as though she is only partially bound to the earth, especially when she stretches out to chase prey or just to run for pleasure. She too is a daughter of the wind.

Dawn paints the eastern-facing buildings a lambent coral. I glance here and there, taken by admiration of one site and then another—until I stop before the seven-tiered House of the Gods that rises like a mountain above me, engulfing the street and opposite buildings in its shadow. The brick walls stretch farther along each edge than I can throw a stone, and as high up. I put my hands on Nami's head and make her look up at the ziggurat. "It is named Linking Earth and Heaven," I tell her.

She is unimpressed.

We proceed just a bit further to Marduk's temple and there, just as I remembered, is the black stone, incised with writing. The angular marks are codes that govern the land. Despite my distrust of their power, I am awed in the presence of this stone.

"Can you read it?"

The voice at my back startles me. A woman has approached so quietly even Nami did not alert me, perhaps because she is absorbed smelling beneath the tail of a dog in the nearest alley. I turn to see a woman almost my height, the quality of her robes declaring her a noble. A scarf draped low over her head hides her forehead and hair, but her eyes are a clear gray settled in a nest of fine lines. I cannot tell if age or the sun's chisel has etched them.

"Only a little," I say, surprised at the sadness in my voice. Suddenly, I miss the mornings sitting with Ishmael in Sarai's tent, learning the history and heritage of our tribe. I miss the sound of her voice instructing us in the long litany of stories. I miss snitching an extra date from the bowl and making Ishmael laugh with a whispered-aside prediction that our grandchildren's heads will split with all they will have to know.

The woman's eyes travel my face and down my body. Instinctively, I increase the hunch of my shoulders. In the past moons, I have had to tie the bindings across my breasts tighter and tighter. Her eyes burn through me as though she can see my deception. If she does, she does not speak it, but lifts her hand to the black stone. "What words can you read of this one?"

I follow her hand, noticing the stains of age on them and relaxing a bit that she will not tear from me what I have sought to hide all my life. Have I been boy so long, I fear being who I truly am? The beats of my heart slow, and I turn to study the words, my teeth chewing on my lower lip in concentration. It was not Sarai who taught us the written word, but Abram, who had been a scribe in Ur.

"A man,'" I say in halting interpretation, "who—?"

"Takes."

"'A man who takes the eye of a noble, if he is a noble, shall give his eye?'"

She nods. "Close enough. And this one?"

"If a man takes a woman to wife, but has no—"

"Intercourse," she supplies.

I begin again, wanting to please this woman as if she were Sarai or my father. "If a man takes a woman to wife, but has no intercourse with her, this woman is no wife to him."

She purses her lips, appearing intrigued with me. "Where are you from?"

By this time, Nami has returned to stand at my side. My hand rests on her shoulders.

"From the land of Canaan and the tribe of Abram."

Her brows rise. "The Abram who fought the kings of Chedorlaomer?"

Despite myself, my shoulders straighten in pride that she has heard of my tribe. As my father often quoted, *News is the fleetest of goods traveling the desert.* "Yes, that is he."

Her mouth twists—in amusement or vexation? "Are you his son?"

"No, I am a cousin of Abram's house."

"And is your father here in Babylon?"

A tightness in my belly reminds me I do not know who my enemies are. Still, I see no reason not to answer her. "No, my father is . . . dead." I am surprised the word emerges without choking me.

Her eyes and voice soften slightly. "My sorrow to your house."

"Thank you, Lady."

I do not know who she is, but my father taught me to read strangers and to learn their desires by listening and observing, so I would know when tongues shaped lies. I gave her the due of her rank without thinking about it.

"Was your father a trader?" she asks.

My brows lift. Did this woman read me as I read others?

The wind shifts, bringing me the scent of her perfume. This is the second time I have inhaled that fragrance, and I almost fall to my knees. The first occasion was as a child when my father and I were allowed briefly inside the temple at En Gedi where the balsam is used by the priests to entice the gods' favor.

"Are you unwell?" she asks.

"I am well." I have forgotten her first question.

"Was your father a trader?" she asks again.

"Yes, he was."

How did this woman come to possess the balsam? Who was she? Was it merely a coincidence? Father had possessed only a few vials of it, at least since I was born, but he could have brought it here . . . or it could have been stolen when the raider slew my father. It could mean our trek across the desert was not in vain, as we so feared. If the balsam is here, Raph could also be.

She looks thoughtful for a moment. "Traders travel and often speak other languages—?" She pauses, but I do not leap into the void of her question. A subtle shift in her expression makes me think perhaps I have earned a bit of respect from her, as well.

"Do you speak other tongues?" she asks directly, the softness gone from her demeanor.

"I do, Lady."

"Do you know the language of the Egyptians?"

"I do."

She considers me. "What is your name?"

"I am Adir, son of Zakiti of the tribe of Abram." My shoulders refuse to hunch, though I instruct them to do so.

Her eyes narrow, her voice now all command. "Come to the king's court in two days at the hour of the sun's peak."

Abruptly, she turns in a swirl of robe.

"Lady!" I call, panic rising into my throat. "Whom do I say sent for me?" I know better than to appear with some vague story about being summoned.

Over her shoulder, she says, "Say you are there at the will of Tabni."

Wonder . . . is the seed of knowledge.

———Francis Bacon

I N A STOLEN MOMENT OF peace, Mika, Chiram, and I sit in the small
walled garden at the back of our house in the shade of an old fig tree,
drinking beer through long reed straws to avoid the floating barley hulls.
Bearing a tray of full cups, our elusive slave appears and serves us, saying
with a slight bow, "He who does not know beer, does not know what is
good"—the first words he has spoken. It seems our hosts are happy for us
to stay as long as we wish.

A chameleon crawls onto a stone ledge, catching Nami's attention. It
is almost invisible, its coloring matching the stone. As a child, I would
sometimes grab one by the tail to see it turn darker. Perhaps it thought
that made it appear fierce. Nami takes a step toward it, fascinated.

I have told neither Mika nor Chiram of my early-morning encounter
the previous day or my summons. I would confide it to Mika, but have
not had the opportunity to speak to him in private. He will not leave
the house.

When the chameleon rotates one of its bulging eyes toward Nami,
she is unable to stand the suspense and lunges, sending the chameleon
scampering into the refuge of a crack. With the sigh of a hunter that has
missed, she settles at my feet.

The garden is lush with leeks, cucumbers, watercress, onions, and garlic, watered by the small canal that runs through it and also runs in clay pipes through the walls into the house. Chiram kneels in the dirt, investigating the size of a garlic bud. "Too early," he sighs, covering it back up.

A grape vine winds up the brick wall that provides privacy, though we can hear the shouts of our neighbors' children and must keep our voices low.

"I should stay inside as much as possible," Mika says.

Chiram looks up at that. "Why? It is your forsaken brother we are here for."

As always, Chiram's resentment fails to provoke Mika. I wonder if Chiram would speak with such contempt had he seen the blue fire in Mika's hands. But Chiram always had little respect for anyone except my father and has never shown any interest in obedience to El. Whatever gods he worships, he keeps silent about it.

"I am fully aware Adir came here because of Raph," Mika responds evenly, "and you are here only because of Adir."

Chiram waves a dirty hand. "A splitting of a hay blade. Why do you stay inside while we are to tromp the streets to find word of your brother?"

I lean toward Chiram. "His name is Raph. Why can you not call him by his name?"

Chiram spits and glares at me.

I close my eyes. Why do I even make the attempt?

Mika stands, towering over us both, spreading his hands. "This is why. If you are to ask questions quietly, my presence will ruin it."

This is true. There is no way anyone with half a mind would not connect Mika with Raph, and no way he could walk upright through the city and not attract attention. I doubt he could stay bent over in the manner he entered the city for very long. The last thing we need is for the people who stole Raph to take Mika. What would I do then?

"Why would anyone here want your brother?" Chiram grumbles, echoing the question that has plagued me countless times. I have not shared anything with him about the box, though he saw the raiders' interest in it when they took Raph. He has not asked about any connection, and I find that strange. Chiram is not stupid. Mean, yes, but not stupid.

"Chiram," Mika says, "the longer you fight against helping us, the longer we will be here."

Chiram cannot argue against this logic. To avoid acknowledging it, he goes to the *dâlu*, a counter-weighted dipper that dips into water and allows one to lift it without effort. He draws a bucket, takes a long drink, and then pours the remainder over his head. It runs down his grimy face and into his beard, beading in the thick fold of his neck. We are not long enough from the desert to lose the wonder of water's abundance here. I wish he would douse himself several times more and lose the stench that clings to him, but turning my head, I sniff my own clothes, and I am not much better, despite my baths.

Finally, when enough time has passed to save his face, Chiram blinks at Mika. "So what is it exactly you want Adir and me to do?"

Mika sits back on the brick bench. "Just see what you can learn. All we know that Raph is here."

"But we do not really know that," I say, weaving my fingers together. "He could have been brought here and then taken somewhere else."

"Or that son of a desert rodent might have lied," Chiram adds, taking a knife from his belt and examining the edge.

"He was not lying," I say. I am certain of this.

"You cannot know that." Chiram's thick finger shakes in my direction.

It is an old argument, one rehashed many times during our long journey across the desert. I could mention the balsam, but I am not certain my father shared the secret of its source, even with Chiram, and I do not wish to endanger the people of En Gedi.

"Perhaps," I say tightly, "we would have learned more if your knives had not been so eager to bite."

"I killed the man who killed your father. Not a grateful bone in your body, boy."

"I—"

"Enough!" Mika's voice is one of command, and we both fall silent. Mika's ire is not easily provoked, and I regret yielding to the lure of an argument with Chiram.

WHEN WE LEAVE the house the following morning, Chiram grasps my shoulders. "Stay within my sight," he says, his fingers biting into my flesh.

"All right," I mumble and crinkle my nose.

As soon as he turns his back, I slip away, disappearing into the throng. He will yell at me later, but his shouts, though they frightened me as a child, have never been more than that. Then a thought arises. Perhaps he restrained his hand only because he would have to answer to my father. Would Chiram strike me, now my father is with the ancestors? And once again, that most perplexing of questions: Why did he follow me across the desert? He says it was to honor his promise to my father, but I wonder if that is really so.

The smells and sights of the bazaar swiftly capture my attention—hills of spices the colors of desert sunset mound reed baskets. Dates, figs, lentils, and barley heap more baskets. The complex scent of spices bites my nose, and both Nami and I catch the tantalizing whiff of meat fat sizzling in sesame oil. Despite the generous breakfast brought by the slave, my mouth waters, and my stomach insists that sufficient room exists should I stumble upon the smell's source. It is unfortunate such aromas must compete with those of men and women who are not wealthy enough to have the bathing rooms or, like Chiram, have simply not availed themselves of the canals or public cisterns.

A man holds out his palm with a well-oiled story about his ill fortune. I ignore him, but am unable to resist the upturned face of a thin child. He grins in delight when I press a small ring of copper into his hand. "May you be invisible to the demons!" he says and disappears. I move quickly along, lest he tell other urchins of his good fortune with me.

At the street's edge, I stop at a display of clothing. With an alertness for movement that rivals the falcon's eye, the merchant catches my gaze and moves in. "This is an exceptional shawl. See the fineness of the pattern and the tight braid of the fringes?" she says. "A lovely gift for your mother or sister!"

I stare at her for a long moment. Finally, scarcely aware of my thoughts, I say, "I will buy it and that one too." I point to a plain wrap that will not draw attention to me. "Do you have a woman's sheath dress to go with it?"

She is taken aback that I do not even ask the price. I note the space behind her goods where she stores other material and slip inside, stripping off my woolen robe and breast bindings. I roll the finer scarf and stuff it into my leather satchel, donning the plainer wrap. When I step out, aside from my short-cropped hair, I am a woman.

Among a thousand women dressed as I am, I still feel I am walking naked through the streets and all eyes are on me. After wearing woolen robes all of my life, the linen brushes my skin like a cloud. However, as much as I hated the bindings on my breasts, I am not sure how I feel about the little jounces caused by my steps. A glint from a display catches my eye, and I stop to purchase a pair of silver loop earrings and endure the piercing. Then I reward myself for the pain by buying a pretty multi-strand necklace of blue glass.

And thus, I present myself at the palace.

"What is your business?" An officious man stops my progress through the chambers.

I repeat what I have told the guards. "Tabni sent for me."

He eyes me with a narrow gaze. "Whom should I announce to the Priestess Tabni?" His emphasis on the word "Priestess" is meant to be a curt reminder of manners, but it is the first actual knowledge I have of her position.

"Please tell Priestess Tabni—" I hesitate, as I had named myself Adir, the cousin of Abram, to her. "Tell her Adira, cousin of Abram, has responded to her summons."

With a curt nod and wave at a series of wooden benches, he leaves.

I settle myself on an empty seat and am at once the object of a searing scowl. The disagreeable expression belongs to a woman who sits across from me. At first, I cannot imagine how I so quickly earned her disapproval, and then I realize I have sat in my customary manner, my legs spread in a position no respectable woman would assume. Hastily, I send my knees together. It will not be easy to change the mannerisms I have spent my entire life cultivating.

The woman sniffs and plucks a cup from a serving tray presented by a slave. I do the same. And then we wait.

I do not wait well. After a long enough time for the sun to shift its position, I ask the man beside me how long he has been waiting.

"Only three days," he says and goes back to the clay tablets he has been studying.

Only three days.

It occurs to me I have an opportunity I may not regain. Besides, it is uncomfortable to have to hold one's knees together for long periods of time.

I rise, paying attention to the way I hold myself, and walk down the long line of people waiting to see the court. In the graceful, unobtrusive manner I have observed in the slaves, I pick up a small tray with a half-full copper cup that has been left on a low table and continue with it down the aisle.

"Slave," a man gestures, "bring us something to eat; it is nearly noon."

I nod, pleased I have succeeded in establishing my new position as household slave merely by changing my demeanor. At the first doorway, I turn and walk through it without hesitation, as if the guard knows me on sight.

He does not, of course, and gives my shorn hair a hard glance. I feel my cheeks burn and lower my gaze even more. His spear blocks my way. "What happened to your hair, girl? Did you displease your mistress?"

At once I understand his discernment that I have displeased a mistress and not a master. Only a woman would punish by cutting off another woman's hair. "You are very astute, sir," I say in a humble, sincere voice, staring at his sandals and hairy toes.

With a derisive snort, he lets me by.

Elated, I absorb the persona of a slave girl who has displeased her mistress and must look and act as if her shorn hair does not bother her. This, I decide, requires an extra boldness to compensate. The next guard who stops me gets a fleeting glare before I lower my gaze. To my surprise, he laughs and reaches for me, pulling me hard against him. He smells worse than Chiram, something I thought impossible. His beard scratches my cheek. "I like women with some salt to them," he says, his hot tongue probing my ear.

My gasp is not an act, and I wrench away from him, very conscious of the fact that had we not been in the king's apartments he could have forced his way on me. I have never felt this vulnerability before. Suddenly, I wish for the rough woolen robe and the bindings I discarded so casually behind the merchant's stall along with the security of being a boy. No wonder my father had supported and encouraged this deception. Women are not safe alone in the world.

It is a realization I always knew, but had never *felt*.

I do not like it.

30

Love work; and hate lordship; and make not thyself
known to the government.

—Shema'iah, *Sayings of the Fathers*

I CONTINUE THROUGH THE EMPTY ROOM in the king's palace, stealing glances at the fine furniture, rugs, and pottery I know must come
from distant lands. The urge to examine the weavings is strong. My time
with the desert women only deepened my interest. From travels with my
father, I could discern differences in patterns and the single knot of the
south versus the northern double knot, but I am certain there are many
variances throughout the world. I want to know how people make their
clothing, the foods they eat, the animals they raise, and the gods they
worship. For a moment, I forget my oath to my father and dream of traveling to distant lands and learning these things.

Then I remember the strength of the guard's hand and his invading
tongue and my father's plea for me to go to Sarai. She would find me a
husband if one would take me. If I were not carrying a tray, my hand
would have found the bridge of my nose. My hair will grow out, and
perhaps she will find a young man who will have me, and I will bear him
children, and we will grow to care for each other. Or perhaps we will find
Raph, and when he sees I have crossed the desert for him, he will realize
his love for me and take me in his arms. Of course, we must go to Sarai

and be married in order to fulfill my vow to my father, but that should not be too much to ask, after all I have done.

I move to another room where several finely dressed people are deep in conversation. There is talk of war and conjecture as to which land poses the greatest threat. I keep my eyes downcast, listening to the conversation for some clue or reference to Raph. The hand that reached the great distance from Babylon to snatch him held a large amount of silver. Could it have been the king himself? And if so, why?

Someone reaches for the cup on my tray and then, realizing it is not full, sighs and turns back to his conversation with another, ignoring me. "The south is a brew of trouble. If Rim-Sin II makes an alliance there and threatens a trade embargo—"

How astonishing. I have never realized the power of a slave to slip through the world practically unnoticed.

But this cannot go on indefinitely. Someone who knows the slaves and what their duties are is sure to expose me. So . . . what am I doing? Can I return to the waiting room without attracting notice?

At that moment, I stop, unable to believe what I am seeing and forgetting I am supposed to look submissively at the floor.

I have slipped into a room where the floor is patterned with small stones and an elegantly clothed man sits in a high-backed chair of carved wood. No one needs to tell me this is the king of Babylon, Samsu-iluna, the son of Hammurabi. Dark, oiled curls of his beard churn down his chest, and a tight cap worked in gold threads sits atop his head. His feet rest on a small cedar chest carved with a crescent and five-pointed star—a chest I recognize!

To one side stands the woman I met in the market, the Priestess Tabni, her position now clearly marked by a gold circlet. Before her and the king, a man kneels. He is dressed only in the simple skirt of the field slave. His broad back faces me, but I would know it anywhere because it belongs to the man I love—Raph!

Unlike Mika, whose height is mostly in his long legs, Raph is imposing even on his knees. His back is straight, though he fights weariness in his shoulders. He keeps them pulled tightly, but I can see the tiny tremble of taut muscles.

Samsu-iluna leans forward, addressing Raph. Everyone's attention is on the scene at the king's feet, and no one pays attention to a slave girl with her tray, even the soldiers at honorary attention on either side of the king's chair.

"You are a stubborn man," Samsu-iluna tells him.

"I have told you all I know," Raph says. "It is my brother who can ascend, not I, and my brother is now somewhere in the far east. I do not know where."

His Akkadian is much better than when he was stolen from me, as good as Mika's.

Samsu-iluna leans back. "Then you will die digging irrigation canals."

Raph says nothing.

"Are you certain you do not know where this 'brother' is?" Tabni asks.

A chill snakes its way into my belly. What would the King of Babylon say if he knew Raph's brother was within his gates? I do not know what Raph meant by "ascending." Is it dangerous? Raph has not been killed, at least not yet. But despite my feelings for him, I would not give Mika into this king's hands, even for Raph's sake. There must be another way to save both.

With a wave of disgust, Samsu-iluna says. "Take him away."

That is when the tray falls with a clatter from my hands.

For a moment, every eye is upon me, and my heart jumps, lodging in my throat. I am not clumsy by nature, but the shock of seeing Raph numbed my fingers. To my surprise, his gaze slides across my face without recognition. His beautiful eyes are weary.

I say nothing to him. My silence shields the fact that Mika is here. I step aside, and the guards escort Raph from the room at spear point. My gaze follows him. I hold myself rooted to my position to keep from running after him. Too much is at stake.

When I turn back, I find Tabni's gaze fixed on me. "Adir?" she says finally.

I straighten, trying to draw my thoughts together. My mouth is dry, and I am unable to speak. Then, amazingly, I feel a firm pressure on my left shoulder, though no one is there. A wave of calmness sweeps through me. When my father would have me translate as a child, he would grasp my shoulder just so to encourage me. Our tribe does not worship the ancestors, but I must blink back sudden tears at the comfort of my father's presence.

I meet the priestess's sharp gaze for a moment and then bow my head in respect. "Adira, actually, Lady. I traveled as a boy for safety's sake."

"I see." She looks over my shoulder. "And who escorted you into the king's chambers?"

"I—" I half turn, as though someone was just with me. "I do not remember his name."

Samsu-iluna shifts on his seat. "So who is this you speak with, Priestess?" He flips his hand at me, his voice tired and bored, dark eyes barely registering my existence.

Tabni turns to him. "A young . . . woman I met by chance yesterday. She says she speaks the Egyptian tongue, and since the envoy's translator died in the crossing, and we currently have no one fluent at court—"

"Excellent!" Samsu-iluna cuts her off with a wave of his hand. "I will not have to try and figure out Bashaa's ramblings, and perhaps we can avoid antagonizing the Egyptians and gaining yet another enemy hovering over us. Find her some decent clothing. What happened to her hair?"

Tabni signals a woman who sweeps me out of the room before I have a chance to answer. Indeed, I do not think the question lingers on the king's mind, for he has already turned to another and is deep in conversation.

WHEN TABNI, FOLLOWED by a young man, appears in the room, I have been dressed in a similar style to the clothing I purchased, but of a much finer quality. She frowns at me. "I had meant to interview you and test your knowledge, not have you to burst in upon the royal court."

I lower my head, my hand to my chest. For a moment, I am distracted by the soft fall of the headdress around my face, a clever addition to my garments, meant no doubt to hide my shorn tresses. "Priestess, please forgive me."

There is no forgiveness in the stern lines of her face. She is obviously not accustomed to young boys becoming girls and appearing unannounced in the king's receiving room. I think she is about to tell me these things, but instead, she waves the young man forward. "This is Bashaa. He speaks the Egyptian tongue."

"Only a little," Bashaa says in Egyptian. "And my accent is rough."

He is a handsome man and looks at me in an odd way that causes my cheeks to flame. I shift my weight, uncertain where to put my hands. His gaze flickers down and then back to my face where it remains, and suddenly I realize he is attracted to me! An act of will keeps my hand from my nose.

"Well," Tabni says, her tongue a sharp blade. "Do you understand him or not?"

My blush deepens. Where is my father's hand now? I can imagine it would be knotted in the back of my clothing, pulling me back into the tent. With that vision, my throat unlocks, but I know better than to smile.

"My apologies," I say to Bashaa in Egyptian. "Please continue speaking."

"Where did you learn the language?" he asks.

"My father is . . . was a merchant. We have traveled to Egypt many times, and I learned the high tongue from Sarai, the wife of Abram, who is the patriarch of my tribe."

He smiles. "Your accent is flawless. I wish I could speak so."

"And where did you learn?" I ask from politeness and not knowing what to say.

"From the court translator who is now, with most unfortunate timing, with his ancestors."

"Was he your friend?"

"No, he haughty, thinking Egyptians better. Not bother with Akkadian."

That does not surprise me. Even Hagar, a slave given as a handmaiden to Sarai, thought herself better than Sarai, a fact she never hid well from her mistress, though she was never arrogant with me, perhaps because I loved Ishmael as a brother. Now she has given Abram a son and been made second wife, so she even more carelessly shows off her status, often infuriating Sarai.

"Unfortunate for the former translator," I say, trailing my hand over the fine cloth of my skirt, "but fortunate for me."

Bashaa's eyes narrow for an instant, and then his face resumes its congenial demeanor, but his next words, still in the language of the Black Land, do not reflect his expression. "Be careful, girl; game this not. Much at wager here. Walk narrow way. Many push aside, over edge, no thought."

His grammar is poor, but the meaning is clear.

31

Warm thyself before the fire of the wise, but beware of their embers, perchance thou mayest be singed.

—R. Li'ezer, *Sayings of the Fathers*

BASHAA CERTIFIES ME AS BEING more skilled in the Egyptian language than he, and Tabni leaves me in a smaller room for most of the day where I fret, worrying about Mika and Raph. Despite the practice I am getting, I still do not wait well.

Finally, the summons comes. This time I am in the king's receiving room by right. It is a lovely place, decorated with elaborate objects of beaten bronze, gold, and silver that I assume were gifts to the king, or perhaps to his father, Hammurabi, the conqueror and lawmaker.

Apart from Bashaa, who stands at my side—a precaution should my tongue thicken with nervousness, or should I make up outlandish tales from the mouth of the envoy—I am a stranger among strangers in the room. Tabni has gone.

"Add nothing," Bashaa reminds me, whispering in my ear. His cheek brushes mine, and I shiver. A man has never touched me like that. It is hardly the guard's rough attention. I wonder what it would be like to lie with a man, to feel his hands on me, and his spear inside me. Somehow my imaginings of Raph never went beyond him holding me close.

Tabni is the chief priestess of Ishtar, the goddess of love. She knows everything, should I care to ask her and should she care to answer. She would most probably laugh at my ignorance. I am past the normal age of marriage now or at least of betrothal, and I do not know the first thing about being a woman. What, I wonder, made me leave my clothing behind the vendor's stacks today and emerge like a butterfly from a cocoon? A butterfly dressed with beautiful wings, but that still thinks like a caterpillar.

The envoy's entrance whips my attention back into the room. He is announced, and I must focus on what he is saying. My heart gallops. I have never been responsible for translating in such a situation. What if my mind wanders and I miss something important? I have gathered from the conversations I overheard earlier, in my brief state as a slave, that Samsu-iluna's kingdom is at risk. People's lives may depend on me.

Pleasantries are exchanged. Tabni has reappeared and stands beside the king. Samsu-iluna offers his regret at the accident that killed the Egyptian envoy's translator and hopes I will be sufficient. At this I draw up my shoulders and my fear vanishes. *Sufficient?*

The envoy brings greetings from his country and king and offers gifts. I translate his words. Bearers enter with beautiful vessels, jewelry of gold, a bird with colors of a rainbow, and an image of a large cat carved of black ebony. Eventually, they turn to real negotiations. Babylonia, it seems, is in need of tin to make bronze. No one says it, but the need for weapons is obviously central. Their supply, which has traditionally come from the southeast, has been cut off by a revolution, and the Hurrians to the north are blocking that route. Tin is critical.

The discussion lasts until mealtime. We all proceed into another room where soft music of flute, panpipe, and harp cajoles the ear. The king and guests sit on cushions before a feast. Tabni and several other dignitaries have joined them. I am expected to stand behind them, my empty stomach churning at the parade of courses—mutton roasted with cumin and leeks, pig stuffed with mint, fish of every kind, cheeses, fine-grained breads smothered with butter and sesame seeds. They all eat and drink beer until long past dark. I give up counting after twelve courses.

Bashaa takes over long enough for me to find the place to make water. I worm my way to a room where lesser staff are eating and pluck a handful of figs and almonds and a boiled duck egg to eat on the way back to the dining area.

When I return, tense silence reigns at the table, and Bashaa is pale.

"What happened?" I whisper, my eyes traveling over the guests. Tabni's hand is gripping her goblet and the king, his eyes reddened with drink, has a most sour expression on his face. The Egyptian envoy appears confused, his gaze darting from face to face.

"Thank Ishtar and Marduk, you are back," Bashaa says, taking me aside. "What does this mean? He recites a long phrase."

I shrug. "It is an Egyptian blessing calling on one of their most important goddesses."

Bashaa's pallor gives way to a deep blush. "I believe I just told Samsuiluna the envoy said he was the son of a pig."

A bubble of laughter rises from my belly, but at Bashaa's stricken face, it lodges in my throat. I take a moment to settle myself into an appearance of seriousness and turn back to the table. Pigs are considered unclean animals in both Egypt and Babylonia.

With a slight bow at the envoy to get his attention, I ask what has been said and then turn to Samsu-iluna. "Most gracious King of Babylonia, if my words caused offense, I offer apology. What I said was the king of Egypt sent you the blessings of our goddess, Bast, in her favored form, the cat statue, that you might be rich with children."

I put in the reference to the statue to add credibility to my interpretation, hoping the king would remember it among the gifts brought to him. Bashaa is in no position to correct or chastise me. There is much at stake here. Wrong words could mean hostilities between these great kingdoms. Canaan would be caught in the middle. It was not so long ago Egypt had held Canaan in her fist. And King Chedorlaomer had come from south of Babylon to claim it. Neither salt nor pitch made Canaan as valuable to the great powers as its location between Babylon and Egypt.

At my interpretation of the envoy's words, it seems the whole table holds its breath and every eye is upon Samsu-iluna.

The sour expression on the king's face melts into a smile, and I can actually hear the exhalations.

I AM NOT allowed to leave the palace for the entire week the envoy remains as a guest. Anxiety has gnawed a hole in my belly. Mika and Chiram will think I am dead or enslaved. I must tell Mika about Raph, but

I am most concerned about Nami. I told her to stay in the house. Would Mika take her out to make water and attend to her business? Would she listen to him or run off to find me? She is not that good at smells. She might get lost in the streets, which are far more crowded and vast than those of Sodom, or someone might recognize her value and take her. My worries spin in circles.

Finally, the Egyptians are gone, and I am called into Ishtar's temple and Tabni's chamber. I force all the fears that are churning in my belly into submission and stand before her.

She sits on a high stool of carved cedar. A patterned necklace of lapis lazuli and silver encircling her throat catches my trader's eye. The rich color lies well against her skin, and the precious stones could not be mistaken for my blue glass beads. The tangy scent of myrrh lingers in the room, but my gaze falls upon a tiny vial. I know it. The hands of the priests at En Gedi sealed that vial. My nose had been correct. Did this mean the Priestess was behind Raph's capture or had the king gifted her with the scent? Either way, I must tread carefully.

"You have done well," she says.

I have done better than "well" and certainly better than "sufficient," but I refrain from reminding her I saved them all from diplomatic disaster. "It was my honor," I say instead.

She slides two bracelets of silver onto my arm. "You have earned this," she admits.

I bow my head and remove the rings, handing them back to her. "You are most generous, Lady, but I do not want your silver."

Surprise flickers across her features, and she narrows her gaze, much as she did the first time she saw me. She is assessing me. "What do you want then? I have little I can give you other than silver or—" She tilts her head at me. "Perhaps a place in service to the Queen of Heaven?"

My hand lifts toward my nose, but I stop it and instead touch the hollow of my throat. To serve the goddess as *qadishtu*, a holy woman, was primarily a matter of choice and going through the rituals, but to be offered a place here at the important temple in Babylon as an *ishtaritu*, a woman of Ishtar, was a great honor, one given only to the daughters of noble families. Tabni must feel she owes me greatly . . . or perhaps she wishes to keep me close for my interpretation skills.

"No Priestess, I do not seek that honor."

"Then what do you seek?"

I look at her. "A slave's freedom."

One silver brow arches. "That might be possible. Whom do you wish to free?"

"The tall man with golden hair I saw in the king's receiving room that first day."

Her face goes still. After a moment she says, "That is not possible." She looks at me with eyes that I have learned miss little. I tread on a very narrow beam, but this is an opportunity I cannot ignore.

"Why do you want him?"

I shrug, careful with my expression. "He is different from anyone I have ever seen, and very handsome. I am attracted to him. He is just a slave, isn't he?"

Tabni stands. "No, actually, he is not."

I say nothing, hoping she will continue.

"He is more a prisoner than a slave. Samsu-iluna is punishing him by having him work as a slave on the canals."

I frown as though piqued by the inconvenience of it. "What has he done to anger the king?"

"It is not what he has done, but what he refuses to do." Tabni rises and goes to the lion statue that sits regally on a small table. She strokes the great cat's back. "It is interesting, is it not, how the goddess chooses the feline to represent her. In Babylonia her creature is the lion; in the northlands it is the panther; in the east, the tiger; and in Egypt, the cat. Why, do you suppose?"

"I do not know, Priestess." Frustration gnaws at me. I do not see how this is related to why Raph has been enslaved.

"I do not know either," Tabni says. "Perhaps it is the nature of the feline. Ishtar's fierceness in battle has weakened the knees of strong men . . . as has her passion." Tabni smiles.

I have the feeling her words are those of someone whose power has been threatened. I think back to what my father told me long ago when we were here. At the time, it was an abstract lesson, but now I reconsider it. In more ancient times the goddess's rule was absolute. Now, although the goddess "chooses" the king, she shares authority with the Babylonian god, Marduk, and perhaps more importantly, with his priests. I decide it is better to be ignorant. "I do not understand."

She smiles at me then. "No, I would not expect you to, being only attracted to a handsome stranger. Let me tell you then, and you can decide
if you wish to pursue this man."

I nod. "My desire for him is strong." I can say this with honesty in my
voice.

She presses her lips into a line. "The love of youth is always strong.
That is Ishtar's blessing . . . and her curse." She seats herself again. "This
man you desire is a shaman from a distant land."

I twist my hand in my skirt. "He seems young to be so much."

She smiles. "He and his brother are from an ancient line of shamans,
priests of the heavens. This man, Raph-el, has refused to call on his power
for Babylonia, and so the king has punished him."

Raph-el. Raph of Heaven or Raph of El, the Creator. So even here in this
land, the messengers of El are known. "What about his brother?" I ask
innocently. "Can he not help Babylonia? Then Samsu-iluna could release
Raph-el."

She sighs. "It is not that simple. In any case, the brother is not here, so
all falls to this one."

I bite my lower lip, relieved that Mika has not been discovered. "Then
I ask you only to let me see him and speak to him."

She looks at me for a long time. "I owe you much."

I lower my gaze and say softly, "This is all I wish."

She laughs softly and looks over at the lion statue. "Ishtar, my Lady,
you will have your sport."

32

Take in your hand large stones and hide them. . . .
—Book of Jeremiah 43:9

WITH TREPIDATION, I APPROACH THE mud-and-reed hut that sits among many in this marshy area south of the city. My beloved is there. I can feel my heart a prisoner in my chest, perhaps in sympathy to his enslavement. No ready words are in my mind to say to him, but the chance has arisen to see him and I must seize it.

A guard bars my way, but I lift my arm for him to see the white cloth tied to it with the imprint of Ishtar's priestess on it. He examines it for a moment and then steps aside. None of the other huts, I note, have guards for the slaves who live within them.

It is dim inside, with only a reed mat for a bed, a clay bowl, and a pot in the corner. The smell is not too bad, and I presume working on the irrigation canals gives Raph opportunity to cleanse himself of sweat and do most of his elimination outside the hut.

He is sitting on his reed mat when I enter, and rises with that warrior grace and wariness I remember. He looks the same, except he has a rough beard and his hair is longer and ill kept. He wears only the short skirt of a slave. His broad chest is deeply tanned. I imagine his light skin has burned and peeled many times before protecting itself by darkening. With relief, I see his arm has not been burned with a slave's brand.

The guard leaves us. For a long moment, I can say nothing, and he is also silent. Then I step toward him.

"Who are you?" he asks.

I stop. I never imagined he would not know me. "Raph, do you not recognize me?"

He narrows his eyes, the blue of them darkened almost to black in the shadows. "You seem familiar, Lady, but—"

Across a desert I have sought him, my mind picturing our reunion a thousand ways, but never in any of those imaginings did he not know me. "I am Adir from the tribe of Abram."

His eyes widen. "Adir?"

I lift my chin. "Adira now."

"How—" He swallows. "My brother, is he safe? Why are you here?"

I move closer, wanting him to embrace me. My skin cries for his touch. "We followed you across the desert." My mouth is dry. "Mika is safe. He is inside the city."

With a sweep of his arms, Raph gathers me to him, crushing me against his chest, then kissing first my left cheek, then my right, and then my left again. It is the kiss of family and not what I have hoped for, but at least I am in his arms.

But to my disappointment, he releases me. "I cannot believe you are here. Why did you come?"

"For you, of course."

He begins to pace within the confines of the hut. "My brother is not safe here."

"What do they want of you?"

He stops and looks at me. "Babylonia is threatened on all sides. The oracle readings of Ishtar's priestess and Marduk's priest are in conflict. They want me to tell them—"

"Tell them what?"

He takes a deep breath. "The future."

I take a moment to consider this. "Tabni says you and Mika are shamans. If you can see the future, why not do so?

"It is not so simple, Adir."

"Adira," I correct.

He smiles. "You make a pretty girl."

My ears burn, and I twist my hands in my shawl to keep them away from my nose. "Why is it not simple?" I ask the question to hide my embarrassment over his compliment. A part of me realizes the irony—I have dreamed of hearing those words, but now that I have heard them, I do not know what to do with them.

"I am not the shaman they think I am," Raph says.

"Oh."

"Mika is."

"Oh."

"I am his brother and his guard. His protection is my life's charge."

I seal my lips to keep from uttering another "oh." He must think me an idiot.

"He is not safe here," Raph repeats.

"What will they do to him, if they find him?"

Raph sighs. "I suppose the king will demand he tell him whatever he wants to know."

"Can he not do that?"

"He might. Again it is not simple. If he does not, they will keep him prisoner until he does. If he is able to answer their questions, they will keep him to answer another and another."

I swallow. "And if he gives the wrong answer?"

Raph grasps my shoulders. "Now you begin to see why it is not a simple matter. You must tell him to leave Babylon and this land."

His grip on my shoulders is harsher than a lover's, but I do not flinch. Any touch is better than none. "But if we leave, they will keep you a slave forever."

"I will find a way to escape, but I cannot go without—"

I think I am about to learn what is in the stolen chest that Mika and Raph carried with them. It sits in the reception room beneath the feet of the king of not just Babylon, but all of Babylonia.

"Adir—"

"Adira. I am—"

But he does not let me finish correcting him. "Did I see you at the palace?"

I am pleased he remembers me. I had not thought he noticed me at all. "Yes."

Raph takes a breath. "Samsu-iluna has something very important that belongs to my people. If Mika knows this, he will put himself in danger to retrieve it."

"The cedar box."

"Yes."

"What is in it?"

"It does not matter. What matters is its return to my people."

He releases my shoulders suddenly, and I feel the void where his touch had been.

"No, I cannot ask this of you. You are only a young boy—"

I am aware of his manipulation at the same time as I feel the rush of insult it produces. "I am not a boy." A week ago, I would have finished that declaration with, "I am a man." Today, however, I say, "I am a woman."

Raph's hand reaches out and squeezes my breasts. "These are real?"

I step back.

His mouth is open. "I thought you were in disguise."

My arms have crossed of their own volition over my chest. "They are real, and I am real." This seems the time to throw myself against him, but I do not. Somehow, nothing I have imagined matches with reality.

The guard steps onto the threshold. "Finish up," he says as if we have been writhing on the ground together. "He must leave for the ditches."

Raph appears to be gathering his scattered thoughts. He whispers urgently, "If you can get the box to Mika, he will leave. He knows his first duty is to his people. Please do this for me, Adira." He says my name carefully. I wonder if he knows the hold he has on me. He is such a handsome man. Surely every woman who meets him falls under his sway.

"We will free you," I say.

He sighs. "You are just as stubborn as a woman as you were a boy."

I laugh, and my fondness for him rushes over me once again.

33

What do people gain by telling lies? Just this, that when they speak the truth they are not believed.

—Aristotle

WHEN I RETURN, NAMI IS so excited, she runs in circles and then jumps on me, placing her paws on either side of my shoulders to lick my chin and take it gently in her mouth. Seldom has she displayed such exuberance. She does not notice or care I am now a woman.

Not so Chiram. He is furious. "Where have you been, Adir? I told you to stay by my side. Do you not ever listen?" Without stopping to draw breath or allowing me to answer, he stomps to within a fist of me. I can smell the beer on his breath. "Why are you dressed as a girl?" he demands. "Do you think yourself some kind of spy? What are those?" He reaches for my breasts.

Warned by Raph's reaction, I step back, and Nami positions herself between us, watching Chiram. She does not growl, but she will spring if he takes another step.

This makes Chiram pause long enough for me to speak. "I am a spy," I say. "Is that not what I am supposed to be doing? Finding out something about Raph without letting anyone know Mika is here?"

"And did you?" Mika asks. He has risen without a sound and steps toward us.

"I did. I have spoken to him."

This stops Chiram altogether from whatever he was about to say.

Mika steps closer, hope smoothing the fine lines beneath his eyes. "He is alive?"

"Yes."

"Where is he? Is he well?"

"He is held captive and made to work as a slave in the irrigation ditches." I frown. "They guard him closely. There is no easy way to flee with him. "

"Who made him a slave?" Chiram asks.

Mika answers first. "The king."

I look at him. "You knew this from the beginning?"

With a shrug, Mika says, "I knew it was a possibility."

I settle myself on my pallet, my back against a wall. Nami lies beside me, putting her head in my lap. I suddenly realize my weariness, but I will not release Mika from telling what he has not chosen to tell.

"What else have you learned?" Mika asks.

I shake my head. "First, answer my questions."

A shadow of impatience crosses his face. I wonder if with his anger, the blue fire will appear, and if he would strike me with it. But I do not allow my expression to change. "I have earned the right to answers."

Finally, he sighs and echoes Raph's words. "You are a stubborn boy." A corner of his mouth twitches. "Or girl."

"True," I say.

Mika begins to pace the length of the courtyard. Moonlight seeps through the fronds overhead, dappling the dirt floor silver and gray. "Raph and I came to Babylon before we came to your land, to Canaan. Raph drank too much one night while rolling stones and bragged we were . . . more than we are."

"What did he say?"

Mika flashes me a look of annoyance, but after a moment he answers, "Raph claimed we were great shamans from the northlands who could rise to the nine levels of heaven and perceive the future."

I wish I could lift one brow as Tabni does, but mine refuse to act independently. Again, I remember the blue fire cradled in Mika's hand. "Can you?"

This time Mika stops his pacing and stares at me. "It is more complicated than that."

Again, words that echo Raph's. I purse my lips in annoyance. I am tired of secrets.

Chiram takes a stick from the cook fire and lights the oil pots. At that moment, Nami rises to her feet, her ears pricked toward the door. A soft triple *thump* confirms her interest.

Chiram scowls. "What does that stupid slave want? It is long past time for food and since what time has he bothered to knock? I will have him on his way." He points a thick forefinger at Mika. "Hold your tale."

This is the first occasion I can recall Chiram being curious about anything.

I am stunned when Chiram reappears, his face grave and annoyed, and steps aside. Behind him, standing tall, despite her compact stature, is a woman. Even in the plain garb she has donned and the dim glow from the oil lamps, I have no trouble recognizing her, not needing the subtle tang of myrtle that accompanies her.

With haste, I scramble to my feet and introduce her. Chiram does not appear impressed, either at the presence of Ishtar's High Priestess or that I know her. Mika's shoulders fall. All our stealth and pretense have been wasted. We are uncovered. I am not such an excellent spy as I supposed. My throat tightens. My actions have thwarted any possibility of Raph's escape, and Mika is now at the mercy of his brother's captors. How could I have been so foolish as to present myself, and thus my friends, at the king's feet?

I will not speak, I vow to myself. If I do, I am sure to plunge us deeper into trouble. If anyone looks closely, they will see the gleam of tears that fill my eyes. I try not to blink to keep them from spilling, and my hand moves to find Nami's head at my thigh. She stands close, knowing I need her presence.

I expect the king's soldiers to pour in behind her, but either she has ordered them to wait outside, or she is alone.

As though she hears my silent thought, she says, "I am alone."

"It speaks for the order in the streets of Babylon that a woman can walk unmolested," Mika says quietly.

She has not taken her attention from him. "Perhaps it is because the goddess has not been forgotten here."

At first, this surprises me. Of course, the goddess is here. The people worship her in every city, though her names are many.

But Mika and Tabni have locked gazes, as though this simple statement from her lips has somehow joined them in a secret understanding.

I am confused, but the tightness in my throat has not eased.

For a long time, silence reigns. Tabni finally breaks it. "You know why I am here."

Mika's brows tighten. "I know Samsu-iluna seeks me."

"What you brought with you is safe," she says.

"What is in the box?" I ask, breaking my vow to keep quiet and listen. My father often chastised me for this fault. But I may as well have spoken to the walls. Neither heeds me.

"Do I have a choice?" Mika asks her.

"I have convinced Samsu-iluna what he seeks can only be accomplished by one who is free of coercion."

"And he believes this?"

A smile wisps her mouth. "He believes sheep can be 'persuaded' into a gate by offering them no other path."

In a sudden shift, Mika spreads his hand. "Our hospitality is in fault. May we serve you food or drink?"

I blink, spilling a tear that has welled. Dare I believe we might not all be enslaved and dragged to labor in the canals? With a furtive wipe of my sleeve at my cheek, I sit straighter. Even so, I do not care for the sound of sheep having only one path to follow.

Like me, Chiram stands against the far wall, his dark, brow-hooded eyes shifting from face to face, waiting to see what enfolds from this encounter.

Tabni shakes her head. "Thank you, but no, I have little time. Samsu-iluna awaits me."

"And if you return alone?"

Tabni's mouth tightens. "Do not tread that path. I do not need to ascend the nine levels to see your future or your brother's and probably of those who travel with you." She does not hesitate in her pronouncement of our doom. "The best of which would be to see all enslaved."

"And the worst?"

With a shrug, Tabni says, "There are quick deaths, and there are slow ones."

"I see."

"Do you?" She looks up at him. "It is not a king's whim that guides Samsu-iluna. His father's kingdom is vast, perhaps too large, and

Samsu-iluna is beset with intrigue and enemies. What the goddess has shown me in the stars of the future and what the god Marduk has revealed to his priest through the entrails of a goat's liver have both been laid before the king. The one's advice is contrary to the other."

Mika rubs his chin. "And he wishes a third insight?"

"Yes. One devoid of politics."

"Nothing is devoid of politics."

She bows her head in acknowledgment, a wry smile briefly at her lips. Then she looks up at him again. "Nevertheless, what shall I report to the king?"

Mika folds his arms across his chest and walks to the open back entrance that looks out onto the garden. He stands thus for long moments. We wait, and no one speaks. Finally, he spins around.

"Take this message to Samsu-iluna. I will seek the future for him, but the price is our freedom to leave . . . with the box."

Tabni sighs. "I have already discussed the terms with him."

"And his answer?"

"He has followed my counsel."

Mika takes a step toward her. "Which is?"

"That all may leave, except you."

I take a quick breath, but hold my tongue.

Tabni crosses her arms. "The king is not his father, but he is not foolish. If you were allowed to leave, what incentive would you have to give him your deities' honest answer?"

"What," Mika asks quietly, "does the king seek to know?"

"Which enemies are the gravest threats, and where to dispatch his forces." She walks deeper into the room, stopping close to Mika. "If you give bad advice and Babylonia falls, you will be here with us to reap the consequences."

Mika's face is still, revealing no emotion.

Nami whines very softly, and I realize I am gripping the skin at the base of her neck. I release my fingers, and they nervously seek the mats behind her ears. It is a constant challenge to keep them free of snarls, and I need something to do with my hands.

Finally, Mika says, "I see now the gate that leads into this ravine."

He too has remembered Tabni's words about the sheep having no other choice than to choose the path through the gate.

"But," he continues, "I have requirements."

"Name them."

"Regardless of what I am granted to see or if I fail, my brother, the contents of the box, and these with me—he sweeps his hand to include me and Chiram—go free with their possessions and with five bracelets of silver each."

Chiram grunts.

Tabni looks grave. "The silver is not a problem and, as I have said, the king has already agreed to let them go. As to the box, that is for the king to decide. What else?"

"Only my brother will touch the box. That is not negotiable."

She nods.

"And this. The rite I will perform has risk . . . and it requires a woman, one who has not been with a man."

With a wave of her hand, Tabni dismisses this. "There are many such girls in Ishtar's temple. You will have your choice."

"No."

I am more surprised than any there that the protest came from my lips. Not only that, but I have stepped forward between them.

Tabni eyes me calmly. Mika has not revealed any emotion until now. And I am not sure what I see on his face. Concern? Surprise? Chiram's eyes are wide. His mouth flaps open and then closes as if he cannot find any words to express his confusion and objection.

"I will lie with Mika." I do not say it as a request.

CHAPTER

34

At sundown he arrived at a good place to set up camp and stopped there for the night. Jacob found a stone to rest his head against and lay down to sleep. As he slept, he dreamed of a stairway that reached from the earth up to heaven. And he saw the angels of God going up and down the stairway.

—Book of Genesis 28:11-12

AS I FOLLOW TABNI UP the stairs of Ishtar's temple, my heart races faster than when I chased after the raiders. My skin glows with heat from several scrubbings. Never in my life have I been this clean. Tabni's holy women have washed me, rubbed me with sweet-smelling oils, lined my eyes with kohl, and done what they could with my hair, weaving saffron-dyed ribbons through it. Tabni gave me a delicate necklace of gold. I wear a thin, white linen dress off one shoulder that brushes my legs like a cloud as I step up and up.

I feel like a lamb readied for the altar.

This is my own doing, I remind myself, though I cannot grasp the exact reason for it. I made an impulsive declaration—for Raph, to save him. Why? Because so much depends on Mika's ability to reach the ninth level, I could not have left it in the hands of a stranger. That is what my mind reminds me, but what do I know of ascending to heaven? Why do I need to be the one to help him up there? He did not ask for me, only for a woman who had not lain with a man. In fact, he had not even known I was a woman until a short time before.

My thoughts wrap themselves around one another. In panic, I instruct my feet to stop their upward march, but it is as if someone has slid a knife between my mind and my body, disconnecting them, and my feet continue to lift and propel me up the stone stairs.

Only Marduk's temple is higher than Ishtar's. Perhaps Tabni's fears are not unfounded. The conquerors of this land, while acknowledging the Queen of Heaven, have gradually reduced her power. I wonder if El will do the same in my land. It would be better if they continued to reign together. Who would want the loss of the goddess's blessing and risk fallow land and barren wombs?

Despite efforts to fill my mind with thoughts of religion, by the time we reach the top, I can barely draw a breath. When we finally emerge, it is not into an enclosed room as I expected, but a square area open to the sky with sidewalls the height of my waist. Four torches burn in each corner. In the center, about a foot's length above the floor, sits a bed of woven fibers. Pillows of fine linen cover the bed and spill onto the floor. At one end of the bed is the cedar chest marked with the carven crescent and star. Beside it, a silver tray rests on a small stand. The tray holds two silver cups, a painted clay jug, and leather packets like those Mika carries in his bag. On the bed's far side, neatly folded strips of cloth are arranged beside a large bronze bowl.

Mika waits for me. He has never seemed so tall or imposing. He also is dressed in a white robe. His flame-colored hair is clean and flows to his shoulders. His beard is trimmed and oiled and gleams in the firelight.

If I had the breath to move, I would turn and run back down the stairs.

For a moment, I stand behind Tabni, surrounded by the five young women who have accompanied me. I am at least a head taller than all of them. Each is beautiful, and all have straight noses. What if Mika is so put off by me he cannot reach even the first level of heaven? I am twice a fool to offer myself.

At some unseen signal, the women dissolve around me like salt in rain, disappearing back down the stairs and leaving only me and Tabni facing Mika.

"You have all you need?" Tabni asks him.

"Yes."

"Then I call on Ishtar to bless you both."

And Tabni also leaves me.

Again, though commanded to follow her, my feet remain rooted.

I stare at Mika. We are alone.

He strides to me, reaches for both my hands and holds them in his. They are warm to my cool, moist ones. "What are you thinking, Adira?"

"I . . . am wondering . . . if I will ever rule my contrary feet again," I say, gasping for breath enough to say it.

He frowns. "What is wrong?"

"Cannot . . . breathe."

"Come here." He pulls me down to the bed and reaches for one of the folded pieces of cloth. "Hold this over your nose and mouth and breathe into it."

My eyes widen in panic. I am already struggling to get enough air; this will make it harder.

"Trust me," he says. "Remember, I am a healer."

I nod and hold the cloth to my nose and mouth.

"Do you feel as if fluid is filling your lungs?" he asks.

I nod again.

"As contrary as it seems, you are bringing too much air into your body."

This seems absurd, but I reason to myself I am the one holding the cloth, so if it gets worse, I can take it away. To my surprise, after a few moments I am breathing easier. Tentatively, I lower the cloth.

"Just concentrate on slow, steady breaths. Control it."

He waits for several moments and then pours a dark liquid from the pitcher into both cups, offering me one. "Only wine," he answers my questioning look.

I drink half of it, glad for the distracting burn in my chest. I need time. "Talk," I say.

"About?"

"Tell me more of your childhood." I want more distractions, and though we had many discussions in the desert, I talked much more than he.

He shrugs. "My people live in caves set into the northland mountains. As a child, I learned to climb before I could walk." He smiles. "Those in the valleys called us The Goat People."

I smile too. "You are too tall to be a goat."

"As I have said, our true homeland is far to the west across the sea, or so our legends say. Where we lived before, that is lost in time's mist."

"Why did you let me be the one?" I do not know why such a question slipped from me. I did not mean to bring us back to the present. Now, I have lost control of my mouth as well as my feet.

"Because you chose it. There is risk in this, Adira, as I told you. You may not awake from it or you may awake . . . different."

He has said this before, but there is a stir of disappointment in my chest. Was I foolish enough to think he might want me? Why? It is his brother I love. That is why I am here. It seems absurd. I am lying with Mika for the sake of Raph. The gods must be laughing.

"Do you think El cares I am reaching for heaven with you?" This has only now entered my thoughts.

Mika's mouth creases. "It is his heaven too, is it not?"

I have not thought of that. Of course, it is. It occurs to me Mika's goddess might not be the same as the ones I know. "What is your goddess's name?"

For answer, Mika tilts his head up at the sky. There is no moon tonight, and the stars are woven thick and close above us in a shawl of light. "She has many names—Bright One, Morning Star, Sacred Knowledge. She is Ishtar, Inanna, Asherat, Asharah, Ashtarte, Lât, Zuhara, and Isis. She is Word and Wisdom." He runs a light finger along my cheekbone. "Tonight, she will be you."

A shiver snakes my spine. Perhaps she is already inside me. Perhaps that is why my body is not obedient to me. I drink the rest of my wine.

Mika's large hands cup my face, and he leans to brush my lips with his.

I pull away, my hand rising to my nose as if to shield it from him.

Firmly, he pulls my hand down and kisses my nose.

I stare at him, which makes him laugh. "You do not think I am ugly?"

"No."

It is the surprise in his eyes that makes me believe him.

"You are many things, Adira, but 'ugly' is not one of them."

"But how can you . . . touch me? Until yesterday, I was a boy to you."

He smiles. "You have not been a boy to me for a very long time."

I gasp. "When? When did you know?"

"Since I first put my hands on you."

My face flames. "What? What do you mean?"

"I remind you again I am a healer. The body is to me as wood to a carpenter or clay to a potter. Do you remember when you fell from your horse and your father called me in to attend you?"

It seems a lifetime ago, but still my chest hurts at the memory of my father's concern. "Yes, I remember."

"The first time my fingers touched your skin and felt your ribs and hip bone, I knew you were not a boy."

I squint at him. "Is that why you were so mean to me?"

He looks away. "I am sorry if I seemed cruel. I needed to keep my distance from women."

I think about this for a moment, and then ask, "You have lost someone?"

His fingers tighten into fists. "My wife . . . and my child."

"What happened?" In all our time together, this is something he has never spoken of.

His jaw hardens. "She and my daughter drank unclean water. An animal died in a pool we drew water from, but they did not know. They died quickly, but in much pain, and I was not there to ease it."

I say nothing, not knowing what to say.

After a long while, he looks up again at the sky and then down at me. "It would have been easier had some Hittite slain them. Then I would have had someone to hate, but I had only myself."

"Where were you when they fell ill?"

He gave a short laugh. "Ah, that is the irony. I was seeking heaven for my people."

"And your wife was not the goddess for you?"

A wistful smile curves his mouth. "She was so once, but the rite requires a woman who has not known a man, remember?"

"I am sorry," I say. There still do not seem to be any right words for such a sorrow.

"It has been two summers," Mika says. "It feels distant and yet, when I remember, I see them lying so still—"

It is only now, in the heart of his pain, I know the true reason I chose to be here with this man. The knowing pierces me. Beneath that little desert acacia tree, death bound us, but I did not know him. I did not know myself. All the nights that followed, when we sat beneath the starred sky and talked—so slowly I hardly knew it was happening—I learned this man—not the angel, but the man. And I gave this man who I was. We did not use lovers' words or touch as lovers. We did not even acknowledge what drew us together. I do not even know if the name of this is "love"; it simply is.

I rise onto my knees and put my fingers over his mouth. Overhead, the stars spread a gauzy canopy over us, a canopy that fades at the edges where the four torches blaze. Our breath mingles for a long moment. The universe stills around us, paused in its infinite spinning. Slowly, I lower my hand and move forward until our lips touch.

Everything is new to me—the softness of his mouth, the warmth of his tongue. I am not certain how he has removed my clothing, but we are naked before one another, and I revel in the starlight that brushes his eyes and tells me I am his goddess . . . at least tonight. He guides me with gentleness until my own thirst matches his.

"We have all of the night," he chuckles at my newfound boldness.

And we take every moment of it.

AT LAST, HE rolls over to kiss the top of my head and sighs, brushing aside a damp curl of hair. "It is time to seek heaven."

"I thought we were already there," I mumble.

He laughs and sits up. I grab for his hip, not wanting to lose the warmth of his body next to mine, and let my hand slide lower. With a long look at the sky, he sighs again and rolls over onto me. "Perhaps heaven can hold a few moments more."

I AM ASLEEP when he wakes me, helping me to sit up. Groggily, I take the cup he puts in my hands. "Drink this," he says.

I looked at his empty cup. "Have you already?"

"Yes."

It is bitter. I wonder what he has mixed into it, and if I will wake from it. While I drink, he kneels before the cedar box and opens it.

My breath catches. Finally, I am to see the secret treasure Mika and Raph have guarded so closely.

Still naked, Mika reaches into the darkness of the box's interior with both hands and lifts something. The muscles cord across his arms and back.

What he takes out is about the size of a newborn child and the color of milk in the starlight. He sets it with reverence at the top of our pallet where it makes a deep indention into the pillows. I touch the cool, flat surface. "A rock?"

Mika strokes it. "Not just a rock," he says.

I lay my hand flat against it and look a question at him.

He presses his hand on top of mine. "In the land of my forefathers, the green land across the sea, it was a dreaming stone in the heart of the most important time-keeper temple."

"The temple with the portals for the stars?" I ask, remembering our conversations in the desert.

"Yes. On a certain night, the goddess, the Morning Star, shines into the temple."

He says more, but dizziness rises up like a fountain in me, and reality seems to split asunder. In one world, our hands remain pressed on the hard surface. In the other, they sink into the stone's heart. As Mika describes it, I see the circular building gleaming white, with long portals cut into the stones. Starlight streams through a precise opening above the lintel stones and down a dark shaft to touch a stone slab.

My mouth has grown thick, as has my mind.

"Lie down," he instructs, pulling me until I settle with my head beside his on the stone. Again, our breaths entwine, and I feel my cheek against the stone while I ascend into a place of mist.

CHAPTER

35

The next morning Jacob got up very early. He took the stone he had rested his head against, and he set it upright as a memorial pillar. Then he poured olive oil over it.

—Book of Genesis 28:18

I AM WITHOUT A BODY OR memories of who I am. Darkness surrounds me, but somehow I know the space is narrow, a tunnel. A circular opening of pure white light lies at the tunnel's end. The light beckons. I must reach it. I do not question why. This is not a place of answers.

With all my being, I strive toward the light, moving by sheer will, because I have no body, no limbs. Closer and closer I come, each minuscule distance hard won, until—if I could find my arm—I could reach out and touch it.

Abruptly, I am snatched away. My eyes open, disappointment flooding me. *I was so close!*

Mika's face hovers above me, lined with concern.

"Come back," he is saying over and over. I remember now hearing him faintly in the tunnel. Did he drag me back? I want to ask him why he kept me from the light when I had worked so hard to reach it, but I have forgotten where my mouth is.

Something cool passes over my face, orienting me to my body.

"It is all right, Adira," he says gently. "You can sleep now."

With a sigh, I fall back into darkness, but there is no tunnel and no light . . . and no dreams.

THE NEXT DAY—OR so I am told—I stand on wobbly legs before the King of Babylonia. Chiram stands beside me, his hand on my arm to steady me. I do not have the strength to shake him off. Crowded along the room's walls are men and women of influence and Samsu-iluna's counselors. On the king's right, grim-faced, stands the High Priest of Marduk, city-god of Babylon. The priest's fingers knead the rich fabric of his robe, which is adorned with Marduk's symbols—a triangular spade and a dragon. To the king's left is Tabni, Ishtar's High Priestess. For a moment, my gaze flickers between the golden, eight-pointed stars entwined on her robe and the memory of stars spun overhead and framed by the four torches atop Ishtar's temple. I waver, and Chiram's arm stiffens, steady as a pole, keeping me upright.

With a rub at my eyes, the scene returns to the present, and I remember the foreseeing given by Marduk's priest contradicted Ishtar's, and for that reason, Samsu-iluna sought Mika and Raph and the magic of the white stone.

Tabni never told us what she had predicted. She is fierce in her loyalty to her king, or perhaps she knows an honest foretelling is all that stands between her land and Babylonia's enemies.

I admire her, and I hate her.

I am changed, forever.

Mika steps forward and inclines his head. Just behind him, Raph guards his left flank, scanning the room. He is no longer dressed as a slave, nor a merchant, as I have known him, but as a warrior, his true self. He is not allowed weapons before the king, but my gaze slides over the muscles of his arms and chest, and the way he stands with his weight balanced evenly between his feet, and I am certain he, himself, is a weapon.

On the other hand, Mika's eyes focus on the king.

"I have spent a good portion of my treasury seeking you," Samsu-iluna says, leaning forward, his voice tight with hope and warning. "Was it worth it?"

"That is for you to judge," Mika says. As always, he is the calm in the storm's heart. *The hands that cup the lightning.*

"Well then, what did your gods show you?"

"I will tell you, according to our bargain, but I ask your word these others with me are free to leave."

A ridge appears in the muscles of Raph's shoulders. He is not happy with the decision to leave his brother.

Nor am I. We cannot leave him here.

Samsu-iluna frowns.

"The word of Babylonia's king," Mika insists, "is known to be good from here to the sea, but I have not heard it from his mouth, only from those who serve him." Mika glances at Tabni.

The king nods, the tension easing a bit from his countenance. "Very well. My word is that all those with you, including your brother may leave. In fact, I will send escort with them to Mari."

"And the silver?" Mika asks.

A smile tugs at the corners of my mouth. Mika would make a good trader.

Samsu-iluna snorted. "And five bracelets of silver."

"Each," Mika insists.

Now the king is smiling. "Each."

"And I am to be released after a year with the same and the chest with its contents."

Despite the fog of my thoughts, I realize the king has been astute enough to keep the dreaming stone with the dreamer.

"You are not one to let a detail slip beneath the water," the king says. "I give my word on it, here before my Council."

Mika raises his hands, palms upward, as if to the heavens' witness. "This then is what the gods showed me."

Silence fills the room, a silence that quivers like a harp string after the last sound has faded.

"There will be trouble from the south—"

My fists clench, my mind assaulted with vague images.

"—and the north."

From what I have heard in the king's halls and the streets, this is not news, but the court leans forward in anticipation. My belly roils. What did Mika have me drink?

From a great distance, I hear Mika's voice continue. "But a mighty army will descend upon the land from the mountains."

Samsu-iluna moves to the edge of his elaborately carved chair. "From which mountains?"

Mika pauses, meeting the king's intense stare. "They attack with the rising sun in their enemies' eyes."

"From the east then," the kings says, falling back in his chair as though released from a bow strung for a very long time.

Mika nods. "They come with horses."

Exhaling a deep breath the king shouts, "The Kassites!" He turns to Tabni. "Priestess, you saw true."

She does not appear happy in her rightness.

I, too, do not care what name he gives his enemies or which of the visions of terror will descend first on this land. Dreams accompanied the poison Mika gave me, but I can make no auguries from the jumble. Behind my closed eyes, the images still crawl over one another like bees on the comb. Where is my own self in this hive that is my mind?

My legs become air beneath me. The floor leaps toward my face, the king's floor of rounded stones, fitted together precisely in nested arcs, pleasing to the eye.

I feel nothing when it strikes me.

I AWAKE ON the road. My head throbs as if wrung and beaten on rocks to wash. For a while, it is clean of thought, dazzled with pain and the perfect blueness of sky that fills my senses. Only slowly do my losses rise in my mind with the stealth of an overflowing bank—my father, Mika, a future that is mine.

I am back on the path my oath made for me. *If I live to fulfill it.*

When I can endure the pain, I turn my head to find I am lying in the bed of a wagon and must sit up to see over the edge. When I do, I promptly vomit over the side. What Mika had me drink has not killed me, but a part of me wishes it had. I want to lie back, but I grasp the wagon's edges to remain sitting and see where I am.

A gray donkey pulls my wagon. I recognize Raph's muscled back ahead leading a smaller black donkey, my Philot. An armed man I do not know walks behind, and two to either side. Chiram leads a camel laden with packs. My head spins again, but I do not lie back until I see Nami. Her bright eyes have caught mine, and her feathered tail sweeps the air. She jumps into the wagon and shoves her nose into my face. Her tongue gives my face and neck the cleaning I'm sure they need, and her teeth gently grasp my chin to assure me of her love.

The ache of my losses eased, I fall back into oblivion, not as deep as before, but a hazy place where reality merges with dream.

THE NEXT TIME I wake, Chiram is wiping my head with a wet cloth. Not gently.

I grab his brawny wrist. "That hurts!"

"Good. Means you are alive."

Gritting my teeth, I sit up, determine to aim his way should my belly heave again. But it does not, the first time in my life I have been disappointed not to be sick. "Where are we?"

"North of Babylon, beside the Euphrates."

Plowing a path through the river's dancing sparkles, a round boat passes by. Its hull is made of stretched hides sealed with pitch. Boats travel only with southbound current, so that orients me. We are traveling north. I note we have left the rich soil of the flatlands in exchange for a more rocky terrain, which gives me an idea of the distance we have traveled . . . and how long I have lain in a stupor.

"What has happened?"

He shrugs. "Mika babbled on to the king about a war and letting us go. You were out cold as a corpse. We set out the same night with this . . . escort." He spits out the last word.

I rub my forehead and feel a tender bump where I assume it connected with the king's floor. Anger churns in my belly. Mika wanted us gone from his sight as soon as possible.

The guard at the forefront raises his hand, signaling a stop. To camp for the night, I presume. At that moment Raph joins us, leaning over the wagon. "Is he all right?"

"She," I correct. I want to ball up a fist and hit him. "How can you just leave your brother?" I croak. "He crossed a desert for you!"

Raph flinches as though I truly did strike him. He stands, and I realize he is going to walk away.

Grabbing Chiram's shoulder for support, I haul myself to my feet. "Wait. Do not walk away from me as you walked away from Mika."

With a grim face, Raph turns back. "Say then what you will."

"I will." I take a deep breath but, for a moment, cannot think. My head pounds, and my mouth tastes like sand.

Chiram clears his throat. "You were about to gnaw his ass."

"Thank you." This must be the first time those words have found their way from my mouth to Chiram's ears.

With a deep breath, I turn back to Raph. "Why?"

His deep blue eyes meet mine, but my heart does not stutter. Anger has given a blade's edge to my focus. I do not know why I thought I loved him. I was a foolish child struck by his beauty and charm.

"Mika," he says flatly, "wanted us to be safe."

"So you let *him* stay in danger? Do you understand what is going to happen there?" Mika had seen the future or perhaps only told a future we could all see. Regardless, war was coming to Babylonia.

Raph's face is without expression, the hard resolve of a warrior set to kill whoever stands in his path.

"Why?" I repeat, aware I am demanding an answer of one of my god's angels, but I would demand it of El himself . . . if he would speak to anyone other than Abram.

For long moments, Raph stands silent before me, and then he glances over his shoulder, checking the location of our guards. "Adira, you do not understand."

"Then explain it," I demand, crossing my arms, "or I will go to these men and tell them we must return." I lean closer to him. "I saw the future too, Raph. I ascended to heaven with Mika. They will want to know what I have seen." It is somewhat a lie, or a twisting of truth, but I am desperate.

A deep crimson suffuses Raph's face. "I swore to keep you safe and out of Babylon."

"Then you must tell me."

"I cannot."

I shrug. "Then you leave me no choice. I do not trust Samsu-iluna."

Chiram grunts. "On that we agree."

I start toward the nearest Babylonian soldier, but Raph snatches my arm, spinning me toward him. Nami watches this with anxious eyes. Chiram scratches his filthy beard.

"All right," Raph says in a harsh whisper. "I will tell you, but only you."

I nod.

Chiram spits.

Raph leads me away from the river. Water carries the sound of voices. We head toward the far side of a hill, passing a shallow cave. One of the soldiers watches us. I see calculation on his face and straighten my spine. That is something I have learned in my short time of being a woman. You are always watched, and there is always conjecture churning behind the eyes of those watching. My days of living carefree are done. Now, I must watch my watchers. This is why women have husbands—to protect them, to keep them safe from such men. This is why my father made me swear to go to Sarai and put myself under her care. If she cannot find me a husband, she will at least take me in as family.

I pull my thoughts from this, because I must be resolute with Raph. If he senses weakness, he will leap upon it.

Behind the hill, I confront him. "Tell me why we left Mika behind. The truth."

"You know the truth, or part of it. Mika too does not trust Samsu-iluna, and he wishes us to be safe from him."

"The fingers of Babylonia are long," I say. "They reached us even in the Vale."

"That is why I must leave you."

"Leave?" I thought I did not love him, but my belly tightens. "Why? Where?"

"I go north. To return to my people."

My eyes narrow in suspicion. "Why would Samsu-iluna be a threat to you?"

Raph shrugs. "I am Mika's brother. If the king has me in his possession, he can force Mika to stay with him."

"Then why let us go?"

"He is a king. He gave his word before his Council. He would lose all credibility if he did not honor his word."

A tiny twitch below his right eye gives him away.

"There is more." I do not say it as a question.

Annoyed, he brushes a hand across his mouth. He and Mika have the same sensitive mouth, I realize, and for a moment, I am snatched into Mika's arms, tasting his lips, feeling him inside me, and a jolt of fire races down my belly. The memory is almost as powerful as the experience.

"Adira?" Raph reaches out his hand. His voice is now full of concern. "Are you well? Do you need to sit?"

I swallow. "I am fine."

"You looked unsteady again."

"I am well," I say stubbornly. "You were telling me the true reason you agreed to abandon Mika in Samsu-iluna's hands and will abandon me to Chiram and these men."

Raph's gaze drops. "I must."

"Tell me then. You owe me that."

He lifts his eyes to mine. "I have the dreaming stone."

"What? How is that possible?" But even as the words left my mouth, I remember Mika's conditions to the priestess: *"Only my brother will touch the box."*

Raph glances over his shoulder, though our position behind the hill not only hides us from view, but from any eavesdropper. "After the ascension, I substituted another stone in its place in the box," he says in a low voice.

"But what if Mika needs to see another future?"

Raph keeps my gaze. "It is more important the stone return safely to our people. We have been its guardians for as many turns of the seasons as the stars in the sky."

I stare at him.

"That is why I must leave you, Adira. I do not wish to. I did not want to leave Mika, but my first duty is to return the stone."

"Why did you bring it to start with?" I practically hiss at him. "Why not leave it where it was safe?"

"We came searching for something more valuable than the stone itself, and Mika thought we might need it to guide our path."

"What is more valuable than a stone that can crack open the portals of the future?"

"Lost knowledge."

Then I remember Mika has already told me this. "Have you then found this knowledge?"

"No. But to lose the stone as well—we cannot allow that to happen."

There is nothing left to say. Raph is telling me his truth. His thoughts are plainly written in his eyes and his stance. He is far easier to read than Mika.

We return to the camp. The sun is hidden now below the horizon, and a chill settles in place of the day's heat. Chiram has a fire made and cooks a stew with meat from a gazelle one of the men brought down. It smells wonderful and sweeps me back to the days of traveling with our caravan. My heart aches that those times will never be again. My father will never call me into his tent to chastise me for some mischief or praise me for some deed well done.

I squat beside Chiram, my longing for childhood overcoming my distaste for him. "Is it ready?"

"No."

The fire crackles.

"What are you going to do when we return?" I ask, surprised I am even interested, but Chiram is the only remaining connection with my father.

He tastes the broth and adds a pinch of something before answering. His gaze finds the camel that has folded her legs beneath her and surveys us with a regal calmness. "I am thinking I now have enough for a caravan of my own."

I nod. The silver he has is enough to fund this.

He picks at his front tooth with a dirty fingernail. "These creatures are not utilized to their capacity."

"The camels?"

He grunts.

"What do you mean?"

"Why do we use donkeys when camels can carry so much more, eat less, and can cross the desert itself?"

I turn this thought over in my mind and cannot find an answer to dispute him. It is a good idea, but praise for him cannot make it past my lips. I try to remember one kind thing Chiram had ever said to me and must give it up without an answer.

Nami returns from her exploring and presses against my side. I scratch behind her ears, and my fingers begin working out the mats. She shakes her head, but I tell her to be still, and she sighs in resignation and settles beside me.

THAT NIGHT, I lie on my back, staring up at the stars, trying not to allow the memories that threaten to tear me apart. Will I ever look at the night sky again without remembering Mika's touch? Will I never see him again?

Beside me, Nami lifts her head and pricks her ears toward the rise where Raph and I had conversed. "What is it?" I ask, my imagination painting a lion behind the hill. She continues to stare, but does not seem agitated, as she would if a predator were lurking. And if she heard prey, she would be after it. After our time in the desert, she often brings small game to me for approval, though she prefers her meat cooked in Chiram's pot.

Something pricks my mind, and I realize none of the soldiers are in sight. They are supposed to guard us, so either they have abandoned that obligation, or they are all together discussing something . . . something they do not want our ears to hear.

I glance to where Chiram snores loudly and Raph lies sprawled in sleep. I had not given much thought to our safety while I knew Raph was with us, but that has changed. He will leave us soon. His path of duty is clear. The stone's safety comes ahead of his brother's life or my safety. I believe he would place it without hesitation before his own life.

Calling on the skills I have honed all my life, I rise and head toward the hill. Nami stays at my side. She knows we are hunting and also moves stealthily.

As we approach, I hear voices from inside the cave and find a place where a boulder conceals us. Signaling Nami down, I hear a man saying, "It is not a plan I care for. Should Samsu-iluna hear we killed them before we reached Mira, he will not be pleased. He swore their safe passage to that city."

"Who knows what will happen to them or their wealth in Mira?" a deeper voice replies. "My contact told me they carry silver—five rings each. Gifts from the king."

"What does the tall warrior keep wrapped in those blankets, is what I want to know." This third voice I think belongs to the man with a wide, jagged scar over his right brow. "He walks beside it every day, never makes water out of sight of it. I would lay a wager it holds a great treasure."

"We will tell the king they tried to run, and we had to kill them."

A spit. "That is the stupidest thing I have heard coming from your mouth, Kuri, and there has been enough of such to fill a canal. What do you say when Samsu-iluna asks where his silver is?"

"If you are so much our better, Puzir, how is it you forget the king will ask the same if we kill them *after* Mira? He will want his silver either way."

There is a moment of quiet.

The voice I now have labeled Puzir says, "Then we cannot return if we wish the silver for ourselves. None of us has a wife. We can find a new place and live like kings ourselves."

"I have a wife," Scar says.

"Is she worth five bracelets of silver?"

Silence.

Laughter. "I thought thus. You can find another woman where we go—a better one with your share."

"And where would that be?"

"A discussion we can have once the deed is done. Perhaps best for us to choose separate paths."

"When then?"

"Night."

"This night?"

Scar sounds eager. I shiver.

"No, tomorrow. We have a long day's trek, and I can plan it."

With a jolt, I realize I will be discovered when they finish their discussion. I wave my hand before Nami's nose and then to my forehead to make sure I have her attention before making the signal for "quiet" and "follow," hunting signals I learned when we lived with the nomads. She rises and trots beside me as I make my way back, my heart beating in my throat at what I have heard.

Even as I slip under the blanket on my pallet, it thuds so hard, I fear the men will hear it and not wait to thrust their knives and still it. My thoughts scramble around until I rein them in. I cannot do anything to arouse the guard's suspicions, but we cannot wait either.

It is not difficult to keep awake now. I do not want to die at the hands of these men. Nami nestles close, and I put my hand on her head. The contact clears my mind, and I can think. If they hold true to the plan I overheard, I may be able to warn Raph tomorrow, but what if our guards change their minds and decide to slay us tonight?

I wait until the sliver of moon has begun her arc across the sky and slip my blanket to the side. Nami pushes against me, stealing the warm space I vacated. "Stay," I tell her softly, reinforcing the command with a hand signal. She lifts her head. In the scant moonlight, she is difficult to see. I know she watches me as I slip to the other side of the wagon where Raph sleeps. He lies on his side with his back to me. He is a warrior, but I am stealthy, and I approach him without alerting him. Proud of my skill, I reach out to touch him, and my heart drops like a stone in water.

Raph has used my old trick. My hand connects with hard rock beneath his wool blanket.

36

If I am not for myself, who is for me? And being for my own self, what am I? If not now, when?

—Hillel, *Sayings of the Fathers*

RAPH HAS LEFT US. CHIRAM is a cook. I am a woman. What can we do against three armed, trained warriors of Babylonia?

What is the right question, Father? Asking this calms my mind enough to think. The right question is this: How can we survive? I do not relish seeing more death, but I am not prepared to see my own. And what would happen to Nami?

Yet what can I do? I have still not recovered from whatever Mika had me drink the night we sought heaven. I would not be of much use in a fight. The guards will return soon, and they will post a watch. Even if I could get to Chiram's pallet without notice and explain it all to him, how would we escape? There is river to our right and desert to the left. Our tracks would show in this soil, and the wind is still. No dust demons here. We would be found quickly.

What if we slipped into the river? I bite my lip. I have not the strength to fight the current, and Chiram cannot swim; he would never do that. I scowl. What good is he? Then I remember Chiram's deadly accuracy with his knives. At least we have that, but again, it does not seem a battle with much chance for winning.

So if we cannot flee or fight, what do we have to bargain our lives? They could simply take our silver, our donkey, and the camel. I consider trying to wake Chiram and explain why I need his silver. I cannot imagine his listening to me or giving it over, so I rise and do what I can.

WHEN I RETURN, I wake Chiram. We have a slim chance of cutting the sleeping guards' throats and perhaps Chiram's knives can take out the one standing watch. Chiram would want to fight. I believe that of him, at least. I kneel beside him and shake his shoulder. He wakes easily, despite the loud snores, and narrows his eyes at me. "What?"

"Quiet," I whisper. "Listen to me."

He sits up, hands going to the knives that stay tucked in his sash even when he sleeps. "What has happened?"

I have no chance to answer. A sound behind me makes me turn and when I turn back, sickle-curved swords prick both sides of Chiram's neck and then the small of my back.

"Where is the warrior, Raph, who traveled with us?"

At first I cannot speak. My chest is filling as it did when I ascended the steps of the goddess temple, but this time not in fear of love.

"He is gone," I manage, concentrating on my breathing, remembering Mika's hand on my arm, his calm voice in my ear: *As contrary as it seems, you are getting too much air.* I slow my breath, forcing myself to ignore the demands of my lungs. *Trust me . . . I am a healer.*

"Get up."

I stand on shaky legs, grateful I am not skewered here and now or savaged. A quick glance at the guard's face—he is the man I call Scar—reveals he is too concerned with Raph's whereabouts to bother with me now. He does not want an arrow in his back or a blade. With a powerful shove, he pushes me forward. "Be silent or I will slit your throat and leave you for the hyenas."

Nami appears, visible only as a darker stain in the dark night. Scar grasps my arm, and Nami growls, a sound low in her throat. "Shut that dog up, or I will kill it," Scar says.

"To me," I say, patting my thigh. At first she does not, keeping her focus on Scar. I pat again, my heart stuttering with fear that she will disobey. It is a moment that seems an eternity until she pads to my side. I exhale, and Scar marches me toward the hillside where I overheard him and his compatriots planning our death.

• • •

I LIE IN the dark of the cave, my hands and feet bound with rawhide strips. What have they done to Nami? It took two men to tie her mouth shut. I am ill with worry for her. I shift, trying to move the cylinder seal my father gave me, which is digging into my chest.

I am not alone. There are sounds of breathing. A familiar stink drifts to me.

"Chiram?" I ask the silence.

He grunts.

I close my eyes.

Chiram shifts. "Where is that good-for-ill, Raph? I thought he was such a mighty warrior."

"Gone," I say. "Back to his people."

"Convenient timing."

I agree, but say nothing. My anger at Raph does nothing for our circumstance. "What do we do?" For a moment I am stunned that this question, this plea, has come from my mouth to Chiram. Never have I turned to him for advice or help, though he has been a presence in my life for its entirety.

There is silence on his part, and I regret my outburst but, finally, he says. "We wait. What else is there to do? Perhaps they will make a mistake."

"And if they do not?"

"We are dead."

I can trust Chiram not to sweeten his words, but the fact is death—at least a quick one—may not be my fate, at least not at first. My mouth is dry as the desert dirt.

Another scent comes to me—blood. "Chiram, are you hurt?"

"Ehh ..."

"Chiram!"

"I did not take kindly to being woken with a blade at my neck."

"Where are you wounded?"

"Well my neck, for one, but that is not serious. That arrogant Babylonian thought I was too fat to move fast." A weak laugh.

"Where else, Chiram?" I insist.

"I imagine there is a lump the size of a salt mound on my head."

"I smell blood."

"Eh, get some rest."

"Maybe I can roll over to you and—"

"Not if they have tied you to a boulder, as they have me." His breathing is labored. "These are no shepherds playing at war, Adir."

"Adira," I say faintly. "My name is Adira."

SO WE LIE in the gravelly dirt, smelling it, tasting it, and feeling the pinch of every pebble as the night crawls its way to dawn.

With the first light, Scar enters with the others—Puzir and Kuri.

Puzir, the taller, speaks. "Now you have had a night to eat dust, we ask you again. Where is the warrior?"

Somehow, Chiram manages to spit through his bloodied lips. "Do not know. Would not tell you if I did."

A hard kick in his back knocks a groan from him.

"Do not hurt him further," I say. "He does not know."

Scar comes and squats beside me, cupping my breast in his hand like an orange. "And do you, sweetling?"

I consider. What would motivate them more—wariness of Raph's return or silver?

The pressure on my breast increases, making me gasp. Silver, I decide. "He is gone to his people."

"Why? And why should we believe you?"

I tell the truth and allow anger to leak into my voice. "He abandoned us to return something of value to his people."

"I knew it!" Kuri rages. "What was it?"

Now I lie. "I do not know. He was too selfish to tell me."

Kuri's fists clench. "She lies! I will beat it from her." He takes a step forward, but Scar puts out an arm to stop him. "What if she does? He is gone and left no track. We have searched and found none."

Scar wipes the back of his hand across his mouth. "Let us return to what's important." He stands and gives me a little kick, not the blow given to Chiram, just a sharp nudge to get my attention.

"We have Fat Man's silver, but what about yours, woman? It was not on your arms or ankles or in your packs. Where is it?"

"I hid it."

Scar gives a scoffing laugh. "When?" I twist my head to see him. My father's knife is tucked in his sash.

I shrug, although it might not be a recognizable gesture from my bound position. "It does not matter. You will never find it."

The blow catches me by surprise and my left ear rings from it. A coppery taste fills my mouth where my teeth stabbed the flesh of my cheek. Another blow meets my silence—this time a kick to my upper abdomen. All the breath rushes from me, and it seems a very long wait for it to return. I hear Chiram cry out in protest and then in pain.

"He does not know," I mutter through torn lips.

This time the blow is to my belly.

Finally, they leave us.

After a while of labored breathing from us both, Chiram asks, "Why do you not tell them? They will keep hurting you."

"If I tell them, and they have what they want, what then?"

A grunt.

"If they beat me to death, they will not find the silver. That secret is all we have."

"They may beat you until you beg for death."

At this I am silent. It is a possibility.

"Where did you hide it?" Chiram asks.

"If I tell you, then they may beat it from you."

"I would not tell those slimy piles of pitch anything!"

"Even to save me from harm?" Why say this? Chiram has never cared whether I lived or died. He shouted at me when I got in his way or stole a piece of food or countless other things.

"A point," he concedes. Then to my surprise, he grumbles. "You were a fine boy; why did you go and become a girl?"

I want to laugh, but it comes out as a choking noise.

"It must have been your mother," Chiram says.

"What?"

"She wanted a boy to give your father."

This was more than Chiram has ever said to me. "I did not know you knew my mother."

"I did. Oh, I did."

There is something in his voice, a longing? Had he cared for my mother?

"I do not remember much about her," I say carefully, afraid he will stop talking.

"She was a beauty, but—"

"What?"

"I have said enough."

"Curse you, Chiram. Tell me about my mother. The truth."

He sighs, a ragged sound. "Why? She is dead."

"Because I am lying bound in a cave and have little to think of but where the next blow will land when those men return. Tell me what you know of my mother."

There was a silence. I hold my breath.

"She was beautiful. Red hair, darker than Mika's. It curled like yours. She wore it mostly in a braid, but down at night."

"How would you know that?" My stomach twists. There is so much I do not know.

"I caught glimpses a time or two when your father lifted the tent flap. She would be waiting for him inside."

Blood drips from the side of my mouth. I wonder if I bleed inside too. The pain is deep.

"Tell me more." It is a demand. I need to know.

He sighs. "She was beautiful and gentle, a helpmate to your father in every way until—"

"Until what, Chiram? What happened to her?"

"When we left to fight against King Chedorlaomer, she was pregnant. She went throughout the camp, telling everyone her son was coming soon and would set things right."

"What did she mean? What was wrong?"

"Nothing was wrong, but the women could not convince her. She seemed to think Zakiti would not return unless she bore him a son. Her mind was not well."

I am uncertain what to do with this knowledge.

"Some said she had fallen under the influence of the desert demons," he says.

"No." I would not believe that.

"She was certain she must have a boy child to make whatever was wrong right again."

"And I was that son."

"I was not there at the birth. She would not have anyone present, save your father. We had only just returned from the fighting, and he would deny her nothing. I can only imagine she was much disturbed when you were not the boy-child she had predicted, or maybe her anguish blinded her, and she thought you were a male. Maybe she made your father swear to proclaim you so. I do not know, but for three summers until she died, she raised you as Zakiti's son."

I marvel at hearing so many words from Chiram. "My father thought to protect me by keeping me as a boy."

"I do not know what nonsense he thought. Maybe he was honoring his oath to his wife. He was a man whose word was more important than his life."

I know that truth as I know my own bones and blood. I swallow. "He taught me to think and act as a boy."

"And so you are here."

"What do you mean?

"It was a son who left his dead father's side to avenge him. A daughter would have followed his wishes and returned to Sarai's tents." Bitterness stains his voice.

I am silent.

CHAPTER

37

What I always feared has happened to me.
What I dreaded has come true.
—Book of Job 3:25

WE LIE THUS THROUGHOUT THE next day. They feed us nothing and only bring a little water. To keep back the blackness that hovers, I live again the night in Mika's arms. Such a tiny moment together, finally acknowledging what we were to each other. I hold it clutched in my mind's palm, a star whose brightness burns back the darkness and burns me with the understanding that it will never be like that again.

I do not ask about Nami. If I show my concern, they may harm her to get me to speak. And I cannot speak until I am ready for death.

"What am I waiting for, Chiram?"

The barest of grunts answers me.

It is a question I revisit when the Babylonians return.

The first kick starts the blood flowing again from my mouth. I can feel my cheekbone shatter and imagine Sarai would not have an easy time wedding me off.

Chiram's groans are subdued, but I scream.

• • •

WHEN THEY ARE at last gone, it is night again, and a wind finds us, bringing the scents of the river. At first its touch is cool and welcome, and then it tears at tender skin. Strange, I have endured what I have endured, yet wind on my skin is unbearable.

"We are near death, Chiram. Tell me—" My lips are so swollen, I am not certain my words are clear enough for him to understand, or why I need to know this. "Tell me why you killed my father's slayer."

His breathing is shallow and labored. "What do you . . . mean?"

"Why did you . . . throw a knife to . . . keep him silent?" It hurts to speak. It hurts to breathe. There are broken things in my chest.

I hear a weak spit. Where does he get the moisture? Perhaps it is blood. "You were about to . . . promise him life—your father's killer."

"You cared so much about my father?"

"He showed me kindness. I fought at his side."

"You loved his wife." I cannot help I know this from only a tone in his voice. My father taught me to hear such things.

A scrabble—nails clawing into the hard gravelly ground—is my only answer.

"One . . . more question, Chiram," I pant, wondering why I do not leave him alone. He is in as great pain as I, perhaps more. In the daylight, his face had been pale as the moon.

"Ask your question."

He did not try to deny he loved my mother.

"Were you truly—?" Pain lances my belly, and I have to pause to wait for it to subside. "Were you going to cook those pups?"

A strangled sound that might have been a laugh worked its way through the mess of his lungs. "I won that . . . dog in a game of stones with a desert chieftain. Thought a pup might take your mind from . . . your herder dog."

I say nothing more. The wet salt that makes its way over the bruised mounds and open wounds on my face and into my mouth is not all blood.

CHAPTER

38

My God, my God, why have you abandoned me?
Why are you so far away when I groan for help?
—Book of Psalms 22:2

I HAVE LOST THE FLOW OF time. Days slip into night and then back to day in an endless loop, and sometimes I cannot even remember why I am holding onto the secret these men want. Or what it is. I cannot tell one part of my body from another. All is pain. *Oh, Father, the moon has fallen from the sky. . . .*

Chiram is silent. There is nothing left to say.

A shadow on the cave floor tells me someone has come. I blink, only able to open my eyes in a narrow slit. Light frames the man who stands in the cave opening.

Like an angel.

Mika holding the blue fire.

But it is not Mika; it is Scar. Today, he is my angel because he will help me die. I remember the secret today, and I will tell him. I will tell him where I hid the silver, and he will kill me. It is a good thing to leave this world, this pain. *I am sorry, Father, that I could not live up to the meaning of my name, that I could not be strong or honor my oath to go to Sarai. My own choices have brought me to this place. Forgive me.*

Scar steps deeper into the cave, closer. Puzir follows.

I open my mouth to tell him before he can strike, but I cannot remember how to speak. I want to laugh; it is such a simple thing, speaking. What are the words? I focus. I need the words first, before I speak them. That is the problem. *The silver is—*

My body shatters into shards of agony. I do not know if he has struck me with a fist or kicked me. The words I had so carefully prepared fragment in my mind, skittering back into the darkness. I reach after them. *No!*

But they are gone.

"Where?" Scar shouts.

I try to look at him to plead with him by meeting his gaze, to tell him I am trying to remember what he wants. He lifts his arm, his face purple with rage or drink, and then it drains to white. He stands in the brilliant light for a long moment before I see the arrow's tip protruding through his chest. As Scar falls forward between Chiram and me, Puzir turns, drawing his sword.

His blade is not clear of the scabbard when another slices obliquely across his neck and wrist, leaving a wet, red line. He staggers, met by a short thrust up through his sternum. The straight blade of a long knife yanks free as he falls, sprawling, over the back of Scar's legs.

I cannot comprehend what has happened. Only that two of my tormentors now lie beside me, and I can see a portion of a leg of the silently downed third just outside the cave entrance.

A figure squats at my side; a hand touches my cheek. I can barely feel it. That is good. I do not want to feel . . . ever again.

"Adira?" He speaks my name gently, but I am unable to speak his, though I know it. *Raph.*

"I am so sorry, Adira. So very sorry."

He gathers me into his arms, and an avalanche of pain crushes me into darkness.

FROM TIME TO time, I rise from black oblivion to see the sky above me, mostly the stars or the branches of a tree where Raph has us rest in the day's heat. I remain in the cart, trying to swallow the water or broth that Raph holds to my lips, his hand supporting my head. Even when

I slip back into the darkness, I am aware of a pressure against my side, an anxious low whine-song. I cannot reach for Nami, but I know she is there. Sometimes I feel her tongue on my wounds, though I cannot bear the pressure on my face, and I pass out from it.

THIS TIME I wake to the sight of smooth, plastered walls. I turn my head slightly to see Raph, his beautiful face clean of travel dust, but drawn and lined with concern. He speaks in a low voice to another man, who carries a leather hide bag similar to the one Mika carries.

"Will she live?" Raph asks.

The man shrugs. "If she has the will, she might." He pauses. "But she might not wish to."

"What do you mean?"

"The bones of one side of her face are crushed. I can do little, but help her pain. And I believe she has internal wounds. I greatly doubt she will ever bear children. What man will want her?"

I hear the words, and they are like a fist in my belly. *No children?* My world has always been filled with travel and trading. I delighted in new cities, learning new languages and customs. Settling with a man and having a family were something for the distant future, but now I understand I will never have such a future. I feel its loss as a deep, keen ache.

Raph looks over at me and sees my eyes are open. He strides to my bed and kneels beside me. I lie in a real bed, I notice, like the one Mika and I lay in atop the goddess's temple. "Where?" I mumble. My mouth seems not to cooperate with my mind's direction, but Raph understands.

"At the palace in Mari. The king has received you in the name of Samsu-iluna."

It is as though I have been traveling far from the world. Every concept is strange.

"Nami?"

Hearing her name, she rises from her place beside the bed, slipping her head beneath my hand.

Raph strokes her shoulder. "She would not leave your side. Those Babylonians kept her tied, but they knew her worth and gave her food and water."

I nod only slightly. My head feels very large, as if it belongs to someone else, and I cannot breathe well from one side of my nose. I am afraid to touch my face, though the pain feels distant. That is a great relief.

"I found your knife," Raph says. "It is with your things."

Trust Raph to think of that. I find comfort knowing that small piece of my father is still mine.

"And Chiram?" My mouth is thick, swollen, and the words are distorted.

Raph looks down and then back at me. "He was dead when I arrived."

I close my eyes. Chiram followed me into the desert, slew my father's slayer, never pushed me to tell where I hid the silver. What kind of man was this man I despised my entire life? I swallow. "Did you bury him?"

"I did not have time, Adira. I did not know if you would survive."

"Go back and bury him."

"If you wish, but not until you are well enough to travel, and I see you to the tents of Abram."

Chiram would be only bones by then, but I can see Raph will not budge on this. The tents of Abram. Yes, that is where I must go to honor my oath. Mika has made his choice, and I must make mine. I signal Raph to lean close. "When you go, find the protruding stone that hangs over the river just behind our encampment. Beneath it, tied to a submerged rock, are my bracelets of silver." I pause to be certain he is listening carefully and, I admit, to rest. Even the act of speaking is an effort.

He waits.

"Those rings did not save Chiram, but they kept me alive. Perhaps they have more to do." I realize I am talking a little wildly, but Raph only nods. "I promise," he says. "Now rest."

"Wait." Uttering so many words has exhausted me, but I take his hand, noticing two of my fingers are heavily bandaged. "Why did you return, Raph?"

"I did not want to leave you, but I had to protect my people's legacy." He answers in a low voice. "I hid it, as you did your silver. I will return to it when you are safe and take it home."

The world begins to fuzz at the edges. "That is good," I say. "I want to go home too." But home has always been wherever my father and the caravan were, and that place has dissolved like a dune of sand in the wind.

PART

CANAAN, 1747 BCE

39

There is no permanence. Do we build a house to stand forever; do we seal a contract to hold for all time? Do brothers divide an inheritance to keep forever; do we the flood-time of rivers endure? It is only the nymph of the dragon-fly who sheds her larva and sees the sun in his glory.

—Anonymous, Ur

WHAT WOULD MY FATHER THINK to see his "daughter of the wind"? That is the first thought that arises as we come into sight of the spreading oak trees of Mamre in Canaan. I am glad he cannot see me. Only the wind can look upon me now without flinching. Raph does well at it, but he is used to me. He was true to his word and stayed with me two moons until I healed. I was still weak, but he was eager to get me here, so he could go back and find his dreaming stone.

I am not eager to face Abram or Sarai or Ishmael. What will my childhood friend think to discover I am a woman, and one with the face of a demon spirit? We often played at discovering one, poking a stick in its hiding place and then running away, screaming in terrified delight at the idea of being chased by it.

Enough, I tell myself. It is not as if I have lost a great beauty. My right cheek is sunken. Two of my fingers have healed in an awkward manner and do not bend correctly. My right eye sees only a blur and my hip and leg ache, causing me to limp, but everything else has healed to the outside perspective.

Inside is another matter.

Philot stops to bray at the scent of other donkeys and sheep ahead. The vibration shakes his whole body and me along with it. I smile.

"It is good to see you smile," Raph says, looking over at me. He walks beside us, his golden hair gleaming in the sun.

I know my mouth is slightly crooked from the pull of skin on the sunken cheek, but what is that? A smile is a smile, an acknowledgment of the peculiarities life brings to startle us out of our desperation. Here I was, but a moment before, sunk in a morass of pity for myself, fear of the future, fear of the past—and my little donkey shakes it away with one bray. If only he could shake away my fears for Mika. They have occupied every step of this journey. What will happen if Mika was wrong about which enemy attacks Babylonia?

What if he was right?

SARAI CONSIDERS ME. We have done with the greetings, the customary food and drink and cursory explanations. Raph has gone. Abram and Ishmael are out checking on the herds. The slaves who were about the duties of the household have been dismissed.

Sarai sits on a stool. Where I would normally be at her feet in deference, I also have a stool because of my injuries. An early lamb that has been hand-nursed lies at her feet. The lamb remains, half asleep, as Nami strides over to inspect her from nose to tail. Nami is not a herd dog, but she understands sheep and goats and calves are not prey, especially when they are in a human's tent. She investigates the rest of the area, the beautiful woven rugs, bronze and copper urns, and the slender, hipless statuette of Asherah, consort of El or of Baal, if one is a city dweller. Nami finishes her inspection and returns to lie at my side with her forepaws crossed.

A slave enters with a strong tea, which she pours into cups. Her eyes carefully do not find my face. I imagine word has spread like the flooding Nile across the encampment.

Sarai has been working on a mending project, but she puts it down in her lap when the slave leaves us, and looks at me. Even now, with silver threading her hair, she is a beautiful woman. Her gray eyes are still luminous and her cheekbones strong, though her lips have a stern line to them and her hands are mottled with brown spots.

I know what she sees, looking at me. I am thankful I do not have to look at myself.

"Here we are," she says, a beginning to a difficult conversation that has creased tiny lines at the corner of her mouth and a furrow of brows above her expressive eyes. I can see how she captivated the Egyptian king. It is telling of her character that she does not begin by offering sorrow at my father's death or my own trials. Sarai is a woman who suffers no wallowing, and this is fine with me. I do not want her pity. I blink, realizing I have been lost in my own thoughts. I must appear stupid as well as disfigured.

"You are still of an age to be a girl, Adira, but I believe I speak to a woman. You have seen much."

She cannot know how much I have seen, and I have no urge to tell her.

"I am grateful for the refuge of your tents," I say. My words come out with some distortion, though I speak slowly and try to overcome the difficulty.

She sits straighter. "We are your family. We owe you more than simply refuge."

"I have been told I cannot bear children." I wish us clear on that. A woman who cannot bear children has little worth in this world. I never cared about such before. My thoughts centered on all that the world offered to see and explore. But now that my step has slowed, I can imagine myself old and alone with no daughter to comfort me, no son to protect me.

Sarai's chortle seems to draw from a deep well of sorrow and irony. It is a contradiction that gives me pause. So long have I been wrapped in my own grief, I have forgotten it was Sarai's barrenness that caused her to give Hagar to Abram as a second wife.

Sarai presses a long finger to her mouth, as if signaling me to secrecy. "We are both barren then, for different reasons, yet I have been told I will bear a son to carry on the covenant that El has made with Abram."

This is the first I have heard thus. "Is Ishmael not Abram's son?"

Sarai's face tightens. "He is, of course." Her hand momentarily clenches the pile of wool in her lap. "I think it is all nonsense. I am too old to bear children."

I am bold when I should be discreet. "Who has said you will bear a son?" This seems very unlikely, given her age.

"According to my husband, El has said it."

I am curious. "You think the word of El is nonsense?"

Sarai meets my gaze without the slightest discomfort. "All the gods are fickle."

I have heard this said in the lands of Babylonia where the rivers ebb and wane and flood with capriciousness. In Egypt, where the Nile's flood can be marked to the precise day and hour, the gods are viewed as steadfast. This, I see for the first time, is reflected in the characters of Sarai and Hagar. Hagar is always hopeful and sees tomorrow as a better day. Sarai is practical and plans for the disaster sure to come.

Sarai strokes the fine wool cloth in her lap. "But I have a little more faith in the potions El's messenger left me."

Would Mika be that messenger? If so, she must mean he gave her herbs the last time my father and I had been here. Or perhaps the third wise man had been the one to give them to her. "Is there any sign?" I ask.

A quiet and beautiful smile melts the sternness from her face. "I will swear you to secrecy with my handmaids."

I nod.

"My moon blood has returned."

This is not exactly a pregnancy, but it is a miracle no less, though I have heard women sometimes stop their moon blood and then start it again. My own has ceased, not from age, of course, but from the blows my belly received. Quickly, I focus my attention back to Sarai, unwilling to return, even in my mind, to that dark cave.

"That is a hopeful sign," I say.

With a trace of smugness, she picks up her mending. "We will see. If I give birth, I will have to suckle the child before all the women to prove it is my own."

This I do not doubt.

"Meanwhile, there is much to do, including finding you a suitable husband."

I want to laugh . . . and cry. "That may be a challenge greater than having a child."

She looks at me critically, seeing all the damage of my flesh and perhaps some that is deeper. "We will see."

CHAPTER

40

For in his days the angels of the Lord descended upon earth—those who are named the Watchers—that they should instruct the children of men that they should do judgment and uprightness upon earth.

—Book of Jubilees

I AM RESTLESS IN THE TENTS with the women, awkward at the tasks assigned to me with my stiff fingers and uncomfortable under the quickly averted gazes. No one speaks of what has happened to me, as if my past is a large hole in the earth everyone avoids.

It is a black fissure for me as well, but when I encounter it, I stop and stare down into its abyss. My father is down there. And Chiram. I never understood how important Chiram was to me. I am still not sure how this is so.

Raph is gone and Mika—I cannot begin to accept that he is no longer part of my life, though it is truth. I see now that what I loved in Raph was what I imagined. But Mika—my love for Mika formed bit by bit, growing from tiny seeds planted in the desert, its roots spreading so unobtrusively that its bloom, at last, was a surprise. Mere distance or time cannot unwind them. His love has changed me as surely as what happened in the cave.

Nami stays by my side, knowing, as she somehow always does, that I need her.

• • •

I SEEK THE refuge and comfort of the herds, sitting alone until Ishmael finds me. It is the first time we have been alone together since my return.

"What happened to your face?" he asks, staring at my cheek.

Startled that this question comes first, I look at him. "A man kicked me and shattered the bones."

Ishmael's mouth tightens. "I will kill him."

"He is already dead."

"Then I will pray to El that his children and his children's children are tormented by demons."

Ishmael's frankness and loyalty melt some of the pain in my chest I thought permanently lodged there. "Thank you, Ishmael."

Taking a seat on the rock beside me, he pulls out a fine bronze knife and reaches down for a stick to sharpen. "Why did you not tell me you were a girl?" he demands, now that we have dispensed with priorities.

"Because it was my father's wish that it be a secret."

He mulls over this. "If you had told me, I would have kept it secret."

I smile. Ishmael and I are like siblings, though we did not see one another for long periods. I was older and showed him how to read the silent language of the donkeys, goats, and sheep, and how to train a dog to herd them.

He applies the blade to the stick and begins to strip off the bark. "Now what are you going to do?"

"It is up to Sarai. If she finds a miracle man who will agree to wed a monstrosity who cannot bear him children, then I will be a wife. Otherwise, I do not know."

When have I decided this? When did marriage become a haven, the place of refuge and safety my father always considered it? A new thought arises, born of this moment. What would stop me from changing back into a man's dress and starting a business somewhere as a merchant or buying a caravan, as Chiram had envisioned? My heart begins to beat, as if it had been a dead thing startled into life, but with it stirs a demon of fear born in a cave across the desert. My childhood efforts with Ishmael to tweak a demon from its hiding place may have resulted only in squeals of imagined terror, but now one rises before me, clawed paws spread wide, mouth agape.

"I will marry you," Ishmael announces.

Again, his loyalty is a healing balm. "I am honored, Ishmael, but you are your father's only heir, and El has promised to make of him a nation of people. You must bear him sons."

Ishmael's blade takes a savage bite from the wood. "Then I will take another wife for that."

I start to protest and then close my mouth. What can I say? His own mother is second wife to Abram and has borne him a child when Sarai could not. It is not an uncommon practice here and in Babylonia.

Then a lance of cold spears my spine, despite the sun's warmth. What would happen to Ishmael should Sarai conceive and give Abram an heir? I know the tale of Sarai's wrath when Hagar boasted she was with child and publicly bragged she was now the favored wife. Hagar may have been a slave, but she had been a king's slave and always carried herself with the pride or implied superiority of the Egyptians.

But Hagar had underestimated Sarai's power. Blood bound Abram and Sarai, as well as vows. Sarai was, after all, not only Abram's wife, but also his half-sister. She had been with him all his life, traveled with him from Ur and then to Egypt, where she lied to the king for his life. He owed her much.

After Hagar's insult, Sarai had gone to Abram. He acknowledged her position as mistress of the household, which included life-and-death authority over the slaves, servants, and their children. In a rage, Sarai confronted Hagar and beat her, and pregnant Hagar fled into the wilderness.

Of course, Sarai relented, and Hagar returned unharmed, but strangely convinced that El had saved her and anointed the child she carried to be the father of a people. She spoke of this to the other servants, who joked, behind her hearing, that the sun had addled her. As it was not a public declaration, Sarai was able to ignore it.

This household, I decided, had as much drama as that performed between the gods in the temples of Ur and Babylon.

I put a hand on Ishmael's arm to get his attention. "Ishmael, what would you do with your life if you were not Abram's heir?"

"What?"

"Just a game," I say. "What would you do if you could choose?"

Ishmael blinks. He has his mother's long, thick eyelashes, black hair, and Abram's dark, luminous eyes. I am certain Hagar would find a willing bride for him.

At my question, those eyes light with the same fire as his father's when he spoke of El. "If I were not heir, I would leave these donkeys, cattle, and sheep and become a merchant like you, travel the world. I want to see all the lands you have seen—the great temples of Babylon and gold-capped tombs of Egypt. I would travel to the middle of the sea and to the desert's heart." Excitement lifted his voice. "I would not have to sit and listen to your stories. I would have stories of my own!"

A portion of my worry eases. Ishmael could do these things if Sarai bore an heir. He would be free. He could lift his head to the wind and taste whatever mysteries and surprises it might bring him.

Just then, Nami leaps to her feet and before I can stop her, she is off.

"What is it?" Ishmael cries, jumping up and dropping the stick he had been sharpening. His knife remains in his hand.

"She has seen something. I do not know what."

Nami stretches out across the grass-tufted plain, her ears swept back like black pennants. I start to call her, but she is so beautiful, so full of grace and so happy to be chasing something, I do not, even though she heads for a herd of cattle.

"A wolf?" Ishmael asks, his hand tightening on the knife.

I shade my eyes. "Could be." But we both know wolves hunt at night. Though our legs are still, we are running with Nami. She carries our yearning for a future and freedom.

Suddenly, Nami dashes left and then right—into the middle of the cattle, which scatter with deep bellows of protest. Nami is oblivious. Her prey, whatever it may be, is in her sight and even if I tried to call her, she would not heed me. Ishmael and I both watch, entranced by her swift turns, thrilled when she flattens out for a straight run. I think we both can feel the wind in her face.

She has left the area where the cattle pasture. We lose sight of her in the high grass, but track her by the startled movement of bleating sheep. Ishmael climbs a stone.

"Can you see her?" I rise to my toes.

"No . . . wait, yes. I think she is close to whatever she chases."

So intent are we, neither of us has heard anyone approach, and we are startled when a long arm reaches out to grab Ishmael's.

"What in the name of the Queen of Heaven?"

It is Eliezer, Abram's steward. Everyone, with the possible exception of Sarai and Abram, fears Eliezer.

Ishmael blanches at the grip on his arm.

"What is happening?" Eliezer demands. His anger reddens the small, sickle-shaped scar on his forehead. Fear spears my heart. The sickle is a sign of the god of death in Babylonia. No wonder Eliezer is shunned. I feel my bones go to water. Eliezer's anger has raised my own god of death—Scar.

Eliezer squeezes Ishmael's arm. "Why are the cattle and sheep running all over the place?"

I cannot speak, but he is not looking at me.

"They are your responsibility, Ishmael!"

"I—" Ishmael begins, but I interrupt him with a hoarse voice and my distorted speech. "It is not his fault; it is my dog that has disrupted the herds." My body is rigid, waiting for the blow to come.

Eliezer barely glances at me and does not loosen his hold on Ishmael. His fierce scowl under thick black brows suddenly reminds me of Chiram, and some of my panic fades, though my heart still pounds in my chest and my mouth is dry.

"Call your dog!" he demands.

"I cannot," I say.

He does not spit, as Chiram would, but now fixes me directly in the path of his piercing scorn. "Why not? What kind of worthless dog do you own?"

Flames scorch my cheeks, and my own anger—ignited in defense of Nami—burns away what remains of the fear. "My dog is worth more than all your herds."

One of those dark brows rise, reminding me now of Tabni. "Is that a truth?" His sarcasm seems muted by surprise that I do not flinch from him. Not many dare Eliezer's wrath.

At that moment, Nami appears with a fat, bloody hare in her mouth. Proudly, she trots to me and drops her prize at my feet.

Eliezer releases his hold on Ishmael. "Well—" He seems lost for the rest of what he planned to say.

"She is a hunter, not a herder." I rest my hand on Nami's slender head. Reaching down, I grab the hare by its ears and hold it out to him. "Perhaps Hagar would appreciate this for her pot?"

When Eliezer and the hare are at a distance, Ishmael gives me an appreciative look. "I have never heard anyone talk to Eliezer like that." He grins.

I grin back, not mentioning that my skin is slick with sweat.

Then we are rolling in the grass, laughing so hard tears leak from our eyes. Nami, panting from her exertions, watches us with perplexed concern.

41

Then one of them [the angels] said, "I will return to you about this time next year, and your wife, Sarah, will have a son!"

Sarah was listening to this conversation from the tent. Abraham and Sarah were both very old by this time, and Sarah was long past the age of having children. So she laughed silently to herself and said, "How could a worn-out woman like me enjoy such pleasure, especially when my master—my husband—is also so old?"

—Book of Genesis 18:10-12

AND SO, I HAVE SPENT most of the spring on Mamre's hills, and Sarai has kindly allowed me to spend much of my time helping Ishmael with the herds. In many ways, though Ishmael is older than Shem, he reminds me of my young desert boy. I hope Shem will one day have his own herd of white camels.

Sarai has required only that I learn cooking skills from Hagar, who is as kind to me as ever, and that I continue my lessons with Ishmael and the other children, as we have always done. I am glad to apply my mind to reciting the familiar stories. Sarai requires we memorize them all. I enjoy the poetry of Ur, especially the *Epic of Gilgamesh* and the "Lament for Ur." They are beautiful and magnificent and sad. In a strange way, feeling the poets' despair gives me respite from my own.

Ishmael also lifts my spirits. He does not stare at my ruined face anymore, but simply accepts it, a gift for which I am grateful. This simple thing—along with the tug of wind in my hair, the sun's caress, the frolic of kids and lambs, the uncomplicated self-interest of the donkeys, and Nami's steadfast presence—gradually begins to heal the wounds that lie beneath my flesh.

The air begins to thicken with summer when Sarai calls me into her tent. I enter and take the short stool that has become my customary seat when we are at lessons. Nami settles at my feet. My fingers work on the mats in the silken hair behind her ears. With a deep sigh, she rests her head on my foot. I do not share her contentment. A tall man with red hair fills my mind's eye. What is Mika doing? Is he safe? I ask every stranger or traveler for word of what has happened in Babylonia—Mika being never far from my thoughts—but have learned little.

Sarai studies me for a few moments, and I remain still beneath her scrutiny until she sighs. "I have pondered what to do for you, Adira."

I cannot but wonder if she has more pondered what to do *with* me, but I do not say this.

"I am happy here watching the herds with Ishmael."

A slight flinch tells me I have identified one of the thorns that prickle her. Ishmael must marry a woman who can bear him children. She is not blind to Ishmael's fondness for me. I cannot stay here. As much as Sarai wishes to have her own child, she is first loyal to Abram and to the vision of making a people for El, regardless of her private scoffing of the gods.

I take a deep breath. "So you have found a husband for me?" I hardly dare imagine who that might be—an ancient widower breathing his last? Why waste the dowry, which Abram will have to supply? But I am silent.

"I have found you a husband."

I wait. It is what I want, is it not? If I cannot stay here, I want the safety of a husband, perhaps one who already has children I can love as my own.

"It is a match of great prestige and honors your father."

"Who is he?"

"He is Abram's own nephew."

Abram's nephew? I know only of three, and all are married. "Am I to be a second wife?" This is a solution, but hardly an honor to my father's memory.

"His favorite nephew, in truth," Sarai says and answers my unspoken question. "And no, you are not to be a second wife."

"I thought Lot was Abram's dearest nephew." It was Lot who had followed Abram from Haran, even to Egypt and back to Canaan. Abram had led men into battle to retrieve Lot from the arms of the king who had taken him into slavery. Then, to solve the inevitable arguments over grazing land, Abram had given Lot lands to the south. Of course, they only "belonged" to Abram in the eyes of El, but that was no matter. Lot was a man of wealth, thanks to Abram's generosity, and had bought the lands from those who had never heard of Abram and his claim.

"Lot *is* Abram's dearest nephew," Sarai says. Her fingers twist together in her lap, a rare sign of discomfort.

"If I am not to be a second wife, then I am confused. Lot has a wife. Hurriya. I met her in Sodom."

Sarai sighs and her eyes, at last, meet mine. "Hurriya is dead."

I take a quick breath. "How?"

"She fell from a cliff."

I remember Hurriya as an overly ample woman. "What was she doing on a cliff?"

"I do not know."

A long silence passes between us.

"Do you have any other questions?" Sarai asks.

"What? Oh, yes." My hand lifts to my face. "Does he know?"

"Yes."

"Then why would he take me?"

Sarai's slender hands fold together. "He has children, and you are the only child of Zakiti, an honorable man of our tribe and family, well thought of, and your father has left you with a fine dowry."

I look up. This is the first I have heard such. "He has?" I had thought Chiram brought what wealth my father had left for me.

"Each time he came here, your father added to your dowry and asked me to keep it safe for you."

Tears fill my eyes at my father's love, but they do not fall. My eyes are dry. Lot has children, but they are older than I. Perhaps we can be as sisters. They will marry soon, if they have not already, and bear children. I will have a family again.

· · ·

THE NEXT DAY I am told Abram himself will bless me. I wait outside his tent, but the sides are rolled up, and I cannot help overhearing him speak with Eliezer.

"She will be fine, Eliezer. Sodom cannot be such a terrible place if Lot is happy there."

"Lot is content because he gets to play the role of Abram's beloved nephew. I am telling you, it is not a place that will welcome a stranger."

"Yes, you did have a bad experience there, but Eliezer, not everyone is alike. There are good and bad men in every city."

"I wash my hands of it then. Bless the child well; she will need it."

I step aside as Eliezer stomps from the tent, not giving me a glance as I enter.

"Father?" I say, giving Abram the respectful title of the family's head. Abram waves me inside. "Enter, Adira."

He sits on a pillow, and I sit opposite him, trying not to wince as I lower myself down, wishing for the little stool Sarai provides for me.

"You are still in pain?" His eyes may be old, but they do not miss much. "A little."

"I would give my right arm to have saved you that, child."

I bow my head. "I am not worthy of such, Father."

He chuckles. "Your father certainly thought so. He spoke of you as if you were the perfect pearl in the oyster's heart. Come closer."

I do, kneeling before him. His hands cover my head like an anointing of oil. A shiver runs down my spine at his touch. He calls on El to bless me and my womb and charges me to bear children to add to El's people and to honor my god and my people and my husband with my obedience.

I will try to be an obedient wife. I will try. For my father's sake.

LOT COMES, AT length, to claim me.

"Let us know if the size of his thumbs is a true reflection of his manhood," one of Sarai's young handmaidens giggles in my ear as they dress and veil me in fine white linen. I remember my curiosity about Lot's thumbs as a child. It is of no interest to me now, other than to hope lying with him will not be painful.

At our wedding, Abram himself asks El's blessings on us.

I feel many things—my oath to my father, my fears, and my hopes. I am not eager for Lot's touch, but I know most women go to the bed of a husband chosen by their family. I am no blushing youth, hoping for a handsome young man, nor even a wiser woman hoping love will grow from respect and intimacy. I am wife to an older widower, a second wife in truth, if not by the letter.

Lot insists Nami not share the bridal bed, so we are alone this night. Incense sweetens the air of our tent, and flower petals adorn the floor. I am reminded yet again of the sacred union with Mika and hope for some tenderness. But when Lot lifts the veil to behold his bride, he flinches—despite the warnings I am certain he has been given—and turns aside, drinking wine until he sprawls unconscious across the bed, crushing the petals.

I listen to his snores until the wild doves announce the morning, torn between relief, and regret that I will never again be the goddess for Mika . . . or any man.

MY HEART IS somewhat lightened when I learn Ishmael and Eliezer will accompany us part of the way on our journey to Sodom. Abram and Sarai and Hagar come out to see us off. Sarai oversaw the packing of my dowry—fine clothes, rugs, and jewelry from Father's travels. I am quite wealthy, but these things, though a reflection of his love, are not my father. Instead of filling my heart, they merely make it ache for him.

Abram lays a hand on my head in a final blessing. "I have asked El to watch over his messengers as you asked, Adira, and I offered a pair of doves for your safety," he says in that quiet, intense voice that always seems to hold me motionless.

I am grateful he remembered my request and honored he has made a sacrifice to El for my sake. "Thank you."

Hagar waits a step away, but when Abram and Sarai are finished, she takes me into her arms. "Be safe, child," she whispers and holds me for a long while. Perhaps I am primed by thoughts of my father, but my throat closes in her embrace and, for a moment, I have a mother. When she finally releases me, she presses a package into my hands. "Honey cakes," she says, and I see her eyes, too, are brimming. "I made extra."

"They are the best, Hagar. They always have been."

She smiles and sniffles. "I know."

. . .

LOT HAS NOT allowed his trip for a bride to interfere with business, and we take five black donkeys with us. They are prize animals and will bring a nice price, though perhaps he will keep a female or two to expand his own herd. He leads the way, riding a donkey like he is a king, but the rest of us walk. He has not given me a glance, and I am just as glad.

Ishmael matches my slower, limping pace at the rear of the herd, helping me keep an eye on them. "We can only go as far as En Gedi," he says.

"Why?"

"Eliezer cannot enter the city."

I wait for the explanation that must follow such an odd statement.

Ishmael pauses, making a show of checking Eliezer's location, to heighten the suspense of his story. Then he rubs his chin, which makes me laugh, as he has no hair there yet to itch. "You have been to Sodom, so you know how they are to strangers."

"It has been almost two summers since I was in Sodom. We stayed at Lot's house. It was during the Spring Rites, and I went among them only once afterward."

"And what was your experience?"

"I stopped only at one place—at a rug merchant's shop."

"And he welcomed you as a customer?"

"He was nasty."

Ishmael smiles knowingly. "They are all like that."

"Why?"

He shrugs. "My mother says it is because of the famine. They hold tight to everything and are suspicious of strangers. Beggars are not allowed in the city."

"But the famine was many years ago, and the whole land suffered," I protest. "And hospitality to strangers is a sacred duty."

"True, but after the famine, the kings from the east came and took everything, all the young men and women as slaves, every bit of wealth and food and all their livestock. Mother says it is no great wonder the cities are wary of strangers."

"But Eliezer is no stranger. He fought with Abram to win back all the cities' wealth and rescue their people. He should be a hero."

"He was," Ishmael said, "but as the summers passed, many forgot, and their attitude toward outsiders hardened. Once, he encountered a man who did not recognize him. The man spoke to him in an insulting way, and Eliezer responded in kind. The Sodomite struck him with a brick."

I remember the scar on Eliezer's forehead.

"What did Eliezer do?"

"He took the man before a judge and claimed damages. The man counter-claimed that Eliezer had asked him for a bloodletting for some ailment and then not paid him."

"That is outrageous!"

"Yes, but the judge found in favor of the local man."

I eye Eliezer's straight, unyielding back. "I would wager that did not lie well with him."

"No."

"What did he do?"

Ishmael grins. "He struck the judge in the forehead with his walking stick and demanded to be paid for a bloodletting."

I laugh in delight. Nami looks up at my outburst, checking to make certain all is well.

"It took intervention from Abram to save him," Ishmael continues, when I am again paying attention. "So you can see why Eliezer cannot set foot inside Sodom."

"At least not until that judge dies."

"At least until then," Ishmael agrees with a smile.

We walk in companionable silence as the sun rises and drinks the morning moisture.

"What are you thinking?" Ishmael asks.

"Only about the sun."

He shades his eyes. "It will be hot today."

Again, I laugh. "A fine prediction, worthy of a shaman. Ishmael, only you would say such a thing."

Ishmael looks smug. He does have a sharp-witted tongue, and I hope Sarai and Hagar find him a wife who will appreciate him.

We do not talk of my marriage but, at length, I say, "Ishmael, there is a thing I wish to know."

"What?"

"How did Lot's first wife die?"

"She fell from a cliff."

"Sarai told me that. What else do you know?"

He shrugs. "What else is there to know?"

"Why did she climb a cliff?"

"Maybe searching for a lamb?"

I sigh. Ishmael translates everything into the world he knows.

"Ishmael, she did not watch a flock. She lived inside the city and over-saw the house and took care of her daughters. The river runs near their house. There was no need to climb anywhere."

"Perhaps she just wanted to see what was up there?"

Although this would have been perfectly true of me—at least before the Babylonian guards robbed me of my agility—the thought of Hurriya doing so seems as unlikely as Lot taking me as wife. I frown. "Perhaps."

42

So the Lord told Abraham, "I have heard a great outcry from Sodom and Gomorrah, because their sin is so flagrant."

—Genesis 18:20

A S SOON AS ELIEZER AND Ishmael turn back, I miss their company, even the stoic Eliezer. Lot pays me less attention than he did when he thought I was Zakiti's son. I find a bit of comfort in the beautiful staff Ishmael gifted me, made from a branch of one of the sacred oak trees of Mamre. It helps with my injured leg, especially negotiating rugged terrain. And, of course, I have Nami. She runs off periodically, but always returns and presses against my leg to let me know she loves me and has only gone to investigate the terrain. She did not do this before my injuries.

We descend the steep hillside, an agony for me, and a feat I could not have managed without Lot's decision to allow me to ride the donkey, more out of frustration at my pace than consideration for me. We cross the plains south of the Dead Sea into the Vale. I try to keep my mind from dwelling on the previous trip when each stolen glimpse of Raph made my heart gallop. So much has happened since that time! How can I be the same person? I know I am not. I am a stranger to myself.

All but two of the donkeys are to be left at Lot's tents. When we arrive, I look out on the rich grasslands and breathe deeply. On the journey here,

I have remembered the stench of Sodom. How did I think I would be happy inside a city? But what choice did I have? Sarai made it clear I could not stay with them, fearing Ishmael would insist on marrying me. And I swore to my father I would follow her wishes for me. Lot is a wealthy man, Abram's favored nephew. No one can say she has not done wisely and generously for me. Yet, I grasp at the chance to live where I can breathe freely. The winds here do not carry the taint of the city or the belching pitch pits. These are Lot's lands. I could be useful here as his wife.

I approach Lot. "Husband," I say, trying out the word for the first time.

He jerks, as if the word is a slap. "What is it? Do you want for something?"

"No." This is a lie. I want for many things—my father, Mika, my life with the caravan, my leg and face whole, but it is foolish to want these things that can never be. "I am well," I say instead. "But I do have a request."

He narrows his eyes.

I angle my face as if I am staring off into the hills, so he sees only the damaged side to remind him of what he will have to gaze upon every day if I stay with him in the city. "I ask to stay here and watch over your . . . our flocks. That is my greatest skill. I fear I am not skilled in keeping a household."

Lot reaches down and plucks a blade of grass, chewing on it. Then he folds his hands across his belly and taps his thumbs together while he considers my request.

"It would make me happy to be here," I add, hoping he has some interest in that, as he apparently has no interest in taking me to bed. This would be a great offense if I were able to bear a child, but I am not, so what does it matter? I do not care to lie with him either.

After a moment, Lot unlaces his fingers and takes the grass blade from his mouth. "No," he says. "You must come with me to the city."

"Why?"

"I need to have a wife present in my house."

That is all he will say. I bite my tongue to restrain my anger. I can see from the veil that falls over his eyes he has some reason he will not share with me for his pronouncement, and no arguing or tears on my part will change his decision.

. . .

TAKING CARE TO skirt the oily pits of pitch, we approach the gates of Sodom. As we pass one black pool, a large bubble catches my attention. Fascinated, I watch it swell, the surface thinning into an oval egg glistening with rainbow colors until finally it bursts. I cough at the noxious smells released.

Lot laughs. "You will become accustomed to it."

I cannot imagine. When I was here before, I endured it, knowing it was only for a short visit, but now I enter the gates of my future home.

Just beyond them is the wide plaza, called simply, I recall, "the Gate," as the foyer in a home is known as the "little gate." The Gate is where much of the city meets to do business or to converse with neighbors. Beyond that sits the temple of Asherah and her Baal, not nearly so imposing as Ishtar's temple. Beside the temple is the king's palace, again a pale reflection of Babylon's. The bricks here are plain, simply covered in a limestone wash. No dyes or beautiful colored tiles adorn the walls; no canals pierce the city's center. The people wear drab clothing, as if unwilling to draw attention. I remember what Ishmael said, and I see Sodom with new eyes. It is a city scarred by famine and fear before my birth; abandoned by the gods when the rivers dried up; and razed by enemies who descended upon it like locusts.

I expect some greeting from the people of Sodom. Lot is a wealthy man, and surely, being the nephew of Abram, one of influence here, but people turn from him or stare with cold gazes.

"Why are they not welcoming you?" I ask.

"They tire of my preaching."

"Preaching?"

"Since the angels of El came, I tell them of El's way, and they despise me for it."

I look up at the goddess's temple as we pass by. Here, at least, an attempt at beauty has been made. There is greenery around the courtyard, and the gates are open. Any man can come here and lie with a holy woman. It is a sacred act that reinforces the fertility of the fields. During the culminating day of the Spring Rite, the chief priestess lies with the king to ensure winter's hold on the land is not eternal, that new life will press up through the darkness of the soil. This has been the way for so long, no one can remember a time before.

I am trying to unearth what Lot means by "El's way." And what does it have to do with the god and goddess of Sodom? I do not understand Lot's meaning. "What," I finally ask, "is 'El's way?' "

He glowers at me, and I see a fire in his eyes more frightening than anger. It is cousin to the way Abram looks when he has spoken to El, but Lot's glare contains ferocity, an assurance that allows no questions, no deviation. "El demands we worship no other god, no goddess!" He has raised his voice so those near us hear him clearly.

He receives angry looks, and a deep foreboding lodges in my chest. I have never heard this from Abram's mouth or my father's. We are to put El above all other gods, but everyone welcomes the presence of the goddess in their house, and most also worship their family's gods. I do not know what would happen should Abram announce that El demands they stop. I wonder if Abram and Sarai know about Lot's pronouncements.

We arrive at last at Lot's house. It is too strange to call it "my" house, even in my mind, though I suppose it is. When I was last here, Lot's wife, Hurriya, laid out a bowl for me to wash my feet and looked at me with suspicion. She was a woman who observed closely, as I did, and something about me made her question my gender. I am almost certain of it, but I will never have an answer to that, unless she sends back a message from the land of the dead, Mot's domain.

We bring the pack donkeys inside to the reed-strewn courtyard, where we are greeted by Lot's household and daughters. Pheiné, the elder, gives me an openly disdainful look. Her sister, Thamma, stares with wide eyes, as one would stare at a man with no arm or a missing ear.

"Why did you bring such a woman home?" Pheiné demands before I can even open my mouth to speak.

"She is younger than we are." Thamma protests. "Are we to call her 'Mother?' "

"Show respect," Lot thunders.

Thamma's foot stamps. "I will not call her 'Mother.' "

"There is no need," I say, realizing I must say something, as Lot's bellowing seems to have had little effect on them. My heart is sinking. I do not think these women will call me "sister" either.

At that moment, a small woman with slender hands enters from the back rooms with an armful of fresh reeds. She is not much older than I. When she sees me, she stops. Her eyes rest only briefly on my face and then drop down to Nami, and a smile flits across her mouth as quickly as a sparrow's flutter. I like her at once. She was here before, but I hardly paid her attention. "Pardon my forgetfulness," I say to her. "What is your name?"

"Lila, Lady."

I nod and open my hand toward Nami. "This is Nami."

"The dog can stay outside," Lot says, beginning to unpack one of the donkeys, who nuzzles the ground looking for dropped bits of grain. The house chickens squawk and scatter.

I stiffen. "Husband, may we speak?"

"What is it?"

My gaze sweeps the area of the little gate. "With privacy, please."

He sighs deeply. "Very well."

I follow him to the room I assume is where he and Hurriya slept. There are beautiful wall hangings and cedar furniture holding alabaster pottery. On one stand is a box inlaid with ivory. I open it to reveal necklaces of cowrie shells and lapis lazuli. They are mine now. The thought brings no joy. No jewels or fine clothing can transform me into a woman of beauty. Men's heads turn to me for a different reason. *Stop this*, I demand of myself. I lift my head and take a deep breath. In the corners, scented oil burns. It is a lovely room, and someone has made certain it was clean and welcoming. I suspect Lila.

"Husband," I say, my tongue still thick around the word. "Nami is not like the city dogs. She never fouls inside a dwelling or tent. She is clean and well mannered."

"A dog is a dog; they are all garbage eaters."

"No, that is not so; she is desert bred as a hunter. She is very valuable."

At this, his expression changes, and I take advantage of what I learn from this. "Someone would recognize her value and steal her, should she be left outside."

"Well," he wavers. "It is your household."

"And I want my donkey to stay also."

"A donkey is no problem, but the dog—"

I lift my chin, ready to fight for my rights.

"Very well, it can remain inside then, but I do not want it near my food."

Relief floods me. If he had banned Nami, I would have sat outside the door with her until embarrassment forced him to allow her in. But I am glad to have crossed that pit without such measures. I take another breath. In the past few moments, he and I have exchanged more words than in all the days since we wed. While I have him in a mood, I ask, "Why do girls of your daughters' age not have their own families?"

He shrugs and turns his back to me, tossing a dusty pack onto the bed. "I will not marry them until they are willing. Hurriya found suitors, but neither girl was satisfied. I cannot blame them."

"The evening meal is ready!" I recognize the voice as Lila's, and before I can ask another question, Lot is through the curtained hanging that separates our sleeping room from the inner courtyard. "Good!" he bellows. "I am as empty as a well in the wasteland. Bring me an ox, and I will eat it whole!"

The meal is mostly taken in silence. I signal Nami to settle in the corner. Lot concentrates on the food, scooping the greasy mixture of lamb and onions onto flatbread. Lila does all the serving. The small brand on her arm marks her as a slave of Lot's house. She keeps her gaze downcast, especially careful to do so when offering food to Pheiné. Thamma, I decide, is a whiner, but Pheiné is the one to watch.

Exhausted, I am happy to retire to our sleeping room, but I am confused when Lot does not follow me. I signal Nami to stay off the bed, and I fall asleep, believing Lot is merely up late, speaking with his family, but when I wake in middle of the night, he is still not beside me. I pull a blanket around me and push aside the curtained doorway hanging.

The courtyard appears empty, save for our pack donkeys and Lila, who sleeps curled around the smoldering fire pit with no covering. I move quietly into the courtyard, Nami a silent shadow beside me. Lot is not in any part of the house or in the back garden. I am perplexed until I hear low voices coming from the room the daughters share.

I move closer to the door, signaling Nami to remain quiet, an unnecessary precaution as she knows from my movements we are hunting, though what and why are beyond her.

At the door's edge, the voices are clear enough:

"Father, why did you bring her here?"

"She is the daughter of Zakiti and it was the wish of Sarai and Abram that I marry her."

"You should have insisted!"

"Pheiné, I will not stand against Abram. He is the word of El!"

"And if mother's fate befalls *her?*"

A sharp intake of breath at that, which I attribute to Thamma.

"Quiet, Pheiné." Lot hisses. "Where is your decency?"

A low sound I cannot quite resolve. "I lost it long ago——"

I step from the doorway and start to return to the sleeping room, then stop and go to where Lila sleeps, covering her with the blanket that draped my shoulders.

CHAPTER

43

The butterfly counts not months but moments,
and has time enough.

—Rabindranath Tagore, *Fireflies*

A S THE DAYS PASS, THEY fall into a pattern. I awake early, because
lying in the bed is painful, and I ache less when I move around.
Taking care of Nami and Philot is my first concern. I want no one complaining about them.

I surprise Lila by assisting her with her chores and especially preparing the food. We cook everything in the cool of morning, spicing it
heavily to ward off the flies. During the day's heat, camel dung or wild
grass smolders to discourage the insects, but adding little or no heat to
the house. Then, just before we sleep, we will build the fire again for
the warmth.

Lila is a small woman, her skin a smooth walnut brown. She wears
her dark hair in a loose braid. Her mother had been a slave from Elam, a
land southeast of Babylonia. Captured in one of the battles against King
Chedorlaomer, she and her mother were brought to Sodom by the victors,
a spoil of war. Her mother died soon after Lot bought them. Lila speaks
little, and it has taken prompting and questions on my part to get that
much of her story. Her hands prepare food with efficiency, despite a missing finger.

Helping her is not all kindness on my part. The few times I venture onto the streets, I receive unkind stares and curses. I do not need my skill at reading men's subtleties to know their displeasure. Despite my attempt to cover my face, I hear more than once, "Leave our city!" I remember how the judge wronged Eliezer, Abram's steward, ruling he had to pay his assaulter for wounding him. Ishmael is right. This is not a city of justice or kindness to strangers.

Busying myself with household tasks gives me an excuse not to go out except in the early morning and at dusk to allow Nami to relieve herself. But I keep her close beside me, not wanting her to run off and be stolen or to mix with the scavenger city dogs. Lila buys whatever is needed at the Gate. She reports that most of the gossip is about the lack of rain, a subject Lot often brings up at the dinner meal. He is convinced it is a sign of El's disapproval.

Pheiné and Thamma spend most of their time in the company of their friends and at their brother-in-law's house. I have not been invited, and neither he nor his wife has come to pay respect to me as Lot's wife. Lot is away much of the day, conducting his business or seeing to the animals on his land outside the city. He rebukes my every attempt to let me live there or even go with him.

Lot sleeps in our bed, but has never attempted to touch me with any intimacy, although he is not unkind. On regular occasions, however, he drinks wine to excess, and I have learned on those nights, he will stumble into his daughters' rooms and not return, unable to look upon my face, I presume, and passing out from drink.

At my instruction, Lila purchased a loom of the type the desert women use. It calms me to weave, though my pace is slow with my damaged fingers. I am making a covering with purple yarns. The dye is made from a coastal shell creature. Our caravan often transported purple cloth at great profit. It is costly, but what else do I have to do with my wealth?

Unfortunately, I can only sit still for a short while. I am not a weaver, nor a wife, but a wild beast, well cared for, but pacing its cage, longing for freedom—or in my situation, limping up and down the courtyard. My longing for Mika is a physical ache. It is not just the night in his arms, but his company I miss—his intense curiosity and sharp mind, his acceptance of me as boy or girl, his gentleness as a healer and his strength. I try to divert my mind from thoughts of him and from my father, but there are times when thinking of them is my only comfort.

I miss the green of the hills and air that is not tainted. Why does Lot insist I stay in this city?

And what happened to Hurriya? This question plagues me. Perhaps, if I were busier, it would not.

ONE NIGHT I awake, sweating, aware I have called out in my sleep. The house is quiet, except for the faint lap of the sea. Lot is in our bed. He makes a noise and rolls over. I wait to make certain he has returned to sleep and then rise and dress, but instead of taking Nami out the door for a night walk, I go to the window. From our house's position, I can see where the far edge of the city wall meets the sea. A section has fallen in, perhaps eroded from the bottom by the sea's occasional corrosive caress in high wind. Every day I have spent time at this window, and I have studied that wall.

Although my leg is weak, my arms are strong, and I hoist myself onto the window's ledge and drop the short distance to the rocky ground. Nami leaps up to the ledge and then down to join me, barely pausing to gauge the jump.

Carefully, we make our way to the edge of the wall. Perhaps, at the time it was built, it did meet the sea. In any case, the narrow spit of land beyond it could not hold more than one person at a time. A person in a boat could access Sodom anyway, so why worry about such a small breach in the wall? The king was concerned with the assault of armies, not a person or two. All cities I ever visited had such weaknesses that no one bothers to address. If I led a military assault against Sodom, I would send one or two people into the city who could open the gates for me. They would not have to find such a spot as this, but merely enter as merchants during the day. Gates and walls exist to keep out predators rather than men.

Once we are beyond the smaller eastern gate, with no more to show for it than a scratch on my shoulder and wet feet, we move toward the cliff, intersecting the path from the gate I followed so long ago. The trail winds up the face of rock, but it is steep. Nami bounds ahead of me, stretching her lithe muscles in delight, but I can only climb a small distance before my leg buckles from the pain in my hip. Only my staff keeps me from a fall.

I sit on the nearest stone and watch the water below stained with the moon's silver. Beyond the moonlight's reach shine the stars that witnessed my birth and the birth of my ancestors, back into the pitch dark of time. They are the same stars that watched me sleeping in my father's tent, that watched Mika and me dying in the wilderness and then ascending to heaven to grasp the future like a dragon's breath. What do these stars think of all our fumbling and grasping, of our insignificant lives that must be to them less than a crumble of salt in the sea?

Nami returns, her tail waving happily, her tongue lolling. No doubt she found something to chase.

OVER THE FOLLOWING moon-cycles, I am out the window almost nightly, leaving Lot snoring if he has come to our bed. Each night I make it a little higher up the cliff before I have to rest and return. I must reach the overlook. Somehow it will bring me closer to Mika to be in a place where we were once together. I have the irrational thought that if I stand there, he will know it, and wherever he is, we will be together.

Once, Nami started to jump out the window during the day, but I caught her and scolded her. She seems to understand. Though she often stares at it, she has not tried again unless I lead the way.

One evening after a good meal, when Lot has drunk enough wine to be in a good mood, I ask to speak with him in the privacy of our room. I know the daughters will be sure to hang about to hear, and I keep my voice low to frustrate them.

"Have you a complaint?" Lot asks, untying his sandals.

"No, I have a request."

He squints in suspicion at me. "What is it?"

"I have brought my dowry to this house—"

"I do not need it," he says quickly. "Do you think I married you for your dowry?"

I would dearly like to know why he married me, but I stay on the path I wish to pursue. "No, you are a wealthy man and well respected." This is not true. The people here were once grateful to Abram for returning Sodom's sons and daughters, wealth, and food after the battle with Che-dorlaomer. But now, they feel Lot has milked that gratitude to empti-ness. His ranting about El is not well received, but taken as an attempt to replace the city god . . . which does indeed seem to be Lot's intent. To Sodomites, El is an elderly, bearded god who drank too much and gave up his throne to his younger son, Baal.

Lot's chest expands at my flattery, and he smiles, pleased. "But," he allows, "it is not an unpleasant thing to have a wealthy wife from a good family." This is as close to praise as he has ever given, and I try to look pleased. He never takes me with him outside the house. I understand a wealthy wife from a good family does not balance an ugly, wounded face and limp. This is not a time to vent my anger or sorrow. This is a negotiation, something I have trained for all my life.

"What is your request then, wife? I hope it is not the same one of wanting to leave the city."

"No, it is not that."

The muscle in his jaw relaxes slightly.

"It is a small thing," I say.

"So tell it."

"Not something that would concern a man of your wealth, although worth a bracelet of silver to me."

Now his interest is certainly piqued.

"What is it that is worth so much to you, but is such a small thing?"

"Merely a slave."

He frowns. "I have many slaves, and they are obedient to you as my wife. Why would you want ownership?"

Of course, that is true, but his other slaves work his lands. When do they have an opportunity to be obedient to me? But I do not say such. I have thought long on this answer, and I make my words casual. "I have never owned a slave, and would like a handmaiden for myself. Of course, I could go out and purchase one at the Gate—" I let the words hang. He is happy I expose myself so little in public.

"No, you do not need to do that. Do you want me to buy you one?"

I frown thoughtfully. "It is most difficult to find the right girl for such a position. I cannot imagine your being lucky enough to find one I would like. Then you would have to sell her and try another."

His fleshy jaw tenses again. He can see how this could require a good deal of his time and effort, and he is not happy about it. "I see."

With a sigh, I say, "Of course, there is a simple solution."

"What is that?" He yawns. Good, he will not want a long argument.

"I would really like to resolve this tonight. I have been thinking about it for a while, and I do not think I can sleep if it is not settled."

Now he is agitated. "What is your solution?"

"Lila would be satisfactory."

"But she is our cook and keeps the house—"

"She can continue that, of course. In fact, she has been serving me as handmaiden in addition to those things anyway. Was she not so for Hurriya?"

Lot flinches at his first wife's name. He has always avoided speaking of her, so now he will want to guide me away from the topic. He will be concerned that if he refuses, I may press him on questions of Hurriya. If he stalls for another day, he risks the possibility of my going out when he is not here and purchasing a slave myself.

"Very well," he says irritably. "She is yours."

"Oh, that is excellent." I hold out the tiny, still-damp clay tablet I had Lila obtain earlier that day. "I knew you would be gracious, so I prepared this. It only lacks your seal."

His brow raises, and then he laughs. "And I not even a silver bracelet richer! You are your father's daughter, Adira. I will give you that."

CHAPTER

44

I am Nature, the universal Mother, mistress of all elements, primordial child of time, sovereign of all things spiritual, queen of the dead, queen also of the immortals, the single manifestation of all gods and goddesses that are. My nod governs the shining heights of Heaven, the wholesome sea breezes, the lamentable silences of the world below. Though I am worshiped in many aspects, known by countless names, and propitiated with all manner of different rites, yet the whole round earth venerates me.

—Apuleius, *The Golden Ass*

LILA THANKS ME FOR ACQUIRING her, but I notice her eyes are red later that day. I do not ask why she has been crying. Perhaps because Lot told her she was now mine, it reminds her she is a slave to be bought and sold.

I am tired from the previous night's climbing. Finally, I reached the top of that accursed cliff. My hip aches, and I am not in a good temper.

"Shall I rub it for you?" Lila asks, seeing my hand on my hip.

"You do not have time. We must prepare the evening meal."

She spreads her hands. "What good does it do you to have me as hand-maiden? You would have done better to purchase another slave."

"I do not want another slave," I snap. "I want a nap."

Her hand flies to her lips, and our eyes meet. We hold it inside for only a moment before we both burst into giggles. I love Lila for this. She makes me see my own absurdity.

. . .

I TAKE MY nap and am deep asleep when Nami wakes me by jumping
on the bed. For a moment, I am disoriented, thinking I am in my father's
tent, sleeping late and must do some chore, only I cannot remember what
it is. Father will not be pleased.

Lila's arm appears, brushing the hangings aside, and then her small
face peers in to see if I am still asleep. When she sees my eyes open, she
says, "We have a guest, Lady."

My hand has found Nami's shoulder. "Who?" I mumble. We have
never had a visitor.

"I do not know him."

I want to roll to my side and return to sleep, despite the troublesome
dreams, but the slant of light through the courtyard behind Lila indicates
I have slept longer than I intended. With a low groan, I rise. My leg is
better for the rest once I work out the stiffness. I sweep back the strands
that have loosened from my braid. It has been long enough to wear this
way for moons. Sometimes, I put my hand on it and marvel at the soft
rope whose length marks my time as a woman.

When I reach the little gate and see the man towering over Lila's small
frame, I am unable to move. Chiram's ghost-spirit stands in the doorway.
For the time between heartbeats, I am swept into the netherworld, for
there can be no doubt I see Chiram before me . . . and then there is doubt. I
blink and realize this man is younger than Chiram, his hair thicker, if that
is possible. Not so much fat on him. The shadow world where the dead
and the gods dwell resolves into this one, and I realize who this must be.

"Danel! Please enter."

The welcome in my voice salves Lila's concern at the burly young man,
and she steps aside to allow him entry into the little gate.

"Lila, this is Danel, son of Chiram, a longtime friend of my father's"—
I swallow—"and of mine."

Lila looks startled that I would bother to introduce someone to a slave,
but she nods to Danel. "May I bring you drink or food?"

Danel, who is only two summers my elder, starts to shake his head,
then apparently remembers his manners and amends, "I would be grateful for a drink of water."

I smile, thinking Chiram would have only grunted a response.

"Of course." Lila goes to the clay-fired urn that holds the water she draws daily from the river, scooping a cupful. Like Nami, she has a gazelle's grace, moving only lightly on the earth, despite her compactness. When she leaves the cup in Danel's hands, he turns his attention to me, and his expression collapses in sadness. Unlike his father's, Danel's emotions have always been etched for any to read. We are almost of equal height, so he looks straight into my eyes. I feel my bad eye wander to the side.

"Tell me what happened to you? And to my father?"

I am not ready for this. "You do not seem surprised I am a woman."

He snorts. "I was. I am. I had heard that Lot returned with a new wife, but only today heard your name and that you were a child of Zakiti. It was confusing, but I came and here you are."

"Yes."

"I don't understand, but I want to."

He hesitates and then, as if he feels the need to explain, says, "When your father was killed, I understood the grief that took you into the wilderness. We searched for you and thought you dead, until the rumors came to us about a tall man with a fire burst of hair and a young boy who were guests of a desert tribe."

I nod. Word in the desert travels faster than a flash flood.

Danel shifted his thick shoulders as if resetting a burden. "Then Father insisted on trying to find you, and he would not allow me to go with him."

There was much said in the silence that followed.

I put both hands on his shoulders. "Your father is dead, Danel."

He takes a deep breath.

"He was as brave as any man I have known," I say.

At this, he looks startled. "Brave? My father?"

I understand his surprise. It is perhaps an odder concept than the fact that the boy, Adir, with whom he was raised, is now a woman. Not that I can remember any cowardly act of Chiram's. He just seemed too self-absorbed to be heroic. Perhaps my father could have told us differently had we thought to ask—Chiram fought at his side in the wars—but as children, we only half-believed an adult had a life before we came into being.

Settling Danel in the courtyard, I tell him the story of what happened from the time I left Lot's tents. I ask Lila to sit with us. She listens to my story with wide eyes, as intent as Danel. When I tell of Chiram's knives finding the back of my father's killer, she gasps. I do not mention the rite on Ishtar's temple. That is a thing between me and Mika and the goddess.

The words about what happened in the cave are difficult to speak, and this is the first time I have given them. Raph did not need them. He could see what happened with his own eyes. Sarai did not ask and though Ishmael did, I said only that a man had kicked me. Danel, however, needs to know that his father never begged for his life, though he was in agony. Danel bows his head, and I know he is fighting tears.

"I never understood what Chiram was to me," I tell him, taking both of Danel's hands. "But in that cave I learned more of the true man. Your father always wanted a caravan of his own, but he risked his savings to bet with a nomad for a dog he intended for me, to salve my pain at losing my herder dog. He searched the desert for me out of concern and loyalty to my father. He was a far better man than I, as a child, saw him to be, and I regret I did not know it then."

Danel takes another deep breath. "You give me a great gift in telling me this. I thank you for that, Adir . . . Adira." A smile plays across his generous lips. "I don't know that I will ever be accustomed to you as a girl . . . a woman."

I return his smile. "I am not used to it myself."

Suddenly, his gaze grows intense, and he tightens the grip on my hands. "Adira, you are in danger here."

I blink. "I know I am not liked—"

"It is more than that. Lot is despised and feared in this city."

If he had not kept my hands trapped in his, one would have drifted to my face. "I know they do not like what he says about Baal and El, but that has naught to do with me."

"I cannot say the people of this city would be kind to someone—" His lips tighten.

"Disfigured?" I finish for him.

He nods. "But I can say that the real reason for their hatred lies in the fact that you are Lot's wife."

"But why? I do not speak ill of their god. I am no threat to them."

"Exactly. It is easier to vent their anger on you."

"What can I do?" I ask him.

"Just be careful," he says, shaking his head. "It is worse that we have had no rain all winter, too easy an excuse for Baal's displeasure at Lot's ranting. If we do not get rain by spring, be careful."

45

The secret of happiness is freedom. The secret of freedom is courage.

—Thucydides

I AM ALONE AT THE LOOM with only Philot and Nami for company when it seems the ground shudders. It is not the first time I have felt it, but Lot assures me it is an occasional happening, not something to concern me, though I recall seeing the fallen stones of buildings when I roamed the city searching for goods for my father.

Perhaps disoriented by the earth's movement, a small brown bird finds its way through the loose fronds thatching the courtyard roof. It flutters wildly from wall to wall, seeking a way out. Nami jumps to her feet, following it, leaping, and snapping. The chickens squawk and flap in distress. Nami understands the chickens are not prey, but she knows this bird is not a chicken.

When she races by me, I grab her. She trembles with excitement. I know she has longed for a chase. I see it in her eyes when she rests her head in my lap and looks up at me. I spend time throwing a bone for her, and she loves that, but it is not the same as chasing a rabbit or an ibex or even a trapped bird.

"Down," I tell her, my hands wrapped around her neck. She ignores the command, struggling against my hold. I do not blame her; it is her nature just as it is the bird's instinct to escape. In its panic, the bird does not realize it could go back up the way it got in. It is difficult to watch the little creature flying again and again into the walls, but if I release Nami, she will kill it. Besides what could I do—limp from wall to wall snatching at it?

At last, it flutters to the ground, exhausted.

Once still, it is not as tantalizing to Nami, and I am able to capture her attention and give her the signal to lie down and stay. She licks my hand in apology for struggling against me. When I am certain she will obey, I rise with the help of Ishmael's staff and go to the corner where the bird sits on the floor, seemingly stunned, though its eyes are open.

Slowly, I reach down and close my hand over it. To hold a bird requires that the grip not be too tight, or it will crush. Yet too loose, and the bird will escape. It struggles once, testing its prison. I am firm, and it quiets, though I can feel the racing flutter of its heart through my fingertips. I remember how Kerit had hooded his falcon to keep it calm, and I tuck the bird, still in my hand, into the dark beneath my robe. Nami looks at me expectantly, wondering, I imagine, if I am going to share my catch.

I hobble to the back window, which is uncovered and open to allow the breeze a path. A lattice normally covers it, but Hurriya had it made so it could be removed and I normally keep it so during the day, even in the winter. I would rather put on a shawl than close it. The chickens sometimes fly up to the sill, but never seem tempted to go beyond.

Beyond the wall's edge, the Dead Sea shimmers. I have learned to see beauty here. Sunset imbues the cliff walls with warm gold. With the morning sun, the salt crystals in the water shoot tiny beams of light to dance just above the surface. So intense is the dazzle, I often wonder if the stars are raining into the sea.

The breeze shifts and I cough, my nose spoiled by the incense I keep burning inside, in part to keep away the flies, but also to cover the smell. Lot says there was not always such a stench. In the days when his wife's mother was a child, she said only on occasion did the smell drift to them.

I remember the first time my father pointed out a yellow seam in the cliffs and had me press my nose to it. It stank of rotten eggs, the same smell that the Dead Sea belches. What has changed, I wonder, to make the sea's belly so discontent?

Lot says if I would stop burning incense day and night, I would become used to the stench. I cannot imagine becoming used to it. It seems more than a smell; the air is often heavy, almost furred. Besides, I buy the incense with my own silver. With the dowry my father left me, I could buy incense enough for my lifetime.

The throb of the bird's heart has eased, and the creature is quiet in the dark of my robe. Perhaps the warmth and sound of my own heartbeat calms it, reminding it of a safe nest with huddled siblings.

I draw the bird out and open my hand. Splaying tiny talons, it fumbles for a perch. When I spread my fingers, the talons wrap my forefinger like a baby's instinctive clutch.

So, here we are . . . woman and bird and sea. The wind shifts again, and a clean breeze lifts my hair, and I remember long ago I was daughter of the wind. "Fly," I whisper.

For a moment, our eyes meet, and we are not predator and prey, but sisters. Then a flurry of wings—and she is gone.

THE NEXT MORNING I determine I will not stay a prisoner in this house, despite Danel's warning. I snatch up the basket and announce to Lila that I am going to market. She looks surprised, but says nothing.

Nami is at my side in an instant, quivering with eagerness to stretch her long legs. The street stirs in dawn's light. Nami does her business, and I kick dust over the puddle. Then she is off to investigate everything within sight of me.

I check the sky, hopeful for a sign of rain, but the clouds are white as the salt mountains that lie to the west of the Vale. Not a drop has fallen since we arrived, though we are in winter's heart, and it is the season for rain.

A woman sits on a bench outside her house, a nursing baby at her breast. The sight stabs my heart, but I smile at her. She covers the baby with the edge of a blanket, as though to shield it from the sight of me. For a moment, I wonder what would happen if Nami and I just kept walking to the Gate and beyond, into the desert. Perhaps little Shem's tribe would find us again. I was happy there. I sigh and remind myself that Mika had been with me then and my chances of finding Shem's tribe or even surviving would be very slim, especially in such a drought.

As the morning passes and the market at the Gate grows thicker with people, I signal Nami to my side. She is a large dog and her protective presence discourages some of the hostility I feel around me.

The vendors, at least, keep their thoughts about me or my husband to themselves, lest I buy from another, but they are free in sharing their concerns about the lack of rainfall. There is plenty of meat. Herders, worried about brown pastures, are killing off their stock. Lot regularly brings in meat. It is grain that is difficult to find.

Though the weather is the talk of every tongue, it is not foremost on my mind. More than a desire to leave the house has driven me onto Sodom's cruel streets. At the Gate, as I shop for food, I shop also for news from the east. "What have you heard about Babylonia?" I ask. "Is there war?"

"There is always war somewhere," one tells me. Another has more specific information, heard from a passing caravan. "Babylonia is threatened from the east, and trouble brews in the south."

I thank him, but this is no more than I already know. I gnaw on my worry for Mika like a dog with an old, bare bone, unable to give it up. Does he ever think of me? I shudder. If so, let him remember me as I was. What would I do if he stepped through the Gate now? Would I run to him . . . or from him? I could not bear his spurning me.

A familiar sound spins me around. I have worked my way among the vendors to a place near the temple. From the steps, a man's voice raises. I know the voice; it belongs to my husband. A crowd has gathered to hear him.

"Baal is a false god!" he cries. "We have no rain because El is angry at Sodom."

"We have no rain," a voice from the crowd shouts, "because Mot has swallowed Baal, and Mot is angry at your words!"

Another man raises his fist. "Leave this city, Lot. Take your family and go!"

"Have you so soon forgotten Abram?" a third man accuses the shouter. "Abram saved Sodom. Is this how we treat his nephew?"

"Abram's god is not ours!" The last speaker turns his head and sees me. "Here is the wife of Lot. Look on her face. Is that a vestige the gods are pleased with? She is an abomination!"

"Go home, Adira," Lot says.

In this, I have no problem finding obedience. But I have not limped past more than a few houses when my head explodes with a pain that brings me to my knees. For a moment, I know nothing but the pain and panic. My breath is shallow and quick, and I cannot move. Then Nami whines and licks my forehead. I put my hand to my head; it is wet with more than Nami's concern. At my feet is a bloodied stone.

"YOU'RE HURT!" LILA says when I stumble in the door. "What happened?"

She makes me sit on the bench inside the little gate while she tends my wound.

"Someone threw a stone."

"Who?" She is indignant.

"I don't know."

My father taught me to find the right question. *What did the people of Sodom want?* I touch the hollow left by the healing of my crushed cheekbone. These people want to live without strangers among them, particularly strangers who reminded them they are not as secure as they imagine themselves to be, but are vulnerable to the world's cruelties. I stir their fears. I can think of nothing to do or say to assure them my fate and the fate of their own previous generations does not await them.

It doesn't matter who threw the stone," I say.

"What do you mean it doesn't matter?" Lila demands.

I look down at the blood on my hands. "I mean that it could have been anyone."

WHEN LOT FINALLY returns, I confront him. "What are you doing?"

He rounds on me. "Do not question me, wife. I do El's bidding."

"So El speaks to you now? And you do not even have to climb a holy place like Abram?" I cannot stop the sarcasm in my voice. My head throbs.

"He sent his messenger to tell me of his displeasure with Sodom's ways."

I gasp. "Mika? You are speaking of Mika?"

"Mika-el, El's angel. I saw him hold blue fire on the hillside. He spoke against the evil of this city."

"He was just surprised—"

Lot's eyes are wide, his face flushed, as he had been on the steps of the goddess's temple.

I swallow what I was going to say. He would not believe me that Mika did not know what the blue fire meant either and that herders had seen such before during storms on the horns of sheep. I can see the fire in Lot's eyes. There is no reasoning with him. Such explanations will only turn him against me.

"We should leave," I say. "What brews in this city is evil. You are right about that."

"El has chosen me to be his voice. We will not leave."

46

Your city has become a strange city; how can you now exist?

—Lamentations of Ur

LILA AND I WALK THROUGH the city with Danel, who keeps watch for anyone who might think to throw a taunt or a stone. A dry wind deposits dust on clothes and skin, and I hold my headscarf over my nose for more reason than to hide my face. Without the season's rain, the river has shrunk into trickles. I recall digging my fingers raw into a dry wadi in the desert, searching for water. Will it be that way here? With every day that the sky withholds rain, anger toward Lot intensifies. He has hired an armed guard to escort him to the market and even to his fields.

The hatred cast toward me as we walk the street is palpable, but Danel is an imposing man. Still, we do not linger. We have been invited to the home of Danel's grandmother Jemia for the evening meal. Lot, Pheiné, and Thamma, not surprisingly, pled other plans.

My discomfort is not just from the hard stares as we pass. I feel as if I have forgotten some part of my body, like my hand or foot, because Nami does not pace at my side. For the first time since Raph found me barely alive in the cave, I am without her. Danel has asked this for the sake of his grandmother, who is old and cannot tolerate animals near her. She does not breathe well, and they make her difficulty worse.

I explained it all to Nami, reinforcing my command not to jump out the window, and then closed the slatted covering. But I expect her to find a way through it and follow me. She found me once in this city, picking out my scent, and once in the desert. Every few steps, I turn, looking for her behind us.

The sun is a round red stone balancing on the western cliffs, spreading a bloody stain across the sky. The air, sucked of moisture, stinks more than usual. Earlier that day, I watched huge bubbles form in the sea and burst with an accompanying stink. Pheiné and Thamma were home, but unimpressed with the sea's activity. Pheiné played her harp, which I had to admit was not unpleasant. I recalled how she had sent smoldering glances in Raph's direction. How jealous that had made me!

Finally, we have heard news from Babylonia. War. Lila made certain to ask details, and I was greatly relieved to learn it had been from the east, as Mika predicted. Each morning, I put aside a small piece of my food and leave it on the sill for the birds to take to El with a plea to protect Raph and Mika. I pray Raph made it home safely with his precious stone. And I pray Babylonia's king takes good care of his sage. Would Samsu-iluna demand more visions of Mika? What would Mika do with only a false stone on which to lay his head?

We pass the layered lime-washed bricks of the goddess's temple. My step slows. I could go inside and ask for sanctuary. It would not matter that I am ugly or that I am the wife of Lot. I could live there for the rest of my days in peace and dignity. The power of that pull toward the temple surprises me.

Perhaps sensing my turmoil, Lila's grip on my arm tightens. As my slave and handmaiden, she would have to come with me. My gaze finds Danel's profile. He walks close beside Lila, between her and the donkeys and street merchants. He steals glances at her when he thinks she does not know. I have studied men's expressions and behavior all my life, and I know as surely as I know anything, I cannot take Lila to the goddess's temple.

We pass through the Gate, the city's heart. Merchants are closing for the day in anticipation of the evening shutting of the gates, packing away their dates and figs, baskets of seeds or beans. Some spread their blankets to sleep near their wares. We pass one such man, who sees us and indicates a hanging section of lamb, its sides scored from the knife's slices and unseen bites of flies. "Not too late," he says, with a grin that displays the gaps between his crooked yellow teeth. Lila shakes her head, and we move on. No beggars line the walls, as there would be in Babylon or any other city. Sodom does not welcome them; a person seen offering a pittance to one would be fined and the beggar expelled.

From the corner of my eye, I catch a glimpse of a young boy running down an alley. Only his back is visible. The way he runs is familiar, though I cannot place it. Dogs bark and chase after him for a short way, and then he disappears around a corner.

The bray of a donkey distracts me. There is a pained quality in it. I stop. "What is it?" Lila asks.

"Wait a moment," I say, watching the scene unfold before us. A man, his back to us, is whipping his donkey for failing to move forward with the wagon he has just loaded with heavy clay pots of pitch. "Move on, you sorry beast of Mot!"

I approach him. "What has this creature done that warrants your beating it?"

He rounds on me. "Who are you—?" The sight of my face stops him, and recognition, or perhaps disgust, widens his eyes. He is a swarthy man with black hair that crawls up his chest to meet his thick, unkempt beard. The unwashed stench of his body overpowers even the efforts of the sea and the debris of the city. From his stance and tone, he is not a man accustomed to challenge.

I do not step back from him. "I am Adira, daughter of Zakiti and wife of—"

He does not allow me to finish, but spits at my feet, "—wife of that son-of-the-underworld, Lot. I know who you are."

"Well," he demands after a pause, "what do you want?"

I point to the blood oozing from the donkey's hide. "Beating your donkey does not work. You must lure it with a treat or startle it forward, but yours is not being stubborn. She has hurt her back foot, either strained it or picked up a stone." I point. "See how she stands with her weight off it."

He grunts and cocks his head, exposing what I could not see at first, a wide scar that runs from the outer corner of his eye to his ear. Despite my mind's assertion that Scar, my Babylonian tormentor, is dead, my body goes as rigid as one of the goddess's poles. I am chilled and sweating at the same time. I have lost my voice, my ability to move.

We remain that way for long heartbeats, the man too stubborn to check my assertion, and I locked in a past terror, waiting helplessly for a

rain of blows, until I feel Lila's hand on my arm. She turns me, and she
and Danel help me walk away. I am surprised my shaking legs remember
how. After we turn down another street, she produces my staff, which I
apparently dropped, though I have no memory of it.

She has me sit on a low wall, once part of a house that has long since
come down, possibly from the earth tremors.

Why has no one repaired it? I think inanely, seeking a distraction from
the reality that I am no longer the person I thought I was—no longer the
girl who would jump on a horse and ride after her father's murderer—
only a woman scarred inside as well as out.

I do not want to weep, not here with eyes on us. I feel the stares, though
Danel has positioned himself so his thick body screens me somewhat.

"Let's go on," I whisper hoarsely.

WE ARE WITHIN sight of Danel's house when, as if to prove Lila's words
true, the ground trembles, followed by a loud boom and the sharp smell
of brimstone. When we recover our balance, we stare one another other. A
long moment of stillness hovers over the street before people explode into
discussion: "What was the noise? Why are the gods angry?"

Danel opens the door and waves us inside. "Grandmother, are you all right?"

There is a groan from the courtyard, and we rush there to find her on
the ground. Danel kneels beside her. "Are you hurt?"

"Maybe a bruise on my hip," she says. "It should feel welcome there
with all the others."

Another woman hurries in with a basket of flatbread balanced on her
head. She sets it down and rushes to Jemia's side. "Do not move," she
commands, her thick hands pressing and prodding. We step back, allowing space for the woman, whose arm bears the scarred slash of a slave
brand. She is as large and brusque as Jemia is small and fragile. I marvel
at Jemia, lying curled on her side on the reed-strewn floor. How can this
woman have produced Chiram? She is even smaller than Lila.

When Jemia's slave is satisfied nothing is broken, she scoops the tiny
woman into her arms and starts to take her to a back room. Jemia makes
a fist and beats it against her shoulder. "No, no! Put me down, Flava."

"You should rest."

The fist does not pause in its assault. "Are you blind, woman? I have
guests. Release me."

With reluctance, Flava sets her gently on her feet. "Remember how long you spent abed the last time you fell?"

Jemia ignores her, straightening to her full height, which amounts to level with Flava's bosom. Despite Flava's hovering, Jemia's dignity belies her stature. "I cannot go to bed every time the ground shakes." Then she turns to us. "Be welcome in my house."

Since we are not travelers, she does not insist on washing our feet, and we simply return to the little gate and remove our sandals.

Lila tries to help Flava serve, but I insist she join us. We sit on cushions around a large clay platter, using flatbread to scoop the pungent mixtures of meats, onions, and beans. Dates, goat cheese, and fresh milk follow the main servings, and then honey cakes almost as good as Hagar's. I appreciate the extravagance of serving such food.

I finally sit back with a rounded belly, leaving something of my portion to assure our hostess there has been plenty to eat. Now it is polite to speak, and I compliment her on the meal and ask questions about its preparation. We meander into conversation about current events. "This new king does not understand his people," Jemia complains. "They never do. I have seen three of them, you understand."

"Grandmother, do not get yourself in a tangle," Danel says.

"I am not tangled. My old eyes see better than yours. This city is fearful and isolated; we are overripe and rotten."

"What do you mean?" I ask.

She slaps her palm against her thigh. "There is closing the gates, and there is closing the gates."

I shift on my pillow, trying to ease the burning ache in my hip and leg. "I do not go out much, and hear very little other than what Lila tells me," I say as apology for knowing little of what goes on in the city.

"What do you make of the explosion, Grandmother?" Danel intercedes, in an obvious attempt to change the subject from politics.

She lifts her shoulders in a shrug.

"Have you ever heard such before?" he insists.

She squints, as if trying to see into a distant memory. "When I was a young girl, there was a noise like the one today. It was down where the pitch pits lie." She spreads her hands wide, her voice dramatic. "The ground cracked open—shooting a tower of flame into the sky!"

"A tower of flame?" It is the first time Lila has spoken.

"Believe me or not," Jemia says crossly.

"I believe," Lila says, her gaze solemn. "The gods are angry with this city."

Jemia appears lost in her memory. "When it finally burned out, foolish children that we were, we went to look down into the crack, pushing and jostling each other, fearful Mot would reach up and grab us."

I remember poking sticks into holes with Ishmael to see if we could wake a demon. "What did you see?" I ask.

She shudders, though it is overly warm from the day's heat. "Mot's kingdom." She pauses, well aware of the drama of her telling. "We saw the layers of the earth, down, down, so deep, there was nothing but black-ness."

"Mot's Tongue," Danel says. "I have seen that place. The older children take the younger there to frighten them. I went, before Father took me with him on the caravan. It is just as you describe, but I never heard of a fountain of fire erupting from it. That must be why they call it a 'tongue.' I always wondered."

I feel my eyes widen, and a sense of doom grips me. Beneath us, in the depths, fire rages, waiting for the earth to shift to release it. Mot's Tongue could erupt anywhere.

"It happened long before you were born," Jemia says. Then, as if it is part of the same subject, she points a bony finger at me. The skin of her hand is creviced like a piece of parched earth. "There are other things that happened before you were born that do concern you." The finger stays extended, but sweeps to include Danel, "And you."

Danel looks perplexed.

Knowing she has our attention, she retracts the finger, folding it with the others in her lap. "I must tell you a story."

"Your father, Chiram," Jemia begins, "was a good boy."

The sense of danger lingers, but I am hungry to learn more about Chi-ram and lean in for her story.

"Perhaps not as quick as others, but steady and dependable," she contin-ues. "You are much like him in that, Danel. When he was a young man, he traveled to Mari to visit his uncle, and he met a beautiful woman. He was warned she had spells of darkness, but he was so taken by her, he brought her home as his wife. They were happy and, in due time, she had a child."

"Which was me," Danel says.

"Yes, it was you. But it was a difficult, painful birth, and something broke in her mind afterward. She seemed to forget who she was and did not acknowledge either her husband or her child. She would wander out into the streets, and Chiram had to find her and bring her home to suckle you."

Danel's hands clench into fists. "I know this, and I know the rest. She disappeared, and Father brought me to you to raise."

"Only for a while." Jemia stops a moment to get her breath. I can hear the faint wheeze, and am now glad I did not bring Nami and make it more difficult for her.

"Danel's father—my Chiram—was almost as lost as his bride," she continues. "He was a shaper of knives, but returning to his profession only made him think of his lost wife, so he tried his hand at various things. He had it in his mind that a traveling caravan had snatched his wife, so he attached himself to various ones, finding a place by hunting and cooking for them. When Danel was old enough, Chiram came for him."

Jemia's watery eyes travel from Danel to me. "Hear now the part you do not know, and I, too, did not know until Chiram came to Sodom after Zakiti died and you, Adira, disappeared into the desert."

Everyone's attention intensifies. Jemia sways a bit, as if the weight of what she knows rocks her off-center. "When Danel was four summers old, Chiram found his missing wife." She looks directly at Danel. "Your mother."

Danel jumps to his feet. "What? Where is she? How?"

"Be calm, grandson."

But Danel will not be. "Why are you telling me this now, in front of guests? I do not understand."

It is Lila's cool, small hand on Danel's calf that settles him. He looks down at her, his mouth tight. She says nothing, yet much passes between them. He sits. "My apologies, Grandmother."

She goes on as if never interrupted. "Many seasons had passed when he found her, and she was the wife of another man, the owner of the caravan."

I draw a shaky breath, putting this together. "My mother? Your son's wife was Talliya?"

Jemia nods and gives us a moment to absorb what she has told us.

Finally, I ask, "Did my mother remember Chiram as her husband when she saw him?"

"No, she did not. And Chiram, though he longed for her, did not claim her. She was married to a man Chiram respected, and she seemed happy."

I feel blood drain from my face, and I stare down at my hands. "When we were captives in a cave in Babylonia, Chiram told me— " I must take a slow breath to relieve the tightness in my chest. "Chiram told me that when he and my father left to fight against Chedorlaomer, my mother was pregnant." I look up. "With me." My mouth is dry. I had not told Danel these details. "Chiram said my mother went throughout the camp, telling everyone her *son* would soon be born, and that would set things right."

Tears glimmer in Jemia's eyes. "Deep inside, a part of her knew she had lost her son."

"She told everyone I was a boy." My own voice breaks over a closing in my throat.

Jemia reaches out and takes my hand.

"And so I was raised," I say, "even after she died."

"And so," Jemia echoes, "Chiram stayed near her. And her son, Danel, was companion and friend to her daughter, though neither knew the other to be family."

Danel takes a deep breath and looks at me, his brows lifting with a sudden understanding. "We, then, are sister and brother."

CHAPTER

47

I looked into the water. My destiny was drifting past.

—Sumerian proverb

I T IS STILL DIFFICULT TO sleep. In my nightmares, a fiery tongue straight from Mot's kingdom burns, coming closer and closer. I wake in a cold sweat, alone. Have my nightmares again driven Lot from my bed?

He has not touched me once, not even a casual brush. I laugh to myself. I will never learn if there was any truth to the talk of large thumbs and the size of a manhood! Affection grows with a marriage, or so I have been told, yet it is impossible to plant that seed in frozen ground. My womb is barren, unless El grants me the miracle he gave to Sarai. But even El needs a man's cooperation. Not that I have tried to interest Lot, even for the sake of hoping the healer wrong. I have not learned affection for Lot. I abhor him. How stupid of me to think I could ever be content here. Daily, he grows more fanatical and puts all our lives at risk.

I worry about Ishmael and hope Sarai gives birth to a girl, though she prays to the goddess for a boy heir, not trusting El in such a matter. What will happen to Ishmael and Hagar if Sarai has a boy? Will he have a chance to live his dreams? Sarai has never forgiven Hagar her thoughtless bragging over Ishmael. Sarai will want her own son to be Abram's heir.

It is a difficult matter, since Ishmael is Abram's first son, but Sarai is his first wife and sister. If I could wager, I would place it on Sarai. She is not a woman who easily concedes defeat. And El has said she will bear an heir.

Pushing aside the bed coverings, I rise and, as always, Nami is instantly awake and accompanies me. I wonder if she knows the moment my eyes open.

I stop in the courtyard to scratch Philot's neck and give him a fig, which he scoops into his mouth with his soft lips. A glance at Lila's sleeping form assures me she has enough coverings now to stay warm—warmer, she claims, than I, because she has the fire.

"It is not fair to keep you here," I whisper to Philot. "I will send you to the fields tomorrow."

Philot nods his head as he eats the fig, as if he says, *You say that to me every day.* I know he would be happier in the fields, and it would remove a burden from Lila, who must bring hay every day, hay that is getting scarcer to find. We could also stable him with the other animals at the far end of the city, but I am stubborn. I want him with me.

On the day after my arrival, Pheiné confronted me about it. "Surely, you do not plan to keep this smelly donkey in the courtyard, as if we were *nomads!*" Her emphasis on the word "nomads" left no doubt as to her distain. I could have told her the desert people felt the same way about city dwellers.

Instead, I said, "He smells like a donkey. What is wrong with that? The city smells far worse."

She ignored this, pointing to Nami. "And the refuse-eater. Can you not put him outside?"

"Her," I corrected, "and she stays with me."

Pheiné tossed her head. "I have lived in this house all my life. You are little more than a child."

"I may be, but I am also the woman of the household. The donkey and dog stay." After a moment, I added, "But you may leave, if you wish."

Perhaps it was not the best way to begin our relationship, and it has not improved since then. Thamma follows her sister in everything, and so, no hope of better there. But what more can be expected from me, a woman so repulsive her husband seeks solitude in his daughters' room? My hope for sisters was crushed the moment I stepped into the little gate. Pheiné and Thamma hate me for reasons I cannot understand. My heart was open to them, but now it is closed. If they do marry and bear children, they will turn them against me.

I move to the window, pulling back the latticework and holding the night coverings aside. The moon has risen, casting a silver shadow on the dark sea. After a while, I sense a presence and turn to find Lila at my side, a woolen blanket wrapped around her shoulders.

"Hurriya had Lot build this opening in the wall," she says. "She wanted to see the sea."

This makes me wonder more about Hurriya. Perhaps we shared a kinship in needing this opening to the world.

"I know you are not happy," Lila says quietly, "but I am glad you are here."

"You are my only friend in this house . . . in this city, I believe."

"What about Danel?" she asks.

"Yes, there is Danel too. My brother." My heart lifts at those words. *I have a brother and a grandmother.*

Now she gives a quiet laugh. "I wonder if he will visit again."

A tone in her voice only confirms what my eyes have already seen. "He is not a wealthy man," I say.

She sees that I have discerned her interest. "That is no matter to me."

"But he is a good one," I add.

The palms of Lila's small brown hands press together at her chest. "That, my mother always said, is enough."

I smile. "My father always said it was as easy to marry a wealthy man as a poor one."

"And by that logic," she counters, a gleam in her dark eyes, "just as easy to marry a poor one as a rich one."

"I believe perhaps Danel will visit often."

We watch the moon together. Nami gives a sigh and settles at my feet.

"Lila," I say at length, "do you know how Hurriya died?"

She gives me a sharp look and hesitates. "They say she fell from the cliff."

"Where?"

She points out the window toward the cliff face where I climb almost nightly, the place where Mika held the blue fire in his hand. It seems at once so long ago and only days past.

"But that is not the truth," Lila says, with a glance over her shoulder.

"How then?" I press.

Lila turns back to the sea, glimmering in the moonlight, her voice hushed. "One morning, she just walked into the water."

I take a breath. "She drowned?"

"Yes."

I remember my experience as a young girl when I tasted the bitter water despite my father's warning. "How?" Only the heaviest objects can sink in the Dead Sea.

"She just walked in, spread her arms wide and lay face down. A boatman saw her, but could not reach her in time." Lila's voice catches. By this, I know Hurriya had been a good woman, kind to Lila. What had she seen that made her embrace the sea and its bitterness? Though I have no answer to the question, some deep part inside me understands.

All the tears she wept are naught but a pillar of salt.

CHAPTER

48

Is there so much anger in the minds of the gods?
—Vergil

I have no rest; only trouble comes.
—Job 3:26

THE FOLLOWING DAY, LILA AND I sit in the dappled light of the
courtyard, teasing lentils from their pods, she on the reed floor, and
I on a small stool like the one I sat on in Sarai's tent. We keep the rugs
rolled up until it is time for a meal, to keep chicken droppings off them.

It is a pleasant morning to shell peas. Two from each pod. Her nine
fingers work twice as fast as mine. She has bought a great reed basket of
them. I still carry the thrust of our talk, but every day she is becoming
more comfortable in the role of friendship I offer her. "This basket nearly
broke my back," she says, a complaint she would never utter in front of
Lot's daughters.

"Why did you choose such a large one?"

She sighs. "It was a better bargain than the smaller."

"Then you should have hired a boy to carry it."

Her dark eyes flash, indignant. "I would have wasted the savings!"

I laugh. It speaks of her character that she is concerned about the
household affairs, though she has no portion in them.

"Well," I say. "We shall have lentil soup and lentil stew and then—"

"Lentil soup," Lila says, catching the path of my humor, "and then lentil stew."

I remember the camaraderie in the desert women's tent in Yassib's camp. Into this opening, I ask, "Lila, how did you lose your finger?"

She hesitates, glancing at my face. "Forgive the query," I say quickly.

"No, it happened a long time ago. I was only a child." She takes a breath. "I do not remember much, just sitting in the dust outside our hut and reaching for what I thought was a stick." She looks up. "The stick came alive in my hand—a newborn viper."

I draw a breath. Even a just-hatched viper is dangerous, sometimes more full of poison than an adult.

"My mother came running at my screams. Before I could realize what she was doing, she pulled out the knife she had in her sash for cooking and killed the snake, then cut off my finger so the poison would not spread. I have done without it most of my life and do not miss it."

I nod. Our deformities, though quite different, link us together in a way a whole person cannot understand.

Nami whines, nosing the basket. I call her to my side before she can knock it over, having no wish to pick lentil pods from the reed-strewn floor.

At a knock on the door, Lila rises with far greater grace than I can manage and goes to open it, giving me time to struggle to my feet. My limitations are not that noticeable now, once I am up and moving, but getting up and down is a challenge.

It is Danel. He has become a frequent visitor. I greet him while Lila goes back to shelling peas. Danel follows her with his gaze, and I smile. He is so obviously smitten.

At the sudden squawking of the chickens and a gasp from Lila, I turn in alarm. She is kneeling on the floor, her back to us. Beyond her, I see that Nami has forgotten my command to leave the basket alone, and spilled the contents. Relieved at the mundane upset, I sigh in annoyance and sympathy. Each day we are confined to this house, Nami finds obedience increasingly difficult.

Lila's hands are full of pods. I take a step toward them to help her collect the spilled beans, but Danel's sudden grip on my arm halts me.

I have missed what he has not. Philot is pulling against his tether, his head up and his tail clamped in fear; the chickens have retreated into the far corners; and Nami's posture is aggressive—her head low, the tufts of short hair spiked between her shoulders. Her legs splay, and tension holds them stiff, ready to leap in an instant.

Only when the floor moves, do my eyes resolve what she and Lila and Danel have already seen. It is not the floor that moves, but a snake, a ribbon of black sliding through the brown reeds scattered on the floor. The soft rustle of scales accompanies the snake's advance toward Lila. She is rigid, but a pod falls from her trembling hand. At the movement, the serpent lifts its narrow head, and I recognize it—a desert cobra.

The air sucks from the room as if a demon spirit has entered.

"Nami, stay," I say quietly, but loud enough to be heard. I am afraid to give her the hand signal and hope she hears me.

"Do not move, Lila," I add in the same tone. Her face is angled to me. I can see her lips tremble to match her hands, and the pinch of skin around the eye visible to me. Other than the tremble, she is motionless, her gaze connected to the snake's, as if they are bound together.

The cobra lifts its head and a section of its body into the air, a thin, split tongue tasting. It is a large serpent. Normally, it would flee from danger, but it does not see well. If it perceives a threat—

I swallow. *How can I reach Lila? What can I do?* My grasp on the staff is as tight as Danel's hand on my arm. I fear if I move, it will strike, but Danel is behind me. "Have you your father's skill with the throwing knife?" I ask him under my breath.

"No," he whispers back. "I would more likely hit her or the wall than a snake!"

"Lila." I try to keep the fear from my voice. She needs to hear only calm and sureness. She must know the beat of her heart calls to the cobra with a sweeter song than a lover's. Perhaps she feels the throb where her finger used to be.

Another pod falls from her shaking hand, striking her lap with a tiny plop.

A swift coil ... and black lightning strikes.

Lila screams.

I pull from Danel's grasp and stagger toward her, ignoring the jabs of pain in my hip and leg. The serpent has latched onto Lila's forearm, sinking its fangs into her nut-brown flesh.

With a swing of Ishmael's staff, I knock the snake aside, and Nami is on it faster than I can shout at her. I raise my staff again, but dog and snake are too entwined to risk another blow. A coil of cobra has wrapped about Nami's neck, but she has clamped down on a part and dances about, shaking her head.

Philot kicks out at them, narrowly missing Nami. Danel has dragged a sobbing Lila to safety. "Adir," he shouts, reverting to the name he has called me all of my life and most of his. "Get back!"

But how can I? I can do nothing more for Lila, but my Nami—

I watch for an opening to apply the staff, but they are now even more intertwined and moving constantly. Finally, it stops, but only appears so. The snake's body remains coiled around Nami's neck. Her teeth bear down just behind the cobra's head, forcing open the curved fangs that drip venom. If Nami releases for a better grip, she is doomed.

The coils tighten in desperation. The cobra does not crush its prey, relying instead on its poison, but I can see Nami's eyes bulge from the pressure. Still, she does not relinquish her position, slowly bearing down through the thick muscles.

It is only now I think to call upon my god. I fall to my knees. I do not know if he will hear me or heed me without the sweet incense of a sacrifice on his altar, and I am not his beloved, Abram, who has his ear. *El, I am daughter of Zakiti of Abram's tribe. You have claimed me as yours. I beg you to save my Nami! Save my heart.*

A strangled sound comes from Nami's throat; she is choking.

"Adira!" It is Lila who calls me now, but I cannot turn my gaze from the dog and snake. I want to cut them apart. My knife! How have I forgotten it? I fumble at my sash, my hands now trembling.

"No, Adira, stay back!" Danel shouts.

As I start forward with a hazy plan to cut the coils from her neck, a sharp crack startles me. Nami gives the head a last shake and opens her jaws, dropping her opponent. It falls with a dull thud beside the basket, still twitching.

I change my plan in mid-lunge, laying the bronze blade into the wound Nami has made and pressing down with all the weight of my body. Behind me, the tail, which has released Nami, whips, snapping up and striking my back. I ignore it, not satisfied until my knife severs the bone.

The shaking that had affected my hands, now courses through my entire body. I turn to Lila. She holds her arm where the snake struck, her face white.

"Find a healer," I snap at Danel.

"Yes . . . I know one close by." He breaks free of his immobility, and he is gone.

Nami steps forward and licks my face with her bloody tongue. I press her to me and then make her lie still on her side while I run my fingertips over every bit of her, hardly daring to breathe, lest they find puncture wounds.

Lila gasps, "Is she bitten?"

I look up and meet her worried gaze. I do not miss that she can show concern for Nami though bitten herself.

"No wounds on her," I say with great relief.

WHEN THE HEALER comes, he inspects Lila's arm and examines her for signs of poison. Then he makes her a poultice. I wish Mika were here, but this man seems to know his business. He says prayers over her and promises to offer a goat to the goddess. I put a silver finger ring in his palm.

"Sometimes no venom is released," he says, curling his long, stained fingers over the ring.

"It was knocked away quickly," I agree, wiping sweat from my face.

"That is very fortunate. The desert cobra requires time to release its poison. I believe she will be fine."

Lila turns to me when he has left. I take her into my arms and let her sob. Danel looks on in the awkward manner of a man who does not know what to do with a crying woman.

At last, Lila sniffs and pulls away from me, touching my shoulder in apology for soaking it.

Nami lies with both paws on the snake's carcass. Pleased with herself, her tail sweeps a clear swath among the floor rushes.

I take a deep breath, my gaze drawn to the severed head of the cobra. "Well," I say on the exhale, "Tonight we will have lentils and snake."

Danel looks on in perplexity as Lila and I burst into a somewhat crazed laughter and more tears.

It is only later, when we have poured tea for Danel, that a thought occurs to me.

"Lila, did you come directly home from the market after you bought the lentils?"

"Not directly," she said. "I went to purchase a new pot."

"What did you do with the lentil basket?"

Her face pales as she grasps the reason for my question. "I left it with the vendor at the Gate." She takes a quick breath. "Surely, you don't think—?"

"Why would anyone put a venomous snake in your basket?" Danel asks, his hands clenching into fists.

"We are hated here," I remind him, thinking of the stone that found my head when I last went out alone.

How can I keep silent? How can I stay quiet?
My friend, whom I loved, has turned to clay.
Shall I not be like him, and also lie down,
Never to rise again through all eternity?

—Epic of Gilgamesh

W HEN WE NEXT VISIT WITH Jemia, I expect Nami's gamboling greeting at the door, her dejection at being abandoned forgotten in the excitement of my return. But she is not at the door. Could she be asleep in the courtyard or the sleeping room? I move swiftly through the house, my heart a stone.

"Where is Nami?" I demand of Lot.

He spreads his hands. Pheiné marches from her room to his side. "He jumped through the window."

"She," I sharply correct, as I run to the window and lean out, calling for her. "Nami! Nami!" *Why did I leave her?* I worried she would try to follow me. Panic beats in my chest like the wings of the trapped bird from moons ago.

Stricken, I leave the house, Lila and Danel at my side, and hobble through the streets like a woman who has lost her senses, calling for Nami, asking everyone if they have seen a black dog that looks like a small gazelle. They know her, yes; she is well known as my shadow, though I am not often out. A few seem to forget I am despised and pity my obvious devastation, but they have not seen her. We search until it is dark.

Numb, I allow Lila and Danel to guide me back.

FOR A WEEK, I search for her, Danel accompanying me. He feels badly that I lost Nami because of his request, but I blame myself, not him. I taught her to jump out the window.

I cannot eat. Lila is concerned and makes me drink water or, better, goat's milk, though I cannot taste it. My behavior disturbs Lot, but Pheiné cannot comprehend it and complains of my laziness. When I am at home, I sit in the window, looking out at the sea. Thamma, in general, ignores me, but once, when Pheiné is not around, she pauses beside me and whispers, "I am sorry." It is a small thing, but I wonder what kind of person she might have been without Pheiné's influence.

At night, when they are all asleep, I climb the hillside. My feet now know this path so well, it does not matter if there is moonlight or darkness. My hands recognize the touch of the stones—which ones protrude and which are smooth and recessed. I know the path, even without the gleam of white on Nami's tail that has always led the way.

CHAPTER

50

"And this is the first law of the luminaries: the luminary, the Sun, has its
rising in the eastern portals . . . and its setting in the western portals."

—Book of Enoch

IT IS ALMOST DUSK. THE wild doves are calling, and we are about to
eat the evening meal when someone pounds at the door. Lila goes to
answer it in my name. She returns with Danel behind her before I have
managed to rise. My usual pleasure in seeing my brother dissolves at his
flushed, sweaty demeanor. "What is wrong?"

Danel takes a moment to capture his breath. "Angels," he says, gulping air, "at the Gate."

"What?" My mind cannot grasp what he is saying.

He takes a deep breath and says more clearly. "Raph and Mika are in
the courtyard inside the Gate." Danel looks toward Lot, who has emerged
in clean clothes from our room, where he was washing off the grime of his
journey from his fields.

"Who is at the Gate?" Lot asks, having only heard part of Danel's an-
nouncement.

"El's messengers," Danel says again.

My heart is a loud drumbeat in my ears. *Mika? Here?* It is impossible;
and yet somewhere buried in my being, I knew he would come.

Danel adds, "The people's mood is not welcoming."

I can barely hear him over the thunder of my pulse, but I understand at once, and so does Lot. Since their presence here almost two summers ago, Lot's preaching has included frequent pronouncements about the visit of his god's angels, hinting their return would mean El's punishment was imminent.

It is obvious to me, however, that Lot is surprised at the angels' return, despite his public predictions.

He points at me. "Prepare. I will bring them."

Danel has caught his breath. "I tried to get them to come to my grand-mother's house," he warns, "but they insisted they would sleep in the Gate with the merchants."

"No," Lot says. "They do not understand the danger. I will bring them." He glares at me as if I am the cause of this problem.

"All will be ready," I manage, my thoughts whirling like a desert dust demon.

We have already prepared the meal, so Lila spreads freshly beaten rugs in the courtyard and shoos the chickens aside. We roll out more guest rugs for sleeping pallets.

Pheiné does nothing useful, but stands in the middle of the courtyard, her hands on her hips. "We have no room for guests with that cursed donkey here."

I ignore her, rearranging the cushions to make a place for them around the cook fire. Pheiné hates being ignored.

"At least that disgusting dog is gone."

I am passing near her, and I spin around without thought, the flat of my palm meeting her right cheek with a loud *smack*. She staggers back with a sharp gasp.

Thamma, who had been helping Lila with the rugs, freezes, her eyes widening. Lila turns her head away, but not before I catch a fleeting smile.

Pheiné takes several outraged breaths before she manages to speak. "You struck me!"

I say nothing.

"You serpent!"

She takes a step toward me. I am taller than she, but she knows I can-not move quickly. I narrow my eyes and grasp my staff tighter. When I do not back away, she stops, her nostrils flaring. "My father will not allow this in his house."

"I am wife here," I say as calmly as I can. "The house is mine, as is discipline of the children."

Her left cheek flames to match the right one. "Children? You are the child!"

"It is true I am younger in age, but it makes no matter. I am wife and this is my household. Now, do something useful or get out of the way."

WE ARE READY when Lot returns. I greet them courteously as they enter, but Mika grabs my shoulders. "Adira!"

I cannot hear for the gallop of blood in my ears.

Raph, beautiful Raph, puts a hand on Mika's arm. "Brother." It is all he says, but like Lila's soft word to Danel, it captures Mika's attention, and he releases me.

I bid them sit on the plaster bench that lines the wall in the greeting room, the same seat where Hurriya washed their feet in the traditional welcome to travelers. How surprised would that young Adira have been to know in only two summers' time, she would be in Hurriya's place. I am dizzy with the disorienting thought and grateful to be on my knees, closer to the earth.

Pheiné positions herself to minister to Raph, angling her face so he does not see the red mark on her cheek. She has avoided speaking to me or acknowledging my existence.

Mika protests when I remove his sandals. I am certain Raph has told him of all my injuries, if he cannot see for himself that I move like an old cow. I keep my head down, grateful for the thick braid that falls over the injured side of my face.

I wash the dust from his feet with tenderness, my hands trembling, remembering the touch of his hands on my flesh. The memory still sears—only so, I tell myself, because another man's touch has not replaced it. And now that half my face looks as if an ox stepped on it, a man is not likely to touch me, unless I slip out in the night during the Spring Rites and keep away from the torchlight. I silently mock that young girl-in-boy's-garb who worried about the slight bump on her nose.

When I am finished, Mika helps me stand. Still I keep my gaze down, though I can feel his desire to have me look at him.

I cannot hide myself when we sit for the evening meal. I sit with Raph between Mika and me. Raph is much easier to talk to. He was at my side when I looked far worse.

"I am glad to see you, Adira," he says, "but you are so thin! What happened to the flesh I put on you in Mira?"

"I too am glad to see you." I smile, aware of the way my mouth twists at the right corner where my cheek hollows into a depression.

"Where is Nami?" he asks.

Suddenly I cannot speak.

"She jumped out the window," Thamma says hastily, her eyes still wide and as full of Raph as Pheiné's.

Raph gives me a look of sympathy. He understands my love for Nami and my suffering.

"Has El sent you because of Sodom's sin?" Lot asks after we have begun to eat. It is not good manners to speak business before the meal is over, but he cannot restrain himself.

"I seek . . . something here," Mika says.

I remember he came the first time seeking ancient knowledge, something from his people's dim past when they lived beyond the sea in a land of rolling hills as thick with green grass as a tightly woven carpet. So many times he has told me of his homeland, that it is as real to me as the desert or the sea outside my window. My gaze travels the white plaster walls of my house. To my surprise, I have to wipe at a tear. Perhaps, I hope, no one saw it.

But I can feel Mika's gaze. He saw.

"If El sent you to find something, I will help you find it," Lot says eagerly.

Mika's jaw twitches. With Mika, this signals irritation. "Do you know then the instructions to build a time-temple of stone?"

Lot's thick lips part. "I know not what this is."

I remember something Mika told me when we spoke out on the desert.

Our oldest name is "Watchers." We have watched the sky from the beginning of time. My ancestors built temples of stone that measured the heavens and brought the goddess into them.

As it had then, a passage from one of Sarai's teachings presents itself in my mind, but this time I speak it aloud: "And they brought me to a place of darkness, and to a mountain the point of whose summit reached to heaven. And they showed me all the secrets of the ends of the heavens, and all the chambers of all the stars, and all the luminaries."

Into the quiet that follows, Pheiné says, "I am certain our guests do not wish to be bored with that old tale." She smiles sweetly at Raph.

Lot's expression clearly conveys he thinks his wife has lost her senses. "Why—?" he begins, but Mika raises his flattened palm toward Lot in a command for silence.

Mika has never taken his eyes from me, and I have nowhere else to look but in them. They are as green as the lands of his ancestors, and they fix on me as if I have uttered the words to the knowledge he has long sought. I blink.

Mika does not blink. "Speak those words again," he says in a voice I have never heard from him.

I repeat the quote.

"Is there more?" he asks, almost hoarse.

"Yes."

"Say it."

I do, the words coming easily to my mind, though I have not recited them since I last sat at Sarai's feet with Ishmael before our journey to Sodom. They speak of Enoch's journey to a high place where he saw El and his angels, a place of many portals arranged in a circle. The angels taught him which stars rose in the circle. Now my heart is beating faster. *This structure, this palace of El's, could it be the time-temple?*

Mika and Raph stare at me.

CHAPTER

51

A stranger has big eyes, but sees nothing.
—African proverb

I AM AGITATED WHEN LOT DECIDES to sleep in our bed. Perhaps he is jealous of El's angels and the attention they have paid me. I need not have been concerned. Lot drank heavily after the meal and snores almost as soon as he lies down. If I had wanted sleep, I could not have found it at his side. When I slip from the room, I am not surprised to see both Mika's and Raph's pallets empty. I *am* surprised, however, to see Lila sitting up against the wall, her blanket around her shoulders.

"Where did they go?" I ask her quietly.

She points to the window.

I almost laugh. "How did they know?"

She shrugs.

My smile dissolves. "What now?" I ask softly.

She does not answer, knowing the question is not hers, but mine. I go to her and she stands, knowing how arduous it is for me to sit on the floor or at least, how difficult to rise to my feet afterward. "You know I often go out that way at night?"

She nods.

"Do you know why?"

She starts to shake her head and then stops. "I believe it has to do with the sorrow in your heart."

I consider her. "You are a wise woman, Lila."

She pulls the blanket tighter. "Will you go tonight?"

This is the question I am asking myself. I turn and step to Philot's side to give him his treat and a scratch. He is getting gray around his eyes and muzzle, as I will here in this house.

Somehow, Philot has settled my mind. I cross the remainder of the floor to the window and climb out. A chill wind from the sea makes me wish I had brought a warmer wrap, but I will not return for one, because I might lose my courage. The soft slosh against the shore is as familiar as my heartbeat. Only the fiercest storm can lift the heavy salt-laden water into higher waves. It is said diving beneath the surface is impossible, that the sea will spew out anyone who tries. Hurriya did not try. She just lay face down upon its breast.

As always when I walk this path, my heart aches for Nami. I still look for her every day, remembering how she chewed her tether and returned to me when the Hurrian horsemen took her. I think I will always look for her.

I climb with care around the fallen stones of the wall and walk the path I have trod so many times. My eyesight is limited on the right side and so when the path turns that way, I almost run into Raph where he sits on a flat stone. His hand flies out with a warrior's speed to catch me as I stumble.

"You are always saving me, Raph."

"You have no debt to me. I should never have left you in the hands of those cursed Babylonians."

I sigh. "Should we count the choices we regret? How do we know what would happen if we chose differently? If you had not left, the guards might have planned more wisely and killed you in your sleep. Then you would not have been there to save me."

"I never thought of that."

"You were waiting for me here?"

"Yes."

I look up at the overhang that blots a piece of the moon, the place where I once sat with Raph and Mika and where Mika held the blue fire. "He is there?"

"Yes, he waits for you."

Another choice. Another path split from the trail. What would it mean were I to turn around and go back to my house with Hurriya's window and my snoring husband?

But I had known what I would do since Philot took his fig—perhaps before that, when I rose from the bed. Perhaps even when I heard there were angels at the Gate.

And so I climb the path, something I could never have done if I had not spent night after night making incremental progress and strengthening my leg in the process. I take my time, trying to slow my heart and bring to my mind what words I will say to Mika, but I can do neither.

Never has the journey up the cliff taken so long or gone so quickly. When I finally begin to climb the last bit, Mika's hand reaches out for me and pulls me up to stand with him on the overhang. Below us is the sea, brushed in a bold stroke by moonlight. To our left, the torches of Sodom flicker against the dark. Wind whips around us, a clean wind tonight, singing in my ears. Mika pulls me tightly against his chest, and the world goes still about us.

When at last he releases me, he holds me at arm's length and only breathes my name. "Adira."

"What do you see, Mika?" I whisper the question, afraid of the answer even in the dimness of the night.

He frowns, taking my face between his hands and tilting it up so I am looking directly at him, the moonlight full on my features. He does not hesitate. "I see the girl who pulled me from a raging flood, the girl who stayed with me and shared her water in the desert and cared for me, though she risked her own life to do so. I see the girl who crossed a wasteland to find my brother, though she could have returned to the safety of her family." His hands still firmly cup my face. He is not finished. "I see the woman who was the goddess for me, though she had never lain with a man, the woman who dared heaven with me. I see beauty and strength. I see the person I wish beside me for whatever time the goddess grants me of this life."

I close my eyes, not knowing what to do with this, though it is what my heart has cried for since I climbed the steps of Ishtar's temple.

Finally, he gives me a little shake. "What are you thinking, Adira? Tell me."

My mouth makes a sound that is part laugh and part sob. "I am thinking I have never heard so many words out of you at once."

He smiles, and pulls me again to him.

I am not certain if the tremble of the earth beneath us is real. In his embrace, I allow myself to stop thinking and simply to be where I am. I absorb the press of his arms, the smell of him, the solid wall of his chest. I do not think of tomorrow or when I must pull away from him.

Finally I mutter, "Why did you come?"

He rests his chin on my head. "I came to see if you found happiness, because without you, I am not."

A bark of a laugh escapes my lips. "I taught you to speak better Akkadian than that."

He gives me another little shake. "Do not jest, Adira. I have suffered without you."

"Then why did you send me away from Babylon?" It is then I realize anger resides in me, nestled between the desire and sorrow.

"To protect you."

"And to protect the stone?"

"Yes, and the stone."

"Is it safe?" I ask with irritation. "I think it should be dropped into the sea."

"It is hidden, but not yet in the hands of our people. After Raph took you to Abram and Sarai, he returned to Babylon."

"I thought you told him not to return."

"Apparently," Mika says wryly, "he acquired some of your love of obedience."

I ignore this. "So the king allowed you to leave as he promised?"

"Of course not."

"Then how did you escape?"

"With Raph's help and the aid of your friend, the priestess, who honored the word of her king, even when he did not."

"Then I am grateful to Raph and Tabni for your freedom."

He smiles and strokes my hair. His touch is tender, yet I feel as if his blue fire crackles down my spine. I step away from him, afraid if I do not, I will never be able to.

"Adira," he says. "No matter what you decide about . . . me, I need the knowledge you have of the tale of Enoch. It is what my people have lost and sought for countless seasons."

"Why is it so important?" I demand.

"It is not just a tale; it is instruction for building a time-keeper temple."

I think about all the description given in the story of Enoch's ascent to heaven, the careful details and measurements of the structure there that Enoch was made to memorize and that the children of Abram now recite.

"My people see time differently," Mika says. "They look into the distant past and the distant future."

"You spoke of this in the desert. Tell me again."

"Long ago, when the great stones came from the sky and fell into the water, the sea rose up and ate the land, destroying the time-temples and all but a few of the priests who knew their secrets. Such destruction could happen again. So the knowledge was spread to other chosen people and lands—to Enoch and others."

"Yes, I remember that now, but why lug that stone around with you? Why not leave it in a place of safety?"

"It is a dreaming stone. We hoped I would dream of where to find the lost knowledge."

"And did you?"

"I tried, but the stone did not speak to me."

"It spoke to you in Babylon."

He looks away then. "I am not certain of that. I followed the rite and did dream of chariots attacking, but who is to say the dream came from the gods or what I had learned listening to the talk of the people?"

I consider this. That he shares his doubts is a gift of intimacy. "So why did you come to Sodom that first time, if it was not at the stone's guidance?"

"We searched for peoples who followed different ways, hoping to find a heritage that preserved the instructions for the time-keeper temples. I heard of the gods of Babylonia and of Abram and El and of this place where Baal and Asherah rule." He took a breath. "I must fulfill my task, Adira. It is not merely my oath. Without it, we will lose the power to read the stars and predict another disaster from the sky."

This is the burden he carries. I look up at him. "I will teach you the words of Enoch."

He grasps my shoulders. "You can teach me as we travel to my people."

I meet his intense gaze, though I feel my bad eye shift to the side, and I hastily look to where red-gold hairs curl almost up to the hollow of his throat. "Lot would never allow that. He will not even let me go to the pastures just beyond the city to tend our herds."

"Are you happy here, Adira? With Lot?"

I do not have to search for that answer, but I do not understand its relevance. "I am wife to him."

"That is not my question."

I sigh. "No, I am not happy." How could I be happy in a city that greets me with stench every morning; daughters who hate me; a husband who cares nothing for me; and not even the comfort of my beloved Nami?

"Then come with me," Mika urges. "The Adira I know would not stay here in unhappiness."

A flame of anger ignites in my belly. "Come with you so you can have your knowledge conveniently at your hand?" *And then leave me.* I am not the woman he thinks he loves. My wounds lie deeper than my face. I am no longer the daughter of the wind. The sight of a scar on a man's face can freeze my blood, turn my bones to wood.

"No, Adira, not for that reason." He takes a careful breath. "I have hurt you, and I did not mean to. I meant to protect you."

"What was done to me was not your fault."

"It would not have happened if I had not sent you away. Adira, I am so sorry. If Raph had not killed those men who hurt you, I would have hunted them down."

I say nothing. He does not understand that the pain of having him and losing him was worse than the pain of blows.

"If I had not let you lie with me—"

"No," I stop him. "That was my choice."

He hesitates. "Was it so . . . unpleasant for you?"

My anger melts. I close my eyes. "No, Mika, it was not unpleasant." This is dangerous ground. I can feel my heart pounding, and my breath is still shallow from standing close to him. How can I explain what holds me here?

I look up at the sky where the brightest stars shine beyond the moonlight's reach. "Your ancestors, the Watchers, studied the stars for time uncounted. As you once told me, 'Every star has its path.' My father tried to teach me I have a place. Trying to be out of that place is like the stars fighting to move outside their path. I am on that path now, and I must stay there." I swallow. "I gave an oath to my father. I cannot dishonor his memory."

CHAPTER

52

I leave no trace of wings in the air, but I am glad I have had my flight.
—Rabindranath Tagore, *Fireflies*

WHEN I LEAVE MIKA AND clamber back down the hillside and
through the window, I lie awake through the remainder of the
night. In the morning, bleary-eyed, I help Lila with the chores, nervously
twisting the silver bracelets that Raph retrieved for me, my part in the
treasure awarded by King Samsu-iluna.

So many emotions have swept over me in the past day. I need to focus
on something simple to keep my feet on the earth. For this, I turn to the
tasks that make up my routine, the first of which is to gather the deposits
Philot has left and take them to the small herb garden located in the back
on the embankment above the sea. For a long time, Lila protested this
was not a job for the woman of the house, but I do not mind. The task
connects me to my childhood, but today, my mind is not on my childhood. Mika's presence has broken loose the dam of memories I so carefully
built. They sweep down the wadi they have dug in my mind, ending
at the previous night's encounter—the feel of his arms around me, his
breath on my hair, the solid wall of his chest against mine.

Lila takes the buckets and joins the women waiting at the eastern gates
for them to open. She has complained that it is growing more difficult to

get water from the river and that soon we will have to depend on the well at the Gate. That is as frightening a thought as the fire I fear is growing underground. We may survive if Mot's Tongue erupts again, but how long will the well give us water? What happens when it runs dry?

Lot wakes and comments on the sleeping forms of Mika and Raph, who have not stirred. "They still sleep?"

"They have traveled for many days," I say. "Let them rest."

But it is not long before Danel knocks at the door. I let him in with fingers to my mouth and speak quietly. "Greetings, Danel. Lila has gone for water." There is no longer need to pretend he comes to see me.

"I know."

This arouses my curiosity. I stand aside for him to enter, which he does, suddenly not able to decide where to put his hands.

"What is it, brother?" I ask quietly. "What disturbs you?"

"I . . . well." He swallows. "I wish to ask you for—?"

I tilt my head, looking at him from my good eye. "For a measure of salt?"

"No, no." Then he blurts, "I want to buy Lila from you."

I take a breath. "No."

If a man's face can fall to his knees, Danel's does so. "I can pay the price," he insists. "I have saved twice an adequate amount."

I open the door and wave him out. "She is not for sale. I will not talk about it again."

MIKA AND RAPH stay as our guests while I teach them the story of Enoch. I learned every word precisely as instructed by Sarai, and so they wish to learn it. Raph is not keen to stay inside and paces the small court-yard, but Mika insists Raph also learn every word. Whether it is Raph's dissatisfaction with his captivity or that Mika, as a healer, has had more practice absorbing knowledge, I do not know, but Raph learns at half the speed of his brother.

I am glad. I dread the day when they will leave.

I am not the only person who is happy with Raph's slowness in learning Enoch's tale. Pheiné and Thamma are both enamored with him, much to Lot's displeasure. But how can he protest? Lot is certain he and Mika are messengers of his god. Still, it is known from the old stories that angels once favored the daughters of man, and the products of such a union were creatures somewhere between divine and man—not a fate to desire for your daughters. Lot finds a reason to stay home when the girls do, which makes for a very crowded house and no chance for me to be alone with Mika. This is both a relief and a disappointment.

One morning, just as I emerge from my sleeping room, Raph surprises me, asking me to escort him and Mika to the market. "Mika needs to replenish his medicines," Raph explains.

"Then I will send Lila for them," I say.

At Raph's sharp glance, Mika speaks up, "No, I must see for myself what is available. I do not know the names in your language."

This does not sound like the complete truth. He could easily tell me the names, and I could translate for Lila, but I know Raph is eager to escape the confines of the house. "Go with Lila," I say. "Rarely am I out, and then only to visit Jemia with Danel. I do not care for the scalding stares of Sodom's residents." And, I admit to myself, I fear uncovering the terror that dwells inside me, especially in front of Mika or Raph.

"Lila left earlier this morning," Raph offers.

"Oh, where has she gone?"

"She did not say her destination, but she left honey cakes."

I know well where she most likely has gone, and it is not to the market. The honey cakes are to appease me.

"Will you go?" Raph says with his most engaging smile.

I cannot help but smile back at him. He is like the sun emerging after a storm. When he smiles, he must be forgiven anything.

Lot is still abed, and Pheiné and Thamma still sleep, or they would insist on accompanying Raph.

I put on a wrap against the morning chill. The hour is still early, so we have the street almost to ourselves. Though water is scarce, the pitch harvest has been remarkable, and clay jars of it cluster around almost every house. Because of its abundance, the price is low and people are holding it for a better day. Even those who do not normally trade in the black gold are buying it.

Mika's long strides carry him ahead, but Raph matches his pace to mine. He wrinkles his nose. "Am I growing more sensitive or is the stench of this city increasing?"

"It is worse. Even Lila says so."

"Why?"

"I think a great fire burns below the earth. Jemia told us of a place among the pitch pits where a tower of fire erupted when she was a child. Before you arrived, the earth began to tremble. I think it is shaking loose foul air trapped below and that is what rises up in the Dead Sea. Perhaps that is how the pitch forms."

"You do not think it is the work of this god, Mot?"

"I do not know if it is or is not a god's work. A sparrow flies with wings. If a god's hand makes the wings and the air, the bird does not know or say. It only sings and flies."

Raph nods. "That sounds like something Mika would say."

"The tremors have seemed stronger the past two moons—since you and Mika arrived, in fact."

Raph glances over his shoulder, his hand drifting to the knife at his sash. "Perhaps the people of Sodom think we are to blame."

"They are primed to think so, because you are guests of Lot. He has threatened that when you come, it will be with the wrath of El. That has not endeared them to you."

"Well, that explains the hateful looks cast our way when we venture out. Not that we have been out of your house more than two steps. You are a hard taskmaster. My head is so full of Enoch's words, I am dreaming of him every night."

I smile, aware, as always, of how it contorts my mouth, but Raph has always set me at ease, even when I was enamored of him. I care for him greatly, but the young girl who could barely hear above the pounding of her heart when he looked her way—that girl was also someone else entirely. How can I be so many different people?

"Raph, what did you wish to discuss with me?"

"How do you know?" He looks startled, like a dog caught with a piece of filched meat.

My contorted smile grows. "Did you think you were so stealthy as to fool me?"

He sighs, but his mouth curves in a self-mocking grin. "I should have known it would not be such a simple task."

"So—?"

He takes a breath. "So, Adira, I wish to ask you to do something for me."

I wait to see what it might be.

With a sideways look, he says, "You did remind me I saved your life."

"Be serious, Raph. What is it?" I shake my head at him.

"It concerns Pheiné and Thamma."

This is not what I expected. Could he possibly wish to marry one of them? Why else would he ask me? "What about them?" I say cautiously.

"I would like you to dissuade them from thinking I am available as a husband."

"Oh. But are you not?"

He hesitates.

"Raph," I ask bluntly, "are you married or betrothed? Why have you hidden this?"

"I have hidden nothing, and I am neither, but I do have someone who waits for me."

I take a moment to absorb this. "Well, why not just tell them yourself?"

"My lover is not a woman."

More than one moment passes while I ponder this. I do not know what to say. Raph is beautiful, clever, gracious, and as fierce a warrior as any man I have ever seen. In many lands, it is not uncommon for a man to love another man. It is generally ignored, as long as he takes a wife and fulfills his duty to her. El has commanded us to be fruitful and multiply. Raph was surprised when he learned I was not a boy, but he accepted me either way. Who am I to judge him? But I am curious. "Do you not wish to have children?"

A glaze films his eyes. "Yes, I do." We are almost at the market, and he slows his gait even more. "But that is not the issue. I have no interest in Pheiné or Thamma, but I do not wish to hurt them."

"You think it would hurt them to tell them your lover is a man?"

"I have rarely told it, but when I have, women seem to take it as a challenge, and things become worse."

"I see."

He clears his throat. "I hoped you would tell them I am betrothed or married. It would embarrass them if I told it, as if I knew they were seeking my interest in that way."

His earnestness makes me wish to laugh, but I do not.

"Will you do this, Adira? I cannot even concentrate on Enoch when they hover over me and peck at each other like the chickens over a pile of grain."

Laughter explodes from me. "Oh, that is the perfect description!"

Raph does not laugh with me, and his expression is so miserable I have mercy. "Of course I will tell them, but you could have just told me you were betrothed or married. Why did you not?"

"I could not lie to you, Adira. Not about something like this."

I stop in the street and embrace him. I have found the unexpected in this wretched place—two brothers.

53

Canaanite sanctuaries included the altar, a standing stone (messoth) and a wooden pole, called an asherah, which was named after Asherah, the mother of the gods of dawn (Schachar) and dusk (Salim).

—Christopher Knight and Robert Lomas, *Uriel's Machine*

TWO MOONS HAVE PASSED SINCE Raph and Mika arrived. Five since Nami disappeared. She is still on my heart. Sometimes I see a shadow of movement from the corner of my eye, and I whirl, expecting to see her leap through the window. But it is always but a shadow.

As spring approaches, the heat intensifies. We must now go to the well at the Gate for water, because it has become impossible to get any from the riverbed. I carry the empty bucket so Mika and Raph can be free to deal with any trouble. We would bring two, but the king has made an edict that each family may draw only one bucket a week. Hardly enough for drinking, and we now carry a stench as strong as the belching sea.

The sea has shrunk from the shore, leaving flat pans of encrusted salt, and it erupts more violently every day, a giant pot of bitter, roiling water, so that even the boatmen cannot safely harvest the pitch. They must wait until the clumps of black tar drift onto land. Disaster boils beneath the earth, I am certain of it, but all my efforts to sway Lot into leaving have failed.

This city is also a pot near the boiling. The Spring Rites approach, the time when Baal is to escape the annual clutch of Mot. If that does not bring rain, I do not know if Lot can hire enough men to protect us.

We join the long line at the well.

"It has never been this hot before Spring Rites," a man ahead of us says.

"Mot fights to keep Baal in his grasp," another replies.

The sun thrusts fiery lances onto every head, glares off the white stones to spear into our eyes. Hot wind spits dust in our faces, and we can only breathe behind the drape of our head coverings. Kohl darkens every eye. My body longs for moisture, sucked dry of it. The only benefit I can name is that people are too lost in their own misery, concentrating on enduring, to give much mind to Lot's wife.

But Raph and Mika have not escaped notice. "Look there!" one of the men in the water line behind us cries. "The strangers come to claim a share of our water!"

My right hand tightens on my staff.

"What do El's angels need of water?" another asks. "Isn't their righteousness enough drink?"

The crowd laughs, but it is a nervous laugh, bordering on madness. This is Lot's fault, his prediction that Raph and Mika's return will signal El's wrath on Sodom. None, however, have dared to throw a stone, even from the anonymity of a crowd—yet.

Sudden cries at the well catch our attention. It is several moments before the word passes back to us. "The allotment is now only a half-bucket for each family!"

The crowd stirs. "What about that woman who took a whole bucket?" Several are pointing to a pregnant woman who is just passing us, walking carefully so as not to spill a drop. A man with a stout staff leaps out of the line and reaches for her bucket.

Mika steps between him and the pregnant woman. Enraged, the man swings his staff at Mika, who ducks before it can strike him. Before I can blink, Raph is between Mika and his attacker, knives appearing in both his hands.

Blood will spill here! Before I can think, I swing what is at hand, instinctively not trusting my leg to support a blow with my staff. Even empty, the *whack* of the copper bucket is enough to bring the man to the ground.

Chaos swirls around us, and men begin fighting one another, accusing their neighbor of taking more than their share of water. Mika snatches an arm about my waist, leaving Raph to guard our escape. We hasten, as quickly as my bad hip allows, along one the streets that spoke off the Gate and end at the Dead Sea.

"Can we get back to the house this way?" Mika asks.

"Yes, but what about our water?" I lick my cracked lips with a swollen tongue.

"We'll return for our portion when this dies down." Mika exchanges a look with Raph.

I read that look. A half bucket is not enough for all of us. Despair wrenches at my chest. *Will they leave Sodom? Am I to lose Mika again?*

"I don't need much to drink," I hear myself say.

"Home first," Mika orders, his brow furrowed.

I HAVE TOLD Pheiné and Thamma their attentions only make Raph more keenly miss his beloved betrothed. After angry outbursts when he and Mika were out, they resumed their habit of spending time away from the house—a blessed relief. Pheiné has regained her custom of loudly expressing dissatisfaction concerning me or Lila, and Thamma has withdrawn into her own world. I imagine this has little to do with Raph, and more to do with what Lila has confided to me, a secret I have not decided how to resolve, one that makes me ill with loathing for my righteous husband.

Raph and Mika claimed a half-bucket ration of water for themselves as well as the family at the well. Both were armed, so no one challenged them, though I am certain this fed the flames of resentment. We are back to one bucket of water for our household.

Today is the last day of the Spring Rites. Tonight at dusk, the goddess will call Baal from the arms of Mot. If he does not answer her and release rain, I fear for the safety of my house. Lot and his daughters are out, leaving me with Raph and Mika, who are reciting Enoch. If El's angels were not our guests, I wonder whether my husband would have left me alone this day.

I am at my weaving when the earth suddenly heaves and twists as though a giant serpent writhed just below the surface. It lifts me and then tilts me sideways, spilling me against the wall with the sound of distant thunder. Confused, I stare at the crack in the plaster that has erupted and raced up the wall like a flooding wadi.

Raph is the first on his feet and then helps me up. By the time I am standing, Mika is also there, his hands hard on my waist, and I forget the rupture in the wall and the protruding lump of earth in our once flat courtyard. The mind is a strange thing, and mine focuses on the heat of Mika's grasp. I can feel it through the cloth, searing into my skin.

"Adira, are you all right?"

I am mute for a moment and then nod, and he steps away, an expression in his eyes that is almost anger. Anger that he cannot have me as his own? That is what I see there, but I have lost certainty in my ability to read the silent language of people, especially Mika's.

Lot staggers in, smelling of beer. I wonder if he left our room during the night, as he often does when he has drunk overly much, though since Mika and Raph have been here, he has always returned to our bed. I do not go out the window anymore. I am afraid Mika waits for me on the cliff.

I look down at the ruin of my weaving frame.

Raph thinks the clearest. "We should go outside."

I am not sure why it would be safer there, my instinct being to stay inside. But I follow his gaze up to the opening above the courtyard where heavy branches cross the courtyard roof, providing support for lighter branches and palm fronds. The support logs have rolled together, leaving a gap.

With Mika and Raph on either side, I am hastened from the house. "My staff," I cry, when we are through the door. Mika ducks back inside to retrieve it. Once it is in my hands, I grasp it tightly, as though it is the means to steady my mind.

Though it is morning, the sky is dark with smoke, and ash falls like black mist, lit with tiny burning bits. The stench of rotten eggs is strong. One of the burning particles falls at my feet. Mika kicks dust over it to extinguish it and then examines it. "Pitch."

People are shouting and pointing to the south. We move our position to see what they see. In that direction, a tower of red flame spears the sky, visible over the city wall.

"What is that?" Raph asks.

I cough in the black, curling smoke that has blown over the city. "The Tongue of Mot. It must be!"

"Mot," Mika says, as if to himself. "The underworld god."

The burning bits of falling pitch stop, but the smoke thickens. People swarm the streets. Many have come to the city from the fields and pastures to celebrate the Spring Rites. I hear snatches of their fears.

"What is happening?"

"The gods are angry!"

"We are doomed!"

Several stare at us. Their ill will strikes like a blow. "Perhaps we should go back inside the house—"

Before I can finish, I see Lila pushing her way through the crowd. When she reaches us, she grasps my shoulders. "Please come!"

"Where? What is it?"

"Hurry," she pants, trying to get her breath. "It is Jemia; she is hurt."

I turn to Mika. "Please go with her to my grandmother. You can reach her more quickly than if you wait for me."

"Only if you let Raph stay at your side," he says, scanning the hostile crowd.

"Yes, I promise. Just go." My gaze darts to his bag to make certain it is at his hip, though it is always there or right beside him. "We will follow."

He is off then, his head and shoulders visible above the throng of milling people, like the decorated asherah poles. Worry for Jemia and the difficulty of staying behind Raph as he shoulders his way through the streets keeps my mind from dwelling on the crowd. Will they blame Lot and me for angering Mot? But for now, they are too frightened to have a solidified intent. I grasp Raph's sash so we will not separate. We move as quickly as my hip will allow.

When we reach Jemia's house, we find the door open and enter. No one is in the little gate, so we go directly to the courtyard. Ash floats down from between newly formed gaps overhead, and I see at a glance that what so concerned Raph in our house has happened here—a log has broken from the courtyard roof and fallen. One end remains wedged among its fellows, but Jemia is trapped beneath the other. Danel attends her, while Mika kneels before the fire, busy with his potions.

I rush to her side, and my heart spasms. I see that no herbs or incantations will save her. The broken, splintered log is embedded in her chest. How her heart is beating around it is a wonder. I take her cold hand and look up at Danel. Tears streak his soot-covered face. He is not much older than I, but now he appears as ancient as Jemia.

To my surprise, Jemia squeezes my hand. "You are here," she whispers.

"Yes, I am here, and Danel is here."

"My grandchildren."

"Yes."

Danel has her other hand. It is all we can do.

Raph positions himself at the door, both his daggers drawn. His understanding of the language might not be as subtle as his brother's, but his warrior instincts recognize a threat.

He is not the only one. Jemia's watery gaze finds my face. "Be careful, granddaughter."

"The earth has stopped shaking," I say, misunderstanding her warning.

"It is not the earth you should beware," she rasps, her gaze flicking toward the street. "Fear drives them. Fear that the underworld god is fighting to keep Baal and spring will not come."

"Do not try to speak," I beg her.

I feel Mika's presence then beside me. "Hold her head."

Danel and I use our free hands to tilt Jemia's head forward, and she drinks from the cup Mika holds. I do not have to ask. I know it is only something to ease her pain.

Desperate, Danel grasps Mika's arm. "Is that all? Are you not a healer?"

Mika's face is grim.

"We can lift the log off her," Danel insists. "It hurts her to breathe. Can you not see?"

With the same gentleness that so surprised me when Mika first touched me on the goddess's rooftop, Mika puts a hand on Danel's arm. "Yes, I see. The potion will help."

"But we must remove the log. Between us, we can."

"No."

Danel stares at Mika.

"If we move it, she will die in even greater pain."

It seems a lifetime before the hope in Danel's eyes changes to agony.

I am weeping now—for Jemia, for Danel, and for myself. My time with her was so short.

Her milky eyes had closed, but now they open, and she releases my hand, lifting it as though searching for something.

"What do you want?" I ask.

Her mouth opens and closes, then opens again in a hoarse whisper— "Lila."

Lila, who had been standing silently behind Danel, ducks beneath the log and comes to the side where I kneel. Jemia's hand fumbles for hers and holds it tightly. Now she has Danel in one hand and Lila in the other. Again, her mouth moves, but she cannot speak. Danel and Lila's eyes meet over Jemia.

And then she is gone.

I marvel at how the body that held that spirit I so loved and respected, that person, is now only a husk. Did Mot's hand reach up and snatch her? Where is she? That she is totally gone is impossible and unbearable.

The loss of her rends anew the place in my chest, the dark hole that opened with the loss of my father and then Nami. Jemia had stitched it together. Now, it is again an aching abyss.

Then I feel Lila's arms around me and Danel. *Family.* It is the only comfort that salves such a loss. We have all lost our mothers and our fathers.

The world is smaller than it was when I woke this morning.

The men pull aside the log, and Lila and I ready Jemia's body, cleaning her and wrapping her in linen. With Danel's help, we choose among the things she loved, a coral necklace, a small alabaster vase from Egypt, a tiny clay imprint of Danel's baby feet. We place that and the necklace inside the vase. Normally, we would take her to the goddess's temple for the rites of the dead, but Danel wants only to give her passage. It is a strange ceremony. Each of us worships different gods, yet somehow, here in this small house, the love we have for this woman makes them all one.

We watch her through the night to make certain demon spirits do not find her body or hinder her spirit in its release. Just before dawn, I instruct Lila to gather food and what is left of Jemia's ration of water. She looks at me with raised brows.

While she does this, I search the house for food that might be easily carried. Danel is lost in his grief and gives no attention to what I do.

At dawn, Danel scoops Jemia's small linen-wrapped body into his arms and carries her out, with Raph flanked on his left and Mika on his right and Lila and me following. I carry the alabaster vase with her treasures and the few things I found in my scavenging in a bag over my shoulder. Lila carries two skins of precious water, concealed by a blanket.

Many people have slept in the street from fear of their houses falling on them. Both gates have been left open for the past several days, welcoming those who have come for the rites. We leave through the Gate. Though I feel the stares, no one bothers our small procession.

As we move down into the rocky slope below the city, it is as if we enter Mot's kingdom. Bluish flame ripples over the tops of the black pits. Likely, the burning pitch spewed by Mot's Tongue ignited them. When the rocky path turns, the fountain of fire rises before us, a towering wall of heat. Black smoke billows up into the already dark sky. We stop, staring at the sight. Lila hesitates. "Will Mot swallow us?"

"We must see to my grandmother," Danel says. "The Tongue is farther away than it appears. But you can return to the city if you wish."

Lila lifts her chin and stays with us.

We pass the charnel houses, taking Jemia instead to the old burial ground where the spirits of her family wait for her. With great care, Danel places her in the large family death urn, removing the linen and arranging her on her side with her legs folded and tucked next to her chest, as the infant sleeps in the womb. We will leave her here for the vulture gods to take her flesh to the sky, and in a year, Danel will return to carry her cleaned bones down the vertical shaft to the circular chamber where she will sleep with her ancestors.

54

The heavens shrieked,
The earth bellowed,
A storm gathered,
Darkness came forth,
A flash flamed,
A fire shot up,
The clouds thickened,
It rained death.
Then the brightness vanished,
The fire went out,
The blaze that had fallen
Turned to ashes.

—Epic of Gilgamesh

WHEN WE EMERGE FROM THE grave chamber, I grasp both of Danel's hands and make him look at me. "Brother, you cannot go back to your house."

For the first time, I have his attention. "Why?"

"Today is the last day of Spring Rites."

He shrugs, uninterested, even though we stand in sight of Mot's Tongue licking the sky. I turn him so he faces the spouting flame. It has not ceased gushing fire, although the rain of pitch and ash has stopped.

"Why has this happened?" I ask him, determined to make him think, though I know he must be numb with his loss.

He shakes his head. "I do not know. Nor do I care."

"I loved Jemia too, Danel. But she wants you to live."

With a sigh, he lifts his hands and lets them fall. "I am alive."

"We must convince Lot to leave this place. All of us."

"What are you talking about, Adira?"

The others stand near, watching and listening, but do not interfere.

I struggle to put my thoughts into words. "I do not think we have seen the worst of this. For the past several moons, the sea has belched foul air."

"It always does."

"Not like this—great bubbles, sometimes strings of them. I spend much of my time by the window, watching it."

Lila nods. "She knows more about the Dead Sea than the pitch fishers."

"What is this to do with me going home?"

"Something is stirred that has been shaken loose." I search for words to explain my fear.

"The gods' anger? You do not believe the rites will appease them?"

I shrug. "Perhaps Mot or Baal is angry at Lot and shook the earth to release the foul air and spit on us, or perhaps El is angry at Sodom and did so, or perhaps it is a matter of the gods we have no hope to understand."

"Or perhaps it has nothing to do with us," Mika says, studying the tower of flame and moving in its direction.

"Brother—" Raph warns. "Leave it."

For a moment, I smile, remembering how Shem and I had to pull Mika away from the mating camels. He is curious about everything. Perhaps that is because the blood of the Watchers pulses in him.

"What does it matter?" Danel is restless now.

I take a deep breath; I know he is full of sorrow now, but he must understand the danger. "Sodom's anger for Lot has been simmering for a long time. This—" I nod at Mot's Tongue. "This may push that anger to boil. You are part of our family. That makes you a target. We are safer all together."

With an indignant frown, Danel says, "Spring Rites are celebrated in all the cities of the Vale since anyone can remember. No one has ever been hurt, save perhaps in a few harmless fights over a woman. The rites are holy."

"Perhaps so. Perhaps I am wrong, but I do not want you to be alone. Jemia would not want you to be."

"She speaks truth," Raph says. "It is plain to see. I know a threat when it lies in the grass." His gaze flicks to me, and he flinches, perhaps belatedly, remembering a time he did not recognize danger when it lay in the hearts of the guards who escorted us from Babylon.

"All right," Danel concedes. "Where will I go?"

"To your sister's house, of course," Lila allows no space for any other thought.

He snorts. "Am I to sleep beneath the donkey?" He turns to me. "Your house will burst apart."

"You will fit in our sleeping room." I do not relish Lot's reaction to this, but Danel is family, and it is my house.

Lila's hands are on her hips, ready to scold him should he refuse. His cheeks flush. "Very well."

I wish we could go the long way back to the city, bypassing the south gate and entering at the eastern gate, which is much nearer our house. But that is not possible, given the terrain from here. We must pass back through the burning pitch pits.

The heat has grown unbearable. Sweats drips from us. Breathing is difficult. Ahead, Danel stops, so I almost plow into his back. "What is it?" I pant.

For answer, he points down to our left. I follow the line of his arm and gasp. Bubbles dance on the surface of one of the pools of pitch. Black liquid, less viscous than the pitch, as if it has mixed with water, oozes from the pit's bounds. It creeps on oily fingers outward from the center.

"What is happening?" I ask.

Danel shakes his head. "I do not know. I have never seen or heard of such."

The bubble quickly becomes a gushing fountain of oily water, sweeping toward us.

Lila clutches his arm. "Mot reaches for us! Let us leave this place!"

We do, with all the speed we can muster in the oppressive heat.

WE RETURN TO the city when the sun has almost set to find the Gate empty. Everyone has flocked to the goddess's temple, which we must pass to reach our house. As we approach, the press of people becomes tighter, making it difficult to stay together, possible only because Mika and Raph have put themselves in front and behind us. Danel and Lila flank me. Mika, by dint of his stature, is able to make a slow path for us.

All of the men wear only a cloth wrap around their loins. The women have adorned their wrists, arms, and throat with gold or silver—or copper, if that is their best. In spite of their terror or perhaps because of it, they are dressed in their finest, their skin smoothed in oil. The women's dresses are a single cloth, tied at one shoulder, leaving the other bare.

When we finally reach the temple, we can see the standing stone and the wooden asherah pole rise over the crowd, the pole's upper portion carved in the slender likeness of the goddess and adorned with ribbons.

At a point almost in front of the temple, we are forced to a halt. Not even a drawn weapon would cut us passage. Wedged tightly, we turn and look where everyone's attention lies—on the third level of the tiered temple. There, the chief priestess stands. She is dressed in white, her throat, wrists, and arms wrapped in Egyptian gold. Tall and slender, she lifts one arm to the sky and reaches down with the other toward the second tier where her chosen consort struggles with a man hooded and robed in red—Mot, god of the underworld.

We are immobile in the press of bodies as the sun crawls toward the horizon and sacred words are spoken. Mika is entranced, but Raph is restless. He is better at swords and at making women's hearts flutter than at religion. Many languid eyes have appraised him, especially those nearby. Mika, too, is the object of appraisal. Either these are people from outside the city, or city dwellers have forgotten their animosity toward Mika and Raph in the heat of the rites.

Sweat runs down my chest and sides and pools beneath my breasts. We have escaped a pot to land in a fire. The heat from so many bodies, so close, is palpable. But the people, rapt at the drama before them, seem oblivious to discomfort. At stake is the fertility of their fields, their anxieties heightened by the presence of Mot's Tongue in the distance. The priestess before them is not a mere woman, but Asherah, the Mother Earth who waits for Baal's seed to bring life to the fields. Below her, the struggling king is Baal, the matching half to the goddess. Together, they are Life. If Baal does not find his way from Mot's embrace to Asherah's, no rain will fall. No grass will flourish to feed the sheep, goats, and cows. No crops or herbs will grow.

Famine.

Half of my heritage is of Abram, but these are also my people through my grandmother, and I am swept up into the single, beating heart that unites the crowd in the mystery enacted before us, the mystery that allows us—mortals of body and blood—a part in the world of the gods.

A man and a woman appear. The man is covered in gold. He is Shapash, the sun god. The woman, who grasps a spear, is Anat, the goddess of war. Together, they fight the hooded Mot on the temple steps, enacting the ancient story.

With a final wrench, Baal breaks free of Mot's arms and ascends the steps to embrace his waiting Asherah. Her hand lifts with aching slowness to her shoulder and unclasps her robe to welcome him. Everything has slowed, as though the air is honey. Her dress drifts to her feet in folds of white, like the salt foam the sea offers to the land. The crowd inhales with one breath. The goddess stands naked in only her gold adornment and reaches both hands to Baal.

I am aware of my body as I have not been since I was the goddess for Mika. I feel the touch of skin on my skin, but I cannot look away. Mika's hand has found mine.

Slowly, all about us, the women reach to their shoulders and loosen the knots there. The sound of cloth falling from so many is like clouds touching, something heard with senses other than the ears. The women step into the open arms of the men.

Somehow, a space has opened around us, as bodies that could not move closer together, do. Mika seems to be the only one of us who still has his senses, perhaps because he has been in the goddess's arms before. He pulls my hand and calls to Raph. I look back at Mika's brother. The centers of Raph's eyes are dark. Is he thinking of his own lover? I stand between Danel and Lila, but their longing for each other crackles around me like the blue lightning Mika once held.

"Hurry," Mika says. "This may be our only chance."

He is right. We shake off the hands that reach for us, and they are soon clasping others. In the sea of hunger and need, we are not hindered, except to keep our own heads above the water of desire that laps at us on every side.

Behind us we hear the chant from the temple, "Aliyan Baal lives; the prince, lord of the earth, is here!"

55

That evening the two angels came to the entrance of the city of Sodom. Lot was sitting there, and when he saw them, he stood up to
meet them. Then he welcomed them and bowed with his face to the
ground. "My lords," he said, "come to my home to wash your feet,
and be my guests for the night. You may then get up early in the
morning and be on your way again."

"Oh no," they replied. "We'll just spend the night out here in
the city square."

But Lot insisted, so at last they went home with him. Lot prepared a feast for them, complete with fresh bread made without
yeast, and they ate.

—Genesis 19:1-3

W E REACH HOME AT DUSK. Lot is furious. "Where were you?"
he shouts. "I forbade you to attend the Spring Rites!" Then he
seems to notice Mika and Raph standing behind us in the little gate. He
clasps his hands, anger melting into confusion.

"I do not understand. Did you smite the people of Sodom?" he asks Mika.

At that moment, Pheiné and Thamma come from their room. Pheiné's
face is flushed, but Thamma is pale. She has been ill for several days.

"Adira is not an obedient wife," Pheiné observes without a glance at
me. "In addition to bringing you shame with her smashed face and limp."

Lila gasps.

I, too, am surprised. Not that Pheiné thought such things, but that she is saying them. Her temper, so like her father's, has galloped free of rein since the last moon. I say nothing. What is there to say? She is right.

Lot shifts his weight. "Daughter, guard your tongue."

"Why?" Pheiné crosses her arms. "It is the truth. She brings you nothing. No status, no wealth to speak of."

Mika, my steady, calm-in-the-face-of-anything, steps forward, his voice as taut as stretched rope. "She is the daughter of Zakiti, as good a man as I have ever met, whose daughter does him honor."

His defense of me and of my father brings tears to my eyes, but he is not finished.

"You cannot see her worth, because your own fears blind you."

This stops Pheiné. "I am not afraid of anything."

He says nothing, but his green eyes bore into her. I would not wish to be the one receiving their glare.

Lot steps protectively in front of his daughter, but his words to her are a warning. Perhaps he fears Mika will cast fire at her. "Pheiné, show respect to El's messenger."

With a sniff, she steps back. "Yes, Father."

I want to slap her again.

To his credit, Lot never spoke to me about striking her because of her complaint about Nami. Or perhaps Pheiné never told him. Not to protect me, I am certain, but to save her pride, or perhaps she feared Lot would recognize my position and not interfere. Lila would never tell him.

Danel pulls his gaze from the ground. He has been in his own world of sorrow. I am not certain he even heard our exchange. "My grandmother died yesterday."

This silences everyone.

Danel looks at Lot. "When the ground shook, she was struck by one of the courtyard roof poles." He sweeps his arm to include Mika, Raph, Lila, and me. "They came to help, but she died. We carried her to the tomb chamber, so the sky birds could take her, and her bones could lie with our ancestors." His gaze is distant. "Where I will one day lie. . . ."

Lila puts an arm on his.

Mika's mouth twists. I know he is distressed at not saving Jemia.

"Mika," I say into the silence, "I wish you to mark Lila as a free woman."

Everyone turns to me with looks of surprise. I lift my chin. "It is best for a healer to do it."

We add dried dung to the cook fire. I take my seal from my neck and give it to Mika. He removes the worn rawhide strip from the center bore hole and slips the cylinder onto a thin rod, holding it into the fire.

"What is she doing?" Pheiné demands of Lot. Pheiné never calls me by my name.

Lot frowns. "She is freeing her slave. It is her right, although it seems an awkward time for it."

"Who is to fix our food and clean the house and—" she looks with distaste at Philot—"see to that creature?"

Despite her whining, Lot does not interfere. He cannot. I have the tablet he marked with his own seal.

Mika takes a little bowl from his bag. My gaze follows the familiar pattern of whorls in the wood, remembering our fight for survival in the desert. When I first desperately dug it from his pack, how magnificent that small bowl appeared! I used it to boil onions for a poultice, to carry water, and to cook whatever I found or Nami brought us. It saved our lives, that little bowl.

Lila sets a bit of the water to boil for him in a small copper pot. Lot is mollified with such a use of water by the fact it was Jemia's portion. The smell of burning pitch drifts into the house. My worries turn to the oily water gushing from the ground. Surely it will run downhill, southward and not threaten the city. But what if it finds other shafts to rise in? I do not miss the irony that we are dying for lack of water, and what might come to us, like the sea beyond my window, is undrinkable. Perhaps Mot's cruel joke on us.

NIGHT HAS FALLEN, and the torches that light the streets are burning. We eat flatbread and stew. Pheiné stands at the door, her ear pressed against it. "The revelry has spread," she says.

Raph's brows rise in question.

Still attentive to him, perhaps hoping she can woo him from his lover, she answers his unspoken question. "On this night, the holy rite yields to revelry. Young men roam, drinking and copulating with any woman who has not the sense to be inside."

"I remember this from our previous visit," Raph says.

Mika frowns. This is evidence of his suspicion that the holy has been twisted in this city.

Raph's words hurl me into the past, to the night when Mika, Raph, and I watched the torches from the cliff overhang. We were too far away to see the details, but the sounds reached us. On that night, my father still lived, my heart ached for Raph's touch, and Mika held blue fire.

"It will be worse tonight." Pheiné's troubled tone pulls me back to the present. Despite her arrogance, she has not been blind. "There are packs of men who will hunt the street. The coupling at the temple is a holy thing, but tonight—"

"Will they come to this house?" Raph asks.

"They never have," Thamma says.

Pheiné shakes her head. "But Mot's Tongue has never erupted the day before the Spring Rites and—" She glances at her father, knowing as well as we his ranting has increased the ire of the Sodomites to a high pitch. "—it has still not rained," she says instead.

"I have said nothing El has not blessed," Lot declares.

To my surprise, Thamma, who sits upon the raised hump of earth in the courtyard as though it is a throne, says, "Has it truly been El's desire that you be so important, Father, or is it your own desire?"

Lot's fingers curl into fists. "What have I raised? Daughters or backbiters?"

She flushes, but does not apologize. It is that kind of night.

"The water is boiling," Lila says to distract us. At Mika's instruction, she pours it over the crushed herbs in his bowl. When he is satisfied with the color, he calls Lila to him and cleans her arm where an old knot of scarring mars her skin. He allows nothing to touch it until it is dry. "You must hold very still, or the mark will not be readable."

Lila nods, her chin high. "I will not move."

She does not, her gaze steady, looking out the window to the sea. The moon has not yet risen, and it is dark. Normally, we can hear the waves, but tonight the sound is lost among the cries from the streets. I wonder what Lila is thinking—of her mother? Her past? Or her future?

Mika places the hot stone cylinder on her arm and rolls it, as one would on clay, leaving the fiery red imprint of the goddess, Lama, on her skin. Wasting no time, he sets down the seal and covers the burn with a thick salve.

"Does it hurt much?" Danel asks, drawn from his sorrow by concern for her pain.

She looks at him, her eyes wet with unshed tears. "I welcome the pain of freedom."

Danel turns to me. "Thank you, Adira. But why? I offered to buy her. I would have freed her myself.

"I know."

"Then why?"

"Then she would have been in your debt. Now, she is not, and it is her choice whether to wed you."

As Danel digests this, another irony pricks my mind. I, who was a free woman, had to marry the man my family chose for me, but Lila, a slave, is now free to marry whomever she chooses. It is a strange world.

The world chooses this moment to become even stranger.

CHAPTER

56

But before they retired for the night, all the men of Sodom, young and old, came from all over the city and surrounded the house. They shouted to Lot, "Where are the men who came to spend the night with you? Bring them out to us so we can have sex with them!"

—Book of Genesis 19:4,5

P HILOT'S EARS TWITCH, AND HE peels back his lip, exposing his upper teeth, a donkey's signal that he smells something strange. It is the only warning we receive before a deep rumble and spate of shaking, lasting no longer than an exhaled breath. This one has thrown Thamma from the mound of raised earth, but not altered the ground. I am thankful Mika was not in the act of applying the freed-mark to Lila's arm.

"El is angry," Lot declares. "But he will protect us. Has he not sent his angels to us?"

I almost laugh at Thamma's rolled eyes, which her father, thankfully, cannot see. Something has changed her since I slapped Pheiné. Perhaps she is no longer in her sister's thrall.

"I hear voices," Raph says, stepping toward the door. Pheiné steps aside, and he opens it. I clump across the floor with my staff and peer under his arm at the living wave of torches that approach.

Raph closes the door. "They are coming this way. Is there a way to barricade the door?"

"Where is your guard, Father?" Thamma asks, a note of panic in her voice.

Lot shrugs. "He left when I could not pay him with water." He lifts his arm toward the door. "I do not fear them. El is my god. He is friend to Abram, my uncle. He will not let me die."

"Everyone dies," Raph snaps. "If you do not wish it to be your day, help me with the door."

He shrugs. "I have nothing to barricade the door, but it will not be needed. In Sodom, it is the worst of manners to disregard the door of another's house."

"These people are angry and frightened, Lot," I say. "And probably drunk, as well. They do not care a whit for manners."

Within moments, they are here. We can see the glare of their torches through the door seams and even at the back window where I have closed the lattice. Perceiving that as the most vulnerable point, Raph draws his sword and takes a stand there. Danel pulls his own knife from his sash. I am glad to see it. City dwellers do not always go about armed, but Danel spent most of his life, as I, on the caravan trail.

Pheiné and Thamma cling to one another, and Lila goes to comfort them. I am amazed at her, considering all she has endured from them. Perhaps being a freed woman is not yet a reality for her. Or perhaps she does care for them, in spite of their ways.

I do not.

The mob shouts. Stones strike against the door with sharp *thwacks*. Philot brays and pulls back against his rope. I draw my knife. I may be crippled, but the man who comes at me, the first one at least, will pay a price.

Suddenly, the noise quiets, sending a chill racing up my spine. A voice shouts, "Lot, don't hide behind Abram's robe!"

Lot moves to the door and shouts. "What do you want?"

Another voice calls out, "We want those men you say are here in the name of your god!"

"Yes, give them to us!" another yells.

Fear, fury, and lust fuel the mob's laughter. The sound washes cold through me despite the sweltering head, an echo of the jeers of the Babylonian guards as Chiram and I lay at their mercy.

The loudest voice raises again. "If these so-called 'angels' do not join our rites and have our women, give them to us, and *we* will know them!"

Lot's face burns with anger. It is a great insult for one man to threaten to rape another. Before Mika can stop him, Lot is out the door, closing it behind him. Pheiné rushes forward, but Mika holds her back. I step close to them.

"Pheiné," I say sharply into her ear, as she struggles, "if Mika has to fight to protect us, he does not need his hands full with you."

She stiffens but is still, and Mika releases her.

"People of Sodom," Lot's voice rises over the din. "Do not do this wickedness!"

"You dishonor our god, Lot! It is Spring Rites. Baal must ascend from Mot's grasp. Are you blind that you do not see the spouting of his Tongue? His anger at Baal's struggle?"

"These men are my guests," Lot cries. "Take my daughters. They have never known a man. Do what you wish to them, but don't touch my guests who are under my roof."

I am stunned, but not more so than Pheiné and Thamma. These men are not here observing the rites of their gods. They hold Lot responsible for disaster. Vengeance and violence drive them.

Thamma begins to cry. Pheiné backs from the door as though to put distance between herself and her father. Mika grasps her arm to get her attention. Her look is one a sacrificial lamb might give at the cut of a knife into its throat.

"We will not allow this," Mika says firmly. "Go back to your sister."

Pheiné stumbles to Thamma's side.

A new voice, full of rage, shouts, "This Lot came among us as a stranger, and now he judges *us!*"

The crowd roars. "We will punish Lot instead! Give him up to us!"

Raph is at my shoulder now, leaving the quieter back window to Danel. He moves me aside and, with a glance at Mika, opens the door, grasping Lot by the back of his robe and hauling him inside while Mika slams it closed and leans against it. Raph adds his weight, as do I, feeling the wood shake with pounding blows. It is only a matter of time before it splinters.

Pheiné whirls on Lot. "What are you doing, father? You would give us up to them for the sake of strangers?"

"They are my guests," Lot says shakily, "and holy men."

I am furious beyond thought. "It is more than that, husband." I spit the last word, tasting its foulness. "It is your precious reputation you wish to preserve, but not for the sake of hospitality." All attention is upon me, even though Raph and Mika continue to press hard against the battered door.

"What do you mean?" Lot's voice is hoarse.

"I mean you would throw your daughters to this mob of men, hoping, if they live, to claim that as the reason they are with child!"

Thamma gasps and begins to cry again. Pheiné stares at me.

"I am crippled," I say, "but I am not a fool. All those nights you spent in your daughters' room were not because you could not bear to lie beside your ugly wife."

I had been a fool, but Lila had told me the girls' moon blood had ceased, and then I understood. My voice lowers, but still pitches above the noise of the rabble. "I know, as well, how Hurriya died."

"No!" Thamma screams. "She fell!"

"Quiet," Lila says to her. "Let all the truth be told."

Lot is as pale as Shem's white camel. "My wife fell from the cliff."

I would give him no mercy, not when he had tried to cover his sin by giving his daughters to the men who hammered at our door. Perhaps Lot had not thought it through, but I know even if those men did nothing more than rape Pheiné and Thamma, with so many, it would be a horrible death sentence. "Your wife, Hurriya, the mother of your children, chose her death and walked into the Dead Sea."

"No," Thamma cries again, and my heart goes out to her, but I cannot stop. "She knew what you did with her daughters, and she could not bear it."

Pheiné bites her lip until blood wells at the corner.

It is a hard thing to know you are responsible for your mother's death. Though both these women are older, I turn to them. "If he came to you when you were children, you are not to blame. Your father should bear the burden."

With a wild scream, Thamma lunges at me, her fingers clawing my face.

The weight of her attack knocks me off-balance, and I stumble backward. Lila pulls her off as Danel shouts, "They are coming in the window!"

57

So Lot stepped outside to talk to them, shutting the door behind him. "Please, my brothers," he begged, "don't do such a wicked thing. Look, I have two virgin daughters. Let me bring them out to you, and you can do with them as you wish. But please, leave these men alone, for they are my guests and are under my protection."

"Stand back!" they shouted. "This fellow came to town as an outsider, and now he's acting like our judge! We'll treat you far worse than those other men!" And they lunged toward Lot to break down the door.

But the two angels reached out, pulled Lot into the house, and bolted the door. Then they blinded all the men, young and old, who were at the door of the house, so they gave up trying to get inside.

—Book of Genesis 19:6-11

THE LATTICE ON THE WINDOW shatters. Danel's knife meets the first man who tries to crawl through. His blade slips into the man's chest. No blood escapes until Danel wrenches it free. Hands reach up from below to pull the man's body out of the way, so another can come through. Blood runs down the inside wall.

For a fleeting moment, I wonder if I brought Danel into danger by insisting he come to our house, rather than protecting him from it, but selfishly, I am glad of his presence.

"Get the women into a room!" Raph yells to Lot, who is staring at the blood on his wall. But Lot stands motionless. It is Lila who herds Pheiné and Thamma into our sleeping room, though not before she snatches one of the cooking knives. I slip my knife back into my sash and move to one side of the window, leaning against the wall for support, my staff in both hands. If a head shows, I believe the stout wood Ishmael chose from the sacred trees at Mamre will do its part.

Just as the door splinters, the world outside the window and around the door seams flashes white, followed by a thunderous noise. I blink, blinded for an instant. Confusion reigns both inside and outside the house.

"What has happened?"

"Which god?"

"Is the world ended?"

I am not certain who asks the questions, but no one answers.

When I can see again, the torches are gone from outside the window, though we can still hear voices at the front of the house.

Danel stands, staring at the bloody knife in his hand. He raises his gaze after a long while to me. "I have never killed before . . . not a man."

"Danel!" Lila has left the daughters in their room to fling herself into his arms. "What has happened?"

There is no answer still, but the smell of brimstone is strong.

A few minutes later, a pair of hands appears at the windowsill. I raise my staff, but the fingers that grasp the edge are small; they can belong only to a child or a small woman.

I know the face that appears briefly to scan the inside, though I have not seen it since I left Yassib's tribe to go to Babylon in search of Raph. I remember the child I saw running through the back streets and suddenly know why he seemed so familiar.

"Shem?"

His eyes track to my voice. "Adir?"

It can be only Shem who calls me Adir in Sodom. I lean over the sill to look down at him. He has a thick covering over his head. Still, I can see he is thin, and his cheeks are hollow. I do not need to see his arm to imagine the slash of a slave mark. There is no other reason he would be here. My belly turns, remembering the happy boy in the desert, so proud of his white camel. "Shem—" is all I can manage.

A smile breaks across his solemn face. "Yes-yes, Adir."

"Adira," I correct without thought.

"I wanted to come before," he says in a rush, "but I could not. My master watches too closely, but he is gone with the celebrations. I saw him at your door; now everyone is scattered."

"Because of the bright light? Did you see it? What was it?"

"A son of Mot's Tongue erupted closer to the city. It is bigger than the first and weeping ash and bits of burning oil. The city is aflame!"

At that moment, I hear Mika cry out that our roof is burning. "Everyone to the little gate!"

"I am closer to the window," I shout to him. "I will go that way!"

Shem helps me down, though I have managed myself many times. Wind from the sea tosses my hair, which has worked its way free of its braid and curls in sweaty ringlets around my face. "Did you say the men are gone from the door?"

"Yes-yes, they are gone."

I relax my grip on my staff. "Why are you here, Shem? What has happened to you?"

"The horsemen returned after you left our tents, Adir. They killed all the men and sold the women and children."

I am sick with the image of this in my mind. "Mana too? Your mother, Shem, where is she?"

He draws himself straighter. "She threw herself at the enemy, her knife in her hand." He looks away and then back at me. "They killed her, but first she drew their blood."

"I am so sorry." I take a breath, trying to grasp all this. "How did you come to Sodom?"

He shrugs. "My master here was once a nomad and still has connections here. Once, when he had drunk too much, he told me that the raiders owed him for information he gave them about you. I was payment."

This spikes my curiosity, but something stings my left arm, and I flick at it reflexively. A small red disc blossoms on my skin. A burn.

"Here," Shem shoves a thick outer robe into my arms. It reeks of old sweat. "Put it on, quickly. I brought it to disguise you, but it may offer protection."

I do. He also hands me a heavy wool head covering in the style a man of the desert would wear.

"Do you wish your dog back?" he asks.

My heart stutters. I grab his shoulders. "What did you say?"

"I know where Nami is. You should come. Quickly, we have very little time."

I try to wrap my arms around him, but he winces and steps back.

"Take me to her, Shem!"

He starts to say more, but then decides not and leads me down the alley that runs behind the houses. To our right, the sea boils great belches. Shem says another tongue of Mot has thrust through the earth. Where is El? Is he watching or wielding? These questions dance in my thoughts like tiny stars around the central sun that is hope of finding Nami. My heart gallops. I want to stop our flight and make Shem tell me she is well, that she will bound out to meet us, her feet light on the ground in her excitement and joy. But I dare not stop.

I take a quick glance down the alleys that connect to the main streets as we pass them. Glowing embers and bits of burning oil have thickened into a rain of fire. Perhaps the wind off the Dead Sea is holding them in the city's heart. I am grateful our house sits on the far northeastern end near the sea. Even though Shem and I track the sea's edge, the foul air thickens with burning ash, and the smell of singed wool makes me grateful for the heavy robe and headdress, despite their rankness. What will happen if the wind fails?

We are fortunate a layer of dirt freshly covers the garbage in the alleyways, making our way smooth. Shem runs ahead and then waits for me, impatient and plainly anxious that I hurry. I do, though it awakens the pain in my hip and leg. The vision of Nami pushes me through the ache. I hope all in my household made it to safety . . . wherever that might lie.

AT FIRST, I do not recognize the building we come to because we approach from the side, but as soon as we reach the front, a stall full of rugs: I know it. We are far from our house, but still near the Dead Sea. The fire has burned holes only in a few of the merchant's wares, though I can see a nearby jar of pitch is burning. The air above it ripples blue and yellow.

I stop as soon as we reach the protection of the awning, though it is thatched and already smoldering in spite of the wind. We cannot stay here long. Shem leads me through the area that is normally a house's little gate, but here is a room stacked with carpets. "I have been to this place before," I say. "Whose shop is this?"

"Katar, my master's."

Then, as clearly as if it were yesterday, I remember when I bought a rug from this man. I can see him clearly—the tiny ring in his left nostril, the hand that roamed in a pattern from chest to oily beard to face and balding head. I never learned his name, but I have never forgotten him. The pieces of what Shem told me suddenly fit together. King Samsu-iluna hired Hurrians to search for Raph, believing he was the shaman of the two. When my father brought Mika and Raph to Sodom, Katar must have gotten word to the raiders that the giant strangers they searched for were with Lot. There are no secrets in this city. Everyone would have known we traveled with the strangers to Lot's tents on the plains south of Sodom. If all had gone according to plan, we would have been there when the raiders arrived, but they were too early, and so my father died protecting his guests' belongings. The raiders hunted for us. Shem was payment by the Hurrians to this rug merchant for his spying.

With a stab of guilt, I wonder if the slaughter of Shem's tribe was provoked by my rescue of the camels or if it would have happened in any case. I will never know the answer to that. *How our choices can return to burden us.*

"Katar wanted to buy Nami," I say to Shem's back. "I think he might have killed me for her."

"He wanted to breed her and sell her pups. She had a litter, but only one is left."

"Is she all right?"

Shem casts a glance over his shoulder, but does not meet my eyes. "I have tried, but—"

At that moment, we pass through the doorway that separates the shop from living quarters directly into the courtyard. Not surprisingly, stained carpets cover most of the floor. Robes are scattered about. In the corner are a stacked pile of copper pieces and perhaps a few pieces of silver. A stout pole reaches up from the center of the courtyard. Bound so close to the pole she can barely turn her head is my Nami.

With a cry, I stumble to her. She does not respond, and it is no wonder. She cannot smell at all through the stench of this room. She is bone-thin and strips of raw skin stripe her back. Her head is turned away from me and rests on her paws. When I touch her, she jerks her head around and snaps and then cringes as if she has learned a blow will inevitably follow.

Tears flow down my face. "Nami. What has this demon of a man done to you?"

"I tried to help her," Shem says over my shoulder. "I brought her water and salve for her wounds whenever Katar left the house, and I cleaned her the best I could. No creature should be treated like this, especially a desert dog."

Katar. The name burns into my heart.

Nami should know my voice or recognize the shape of me, but her eyes are glazed and unseeing, and I am still swathed in the robe and head-covering of a man. "Shem, whose robe do I wear?"

"Katar's." Shem moves his feet in a nervous shuffle, as if anticipating the outcome of his actions on his master's return.

This explains Nami's reaction. I smell like her hated one. Turning my hand so the back of it is presented to her, I slowly move it toward her nose, so she can catch my scent.

A low whine issues from her throat. If she were human, I would say it is a sound of one who has lived the dark of endless nightmare, dreaming of a rescuer, yet when such appears, she fears it is not real. So it was with me in the cave beside the river when Raph came.

Gently I stroke her head and whisper, "I am real, Nami. I am here."

She cannot move her head far. Katar has tied her so she cannot chew through the rope, but my knee is close and she rests her head on it.

I keep one hand on her head and slip my knife from my sash to work on the thick rope. "Run back to my house, Shem. Find Mika, the tall man with hair the color of Mot's Tongue. Bring him. Neither of us can carry her."

Shem hesitates. "Do not let Katar find you here. He will kill you."

"Run." There is no place for argument in my voice.

As I work my knife against the rope, Nami is completely still, though I can see her neck is raw from pulling against her bonds. It must torture her.

I have almost cut through it when I hear a loud shout from the front shop. "Shem! Where are you, boy?"

When there is no answer, he bellows, "I will flay what is left of your skin from your back. Gather the best pieces and my gold. This city burns!"

My back is to the door, but I do not turn. I am determined to free Nami. The blow to my side spills me sideways. My body has forgotten how to draw a breath.

"Thief!" Katar shouts. "Who are you? I want to know your name before my blade peels the skin from your throat."

Shaking with the effort, I gasp a breath and roll to my side, my hand searching in vain for my staff. "*You* are the thief. This is my dog."

He squints at me, his eyes not adjusting quickly to the dimmer light inside the house. The small ring in his nostril quivers with his rage. "Who are you?"

I need time. I should reason with him, stall to give Mika time to reach us, but what comes out of my mouth is not reason. "I am Adira, the daughter of Zakiti, wife of Lot."

"You are a woman?"

Through the pain in my side, I feel another irony. Here I am, once again clothed as a male in the city where I first met this man, this demon.

"I am the owner of this dog you have tortured."

"You are the ugly, barren wife of Lot?"

"I am Lot's wife," I say because I, who have always been glib of tongue, cannot think of anything else to say.

"Well, your husband sold this dog to me."

The air rushes from my lungs again, though no blow has been struck. "What?"

"He brought her to me; you have no claim. Not that I care what a woman claims."

I do not doubt his words. I thought Nami had jumped through the window to chase after me, but now I know the truth. I can imagine Pheiné in Lot's ear at night in the bed he shared with his daughters, complaining of Philot and Nami and most probably . . . me. Nami had been the most convenient to be rid of when Lila and I visited Jemia. Philot would most likely be the next to disappear. And then me? If I did not throw myself into the sea in despair, would they have nagged Lot to be rid of me? He married me to keep up a show of righteousness. Of that I am convinced. But once his daughters became obviously pregnant, what then?

"So, wife of Lot, what should I do with you? You are a thief in my house. It is my right to slay you, but perhaps first I will cover your ruined face and see what is between those long legs."

If ever I needed the skill of negotiation I had honed at my father's side, it is now; but instead, I say stubbornly, "Nami is not yours. She was not Lot's to sell."

I see the kick coming but I am not able to do more than try to roll away. Instead of my chest, it falls across my shoulder. Pain lances down my left arm. I ignore it and force myself to hands and knees, but I cannot rise quickly enough, and he is on my other side with a blow. The shock of it stuns me; my entire side burns with pain. I have rolled back toward Nami, and I huddle against her side. With the knifing pain, my thoughts fade into the nightmare of Babylonia, into the cave where I can only lie awaiting the next blow. *Where will it land? When will it end? When can I die?*

I am drifting . . . to heaven or the sea's embrace?

From somewhere, a sound pulls at me. At first, I cannot understand what the sound is or why it has the power to drag me from my salvation into a scene from my past:

Green points of light glare from that dark, a predator's eyes—a stalking wolf. Then a dark shape with white markings moves between us with a low growl, and I realize this is the sound pulling me from the darkness—the growl of a dog protecting her pack.

I am jolted into awareness of the hard ground pressing against my cheek; the ache of each breath; the smell of burning wood and pitch; and the stench of urine. But the sound is the same as in my dream; it is Nami. She has snapped the frayed cord of her rope, completing the job of my knife, and struggles to her feet.

My heart wrenches at the sight of her so decimated. How is she standing? But she is, legs splayed, more ribs than flesh, teats hanging low. She staggers between me and the man who hurt her so many times that she cringed from the smell of him. She does not cringe now.

But he is not afraid of her. How can he be? Like me, she is too crippled to dodge his blow, a fierce kick that sends her into the far wall, where she sprawls, twisted and still . . . *so still*.

The heavens stop their turning. I cannot think, cannot breathe. I lie on my stomach, one hand trapped beneath me, the other flung out into the soiled blankets that had been the boundaries of Nami's world. Needle teeth find a finger of my outstretched hand. A pup, the last pup, has found its way from the blanket folds. Hunger has driven it to latch onto my finger.

Nami's pup.

I promised her, so long ago, that I would find a way to protect her pups, and I failed.

From the corner of my eye, I see him coming.

I will not fail her again.

The pup's movements have uncovered something else in the blankets' folds—my knife, my father's knife.

Katar goes to one knee beside me and grasps my shoulder, sending a bolt of pain down my arm and side as he flings me over onto my back, bunches my robe in his hand, rips my underclothing and falls on me. I do not move until he is on me.

With all my strength, I strike downward, plunging my blade into the base of his neck.

58

At dawn the next morning the angels became insistent. "Hurry," they said to Lot. "Take your wife and your two daughters who are here. Get out right now, or you will be swept away in the destruction of the city!"

When Lot still hesitated, the angels seized his hand and the hands of his wife and two daughters and rushed them to safety outside the city, for the Lord was merciful. When they were safely out of the city, one of the angels ordered, "Run for your lives! And don't look back or stop anywhere in the valley! Escape to the mountains, or you will be swept away!"

—Book of Genesis 19:15-17

W HEN SHEM RETURNS WITH MIKA and Raph, I am still beneath Katar's body. If it were not plain from the knife piercing the back of his neck that he is dead, I think both Raph and Mika would have decapitated him on the spot.

For a moment, after pulling Katar away and realizing I would live, Mika turns his anger on me. "What demon stole your mind, Adira? Why did you come here alone?"

Not, why did you come? But, why did you come alone?

"I love you," I say.

He stops his ranting to stare at me, then he laughs, a sound edged with madness. I have never seen him this angry or this wild. Raph puts a hand on his shoulder, anchoring him, as only a brother can.

"Help me stand," I say. They do, and I force my face to stone so they do not see the pain. "My staff." Despite my efforts, the words emerge in a gasp.

Raph retrieves it. Steadied, I make my way to Nami's body and sink to my knees. "Oh, my poor, brave friend," I mutter. "He will never hurt you again." I am sick with sorrow for her and for the pain she has endured. Could any man be as loyal and loving? The cavern in my heart seems vast and dark. Is life only about losing what you love?

"Adira, the roof is starting to burn," Raph says urgently.

"I will not leave her. She would not leave me."

Raph starts to speak again, but Mika steps forward. "I will carry her." I nod.

Before he can reach for her, Danel's voice is calling in the outer shop. "Adira! Are you here?"

It is Raph who answers. "We are here, in the courtyard!"

Danel enters and sets down a bulging pack, Lila close behind him. Lila comes at once to me. "Adira, are you all right?" Then her gaze falls to Nami and she gasps. "Is that *Nami?*" Her hand flies to her mouth.

I understand her question. This broken body is hardly the beautiful, sleek animal she knew.

Shem also joins us. He kneels beside me, his face grave and streaked with soot. "She was always gentle with me. She let me hold her pups."

The pup. I had forgotten it. "Bring it to me," I tell Shem, pointing.

He goes to root in the soiled blanket and pulls out a squirming pup, its eyes barely open. "The last one," he says, pressing it against his chest. Shem's steps are slow to my side, and his lower lip quivers as he holds it out to me. "A male. The best one. I hid him when buyers came."

The pup has Nami's black coat and white legs and the same whimsical gold-brown slashes above his eyes. I slip him inside my robe, as I had done so long ago with the pup from Nami's first litter. He snuggles against me, as if he knows my scent. It is a comfort to have him there.

"Come with us, Adira," Danel says.

I am confused and too soon from the darkness of my nightmares. "Where?"

"To Harran, where we have other family. Will you come with us, sister?"

I blink at him. "Lot has agreed?"

Danel looks away and then back at me, his shoulders taut. "No, he refuses to leave Sodom, though it burns. A twin to Mot's Tongue rains ash and burning pitch on the city, perhaps on the fields below and other cities of the Vale. Who knows if it will ever end or what might happen next."

"Why does Lot refuse to leave?"

"He says El would want him and his family to stay, as proof to the people his god is mightier than Baal or Mot."

What would it be like to have such surety as Lot of the god's intentions? My thoughts turn to Pheiné and Thamma and the unborn children they carry. If the city burns, those babes will die before they are born, and they do not deserve that, any more than this pup next to my heart.

My gaze lifts to Mika. In Lot's eyes, he is El's messenger, the angel who held a god's blue fire in his hand. "I know how to make Lot leave," I say.

Danel does not ask, but trusts me in this. "Should we wait for you?

"No, do not wait. I do not even know if Lot would go to Abram. You must leave the city now."

Danel hesitates and then comes forward to help me stand and to embrace me. "I am sorry for all the trouble I gave you as a child," he says into my ear.

I bury my head on his shoulder. "I am grateful for it . . . now." I reach out an arm to include Lila, and we remain that way for a moment.

When we part, I work two of the bracelets of silver from their place on my arm and give them to Danel. "Purchase a caravan if you wish," I say. "It is what your father wanted."

He hesitates. Lila snatches them from my hand and works them onto her own arm. Practical Lila. She knows what it is like to have nothing. "We are grateful, Adira," she says.

I glance at the burning roof and move to the plaster ledge running the length of the wall. It is not under the opening above the courtyard, so if a log falls, it will not impale us, as one did Jemia. Sweat pours from us. The fires have heated the bricks. They will not burst into flames as the wooden poles do, but if the fires get hot enough, the mortar between will dry into dust. I need not worry about that, because we will be cooked before that happens.

I call Shem to me. His eyes are bright with tears. "You have slain my master," he says. "I am your slave now, Adir."

"No, you are not. You are free."

His dark eyes are wide. "Then I will go with you as your companion.

What if you must go again into the desert?" There is a note of desperation in his voice. "You will need me."

"I promise you I will not go again into the desert. I have had enough of deserts. But I have a task for you."

"What?"

"You must go with my brother, Danel, and Lila. They will go through Abram's lands. There you will find Abram's second wife, Hagar. Show her this." I reach to my neck and remove the cylinder seal that has hung there since my father put it into my hand. I place it around Shem's neck with another ring of silver from my arm. The cylinder hangs to his belly, so I tie a knot in the cord to shorten it and hide it beneath his robe.

"Adira," Raph says. "We have to leave."

The house is beginning to fill with smoke, but I barely glance at his sweat-streaked face. I must do this. "Shem, show this seal to Hagar and tell her I wish you to be part of her family, a companion to her son, Ishmael."

"Hagar and Ishmael," Shem repeats, burning the names into his memory.

If Sarai gives birth to a son, Ishmael would be in danger. Sarai was a good woman, but she would be fierce in protecting her child's inheritance. Hagar always insisted that El promised Ishmael would also be the father of a people. If so, they would be a people of the desert.

"Ishmael may not know it," I say gravely to Shem, "but I think he may be spending time in the desert. He will need you."

Shem looks unsure.

"Teach him everything you know about camels."

Only then does he smile. The first one I have seen on his face in this dark city. It transforms him into the boy I had known, so proud to show off his prize white camel, so quick to offer me, a stranger, his friendship. I draw a deep breath, preparing myself to do the most difficult thing I have ever done. Without allowing myself to think about it, I draw the sleepy pup from my robe and hold it out to him. "Name him Zakiti," I say. "You and Ishmael will need him to hunt for you."

Tears fill his eyes. I imagine this pup was the only comfort he had as a slave to Katar.

When they are gone, I return to Nami's side, despite the crackle of flames above us. Mika kneels, sliding his arms beneath her. Her body will not be a great burden; she is so thin.

He stops.

"I will find a piece of carpet to cover her," I say, thinking he is considering the journey back to my house.

"This dog—" Mika's voice is tight. "Nami is not dead."

My heart flutters. "What?"

"She is still warm. The body should have cooled by now, even in this heat." He runs a hand over her prominent ribs, leans down to press his ear to her.

I am suspended over a chasm, hanging onto a rock. A rope dangles just beyond my reach, but I must let go to reach it, and if it is not truly there or is pulled away at the last moment, I will fall forever. Once again, I cannot breathe.

"Her heart is strong, Adira!"

"I know that," I hear my own voice say and force my lungs to inhale. "But is she . . . dying?" I cannot bear to have her back and then have her go away. Nor can I have her suffer if there is no hope.

Mika is only a healer now, his fingers probing. He peels back her eyelid, exposing it to light. "She is breathing very shallowly. I think her ribs are broken. The question is whether she bleeds inside. She is very weak. Is there water?"

I move quicker than I thought possible, aware of the sharp pain in my own ribs. There has not been time to tell Mika of the blows I received. I return with water from an urn in the shop area and a small bowl.

Mika holds the water at Nami's nose, but she does not stir. He takes a piece of cloth from his ever-present leather bag and dips it in the bowl, then lifts the edge of her muzzle and squeezes it into her mouth. Her tongue moves, and she swallows. He gives her a little more. "Only a little just yet," he says to her.

Above, the roof burns fiercer.

From the doorway to the front shop, Raph calls over his shoulder. "People are coming in, taking whatever they want. The streets will not be safe!"

"We just have to get out," I call, coughing from the thickening smoke, and pull an end piece free from my head covering to shield my mouth and nose. I look at Mika. "The back alley that runs along the seashore. It is more passable."

I wish for a window, but there is only one doorway out of this house.

As if to seal our difficulties, a thick, blazing log falls with a loud crash into the courtyard, blocking our path.

We can hear Raph engaging the looters, trying to keep a way for us to the outside. I consider the burning log. I could not jump over it. Mika could, but not with a burden in his arms. I want to tell him to go on, to leave Nami and me, but the words will not come out. I do not want to die. Not if Nami has a single breath in her, and not if we can save those innocent babies sleeping in my stepdaughters' wombs.

I can still smell the stale urine on my hands. It is a wonder Danel and Lila could bear my embrace, but it gives me an idea, and I hobble to the soiled, wet blankets that Nami was forced to lie on. I slap them across the log where the fire is lowest. Mika quickly sees what I am doing and joins me. There is a sizzle and steam, and the flame begins to eat the blanket but I throw another one and another until we have a narrow bridge we can cross.

Mika is standing now, Nami draped in his arms, and he steps across, waiting close on the other side, so I can use his shoulder as a brace.

When we reach the front of the shop, we find Raph has cleared the place. His sword is bloody, but there are no bodies. I grab sections of carpet to drape over Nami and Mika to protect them.

CHAPTER

59

Then the Lord rained down fire and burning sulfur from the sky on Sodom and Gomorrah. He utterly destroyed them, along with the other cities and villages of the plain, wiping out all the people and every bit of vegetation. But Lot's wife looked back as she was following behind him, and she turned into a pillar of salt.

—Genesis 19:24–26

Go to the edge of the cliff and jump off. Build your wings on the way down.

—Ray Bradbury, *Brown Daily Herald*

I SIT IN THE LITTLE GATE of my house, Nami at my feet, her head resting on my foot. I have stayed with her all night, getting her to drink and even eat a little, although she will only do so from my hand.

While I struggled with Katar, the men—Mika, Raph, Danel, and Lot—cleared the logs from the roof, and the women removed all the dried reeds from the floor. The bits of flaming pitch from the Tongues of Mot seem to come and go in waves, but they now fall through the opening, burning out in the barren dirt. It is sweltering hot with no relief—even the wind from the sea is hot—and I cannot imagine Mot's own caverns stinking worse, but we are safe for the moment. The ground has shaken twice since our return, not as hard as the first time, but I feel they are but precursors to something worse. Perhaps the gods are fighting over this city, though why they should want it is beyond my understanding.

Mika played the part of El's angel, and told Lot he must leave with his family. Lot has gone to convince his third daughter, whom I have still not met, to come with her husband and children. Raph has gone with him for his protection. The streets are clearer now, with people huddled in their houses, but those who do come out know no law or restraint.

Pheiné and Thamma are, for once, being useful, gathering food and supplies. They must take only what they can bear themselves, because Philot will be carrying my belongings and Nami. I have made a place where she can rest if she will tolerate being carried.

Mika sits beside me on the plaster-covered bench, stretching his long legs before him, and frowns. "I do not know why Lot insists on my status as his messenger or angel."

"Mika, do you not think the blue fire was El's mark?"

He looks very serious. "I do not know what that was, or which god sent it, or why. In my mind, men often make what they do not understand into signs from the gods."

"Are you then not a messenger, an angel?"

He scowls, always discomforted with this. "Not that I am aware."

"Perhaps angels do not always know who they are."

Something changes in his look, and he touches the knot on my nose with his fingertip. I remember when he kissed it, and tears suddenly fill my eyes.

Mika says, "I commanded Lot to lead the way out of Sodom and not look back."

I nod. "That is best. He will not want to go at my pace." And I have no wish to even speak to him. I do not know how to deal with my anger toward him for the lives he has mangled, both mine in taking Nami from me and those of his daughters. If it were not for my oath, I would do as the nomad women do and "turn the entrance of my tent" from him.

To my surprise, Mika takes my hand with one of his. I have large hands, but his swallow them. With the other, he turns my chin, so I am looking at him. "Adira, I do not want you to go with Lot."

This takes me off balance, but does not surprise me. He said as much on the hillside.

"I want you to come with me."

"Where are you going, Mika?"

He sighs. "First to my people, to teach them the words of Enoch, and then I wish to find the land of my ancestors. The land of green hills and sparkling rivers where my people built the time-temples. I wish to see one, to look through its portals at the rising stars. And I want you to be there with me."

I stare at him. Leave Lot? I feel nothing at the thought, except a strange lightness. And I am no mother to Pheiné or Thamma. But I see my dying father. "I swore to my father by our god I would obey Sarai, and she gave me to be Lot's wife."

Mika's free hand joins the one that holds mine. "Is the oath to your god or your father?"

I think about this for a moment. "To my father. I have told you all my life he tried to mold me into obedience, to be like the stars who know their path across the sky. I have never been able to do that, to honor him as I should. I cannot dishonor him now."

"Adira," Mika says softly. "You are right, most of the stars have fixed courses, but there are a few that do not. The morning star, for one, is a wanderer and makes her own path. You are such a star. You must make your own way, or your heart will shrivel."

My heart seems to hear him and beats faster with his words, but my mind can only find one thought: "I swore to my father."

We both hear Lot's bellow on the street outside.

Mika squeezes my hand to capture my attention again and says, "I once ignorantly declared that 'Truth is truth.'"

I remember those words from a night two springs ago. Mika, Raph, and I looked down at the people of Sodom celebrating Spring Rites. Raph had said, *"You cannot expect them to honor our truths. They have their own."*

And Mika had replied, *"Truth is truth."*

"Adira," Mika says, bringing my attention back, "do what you must, but think *why* your father made you swear that oath. Be true to what made him ask it."

I cannot think. Too much has happened.

"I will wait for you," he says gently, "in the cave at the overhang in the cliff."

WE ARE AN odd sight in the dawn light, climbing the trail that leads out of the eastern gate, the trail I strove to master each night before Mika and Raph came. We all wear thick clothing that leaves only enough space to see and breathe. Even Philot is covered with carpets. He bears this without complaint, as he has always done. At first, Nami was not happy with her position atop him, but I stroked her and calmed her, and I keep one hand on her to reassure her. She seems now to understand, or perhaps she just trusts me. We have traveled many roads together.

Ahead, Lot leads the way, having instructed us all not to look back, on pain of El's wrath. Even though I know every rock and turn of this path, he has quickly put distance between us. On either side of him, Pheiné and Thamma struggle with the climb and their burdens. It was difficult for them to leave so much behind and to face bearing their children in a strange place. I wonder what story Lot will give for them, and whether he will admit to being the father of his own grandchildren. His third daughter refused to go with him.

Behind us there are screams and the sound of rushing, gurgling water. I do not look.

As we readied to leave, people rushed by us, carrying hastily gathered goods and supplies. Only one stopped to tell us that black water bubbled up from the sandy ground at the Gate, as though Mot now vomited into Sodom. I remembered what we had seen on our return from burying Jemia, and could imagine it. I wondered if Mika could see it from his position on the cliff, but most likely he and Raph had sought the shelter of the shallow cave. Another person running by us yelled that the black water had grown and was consuming the city. The streets were almost as crowded as they had been during the Spring Rites.

I hesitate, thinking of Jemia's body. Would the black water take her? But what could be done? If it spread that far, it would flood all the grave chambers. I look up, hoping her spirit has gone to the sky.

As we join the throng pushing through the eastern gate, I wonder how all these people will manage to climb the narrow path up the cliff, but every one of them turns south toward the river, hoping, I imagine, to find safety in one of the other cities or the fields beyond. Mika had told Lot to seek the mountains, not the plains, and he has obeyed.

Now, only we climb the cliff. There has not been much time to think on Mika's words to me. My mind seems determined to scatter my thoughts, like seeds in the wind, rather than help me to a decision. I can see ahead the bend in the path that leads to the ledge where Mika waits. I have only a few steps before I must make my choice.

Choice—is it truly ours, or are we waves carried by the wind, our destiny set in a final heave upon the shore?

In the cave along the river, I chose death. Yet it did not come at my call. I was not able to speak the words to bring it. Raph's choice to return for me gave me life and allowed me to honor my oath to my father and my commitment to family.

The tangle of choice goes back further. At my birth, my mother chose for me, laying the persona of male upon me. My father chose not to contradict it, perhaps at first only to pacify my mother. But when she died, he chose to keep that secret and make it ours. Then he made me swear to return to family, to Sarai. Why?

Mika has urged me to answer this question.

I stop where the path splits, and Philot stops with me.

I am no wife to Lot. I do not need to "turn the entrance of my tent" as the nomads do. *If a man takes a woman to wife, but has no intercourse with her, this woman is no wife to him.* This is the wisdom and law of Babylonia. It is not my vow to Lot that causes me distress, but my vow to my father.

I hear his voice: *Understanding comes when the right question has been asked.* It is suddenly clear to me—as was the answer to the riddle of what the man who bought salt really wanted. The right question is not, would I dishonor my father by disobeying him; the right question is—why did he have me swear to obey Sarai?

And with the right question comes the answer: not because he wished to make me like the stars with fixed paths, but out of love for me, to keep me safe, and to give me a chance at happiness.

I have had neither safety nor happiness at the hands of Lot.

Beneath the thick coverings, Nami licks my hand. I turn, looking back and down over the smoking ruin of Sodom, the burned city, its streets and buildings partially eaten now by a growing black stain. Will it indeed consume all of Sodom, leaving nothing of witness to the city that once stood here?

Down in the rocky plain, Mot's Tongues spout flames, their fury burning, and fire engulfs most of the city. Closer, below me, the sea strokes the cliff's edge, leaving crusts of salt. In the distance, I can see smoke rising from Gomorrah as well. Perhaps El has chosen to destroy these cities, these people who follow the goddess's way. Perhaps, he wishes to leave Baal in the clutches of Mot and claim Asherah as his own queen.

Or perhaps Mika is right, and this devastation has nothing to do with the gods. But in the wake of the fury below me, such would be difficult to believe.

Truly, it does not matter what I believe. The story will be told as it will be told. I lift my face into the wind that blows from the north, a wind clear of the stench of Sodom, perhaps blown from a distant land of flowing streams and green grass.

And then I turn onto the path that leads to the overhang and the cave where Mika waits. No doubt my life will be forgotten on the lips of those who speak of what happened here—nothing more than a pillar of salt—but I am again who I am, a daughter of the wind.

ABOUT THE AUTHOR

T.K. Thorne is a retired police captain in Birmingham, Alabama, USA. She holds a master's degree in clinical social work from the University of Alabama and currently works as the executive director of the business improvement district in downtown Birmingham. Her writing has won awards for poetry, fiction, and screenplays. *Noah's Wife* is her award-winning debut novel. T.K. describes herself as a writer, humanist, dog-mom, horse-servant, and cat-slave.

The author invites you to her website for behind-the-scenes information about the writing of *Angels at the Gate*, book club questions, and to sign up for her private newsletter list. If you enjoyed this novel, please write a review or post it on your social media and share!

www.TKThorne.com

Facebook: T.K. Thorne | Blog: TKs-Tales.com | Twitter: @TKThorne

AUTHOR'S NOTES

WHAT IS THIS STORY?

An assortment of oral and written comments and stories accompany both Jewish and Islamic tradition and their primary source texts, the Hebrew Bible (Tanakh) and the Koran. In Judaism, those commentaries are known collectively as *midrashim*. As with my previous novel, *Noah's Wife*, this story is "my *midrash*," my commentary—my imagination layered on a foundation of archeology, historical theories, and ancient writings. For ease of reading, I chose to quote Biblical text primarily from the New Living Translation. On occasion, I used brackets for clarification or to substitute a word or phrase from the Chabad.org translation of the Tanakh.

UNRAVELING THE KNOT OF "WHEN?"

In a historical novel, the first challenge is to determine when the narrative takes place. According to the Bible, Lot was the nephew of Abraham (Abram), which sets the story "in the time of Abraham," but controversy swirls around Abraham himself. Was he a mythological figure or a real historical figure, or some mixture? The three major religions of the Middle Eastern and Western civilizations trace their roots to this one man. Scholars also disagree about his era, which likely occurred in the Middle Bronze Age, spanning 2100–1500 BCE. The Elba tablets (discovered in Syria in 1976) mention a city called *Sadam*, which some believe was Sodom, and that would place the era of Abraham between 2950-2000 BCE—but this is hotly debated.

Based on David Rosenberg's research in his book *Abraham: The First Historical Biography*, I placed Abraham at approximately the time of Samsu-iluna (1749–1712 BCE), the king of Babylonia and son of the famed Hammurabi. Samsu-iluna's kingdom fell to invasion by peoples living on his eastern border, who attacked Babylonia from the mountains in two-horse chariots.

The Babylon of the period in which *Angels at the Gate* is set has not been excavated. Therefore, we cannot know its architecture or way of life, but we have detailed descriptions of the city in 300–400 BCE. We also have clear descriptions of earlier Sumerian cities based on archeological findings and writings of the day. One of the more emotional moments in my travels came when I stumbled upon several of the beautiful blue-tile segments of Babylon's wall in an Istanbul museum. The famed glazed walls date from King Nebuchadnezzar's day (605–562 BCE), much later than this story; however, he may have modeled them after existing walls and art, as the ziggurats and other structures of his city were built on earlier Sumerian designs.

What Was the Religion in Abraham's Time?

The second major research challenge to writing *Angels at the Gate* was determining the religion actually practiced by Abraham, the population of Sodom, and the desert nomads. As Raphael Patai states in his book *The Hebrew Goddess*, "The average layman, whether Jew or Gentile, still believes that the official Hebrew religion was a strict monotheism beginning with God's revelation of Himself to Abraham. [But] scholars date the origin of Hebrew monotheism a few centuries later, during the days of the great prophets." Archeological sites provide increasing evidence of this. The earliest Hebrews took ideas about deities from their native land—Canaan and Mesopotamia. For this reason, I have used the small case for "god" throughout.

I also chose to name the earliest Hebrew tribal god "El," rather than "Yahweh," as there is evidence the name Yahweh developed later. El is the word contained in the Hebrew word, "elohim." Elohim is a plural word in Hebrew; possibly it originally meant God, the Most High, or God the Highest [of the gods]. The "watchword" of Judaism is the phrase, "Hear, O Israel, the Lord our God, the Lord is one." The word "one" (*echad*) in that phrase can mean "one" as in "there is only one," which is the common interpretation; but it can also mean "first." This would make the interpretation read as "Hear, O Israel, the Lord our God, the Lord is first among the gods." This echoes, "Who is like you, Yahweh, among the gods?" (Exodus 15:11).

The first commandment is "I am the Lord, thy God who brought thee out of the Land of Egypt, out of the house of bondage." It is interesting that the text says, "I am the Lord thy God," not "I am the Lord, God," as if identification is necessary. The rest of the commandment reads, "Thou shalt have no other gods before me" (Exodus 20:3). Does this mean no gods should be placed above God, or no additional gods should be worshipped? Either way, the question does not seem to be whether other gods exist, but rather, which one is to be primary and worshipped by the Hebrew people.

The roots of El are to be found in the land where the Hebrews arrived or arose—Canaan. Writings discovered in the city of Ugarit (Syria) and dated around 1300–1400 BCE name El as the chief and creator god. He was the consort of the goddess Asherah, the mother of gods. The city-states of Canaan acknowledged the pantheon, but each city had their own special god (also true in Mesopotamia), usually the husband/companion of the goddess.

In later times, Hebrews came to call their god Yahweh, rather than El, and El was used as a more general term for god or God. For example Israe-el (land of God), Anan-iel and Rapha-el, (angels), etc. Canaanites believed that Baal overthrew his father El and became the consort of his mother, Asherah. There is scholarly thought that the Hebrews believed the same thing, only Yahweh (not Baal) became the highest god (the Elohim) and took Asherah as *his* queen. Artifacts from 700–800 BCE bear inscriptions that read "Yahweh and his Asherah." The terminology becomes even more confusing. Some think Baal and Yahweh originally may have been the same god. In any case, over time, "Baal" in Akkadian came to mean simply "master" or "lord." In *Angels at the Gate*, I chose to have Baal and Asherah as the deities worshipped in the city of Sodom, to reflect a tension between the nomadic Hebrew tribes and the Canaanites in the cities.

WHAT ABOUT THE GODDESS?

Just as there were many gods in Israel's Bronze Age, the goddesses were many, or at least had many names and forms across the Middle East and across time—Asherah, Anat, Anath, Astarte, Ashtoreth, Ishtar, Isis, and Athirau-Yammi, or Yam Nahar. For thousands of years, prior to the emergence of the Hebrews, the goddess reigned in

Anatolia (Turkey) and across the Middle East. In fact, the old name for Turkey, Anatolia, means "Land of Mothers." Even in much later times, the feminine remained an entwined and yet mysteriously distinct part of the Hebrew God, known as the *Shekinah*, the holy spirit or presence of God.

Asherah was also known as the goddess of healing. She was represented by a tree or pole. (Perhaps that is the origin of the spring Maypole rites.) Snakes, symbolizing wisdom and renewal, were often associated with her and other goddesses. Moses and Aaron carried staffs (poles) as symbols of power, and the concept of snakes and staffs—later associated with the Greek god Asclepius and the Hebrew Essene priests—became the symbol of healing, as it still is today.

After the first destruction of the Temple and the Babylonian exile, Biblical prophets (and/or Biblical authors) made great efforts to separate the Hebrew religion from the Canaanite religion, and the goddess was "demonized." Perhaps this is why Eve, a woman, was blamed for listening to the snake who offered the fruit of the tree of knowledge in the Garden of Eden.

The concept of a personal god (as opposed to a city god) probably originated in Mesopotamia—in the Sumerian kingdom, of which Ur was the primary city. According to Genesis, Abraham came from Ur. In Sumer, there were "high" gods, as well as family gods who interceded with the high gods for the people. We know this from the many cuneiform writings uncovered there. In *Angels at the Gate*, Abraham brought this concept to his tribe, but modified it so that his personal god became a personal god of his tribe, a god that did not reside in one place or in a statue, but existed wherever his people were. It was a tremendous leap in the concept of the nature of the divine.

WHO WERE THE ANGELS?

Perhaps the greatest challenge in writing this story was the question— Who were the angels? Angels in the Hebrew Bible weave in and out of the narrative as God or sons of God or messengers of God. They usually appear as men. "The *Lord* appeared again to Abraham near the oak grove belonging to Mamre. One day Abraham was sitting at the entrance to his tent during the hottest part of the day. He looked up and noticed three *men* standing nearby. My *lord*," he said, "if it pleases you, stop here for a while." (Genesis 18:1; italics mine.)

Some scholars believe the Hebrew phrase "sons of God" (*bēnê elîm*) is related to a phrase from a Ugarit (Canaanite) text for the sons of El and Asherah (*bn il*). Some biblical translations have used "angels" in place of "sons of God." The Book of Enoch and the Book of Jubilees both refer to the "Watchers" as "sons of God."

The English word, "angel" is used for the Hebrew word *mal'ākh*, which simply translates as "messenger." Sometimes the phrase *mal'āk 'al'ākhîm* appears or *mal'āk YHWH*, which have been interpreted as "messenger(s) from God, an aspect of God, or God himself as messenger."

It has been suggested that the divine council imagery of Mesopotamia, Egypt, and Canaan may have influenced the Jewish understanding of angels as a "heavenly host" over which God presides. It was not until 200-500 CE that theology and art gave angels the physical characteristics (wings and halos) we now associate with them.

The controversial book *Uriel's Machine* by Christopher Knight and Robert Lumos offered an intriguing possibility. *Uriel's Machine* makes a case for a connection between the Middle East and the European megalith builders, particularly in the structures of Stonehenge (England) and Newgrange (Ireland). Israel and Egypt are the only locations where standing stones and stone circles (gilgal) are found outside Europe. In the Book of Kings, there is a description of Elijah repairing an altar of the Lord with twelve stones and a ditch around it—the elements of a henge, such as Stonehenge. The typical Canaanite sanctuary included a standing stone (messebhoth), an asherah pole, and an altar.

The Book of Enoch (one of the books of the Dead Sea scrolls not included in the biblical canon) provides lengthy and particular descriptions of the prophet Enoch's ascent to heaven, where he is shown God on his throne and the portals around the throne through which the moon, sun, and stars are visible at different times of the year. Knight and Lumos match with precision Enoch's description of the throne and portals—which Enoch has memorized under the tutorage of the angel Uriel—to the ancient stone megalith of Newgrange in

Ireland, an amazing astronomical instrument. They theorize that the vanished builders sought out others (Enoch being one) to give instructions on how to build the structures so their knowledge would not be lost. Those scientist-priests, known as Watchers or Angels or by archeologists as Grooved Ware People, disappeared around 3150 BCE, the time of a large comet impact. Where did they go? Knight and Lumos believe they scattered into the Middle East and Asia, with some remaining in Canaan and "becoming the giants of biblical legend," eventually passing their lore to the stone masons who built Solomon's temple (without the aid of metal tools). Thus, they may have been the founders of the traditions of modern-day Masons, whose rites specifically exclude metal.

CYLINDER SEALS

Mesopotamian cylinder seals were used primarily to roll on soft clay to create a raised surface that would identify the user. They were used to mark documents and inventories and were made of different materials and decorations. I created the use of a cylinder brand to mark a freed slave for the purposes of my story.

CAMELS & HORSES?

Another debate among archeologists is the domestication of camels and horses during this time period in Israel. Although archeologists believe camels were most likely not domesticated in Israel until around 900 BCE, there is evidence of the domestication of dromedary (one-hump) camels as early as 2600 BCE in Iran. Bedouins (nomads) ventured into the Arabian Desert around that time, bringing with them the prototypes for the Arabian horse breed. Evidence of horseback riding dates as far back as 3000 BCE in northern Kazakhstan, and horse bits from the Middle Bronze period have been found in Israel. Finding a bronze bit from my story's time period in an Israel museum was another exciting moment for me. Drawings of horse chariots date to 2000 BCE in Mesopotamia and 1500 BCE in Egypt. A horse stable from a later period has been found in the Negev desert, proving horses could negotiate the area.

Dogs?

Genetic research indicates that all dog breeds originated from the gray wolf of the Middle East. Nami was a saluki, one of the oldest known breeds of dog and considered the royal dog of Egypt. Unlike many other breed of dog, the saluki's DNA appears to have deviated very little from its origins. Salukis are sight hounds, bred to be desert hunters and companions, and are to this day prized by the Bedouins as part of the family. Nami became a strong character as I wrote this book, and I loved her, but I didn't know the right ending for her until I got there.

The Fate of Sodom & Gomorrah?

The Great Rift, a geological tear in the earth that starts in Africa, runs up the valley between Israel and Jordan, cupping the Dead Sea. (I decided not to call the Dead Sea the "Salt Sea" as the Bible does, to avoid confusion— obviously, the Mediterranean, the Atlantic, and the Persian Gulf are all salt seas.) It is the lowest place in the world not below water. Earthquakes are no strangers there. For all the searching, the "five cities of the plain" mentioned in Genesis have not been positively identified, although there are some ruins in contention.

The Genesis story calls for fire and brimstone (burning sulfur) from the sky. Volcanic activity is the first scenario fitting those criteria. But there is no indication of volcanic activity in the time period near the area where Sodom was supposedly located. Most theories place Sodom south of the Dead Sea, although some lean toward north of the Dead Sea. Some even put the "cities of the plain" in Mesopotamia.

Meteorites are another possibility, although most meteors that enter Earth's atmosphere burn completely. There is no evidence of significant impact craters in the area. A large meteor might, however, explode before impact in an "air blast," as the 1908 and 2013 events in Russia illustrate (along with a theoretical explosion in 3123 BCE, as documented by a Sumerian astronomer). An air blast explosion could have destroyed the cities and fits the evidence of burning that can be found at the remains of several settlements in the area.

One such archeological dig is Tall El Hamman, a gated ancient city to the north of the Dead Sea. The time period there (Middle Bronze) is close to the estimated time of Abraham. One of the problems with the Hamman site being Sodom is that there are many cities (more than five) clustered around it, while to the south of the Dead Sea there is some evidence that there were five cities that could match the Biblical reference to the "five cities of the plains." Biblical references indicate Lot wandered "as far as Sodom." Ezekiel 16:46 indicates that Sodom is to the *south* of Jerusalem. The Hamman site (in the northern plain or Kikkar) is to the *north* of Jerusalem. Also, the pits mentioned in Genesis are located in the southern region of the Dead Sea.

Some believe the ruins of Bab edh-Dhra, a city near the southeastern edge of the Dead Sea, might have been Sodom, and there is evidence of burning at the site and a large burial ground nearby. However, it is believed that Bab edh-Dhra burned around 2350–2067 BCE, which is two to four hundred years before the commonly believed time of Abraham (1800-1500 BCE). A possible sister city, Numeira (Gomorrah?)—which also shows evidence of burning—exists nearby, but the time period of that city is closer to 2600 BCE.

Of course, assuming the Biblical stories are actually based on real events, the legends of burning cities might have been superimposed onto a later time, but there is another puzzlement. The time periods *between* the various sites of "burned cities" are hundreds of years apart. Are we to believe that three or more meteor air blasts occurred hundreds of years apart in this relatively tiny section of the world? Or is there another explanation for the several burned cities over a varied timespan in the area?

Bitumen (tar) was called "pitch," and we know it today as asphalt. It is a natural product of petroleum existing underground in the area. Bituminous limestone releases asphalt and gaseous matter. With shifts in the earth, the asphalt rises up in the Dead Sea, as do sulfur fumes. Both occurred more frequently in the ancient past. Historians, including Diodorus Siculus (60–21 BCE) and Flavius Josephus (37–100 CE), confirm the harvesting of asphalt by boat. In the Dead Sea region, there are underground areas of methane, asphalt, and sulfur. Earthquakes might bring these materials into contact with each other underground, a volatile mix that could spontaneously erupt and emit flames of burning sulfur (brimstone) and pitch. I used this concept for "Mot's Tongue."

Assuming none of the ruins mentioned are the remains of Sodom and her sister cities, a great mystery surrounds the "cities of the plain" referred to in the Genesis story. What happened to them? Mud bricks made primarily of clay were a common building material during the Bronze Age. Clay hardens when exposed to heat. If the temperatures are high enough, it takes on a glassy structure. But limestone, the most abundant material in the area, is not flammable. If none of the cities mentioned above are Sodom (and none, except the northern El Hamman site fits the time period) what could account for the fact that there is no trace of the burnt city in the Abraham time period south of the Dead Sea?

One possibility is a geological process called liquefaction, where the shaking of saturated (waterlogged) ground causes an increase in water pressure and water can rush to the surface (i.e., the ground turns to water), as has happened in disasters in New Zealand, Japan, and the United States. On a slope, this can become a landslide. In earlier times, the climate in Israel was wetter, and a city built at the edge of the Dead Sea would rest on ground vulnerable to such saturation. Scientists put this theory to a test by building a model city and using a centrifuge at Cambridge where they replicated a 0.6 earthquake in conditions around the Dead Sea in the Early Bronze period. The effects were catastrophic. The ground turned to quicksand (blackened in *Angels at the Gate* by deposits of pitch), and the model city sank to the bottom of the Dead Sea.

Indeed some scholars believe that what is now the southern section (or part of the southern section of the Dead Sea) was once a fertile plain fed by the eastern river washes and that is why the Bible refers to the kings of Sodom, Gomorrah, Admah, Zeboyim, and Zoar joining battle in the "Valley of Siddim, which is the Salt Sea," a statement that surely is not meant to mean that the kings fought a battle *in* the Salt Sea (Dead Sea) but in the Valley of Siddim, which is [now] the Salt Sea. Perhaps the burnt city of Sodom will one day be found at the bottom of the Dead Sea, or perhaps the mystery will endure.

LIST OF CHARACTERS

*ABRAM (ABRAHAM): son of Tehrah
ADIR: Adira's name as a boy
ADIRA: daughter of Zakiti, and Lot's wife
ANAT: Canaanite goddess of war, and sister to Baal
ASHERAH: Canaanite/Hebrew mother goddess
BAAL (BA'AL): Canaanite god, son, and consort of Asherah
BASHAA: Egyptian translator in Babylon
*BERA: deceased king of Sodom
*CHEDORLAOMER: king of Elam (a kingdom southeast of Babylon)
CHIRAM: caravan cook, Danel's father
DANEL: Chiram's son
DUNE: Adira's gelding
*ELIEZER: Abram's steward
FLAVA: Jemia's servant
ANAN (ANAN-EL): companion of Mika and Raph
*HAGAR: Sarai's handmaiden and Abram's second wife
*HARAN: son of Tehrah, Abram's brother, and Lot's father
HURRIYA: Lot's first wife (Canaanite)
*ISHMAEL: Hagar's son
JEMIA: Danel's grandmother
JERAH: young desert man with falcon
KATAR: rug merchant
KERIT: son of Yassib
KURI: Babylonian guard
LAMA: Ur goddess on Adira's seal
LILA: slave in Lot's house
MANA: wife of Yassib
MIKA (*MIKA-EL): messenger of El
MOT: Canaanite (Ugarit) god of death and the underworld

NAMI: Adira's dog
PETRA: daughter of Mana and Yassib
*__PHEINÉ:__ Lot's daughter (Book of Jabel)
PHILOT: Adira's donkey
PUZIR: Babylonian guard
RAPH (RAPHA-EL): messenger of El
SAMSU-ILUNA: king of Babylonia
*__SARAI (SARAH):__ Abram's wife
SCAR: Babylonian guard
SIDILK : Hurrian raider
SHEM: young desert boy
TABNI: priestess of Babylon
TALLIYA: Adira's mother (goddess of the dew, daughter of Baal)
TALMET: boy of Abram's tribe
THAMMA: Lot's daughter (Book of Jabel)
YASSIB: nomad chieftain
ZAKITI: Adira's father

---

* Biblical names

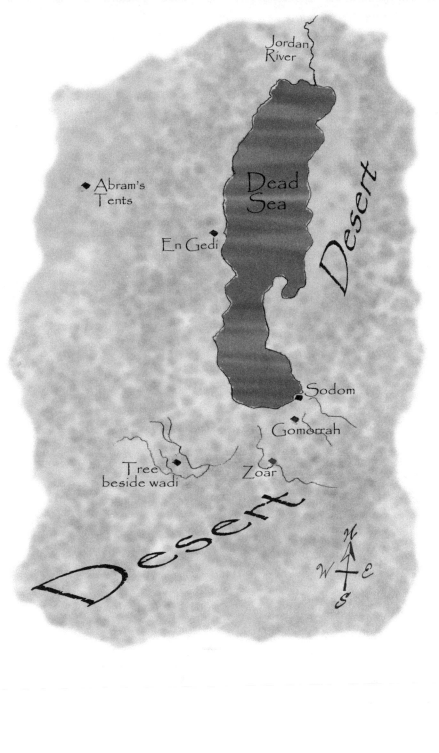

SELECTED BIBLIOGRAPHY

International Masters Publishers. Ancient Civilizations series. *Ancient Mysteries: The Dead Sea Scrolls.* AB. Montoursville, Pennsylvania, DVD, 2008.

Arnold, Jennifer. *Through a Dog's Eyes.* Spiegel & Grau, Random House, New York, 2010.

Balter, Michael. *The Goddess and the Bull: Çatalhöyük: An Archaeological Journey to the Dawn of Civilization.* Simon & Schuster, New York, 2005.

Barber, Elizabeth Wayland. *Women's Work: The First 20,000 Years— Women, Cloth, and Society in Early Times.* W.W. Norton & Company, New York, 1994.

Bertman, Stephen. *Handbook to Life in Ancient Mesopotamia.* Oxford University Press, New York, 2003.

Bratcher, Dennis. "Baal Worship in the Old Testament." Consultation on the Relationship Between the Wesleyan Tradition and the Natural Sciences, Kansas City, Missouri, October 19, 1991.

Braun, Joachim. "Music in Ancient Israel/Palestine: Archaeological, Written, and Comparative Sources." William B. Eerdmans, Grand Rapids, Michigan, 2002.

Cecil, Jessica. "The Destruction of Sodom and Gommorrah." BBC, London, 2011.

Cline, Eric H. *From Eden to Exile: Unraveling Mysteries of the Bible.* National Geographic, Washington, D.C., 2007.

Feiler, Bruce. *Abraham: A Journey to the Heart of Three Faiths.* Harper Perennial, New York, 2002, 2004.

Geva, Hillel. "Gezer." Jewish Virtual Library, The American-Israeli Cooperative Enterprise, Chevy Chase, Maryland, 2012.

Westbrook, Joel and Fields, Ed, Executive Producers. *Biblical Mysteries: Sodom and Gomorrah.* Union Pictures and Alexandria Productions, Goldhill Home Media, DVD, USA, 2008.

Hillel, Daniel. *Negev: Land, Water and Life in a Desert Environment.* Praeger Publishers, Westport, Connecticut, 1982.

Johnson, Julia. *Saluki, Hound of the Bedouin.* Stacey International, London, 2005.

Keohane, Alan. *Bedouin: Nomads of the Desert.* Kyle Cathie Limited, London, 2008.

Knight: Christopher and Lomas, Robert. *Uriel's Machine: Uncovering the secrets of Stonehenge, Noah's Flood, and the Dawn of Civilization.* Fair Winds Press, Beverly, Massachusetts, 2001.

Kurlansky, Mark. *Salt: A World History.* Penguin Books, New York, 2003.

Leifert, Harvey. "Chemical Warfare 1.0." Natural History, Research Triangle Park, North Carolina, April 2009.

Losleben, Elizabeth. *The Bedouin of the Middle East.* Lerner Publications Company, Minneapolis, Minnesota, 2003.

MacQueen, J. G. *The Hittites and Their Contemporaries in Asia Minor.* Westview Press, New York, 1975.

Meshal, Ze'ev. "Did Yahweh Have a Consort?" Biblical Archeology Review, Boone, Iowa, 1979.

Neev, David and Emery, K.O. *The Destruction of Sodom, Gomorrah and Jericho: Geological, Climatological, and Archaeological Background.* Oxford University Press, New York, 1995.

Mieroop, Marc Van De. *King Hammurabi of Babylon: A Biography.* Blackwell Publishing, Oxford, United Kingdom, 2005.

Mitchell, Stephen. *Gilgamesh: A New English Version.* Free Press, New York, 2006.

Patai, Raphael. *The Hebrew Goddess.* Wayne State University Press, Detroit, 1990.

Pellegrino, Charles. *Return to Sodom and Gomorrah.* Avon Books, New York, 1994.

Peterson, Daniel C. "Nephi and his Asherah." Journal of Book of Mormon Studies, Volume: 9 Issue: 2. Maxwell Institute, Provo, Utah, 2000.

Rosenberg, David. *Abraham, The First Historical Biography.* Basic Books, New York, 2006.

Roux, Georges. *Ancient Iraq.* Penguin Books, New York, 1992.

Rugh, Andrea B. *Simple Gestures: A Cultural Journey into the Middle East.* Potomac Books, Dulles, Virginia, 2009.

Shanks, Hershal, Editor. *Ancient Israel: From Abraham to the Roman Destruction of the Temple.* Biblical Archaeology Society, Boone, Iowa, 2011.

Stone, Merlin. *When God Was A Woman: The Landmark Exploration of the Ancient Worship of the Great Goddess and the Eventual Suppression of Women's Rites.* Harcourt, Inc., Boston, 1976.

Tubb, Jonathan N. *Canaanites (Peoples of the Past).* University of Oklahoma Press, Norman, Oklahoma, 1998.

Ullian, Robert. *Frommer's Israel.* Wiley Publishing, Inc., Hoboken, New Jersey, 2009.

Vincent, Norah. *Self-Made Man: One Woman's Year Disguised As a Man.* Penguin Books, New York, 2006.

Walker, Barbara G, "Shekina." *The Woman's Encyclopedia of Myths and Secrets.* HarperCollins, New York, 1983.

Wroblewski, David. *The Story of Edgar Sawtelle.* Ecco/HarperCollins, 2008.